ELIZABETH EDMONDSON

The Art of Love

HARPER

This novel is entirely a work of fiction.
The names, characters and incidents portrayed in it are
the work of the author's imagination. Any resemblance to
actual persons, living or dead, events or localities is
entirely coincidental.

Harper
An imprint of HarperCollins*Publishers*
77–85 Fulham Palace Road,
Hammersmith, London W6 8JB

www.harpercollins.co.uk

This paperback edition 2008
1

First published in Great Britain by
HarperCollins*Publishers* 2007

Copyright © AEB Ltd 2007

Elizabeth Edmondson asserts the moral right to
be identified as the author of this work

A catalogue record for this book is
available from the British Library

ISBN-13: 978-0-00-722378-7

Set in Sabon by Palimpsest Book Production Limited,
Grangemouth, Stirlingshire

Printed and bound in Great Britain by
Clays Ltd, St Ives plc

THE ART OF LOVE

Born in Chile, and educated in Calcutta and London before going to Oxford University, Elizabeth Edmondson is a full-time writer.

Also by Elizabeth Edmondson

For Rosie Buckman
With love and gratitude

PART ONE

ONE

'If I'm not Polly Smith, then who am I?'

'What a profound question,' said Oliver Fraddon.

The two of them were standing side by side in a gallery at Somerset House, home of the Register of Births, Marriages and Deaths for all the counties of England.

'The world in little, one might say,' Oliver went on, looking along the floor-to-ceiling shelves filled with thousands of large red ledgers that contained the transitions of millions of lives, present and past. 'All of us written down here, captured, immortalized. Volumes full of names and identities, A to Z, plain and extraordinary. We're born, we marry – or some of us do – and we die, and each time we are set down on a page in here. A frightening thought.'

'Never mind the frightening thought, what concerns me is that I'm not among those immortalized here,' Polly said.

'Very true. I suggest we go back to the desk and ask the recording angel for help.'

He led the way down the metal spiral staircase, warning Polly to watch her step. 'Or you'll end up as a new entry under Deaths.'

The clerk standing behind the long wooden length of the

main counter had not a touch of the angelic about her. She wore pince-nez attached to a thin chain and had a harassed air. Oliver addressed her. 'This young lady seems to have gone missing.'

The clerk looked at Polly with worried, faded grey eyes, eyes that were kinder than her pinched mouth. 'Oh dear. Can't find yourself? Not where you should be? Your name is Smith, you say. Well, there are rather a lot of Smiths, but in the end there's only one of you. It comes down to having the right dates and the right address. Once we're sure of that information, we can find you. Unless,' she added, her voice sharpening, 'unless you're a foreigner.'

'Do I look like a foreigner?' Polly asked, indignant, not because she minded being taken for a foreigner, but because she wanted to assert her rightful place, numbered among all her fellow citizens here, in those large red books.

'No, but if you were born abroad, even if you were as English as me and Mr Grier over there, then you wouldn't be in the main part of the registry, but in the records we keep elsewhere.'

'In the nether regions?' suggested Oliver in Polly's ear. 'The brimstone section, with devilish clerks scurrying to and fro.'

'It doesn't arise,' said Polly, 'I was born in Highgate. 11, Bingley Street, off Archway. My mother still lives there. On May the first, 1908.'

'Only there is no entry for her in the relevant volume,' Oliver said.

The angel was impressed by Oliver, Polly could see that. If it had just been her standing at the desk, in her old mac and wine-coloured beret, she'd still be waiting for the clerk to look up from her card indexes and paper. It had been Oliver, every inch the gentleman in his tailored suit, who had commanded her immediate attention. Just by being there. It was unfair. But useful, she told herself. And of course, the minute he opened

4

his mouth, there was the accent, proclaiming him a product of the upper classes, with all the easy authority that Eton and Oxford gave to the Olivers of this world.

So the woman in the pince-nez had been helpful. Had gone back with them to the red books, had found the one that should have contained the entry for Polly. 'Polly's short for Pauline,' she told the woman, but it made no difference. There was no female Smith, initial P, born in Bingley Street, Highgate on the first of May, nor indeed at the end of April or the middle of May. There was a Thomas Smith, born in Priory Gardens on the second of May; that was as close as she could get.

The clerk closed the book, and Oliver courteously took it from her to replace it on its shelf.

'You'll have to get the correct details from your parents,' the clerk said. 'If you were born in a nursing home, perhaps in the country, you might have been registered there. I expect your father registered you, and he mightn't have realized he should have done it where you lived, and not where you were born. Ask him.'

'I can't, he's dead.'

'In the war?' the clerk said, with a sudden and unexpected flash of sympathy. 'I'm sorry. But your mother will know. And doesn't she have the original certificate?'

'Good question,' Oliver said, as they came out of the grandeur of Somerset House into the noise and bustle of the Strand. 'That would solve all your problems.'

Polly grinned. 'I dare say in your stately home everything is in perfect order, but Ma's not very organized with papers. They're stowed away in boxes, only not so you can find anything. She takes care with her music, she can always find a piece of music she wants. Papers are different, and after all, it was more than twenty years ago. I asked her, of course I did, but she got into such a fret, positively alarmed when

I said I'd look through all her stuff, that I thought it would be easier just to come here and get a copy. They don't need the original for a passport, do they?'

'A copy from Somerset House passes all scrutiny,' said Oliver. He drew her to the side, out of the way of passersby. 'So what now? Honeymoon cancelled? Come to think of it, wedding off, I'm sure you need a birth certificate to get married.'

'The wedding isn't cancelled, because no date has been fixed. Just January.' Which was now only a few weeks away. 'Roger told me to see to the passport so that there wouldn't be any hold-ups. He likes to be ahead of himself. And what I'm going to do now,' she said, suddenly decisive, 'is catch a tram and go home and interrogate my mother.'

'Then I shall escort you to the tram stop.'

They walked along the Strand towards Aldwych, Polly thinking, Oliver watching her. A pigeon landed in front of them and then took off with a whirr, the colour and shape of the grey wings catching Polly's eye. Grey, but so many shades of it, from almost white to rich purple. And the energy of the movement, effort blending into the smooth ease of flight.

A grey bird on a grey day, but the dismal skies above them had no colour nor shape nor energy. There was the hint of sulphur in the air that warned of approaching fog; the crisp autumn days of October were over and now London had descended into the sullen dreariness of a damp and cold November.

'The dark days do make me miserable,' Polly said, as they crossed the road. 'I spend most of the winter pining for spring and longer days. I never feel really happy in the winter. It's the cold and the general dimness, I suppose.'

Polly and Oliver went down the steps to the tram station at Aldwych. Oliver took her hand and kissed it, as was his habit, then saw her on to the waiting tram, raising his hat as she climbed on. Oliver always wore wide-brimmed hats in soft browns and greys. She ran up the stairs to the upper deck and snatched a window seat from a burly man with a brown parcel. As the tram rattled off and emerged into Kingsway, she saw Oliver walking back towards Aldwych. Among the hurrying crowds, heads down, faces red from the cold, clad in drab coats and suits, his exquisitely tailored figure and hat made him stand out, as did his languid stride.

The tram plunged underground into Kingsway tunnel.

Polly both loved and hated trams. The clatter and banging and restless swaying disturbed her, but there was a comfort in travelling on a vehicle that ran on its tracks so purposefully and undeviatingly through the chaos of all the thick London traffic. And this particular tram, the Number 35, was part of her life. She had travelled on it every school day to and from her school, and then later on, when she won a scholarship to art school, had ridden on it into the heart of London to her college.

The journey to her old home took forty-five minutes, through the streets of northern London and up into Highgate. She got off at Archway, just as she always did; she could have walked blindfold from the tram stop to her house, and in fact, more than once, going home in a bad fog, she might as well have been blindfolded.

Polly hoped that they weren't in for one of those terrible pea-soupers, which caught in your throat and always made her feel sick and headachy. She loathed the days when it was as if the sun never rose, and the sounds of London – traffic, voices, street criers, bells – were muffled by the smoke-laden, noxious greenish-yellow air.

She walked along Bingley Street to number 11, pushed open the gate and climbed the steps up to the front door, which was painted a dark green colour and sported a brass knocker in the shape of a pixie. From the window to the right of the front door, she heard the wavering sounds of a piano scale. Her mother had a pupil. She looked at her watch. Ten to five, so the lesson would probably finish in ten minutes. The front door was on the latch, and she opened and shut it behind her quietly. Inside, she took off her mac and beret, unwound her woolly scarf and hung them up on the hook behind the door. Then she walked down the hall and into the kitchen, warm from the stove which her mother kept going all the time in winter. She put the kettle on, and sat down at the scrubbed wooden kitchen table, her feet automatically curling round the legs of the chair as they had done since she was a little girl.

The kitchen overlooked their small garden, a constant affront to the neighbours, whose neat herbaceous borders, squares of lawn and regimented vegetable patches tucked away at the bottom of each matching garden proclaimed the right horticultural instincts. The garden was the one place where Dora Smith's restrained nature seemed to give way to something more reckless. She packed the space with plants, not in neat lines, but more, Polly always liked to imagine, as a jungle would be. Dense and profuse, and nothing small except the soft swathes of violas and the snowdrops which nestled under the overhanging branches of shrubs and bushes.

But no London garden looked inviting in November. It had a forlorn, end-of-season look to it. The piles of crisp autumn leaves had vanished, leaving just a few soggy remnants on the ground or clinging to the twigs of the trees. The evergreens added a touch of colour and life, but even they had a grey tinge, as though the misty air had got to them as well.

The kettle came to the boil in a flurry of steam. Polly warmed the brown teapot, spooned in the tea, and left it on the stove to brew. The door to the front room opened: voices, thanks and goodbyes, the front door opened and shut, and Polly's mother came into the kitchen.

'I heard you come in,' she said. 'You've made tea.'

'Have you got a five o'clock?'

'No. I should have, little Sally Wright, but she has a bad chest, and she isn't allowed out when the weather's like this. Just as well, for if she did come, it would be half an hour of cough, cough, cough. She's a musical child, though,' she added, wanting to be fair. 'But I've another pupil at half past. Pour the tea, Polly. Do you want a biscuit?'

Polly took a biscuit and chewed it absent-mindedly, for a moment at a loss as to how to broach the subject of the birth certificate.

Then she plunged in, what was the point in beating about the bush? 'I went to Somerset House today, to get a copy of my birth certificate.'

Dora Smith put her cup down so hard that it rattled the saucer.

'You aren't still set on going abroad for your honeymoon, are you?' she said. 'I don't advise it, you'll catch some dreadful disease, it's not very clean over there.'

'How do you know? You said you'd never been abroad,' Polly said, rather crossly.

There was a pause. 'My . . . It's what people say happens to everyone who goes. And you don't speak any foreign languages, at least if you do, your French teacher never found out about it, your French reports were always shockers.'

'Roger speaks German and French. Besides, even if we weren't going abroad, I have to have the birth certificate to get married. That's what he says.'

'I really do not see why you're in such a rush to get married. Roger still has to finish qualifying, and—'

'He is qualified.'

'Then why is he taking more exams?'

'You have to, if you want to be a hospital doctor.'

Polly felt she hadn't got to the bottom of her mother's ambivalent attitude to Roger and her engagement. Dora Smith was a woman with two distinct personalities. The one Polly knew best was the sensible, practical woman, who shared her neighbours' attitudes and opinions, among which was the certainty that the main purpose of a young woman's being was to find herself a good, reliable husband, in a respectable way of life, and settle down with him to be a good wife and mother. Within this conventional scenario, Roger was a gem. A doctor was better than the daughter of Ted and Dora Smith might have hoped for, and a catch to brag about to her friends, if Dora were given to bragging, which she wasn't.

But Dora Smith had another side, the side that had been dismayed at Polly's precocious artistic talent, that had refused to praise her exceptional promise, yet who had fiercely asserted the need for Polly to do her art as well as she could. 'If you're an artist, then you have to be trained properly, to become as good as you can be. It's not the same as having art as a hobby. One's professional and the other's amateur.' And it was that Dora Smith who had said, clearly and unexpectedly, 'If you marry Roger, the light will go out of your painting.'

To which Polly might have replied that the light had already gone out of her painting, and so what difference would it make, but that wasn't an acknowledgement she was going to make to anyone.

'Can we get back to the birth certificate? Are you sure you can't find the original? I don't see how it can be lost, one doesn't lose something important like a birth certificate.'

Dora Smith didn't answer, but took a sip of tea, her gaze wandering away from Polly as she looked out of the window. The clock ticked, the stove gave its familiar creaking sound as it cooled, the cat flap on the back door rattled and a large tabby cat slid through it. He gave Polly an uninterested look with his round, golden eyes, swished a stripy tail and went to investigate his food plate.

Still Dora said nothing.

'I'm not there, in Somerset House,' Polly persisted. 'There's no Pauline Smith registered, not on that date, not anywhere in Highgate. Was I born somewhere else? In a nursing home?'

Her mother sighed, and Polly saw that her eyes, when she looked back from the window, had a glisten of tears in them.

'Ma, I'm sorry. What is it? What's the matter?'

The words came out in a rush. 'You weren't born in Highgate, you were born in Paris. I haven't lost your birth certificate. I burnt it.'

'Burnt it?' Polly couldn't believe her ears. 'Burnt it? Why? When? Just to stop me going abroad? And how could I possibly have been born in Paris? You've never been to France, you said so yourself.'

'I burnt it when you were a baby,' said Dora Smith, with a sigh. 'Oh, dear, why did this wretched man want to take you abroad. Or marry you at all? Bringing it all up. I had hoped . . .'

'You had hoped what?' Polly felt a cold sensation in her stomach. Paris?

'You'll need all the details if you really must have a passport. I'll write them down for you.'

Polly watched her mother as she got up and went to the drawer where she kept scraps of paper. She smoothed out the back of an envelope, and wrote in her clear italic hand. Then she passed it to Polly, and went over to stand at the sink.

Polly stared down at the elegantly inscribed words.

'This makes no sense,' she exclaimed. 'Who's this – I can't even pronounce it – this Polyhymnia Tomkins?'

'That's your real name,' Dora said, leaning on the sink and running the tap, so that Polly had to raise her voice to be heard.

'Tomkins? I'm Polly Smith. How can I ever have been called Tomkins? And Polyhymnia? That's not even a proper name.'

'I'm not your mother,' Dora said. 'And Ted Smith wasn't your father.'

TWO

On the tram back into the centre of London, Polly sat unseeing, not noticing the people around her, or hearing the grumbles of two women in the next seat about the weather, not aware of the bell clanging, the swaying as the tram went over points, oblivious to everything outside herself, as she tried to make sense of what her mother – who was not her mother, after all – of what Dora Smith had told her.

What kind of a mother could she have been, this woman who had abandoned her so casually into the care of her sister when she was only weeks old, and never saw her again, who clearly didn't care whether she were alive or dead?

What kind of a mother would call her daughter Polyhymnia?

'Polyhymnia's one of the muses,' Dora Smith told her. 'The muse of sacred song.'

Sacred song indeed. Well, no one could have been more wrongly named, because, to Dora Smith's dismay, Polly had no ear for music at all. She had ground her way through piano lessons until both of them had given up with relief, and she couldn't hold a tune; singing at school had been a case of miming and mumbling, under the constant frowns of the singing mistress.

13

Dora Smith had been less than forthcoming about her sister, Thomasina. That was another ridiculous name. 'We went our separate ways,' was all she would say. 'We weren't at all alike.'

'Where is she? Is she still alive?'

'I don't know, and that's the honest truth.'

'How could you lose touch with a sister? If I had a sister . . .'

Which was an unkind thing to say. Of course, if she, Polly, wasn't the Smiths' daughter, then Dora Smith had never had children of her own. Polly had asked, when she was a little girl, why she didn't have a brother or sister, and Ted had put down his newspaper and frowned at her, saying that wasn't a suitable question to ask. Later, when she was in her bath, being soaped and flannelled from nose to toe by her mother, Dora Smith had said with a sigh that she wished Polly did have a little brother or sister, but fate had chosen for her to be an only child.

I couldn't have had better parents, Polly told herself fiercely.

Dora Smith had said, with a world of sadness in her voice: 'You are my daughter, Polly. You're the only daughter, the only child I had. Ted loved you as if you were his own, and well, a niece is close. A sister's child. You're my blood, that counts for a lot.'

Only it didn't seem to count sister to sister, not if Thomasina had walked out on her sister and her baby's life with never a backward glance.

'Why Paris?' Polly wanted to know. 'What was she doing in Paris?'

There it was again, Dora's obvious reluctance to answer questions. 'She was a bit of a gadabout, restless, never happy in one place. She had friends in Paris, I suppose.'

Illegitimate. Polly stared out into the chilly darkness, vaguely

14

lit by the headlights of cars and streetlights gleaming dully through the thickening fog. She was illegitimate.

'What you're saying is that I'm a bastard,' she had said, raging at Dora.

'Don't use that word. Not ever.'

'It's the word other people will use. Didn't that ever occur to my mother?'

'Your mother . . . your mother was an unconventional person. She wouldn't – that is, what people in general might consider a stigma, wouldn't be to her. I remonstrated with her when she arrived on our doorstep with you in her arms. I said she should marry your father, so that you wouldn't have the disgrace of illegitimacy, but she said no healthy baby could be any kind of a disgrace.'

'That was big of her.'

'They'll give you a short birth certificate at Somerset House,' Dora said. 'One that doesn't have any blank spaces. Thomasina refused to fill in any details for your father.'

'It was an English birth certificate, though? I am English?'

'Of course you are,' said Dora, shocked. 'As English as a Chelsea bun. At least she had the sense to register you at the consulate there, that's what you do, for English babies born abroad. Go back to Somerset House with those details I've written down, and they'll find the entry all right.'

It was extraordinary to think that all these years she'd lived as Polly Smith, and in fact she was no such thing. Her passport would proclaim to the world that she was Polyhymnia Tomkins. A stranger. She couldn't think of herself as any such person. Polyhymnia Tomkins was the fabrication, she was the person who didn't exist, not Polly Smith.

'You always said Polly was a pet name for Pauline.'

'Ted said we couldn't have a girl called Polyhymnia. He said you'd be teased at school, and the neighbours would think it odd.'

'Did you live here when I was born?' Polly had asked her mother. 'Here in Bingley Gardens? You told me you'd always lived here.'

'We didn't. We lived in South London, in Putney, when Ted and I were first married. When you arrived, Ted said we'd have to move. He'd been with the London, Brighton and South Coast Railway, but he didn't mind moving to north London because he'd applied for a better job, with the Great Northern. It was a promotion, so he was pleased about that, only it was a long way to travel right across London to Kings Cross every day. So we moved to the other side of the river, where no one would know that you weren't our child.'

No parents could have done more for her than Ted and Dora Smith had done, Polly knew that. It was unreasonable and ungrateful of her to be angry with Dora for never telling her who she really was, but she wasn't feeling reasonable or grateful.

'I knew I'd have to tell you one day, only the right moment never seemed to come. And I came to forget that you weren't really my daughter.'

And to all intents and purposes, Polly was their daughter. She didn't remember Ted Smith very well; she'd been seven when he went away to fight in France, and nine when the telegram came saying that he'd been killed. What with the savings he had left and what Dora had made with her piano lessons, she had never lacked for anything, and she hadn't lacked for love, either, Dora was lavish in that commodity.

Dora had seen to it that Polly worked hard at school, found the money for extra art lessons when it became clear how gifted she was, and instead of having to leave school at fourteen to earn her keep like several of her friends, she was allowed to stay on and try for the scholarship to art college. Dora Smith had paid for the extra that the scholarship didn't cover, making sure that Polly had everything she needed.

Not for the first time, Polly found herself wondering about Dora and her mother's family. There had been two sisters. Did she have any uncles? What about her grandparents? Dora had always been reticent about her family. 'My parents were quite old when they had me, and they're long since dead,' was the sum of the information she was prepared to give Polly. Where had they lived, where had Dora – and, of course, Thomasina – grown up?

'Oh, various places,' was the evasive answer to that question.

Polly came to with a start. The tram had reached Kingsway, and everybody except her had got off. 'Hurry along there,' the conductor said, his face pinched with cold. 'Haven't got all day, you know.'

Polly felt strangely discouraged as she walked through the Georgian streets to the house in Fitzroy Street where she lived. She let herself in, the familiar smell of wet shoes and overcooked cabbage washing over her. Her landlady was mean with light bulbs, and the light in the stairwell was almost as dim as the foggy world outside the door. Polly climbed the four flights of stairs to the top floor. She opened the door to her attic room, took off her mac and hung it on the back of the door. Then she removed her damp beret and ran her hands through her hair.

Did she want to bother with a passport at all? Not to have one would mean she couldn't go abroad. Nor, according to Roger, could she get married. Was that true? Vague ideas of special licences flitted through her head, but Roger would expect her to produce a birth certificate in any case, he'd want to file it away with all his other documents.

The moment she had a passport, it was hullo, Polyhymnia

17

Tomkins, goodbye Polly Smith. Yet, legally, she supposed, she was already Polyhymnia Tomkins, always had been Polyhymnia Tomkins. It was Polly Smith who did not exist.

What's in a name? she said to herself.

A lot. A name wasn't just a series of letters arranged in a particular way. A name was a person. It could be more than one person, there were probably dozens, hundreds of Polly Smiths up and down the country. But each one was identified by her name. Without a name, you weren't a person. It would be impossible to be truly human without a name. You gave a pet a name, a cat, a horse, a tamed magpie, even, was marked out from others of its kind by its name. Although animals were different, a new owner might change a creature's name. It was a mark of humanity that your name was an integral part of you.

What about orphans, who were adopted and given a name by their new parents? Or, for women, marriage changed your name, you became Mrs Roger Harrington, or even – since she had noticed that the servants in Bryanston Square called Roger 'Mr Roger' – Mrs Roger.

Spies changed their names, and so did criminals on the run. Authors wrote books under pseudonyms. Actors and actresses had stage names, look at her friend Tina Uppershaw, born Maureen Scroggs. Film stars who started life as a Mavis or a Ken became a Carole or a Ronald, with a new surname that would look good in lights.

For Polly, names had a special dimension. She saw letters in colour, and words and names were a glowing blend of those individual colours. Polly was slate blues and greens with flashes of light and yellow. Pauline was another colour, a darker one, but since she never used it, it didn't bother her. Smith was brown and maroon with touches of grey. Whereas Polyhymnia was a much more complicated palette of light and dark, warm and cold colours making an intriguing but unfamiliar whole. Tomkins was a grey and pink name, with a touch of wine at the edges.

Polly sighed. This was making her head ache even more, she must stop these thoughts going round and round in her mind. She made herself focus on her surroundings, she had long ago discovered that to live entirely and intensely in the present moment was a cure for most ill moods and worrying times.

Polly's room was perfect for an artist. It had a north-facing skylight and a dormer window looking out over a parapet to the smoky chimneys of London. Her narrow bed, covered in a blue and yellow cloth, was set under the eaves, which meant that she had to sit up carefully in bed, so as not to crack her head on the sloping ceiling. Her clothes hung on a rail behind a curtain and she kept the rest of her things in a large chest of drawers set against another sloping ceiling, which left space behind it for her suitcase and various other possessions. The floorboards were uncovered, except for a small blue rug beside the bed. By the door was a washbasin, a great luxury. The bathroom was two floors down, and shared with the other occupants of the house: her landlady, Mrs Horton, her daughter, who was a nurse and kept odd hours, and three other lodgers.

Polly looked around her room, seeing it not as the haven it had been to her, a haven and a workplace, with her easel set up in the centre of the room, her paints and tools on a table beside it, not the place where she lived and worked, but a place inhabited by a stranger.

She crouched down beside the gas ring on which she boiled her water and did all her cooking, turned on the gas, which came on with a hiss, and struck a match. The burner lit with a soft popping sound. She had a saucepan with soup she'd made the day before and she put it on to heat.

This room belonged to Polly Smith. Only she wasn't Polly Smith.

She sat down at the table and opened a sketchbook. She unscrewed the cap of her favourite fountain pen, and with a few swift strokes, drew herself. A realistic self portrait; this was the face that looked out at her from the mirror, was caught in snapshots or, looking severe and criminal, the face in the photo which she had had taken for her passport.

Then she drew another figure, a faceless young woman, dressed not in a limp skirt and jumper, but in a trailing robe. She added a sleek hairdo and whorls of smoke rising from a cigarette in an absurdly long holder.

Polyhymnia Tomkins, sophisticate.

Now her pen was working rapidly, and more featureless figures danced off the page. A Grecian woman, in flowing robes, swirling down on a parson sitting at an organ. Polyhymnia, Muse at work. Next came a woman dressed in breeches and a pith helmet who was gazing at a supercilious camel. Beneath that she wrote, Polyhymnia Tomkins, explorer.

Then a woman in a sensible tweed suit pushing a pram with a felt hat on her head. That was Mrs Roger Harrington. Of course, when she married Roger, she wouldn't be Polly Smith in any case, she would lose both Smith and Tomkins, for ever. And as to the Polly, she would just go on being Polly as she always had done.

This prospect didn't cheer her up as much as it might have done. She would have to tell Roger, of course. Tell him that he wasn't marrying respectable Polly Smith, daughter of the respectable Mr and Mrs Smith of Bingley Street, but Polyhymnia, bastard daughter of Thomasina Tomkins, father unknown.

Father unknown. Was there any way you could discover who your father was, when your mother vanished without saying? Why hadn't Ma – who wasn't her mother, but her aunt, how could she ever get used to that? – questioned her real mother more vigorously, insisted on being told who was

20

the father of her child? Or made an effort to find this out, while the trail was still hot and it might have been possible to discover who Thomasina's friends were, and who among them had been more than a friend?

Of course, her mother might have had dozens of lovers. Might even have been – no, she wasn't going to think that for a moment. There had been an exasperation in Dora Smith's voice when she reluctantly spoke of her sister, but no moral disapproval. She wasn't much given to moral disapproval, which was another thing that singled her out from her neighbours.

A married man, probably, thought Polly with all the cynicism of her twenty-five years. An old story, and a simple one: an affair which could never end in marriage. The man refusing to acknowledge a child, or maybe Thomasina too proud or too kind to threaten her lover's marriage. France was a Catholic country, if the father were a Roman Catholic, then the situation would be hopeless, even if her father had wanted to marry her mother.

Could she find out more about her mother, somehow? She wouldn't have Ma's help if she tried to, that was clear. 'I'm not going to say another word about Thomasina, and that's final. It's all over, it's all in the past, and that's where it will stay. No good ever came of delving into the past.'

There was no arguing with Ma when she had that look on her face. The Inquisition wouldn't have been able to get anything out of Dora Smith once she'd made up her mind.

Wild thoughts of employing a detective flitted through Polly's head – only how could she possibly afford a detective? She could try herself to find out more, but where would she begin? Tomkins was such an everyday name, not quite as ordinary as Smith, yet there must be thousands of Tomkins in the British Isles. Since she hadn't the slightest idea what part of the country Dora or her family came from, it would be pointless trying to find out more.

The soup bubbled and rose to the top of the pan, and Polly only just whipped it off before it dribbled down the side of the saucepan. She poured it into a bowl, spread a thin layer of margarine on a slice of bread and, pushing aside her sketchbook and pencil, set the soup on the table.

She ate slowly, looking into the distance, not seeing her familiar surroundings, but a strange place, full of people she didn't know. A world to which she was connected, but one where she had no presence or substance. She shook her head. Then she glanced at her wristwatch. Oh, Lord. Ten past eight, and she was supposed to meet Roger at twenty past, when he came off duty at the hospital. She gulped down the last of the soup, dumped the bowl and spoon in the basin, pulled on her mac, rammed her beret on to her head, picked up her shoulder bag and ran out of the room.

THREE

Dr Roger Harrington was waiting at the corner as Polly came panting up. Sturdy, good-looking, he had an air of competence and a cleft to a strong chin that betokened a firm if not obstinate nature. This evening there was a weary look about his eyes, not surprising when he'd been on duty for more than twelve hours.

'Really, Polly, you must try to be more punctual,' he said, as she put up her face for a kiss.

'Sorry,' said Polly.

'I thought we'd go to the pictures, but we'll have to buck up if we're going to get there on time.'

Polly had to jog to keep up with him. 'What's on?'

'We're going to see *The Mayor of Hell*. James Cagney.'

Polly sat through the film with the action on screen barely registering in her mind. Somehow, that evening, she must tell Roger what she had discovered: that she wasn't who he thought she was, that he was engaged to a woman who didn't exist, and instead had attached himself to the illegitimate offspring of Thomasina and God knew who.

It was made worse by the fact that Roger, after the film was over – a film that he said he'd really enjoyed – was full of his latest medical interest. 'Heredity is the key to everything,' he was saying. 'That's what makes us what we are. There's no getting away from it. Just like with racehorses, who your parents and your grandparents and great-grandparents are determine just who and what you are.'

'I don't know much about my grandparents,' Polly began, seeing an opening.

'It doesn't matter. I've seen photos of your father, a fine, upright man, and he died bravely, so he clearly had a good character. That's what counts. And there's nothing wrong with your mother, she's healthy and reasonably intelligent. Hard-working, responsible, look what a good job she's made of bringing you up single-handed, there's no reason why you won't be the same. And she's artistic, and so are you. With her it's music, with you it's paint, but it's all the same. Temperaments and choices are predetermined you see, by our genes.'

Polly wasn't sure what genes were, and felt that she'd rather not know.

'And here I am, a doctor and the son and grandson of doctors. It's in my blood.'

Polly could see a number of objections to this. There was Shakespeare, the son of a glover, or had his father been a butcher? No literary genes there, unless his mother had been a poet in secret, but she had a suspicion that the female line didn't count as much in Roger's thinking as the male one. 'What about someone like Leonardo da Vinci?' she said, tucking her hand into his.

'What's he got to do with it?'

'His parents weren't artists. He was illegitimate, you know.'

They were under a streetlight, and Polly could see the frown on Roger's firm brow.

'Was he? That's something that we, as a nation, are going to have to be very careful about, now that all this new stuff about heredity is being discovered. It's too risky having children growing up who don't know who their fathers were. Besides, the chances are that the children of a woman who isn't married will inherit her lax morals, and will go the same way themselves.'

No, this wasn't the moment to tell Roger about Polyhymnia Tomkins.

At Polly's house, he took the key from her and opened the front door. Then he gave her a chaste kiss and walked briskly away. Polly stood for a moment in the doorway, watching his upright retreating back.

He never came up to her room with her in the evening. The only time he ventured there was in broad daylight, at teatime, and then he left the door open. 'You don't want to get a bad name with your landlady or your fellow lodgers,' he told her.

What if he was right, like mother like daughter, and she was destined for a wild life of immorality instead of a safe marriage to a good man? Yet her life so far had hardly been characterized by sexual recklessness.

Polly's first fling had been a minor one, a step taken in a spirit of determined curiosity with an older man, a friend of Oliver's who had invited her into his bed when she was spending a weekend in the country, a bohemian household ruled over by a famous painter, where it seemed that bedroom doors opened and shut as a matter of course. He was an attractive man, but she hadn't enjoyed the experience greatly, He had laughed at her and said that the worst was over, and once she lost her heart to a man, she would find sex exciting and ecstatic.

Then she met Jamie, a fellow artist, and she discovered that Oliver's friend had known what he was talking about. Jamie; no, she wasn't going to think about Jamie, brilliant, erratic, blissful in bed, funny – and, like so many of his contemporaries,

25

with his soul scarred by four years of war that he'd been lucky to survive.

Polly pulled the pillow over her head to shut out her thoughts as well as the sounds of the dachsund on the other side of the street, who barked every night until his mistress came home, and she felt nothing but gladness that the day, a day which had held such astonishing revelations, was over.

Tomorrow, she would go first thing to Somerset House and get that damned birth certificate.

Polly Smith was a sound sleeper, oblivious to the world almost the moment her head touched the pillow.

Polyhymnia Tomkins, it seemed, was troubled with insomnia. Polly woke at four in the morning after several restless hours. She slid out of bed, pushing damp hair back from her forehead, why was she so hot? She drank a glass of water, and looked around for something to read, anything to take her mind off the thoughts that were driving round and round in her mind.

Her eye fell on her passport photo, clipped to the passport application form. It was waiting for the birth certificate, so that she could take it to the Passport Office in Petty France.

What was it that it said on the accompanying instructions? The photograph had to be signed by an MP, a JP, a solicitor, a member of the medical profession, a clergyman. Who had to declare, in solemn words, that the photograph was a true likeness of . . . of whom?

How could anyone declare that the photograph was a true likeness of Polyhymnia Tomkins, when no one in the whole wide world knew or had ever known Polyhymnia Tomkins?

She'd intended to go to her old school to ask the headmistress to sign it. How could she look Miss Murgatroyd in the eye and say, 'Actually, I'm not Polly Smith, and the woman you knew all the years I was at school as my mother is no such thing. I'm her sister's illegitimate daughter.' Polly grew pale at the thought. Who could she ask to sign it? Could anyone sign it, given the circumstances? What would people think of Dora Smith if word got out that the girl everyone knew as her daughter was in fact her niece, father unknown?

The feeble grey light of a November dawn was spreading across the sky before Polly fell asleep again, and when the alarm clock went off with raucous enthusiasm, she felt as though she'd had no sleep at all.

Well, she might as well get the birth certificate, she told herself as she washed in the basin. After that she would have to tackle the problem of the photograph.

This time, she went alone to Somerset House. Last time – was it only yesterday? – she had gone with a light heart, a sense of being on her way to the excitement of going abroad. Oliver had been with her, now, on her own, she found the imposing eighteenth-century building had a sinister air to it.

She hoped, unreasonably, that there would be a different clerk on duty, but no, the woman who was sitting at the enquiry desk was the same one, grey hair twisted into a severe bun, grey eyes enlarged by the pince-nez, eyes that didn't look at all kind this morning, but full of suspicion.

'You were here yesterday,' the clerk said accusingly.

'I was, but it's a different name I'm looking for now.'

Polly hoped she was speaking with calm self-assurance, but the woman's eyes glinted with malicious understanding.

'Not who you thought you were? We get that all the time. They say it's a wise child who knows its own father, don't they? If you've got the details right this time, you should have no trouble.'

She went back to the cards she was filling in.

Polly cleared her throat and waited.

The woman looked up. 'Well?' she said sharply.

27

'You said yesterday that people born abroad weren't in these books.'

'Are you now saying you were born abroad? Are you sure you're English?'

'Quite sure.'

The woman banged her hand down on the bell on the corner of her desk, and after a short pause, a lugubrious individual in a brown linen coat appeared.

'Mr Grier will show you where to go.' And, to Mr Grier: 'Foreign.'

She bent her head again, and Mr Grier looked at Polly. 'Which country?'

'France.'

'This way.'

They went out of the big room with its serried ranks of ledgers and along a corridor, then out into the central square. 'It's in a different section,' he said, pushing open a door and standing back to let her through. They went along another passage, and he stopped at a door with a single word written on it: 'Miscellaneous'.

It was a small room, with more of the red bound ledgers, but only a handful of them compared to the room they had left. 'France,' he said, hauling a volume down and laying it on the high wooden stand, which stood against one wall in a narrow gap between the shelves. 'Leave the volume here when you've finished, I'll put it back.'

Miscellaneous. That was what she was, miscellaneous. Wasn't there a famous aristocratic woman in the eighteenth century who'd had so many children by various fathers that they were given the surname Miscellany?

The book opened at the year 1920 – how few English people seemed to have been born in France. After the war, they would mostly have been diplomats' children, she supposed. Perhaps, being so close to England, women preferred to come back home to give birth. She turned back the pages until she came to 1908. And there, halfway down the page, she found the entry. Polyhymnia Theodora Tomkins.

She had a middle name; Dora Smith had never mentioned that. Theodora, Dora's own name. Perhaps the sisters hadn't been quite so estranged, after all.

She copied the details on to one of the slips of paper provided in a wooden box on the stand, and retraced her steps to the main desk. She handed the slip to the clerk, signed the form, which was filled in with firm, clear letters, and wrote her address.

'It should arrive within the week,' the clerk said. 'You want a short certificate, do you? I see.'

Polly felt her colour rising, she resented the clerk's knowing look. A short certificate, proclaiming her illegitimacy to the world, was to be despised.

That's that, she said aloud as she stepped out into the Strand. The first step had been taken to bring Polyhymnia Tomkins to life.

Perhaps as Polyhymnia she would turn out to be quite a different creature from her old self. Even if she were Polly Tomkins – and no one would use a name like Polyhymnia on an everyday basis, for heaven's sake – a Polly Tomkins must be a different person from a Polly Smith.

Or was that so? If Polly Smith married a Mr Tomkins, would she be different from when she used her maiden name, was a Tomkins in essence different from a Smith? Would she become a different person when she was Polly Harrington?

Yes, she would be different, because she would be a wife, and in due course a mother.

The thought depressed her.

The last traces of the previous day's fog had been blown away by the brisk westerly wind that brought instead gusts of rain sweeping across the city. People walked quickly, heads down, black umbrellas held aloft. Polly didn't have an umbrella, she had given up on umbrellas a long time ago, since, unless it was raining and the brolly in her hand, she invariably left it somewhere. She turned up the collar of her mac and stood for a moment in a tobacconist's doorway, out of the rain, while she decided what to do.

She could go back to her studio and work. No; the painting on her easel at the moment wasn't coming out as she wanted it to, and it grew more unpleasing by the day. Figures on a street, but as Oliver remarked, it looked like the worst excesses of the industrial revolution, with gaunt figures against a backdrop of chimneys.

'It's London.'

'Never. It's undoubtedly some dreary northern street, you've caught the spirit of disillusion and hopelessness wonderfully well.'

'It's meant to be Russell Square in the rush hour.'

'One day, Polly, you'll find what you really want to paint, and it won't be rat-coloured figures in a dismal landscape, no, nor those fetching but trivial book jackets you do for WH Smith. Nor touching up flower paintings in Rossetti's workshop.'

'The jackets and the flowers make me money.'

'Of course, and even an artist must live, if only on eggs and soup. I daresay you could make an excellent career out of nothing but the book jackets; they have a charm which is, you don't need me to tell you, quite lacking in your paintings.'

His words had stung Polly. No artist himself, he chose to find his company among artists, and was renowned for having an eye and an unerring instinct for putting his finger on the weakness in any artist's work. And Polly, honest with herself, had to admit that her art was never going to please her or anyone else unless it changed dramatically.

Her friend, Fanny Powys, happy in her own work of silkscreen printing, had tried to cheer Polly up.

'Oliver doesn't bother to make his sharp remarks about painters he doesn't think have any talent. If he's polite, you know that artist's a no-hoper.'

And Fanny should know, for it was at the private view of an exhibition of her prints that she had introduced Oliver to Polly. Polly, her attention entirely on a vigorous design taken from the whorls of oyster shells, had paid scant notice to the tall man who remained standing beside her.

'It's a matter of patterns,' he said. 'That's what makes Fanny's work different from most of her kind.'

And Polly had found herself drawn into a lively discussion about silkscreen printing, which led to wider topics of contemporary art. Polly was amazed that Oliver, who was, he had at once told her, not an artist, should have such an eye, such a quick appreciation of what artists such as Fanny were about.

'I grew up surrounded by paintings and works of art,' he explained. 'My father is a collector, and very knowledgeable. He's always been interested in the artists of the day as much as in past masters, and so I follow in his footsteps.'

Polly disagreed with Oliver about the work of several painters, and the argument was continued over supper at Bertorelli's, the restaurant that was to become their favourite eating place.

Polly had taken an immediate liking to Oliver. 'We are snip and snap,' she explained to Fanny. 'Oh, it's not sex, although I suppose . . . No, it really isn't. Affinity, that's the word.'

'A strange affinity,' Fanny said drily. 'Polly Smith and the Hon. Oliver.'

'Hon.?'

'His father's a lord. Didn't he tell you?'

Polly pondered on this piece of information. Did it make

a difference? No, Oliver was Oliver. Of course he had another life, far removed from the impecunious day-to-day existence of artists like herself. Yet he was, in his way, one of them. 'He's a friend,' she told Fanny. 'We like one another's company. Our minds are in harmony. That's enough for me, his being an Hon. is neither here nor there.'

A man in a dark coat said, 'Excuse me,' in affronted tones, as though Polly were standing there with the express intention of keeping him from his tobacco, and she moved out of the way, back into the full force of the wind and the rain.

She made up her mind. She would go back to Highgate, and consult Ma about the passport photograph. Maybe she could suggest who could sign it for her.

Dora was at her piano; even on her busiest days, she never did less than two hours' practice. In the kitchen, Mrs Babbit, the char, was singing loudly to herself as she turned out a cupboard.

'How can you play with that noise going on?' Polly said, as she always did.

'Focus,' said Dora, as she always did. Polly, somewhat hesitantly, because she didn't want to sound accusatory, explained her problem.

'I never thought of that.'

'If I'm illegitimate, which I am, then that's a fact, and there's no point denying it,' Polly said.

'And no need to go broadcasting it from the rooftops, either. I've protected you from that all these years.'

'And it wouldn't be good for you if word got around. I don't live here any more, but you do. I've been racking my brains, but I simply don't know these professional kind of people, except the vicar here, and Miss Murgatroyd.'

'It'll have to be Dr Parker,' Dora said. 'He knows you aren't my daughter, and he'll sign it for you.'

'You told him?'

'When Ted and I were still hoping for children. He's never said a word to anyone all these years, he won't say a word now. Go along right away, and you may catch him before he sets off on his rounds.'

Polly arrived at the doctor's house just as he was putting his medical bag into his black Wolseley. As she called out to him, he looked up with the long-suffering expression of a doctor trying to get away, but he smiled when he saw who it was.

'I thought you were another patient.'

'Well, I am, I suppose, but I'm not ill. I'm never ill.'

'So what can I do for you?'

'It's a photograph, for a passport. It needs a signature. I thought . . . Ma said . . .'

Dr Parker was suddenly alert, and he drew his bushy brows together. 'Passport, eh? So Dora's had to come clean at last, I suppose.'

'Yes.'

He ran his eyes down the form. 'I've done this often enough before.' He opened the car door. 'Can't do this standing in the rain.'

The car smelled musty and leathery. Comforting, somehow. He rested the photo on the steering wheel and took a fat black fountain pen out of his inside pocket. He unscrewed the cap and turned the photo over. 'Read out the exact words, Polly, and then you can tell me who you are.'

'Polyhymnia Tomkins, I'm afraid.'

'Good God. Let's hope I can spell Polyhymnia.'

'P–O,' began Polly.

'It's all right, I can remember enough of my classical education to cope with that. One of the muses, wasn't she?'

'Yes.'

'And Tomkins was Dora's maiden name. You're her sister's child.' And then, catching sight of the bleak look on Polly's face. 'Cheer up, young lady. As a doctor, I could tell you, if I didn't know how to keep my mouth shut, how many people even in this small part of London aren't quite what or who they think or say they are.'

'What do you mean?'

'Daughters who are actually granddaughters, sons who were born a year after their named fathers went away to the war, married couples who never went before a priest or a registrar. Your secret's perfectly safe with me, Polly. Besides, you'll soon be Mrs Harrington, and no one will know or care what your name was before that.'

'No,' said Polly, as he wrote on the back of the second photograph and handed it back to her.

'Tuck those away safely, or the ink will run in the wet and it'll be all to do again. Are you going abroad for your honeymoon?'

'Roger likes mountains, so it's to be the Alps.'

'The mountain air will do you good, bring some colour back to your cheeks. As your medical man, I can tell you that you're looking a bit peaky.'

'I don't like the winter. And I'm not sure about mountains. It'll be cold.'

'But bright.'

The birth certificate arrived in a brown envelope, stamped OHMS. Polly hesitated, then pulled it out and read it. Brief was the word. Name, place of birth. She would go today to the Passport Office; if she put it off, she might never do it, but once she'd handed over the form and the photographs and the birth certificate, it would be out of her hands.

What would Roger say when he asked for the birth certificate? Would he ask why she didn't have a full one? Could she pretend she asked for a short one because it cost less?

That wouldn't be quite honest, she must pluck up her courage and tell him the truth about her parentage.

With this uncomfortable thought in her mind, Polly went off to Petty France, to wait on a hard wooden bench before being called up to show her papers, hand in the forms and address an envelope to herself. The passport arrived three days later, dark blue, embossed in gold with the royal coat of arms, and filled with stiff empty pages.

And there, written in an official hand was her new identity, Polyhymnia Theodora Tomkins. Born Paris, May 1, 1908.

FOUR

As a child, and indeed until she left her home in Highgate, Polly had disliked Sundays. Not because the Smiths were tyrannical Sabbath-keepers, but because of the general dreariness of the day. Almost, she wished Dora had been a churchgoer, since friends and neighbours who did attend divine service on Sunday mornings seemed to enjoy their day much more than the Smiths did.

Dora, however, was an agnostic. 'I'm not saying there is or isn't a God,' she told Polly. 'That's for everyone to decide for him or herself. On balance, I'd say there's more to life than what we can see, music is proof of that.' Dora had a fine contralto voice, and sang with the London Bach Choir; they had just given a performance of the St John Passion, 'And I defy anyone to listen to Bach and not be touched by a greater spirit. One thing I'm certain of, which is that any God there happens to be isn't in attendance at St Jude's on a regular basis at eleven o'clock on Sunday mornings. Nor at any other time. I shouldn't have any respect for a deity who chose to be in that place in that company.'

So Dora spent Sundays catching up with herself, as she put it. She took in a Sunday paper, which she read in the morning. In the afternoon, she listened to the wireless and did some mending. In the evening, she usually went round to the Mortimers at number 19, to play cards. All of which, to the young Polly, spelled boredom. Sunday was a tedious day, twice as long as any other day of the week, a day when she felt caged and confined. By Sunday evening, she was longing for the day to be over and for Monday to come.

Once she had left Bingley Street, Polly's Sundays improved. She often spent the day with friends, discussing Life and Art, and, in good weather, going on the river or borrowing a bicycle and going for long rides into the country. On Sunday evenings, there was always a group of convivial souls gathered at one or other of the pubs they patronized.

All that changed once more when she met Roger. In fact, her more cynical friends claimed that it was because of Sundays that she had got engaged to Roger. Roger was at his best on Sundays, more relaxed, warmer, his mind not so engaged with his work. However, he was still a punctual man, Sunday or no Sunday, and Polly cursed when she looked at the clock and saw the time. Twenty-five past ten. That was the penalty for idling in bed, but on a winter morning it took a lot of effort to leave the warm covers and get dressed in a room so cold that the windows were still frosted over halfway through the morning.

Damn, there was a hole in her lisle stockings. Would it show? Yes, it would. She had approximately five minutes before Roger would draw up outside the house and give three short blasts on his horn, expecting the front door to open at once.

Too bad, he'd have to wait. She found her sewing kit, and with the stocking still on her leg, cobbled the edges of the hole together. It didn't look good, but it was better than a patch of bare leg showing through. Toot, toot, toot. There was Roger. She dragged a comb through her hair; she had slept on a lock which now jutted out at a strange angle, well, it couldn't be helped. She tucked her hair up into her beret, grabbed her handbag, and hurried down the stairs.

Roger was standing beside his MG, looking at his watch. 'Really, Polly, I don't know why you can never be ready on time.'

'Good morning, Roger,' she said, giving him a peck on the cheek. He held the car door open for her and she got in. 'I found a hole in my stockings, I had to mend it, imagine what your mother would think.'

He glanced down at her leg. 'Those are terrible stockings, anyhow, why don't you get yourself some decent ones?'

'I'm broke.'

'I don't know what you do with your money, you never have a penny.'

'I don't have many pennies to start with.'

'When we're married, I'll give you an allowance, but you'll have to keep track of where it goes, keep accounts and so on.'

The sun had straggled out after days of greyness, and Polly felt too cheerful to let the thought of keeping accounts daunt her. 'I expect I'll manage. And I'll have my money from the workshop as well, besides what I earn from . . .'

'The workshop?' said Roger, accelerating with a throaty roar of the car engine. 'Certainly not. I can't have my wife going out to work, let alone in a place like that.'

Now the sun seemed much less bright. 'But Roger . . .'

'No buts, Polly.' He turned his head and gave her a warm smile, that particular smile was one of his most likeable features. 'Come on, Polly, you know it isn't the thing. Not for a doctor's wife. Of course you must keep up with your art, do those book jackets and so on, and you said you were hoping to get some illustrations to do, that'll bring you in a bit of pin money. That's quite different from going out to work at that place. If you want to fill in your time to some purpose, I'm sure we could find you a suitable position at the hospital, at the welfare section, perhaps.'

There were, Polly realized with a sense of apprehension, a lot of things she and Roger had never talked about. Not because he found it difficult, but because he didn't think there was anything to discuss. So much for Roger's vaunted socialism, so much for equality. The Rogers of this world were a great deal more equal than the Pollys, that was the fact of the matter.

Roger took a sharp corner with a screech, and Polly clung on to the door. Behind the wheel of his car, Roger changed from a sensible, almost cautious man into a daredevil; thank goodness on a Sunday morning there wasn't much traffic about. 'I don't want to give up my work.'

'Polly, be reasonable. You'll be starting a new life, you'll be a new person, Mrs Roger Harrington. It wouldn't be at all suitable for you to carry on – it's not really the kind of job that – well, it isn't suitable, that's all. Besides, we'll want to have children, a baby will put a stop to all that kind of thing.'

Roger hadn't been impressed by the workshop on the one occasion he had been there. He'd come to pick up Polly, and Sam, spying him in the yard below, had called to Polly that her young man was here, and shouted to him to come up.

Roger hadn't taken to Sam – 'What an extraordinary young man, I'm not sure it's quite the thing, Polly, you working up there alone with him.'

Sam hadn't been any more flattering about Roger. 'Can't you do better than that, Polly? Look at his mouth, he's quite handsome now, but that's going to get more and more rigid as the years go by. I smell a disapproving man, you want to watch out, it'll be disastrous getting hitched to a man who disapproves.'

39

'What rubbish you do talk,' Polly had said, annoyed, but then, at Roger's remarks, she had had to swallow her amazed laughter. 'I'm perfectly safe with Sam, I assure you. And mostly Mr Padgett's there as well, and other assistants who come and go. Honestly, what do you imagine? Wild lust among the paint tubes and the canvases?'

'I do wish you wouldn't say things like that.'

Polly usually found Roger's prim ways rather endearing, but this time it annoyed her. 'Oh, Roger, can't you see at a glance that Sam's as queer as a square button?'

'No, I cannot, and I don't like to think that you could. Do you realize what you're saying? Do you realize that it's a criminal offence? Never mind. I put it down to naivety. As a medical man I have some understanding of such people, but it's wholly inappropriate for you to make such remarks, you don't know what you're talking about.'

She wasn't going to argue, not now, not this morning, and here they were, in Bryanston Square, and there was Roger's sister, Alice, waving at them from behind the wrought-iron railings of the first-floor balcony.

Roger screeched to a halt in front of the large terraced house, and went round to open Polly's door. The front door of the house was already open, and Dr Harrington, Roger's father, came down the shallow steps, smiling a welcome. 'Come in, my dear, come in, you must be freezing, driving in that open car of Roger's, really, it's high time he bought a saloon.'

And up the stairs to the drawing room, where one of the other Drs Harrington, Roger's mother, sat in a comfortable chair with her youngest grandchild on her lap, looking pleased, and telling Alice to ring for Foster to bring fresh coffee.

Polly let out a sigh of pure pleasure. The Harrington family were, to her, like something out of a book: read about, dreamed about, but known not to exist outside the pages of a story. But they did exist, here they were, and what was even more wonderful, she was part of the family, or soon would be.

The drawing room was large, with tall sash windows that looked out over the green garden of the square. It had a formal marble fireplace in which a substantial fire was blazing. Everything in the room that could shine, shone: the brass fire surround, the window panes, the large mirror on the wall, the polished surfaces of the tables.

Roger had an older brother, Edward, another Dr Harrington, a rising man in his field of eye surgery, who was married to Celia, herself the daughter of a distinguished consultant. She was a qualified pharmacist, and an asset to her husband. Alice was Roger's younger sister, still a schoolgirl, she rather frightened Polly with her ferocious personality, and it always surprised her when Alice expressed admiration for her calling as an artist.

'It's a vocation, isn't it? Just like my family think medicine is. I mean, you have to do it, whether you want to or not,' she had said to Polly the first time Roger had brought her home to meet his family. 'Writers are the same, they get twitchy if they don't write. Does Roger understand that, I wonder?'

Celia came and sat on the sofa opposite Polly. Polly braced herself, for although Celia was always kind and polite, Polly knew quite well that Celia felt it her duty to fill Polly in on various matters of life that would be important for any woman married to a Harrington. 'You've had your hair cut, I see,' was her opening gambit.

No, strictly speaking that wasn't true. Polly had cut her own hair. Thick, straight and heavy, she trimmed it into an approximation of a bob, leaving it long enough to pin up if she wanted it out of the way.

'I can recommend my hairdresser, Miss Lilian, at the Westbury Salon.'

'Thank you,' said Polly, hating the sound of Miss Lois, but having to admit to herself that Celia's sleek cut was a delight.

Lunch was announced, and they went downstairs to the dining room, a handsome panelled room on the ground floor, with portraits of earlier Harringtons looking benignly down from the walls.

Sunday lunch at the Harringtons was always the same. Soup, a joint and a pie.

Always plentiful, always beautifully cooked, always delicious. Today it was a thick leek and potato soup, followed by roast beef and Yorkshire pudding, with roast potatoes, buttered parsnips and cabbage.

Edward turned to Polly as she was about to take a mouthful of Yorkshire pudding smothered in rich gravy.

'Have you and Roger settled the day yet? January's not far away now. Then off to the Alps, how I envy you.'

Roger wiped his mouth and laid his napkin beside his plate. 'Slight change of plan, actually,' he said. 'Sorry, Polly, I'd meant to tell you before, but I thought I might as well tell everyone at the same time. I only heard on Friday. The fact is, I've been offered a chance to go to America – you remember, Father, I told you I might apply for one of the Leadenhall Awards? Well, I've got it.'

A minor uproar broke out around the table, with mingled congratulations and questions. A success for any one of the Harringtons was felt by them to reflect well on the whole clan.

'What does it entail?' Dr Harrington senior asked.

'I get six weeks in Boston, all expenses paid, and a chance to work with some of the top men in the field.'

Polly said nothing. Alice too was silent, and she looked

directly at Polly. 'You don't mind a bit, do you?' she said in a soft voice.

'No,' Polly whispered back.

'I am sorry, old thing,' Roger was saying to her. 'I didn't tell you I'd even applied, because of course I never expected to get a scholarship, the competition's fierce.'

'Why don't you get married at once and go to America for your honeymoon?' said Celia brightly.

Polly looked at Roger, alarmed. Of course, she'd love to go to America, but . . .

'Impossible, I'm afraid. It's definitely just me, there's no provision for wives. You won't mind, Polly, will you? After all, since we've been engaged for more than a year, two or three more months are neither here nor there.'

'No, of course I don't mind,' Polly murmured, trying to hide her relief. For goodness sake, what was the matter with her? She was genuinely fond of Roger, if not exactly passionately in love; he represented stability, security, safety, and when she was married, she would acquire what she'd never had: a family. A brother and a sister, and Dr Harrington the father she didn't have. If Roger's mother was a trifle too austere to count as the maternal type, well, she had a mother of her own. Two, in fact. Quite enough for anyone.

That brought her up short. Could it be that Polly Smith, daughter of Ted and Dora Smith, was perfectly ready to marry Roger, but that Polyhymnia Tomkins, daughter of Thomasina Tomkins, would rather marry quite a different sort of person – or not get married at all?

At least this meant that she could postpone the day when she had to come clean to Roger – and to his family, he shared everything with his family – about who she really was. How would they react when she revealed that, instead of being the daughter of respectable people, not on a par with the

Harringtons as to background and wealth, of course, but just about acceptable, she was illegitimate? What would they say to a bastard in the family? Dr Harrington liked to think of himself as broad-minded, but Polly had an idea that Roger's mother might have been happier if Roger had become engaged to another Celia.

Polly had never subscribed to the school of getting unpleasant things over with; she always lived in hope that if you put off what was disagreeable, it might go away, and she had found this was often the case.

'When do you go?' Mrs Harrington was asking Roger, and Polly knew she was thinking of suitable clothes and packing. 'Isn't Boston terribly cold in the winter? Did you order a new overcoat? Will it be ready in time?'

'I sail on Saturday. On the *United States*.'

Should she be wrinkling her brow and worrying about whether Roger would have enough warm socks? Polly asked herself. Bother socks, let him worry about them himself.

'I'll be back by the end of January, so we can get married in February. Which reminds me, you'll need a passport.'

'I got it,' said Polly. Oh, God, Polyhymnia Tomkins; surely her duplicity, her new identity must show in her face; go away, Polyhymnia Tomkins, she said inwardly; you aren't wanted in Bryanston Square.

Roger raised his eyebrows to heaven. 'I know what you've done, you've got one in the wrong name.'

'What?' Polly said, her voice squeaky, how did he know?

'You've got a passport in your maiden name, haven't you? Whereas you need one in your married name. What a nuisance, but you can turn it in and I'll put you on mine. I thought it would be advisable for you to have one for yourself, in case we have to travel separately at any time, but I don't suppose that will ever arise. Meanwhile, you'd better give it to me, I'll see to it, and I don't think that room of yours is a safe place to keep valuables.'

'I left it at home. In Highgate. With my mother,' Polly said swiftly and untruthfully, shocked at how easily the lie sprang to her lips. She dug her spoon into the apple pie which had been set in front of her. It was covered in clotted cream sent up from Devon, where the Harrington family came from and had a holiday house, and she rolled the food around in her mouth, barely able to swallow it.

'A walk in the park?' Dr Harrington suggested when they had had coffee upstairs in the drawing room. The walk was part of the ritual, and today Polly, sleepy and disturbed, was more than willing to get out of the house and walk herself back into a good humour.

The park in question was Regent's Park, looking rather forlorn in the fading light of a winter's day. Polly linked arms with Roger, and Celia walked on her other side, talking across her to Roger about Alice. 'I'm pleased to see her take her school work seriously. She needs to buckle down to her books and really apply herself if she's going to get a place to study medicine.'

Roger nodded.

'Does she want to be a doctor?' Polly asked.

Celia had a particular laugh which had nothing to do with mirth. She laughed now. 'Of course she wants to be a doctor. She's a Harrington. She's lucky, she's got the brains for it, and of course the family will help her get a place, only she must get good results in her exams. Women can't get in on rugger and good humour, they have to be twice as good as the men on the academic side.'

'What would she do if she weren't a Harrington?'

'Don't be tiresome, Polly,' said Roger. 'She is a Harrington, it's irrelevant.' And then, with a flash of irritation, 'I suppose she's been going on to you about how she wants to be an actress. It's nonsense, childish fantasy, there's no question of it. Wanting to go on the stage, I ask you!'

A chill came over Polly that was unconnected with the icy wind that had sprung up and was blowing the last leaves of autumn across the path. A squirrel ran down a tree, and sat upright, looking at them with beady eyes before springing away.

'Does Alice have no say?'

Roger looked at her in surprise. They were much of a height, for he wasn't a tall man, and Polly was tall for a woman. 'A say? Of course she has a say. She has plenty of say, it's impossible to shut her up.'

'No, a say about being an actress.'

'I've told you, it's just a silly idea she has. She'll grow out of it. She's got too much sense and too good a brain to go in for anything so foolish.' Roger put his arm round her waist and gave her a squeeze.

'If we had a daughter, wouldn't you let her do what she wanted?' Polly said, looking at the ground as she walked.

'Parents know what's best for their children, and I'd hope that any daughter of ours would be too sensible not to want a decent profession, at least until she married, and medicine, if a woman chooses the right field, general practice or paediatrics, can be combined with marriage and even motherhood. Don't worry about Alice, Polly. She'll want to be a dancer or some such rubbish next week, and I dare say a balloon pilot the week after. You know how girls are at that age, all this acting business is just a passing fad.'

Polly remembered how she was at that age, absorbed in her painting and drawing, fascinated by colour and line and perspective, spending all her spare time in galleries or looking at pictures and sculptures in books, intoxicated by the beckoning world of the artist.

Polly had got engaged to Roger on the way home from a Sunday spent with his family. Warm and secure, she had wrapped herself in Roger's embrace, welcoming the tweedy solidity of his arms, the lingering scent of pipe tobacco. Now she suddenly felt she was looking at him and his family as though through a shattered pane of glass, with the tranquillity and security distorted and broken into a thousand pieces.

FIVE

'Happy families! You've too much sense to be taken in by a happy family,' Oliver said to Polly that evening, as they sat side by side on a settle covered in faded red velvet in the Nag's Head. Polly, who had drunk two glasses of burgundy at lunch, was drinking lemonade, while Oliver had a whisky and soda. It was quiet, on a cold Sunday night. A fire burned in the old-fashioned grate, and the pub cat, a large ginger tom, was curled up on the chair opposite.

Oliver had come round with uncannily good timing, to find Polly sitting on her bed in something like despair.

'Come on, Polly, it's not like you to be down. What's amiss? No, don't tell me. Put on your coat and hat, and we'll go for a drink. Then we can share our tales of sorrow.'

Polly looked gloomily into her glass of lemonade. 'It's just that life's a bit fraught at the moment,' she said finally. 'Why share our sorrows? What's up with you?'

Oliver was an equable man, who took life lightly, often amused, sometimes sarcastic, inclined to be free with his tongue and opinions, but always in a slightly detached way.

I feel closer to him than I do to Roger, Polly said to herself.

Roger's a fiancé and a lover, but he isn't a friend. I don't think he ever will be a friend.

'Bertram – well, Bertram and I are washed up, that's all,' said Oliver. He took a big swig of his drink. 'I think I need another one of these.' He got up and went over to the bar and sat down again. 'Sorry, Polly. I don't think you need to hear about other people's problems.'

'You aren't other people,' said Polly.

Polly had discovered that Oliver was a homosexual by the merest chance; that is, she had gone to his flat, at his request, and had found him in bed with a man. Both of them naked, Oliver's friend severely embarrassed, snatching up the cover to conceal himself, Oliver stark naked and still aroused, laughing at her expression as she tried to back out of the door.

'Oh, come in, Polly, and don't be missish. Bertram, come out from under that sheet, for Christ's sake. This is Polly, not the police come about the vice.'

He had lazily put on a silk dressing gown. 'I quite forgot I asked you to bring those prints round, Polly.'

Bertram, his face scarlet, came out of the bedroom tucking his shirt into his trousers. 'For Christ's sake, Oliver.'

'Polly, this is Bertram. An old, and as you can see, a very close friend. We were at school together. A long time ago, but affections can linger. Now, don't get worked up, Bertram. One thing about Polly here is that she is utterly discreet and completely trustworthy. There are few people I would trust not to spread this delicious piece of scandal around London, and lucky for us, Polly is one of them.'

Polly sat down on Oliver's elegant sofa with a thump. 'I'm so sorry. What an awful thing to do. I didn't realize . . .'

'Is it so much worse than finding me in bed with a woman? Yes, I suppose it is.'

'You do understand, don't you?' Bertram said, sitting down

on the matching sofa opposite and gazing solemnly at Polly. 'You do understand that if this ever got out – well, it mustn't for both our sakes. Oliver simply can't take any risks, not after—'

A warning look from Oliver silenced him for a moment. 'Well, I won't go into the reasons. And as for me, no one has any idea. That I – that I'm . . . You do see, don't you?'

Polly did. Some queers weren't bothered one way or the other, such as Sam, who was quite open about his inclinations. That worried her, because you read in the papers about people, even famous people, being had up for accosting other men.

'It's a private affair,' said Oliver, watching her. 'Not like picking up guardsmen or boys in the park, you know. Think of us as a couple, but a couple who have to keep their relationship secret.'

'If my family ever knew . . .' said Bertram. He took out a silk handkerchief and passed it across his brow. He was a good-looking man, with light brown wavy hair and deep, dark blue eyes. He smiled at her, his face relaxing for the first time, and she smiled back.

'Don't worry,' she said. 'I wouldn't have had this happen for the world, but your secret's perfectly safe with me. Truly it is.'

She rose, wanting to get away.

There had been a time, when she first met Oliver, when she might well have fallen in love with him. She had never felt such a rapport with a man; she felt utterly at ease in his company, even when she barely knew him.

And now Oliver had lost Bertram? 'That's dreadful, Oliver.'

His mouth trembled, and he bit his lip to control it. 'It is, rather. When you love someone as much as I do Bertram, one can't imagine life without him.'

'But why? Has he found someone else?'

'He's getting married,' Oliver said flatly. 'He's decided to put what he calls "all this" behind him, and he's marrying a nice girl. A friend of his family. Suitable in every way. His family are thrilled. He wants me to be best man.'

'He wants you – oh, Oliver, no! He can't ask that of you.'

'It seems he can. However, since he's getting married next month, and I plan to be in France for the whole of January, he will have to look elsewhere for a best man.'

'You sound bitter. I'm not surprised.'

'No, I'm not bitter. In a way, I always knew it would end like this. Bertram has never liked the cloak and dagger side of such a friendship, the secrecy, the effort to keep it all hidden. Some of us thrive on it, he doesn't. He yearns to be respectable, like everyone else. Sad to say, he has an essentially bourgeois nature.'

'But if – if he's the way he is, how can he marry? The poor girl, she doesn't know about you and him?'

'Good heavens, no. I don't suppose she even knows that such relationships exist. No, she doesn't know, and Bertram is definitely not going to tell her. He's going to walk down the aisle with his radiant bride on his arm, and from then on, he'll be a normal man. He wants children, of course. That's a strong pull. That's one thing we can't give each other. Oh, hell, Polly, why is love so beastly? You're so fortunate, with your staid Roger and the whole world beaming approval, you don't know how lucky you are.'

'I thought so, but I'm not so sure.'

'Lovers' tiff?'

Polly pulled a face. 'Can you imagine having a lovers' tiff with Roger? Arguing with him is like disagreeing with a brick. No, it's just that I saw a side of him today that I didn't know about, and I didn't care for it much. He's going to America, sailing at the weekend. To spend time with American doctors in Boston.'

'Is he? How long for? I thought you were all lined up for a wedding in the new year.'

'Not any more. It has to be postponed until he gets back, sometime in February.'

'And you aren't upset?'

'No, not at all. I don't mind being engaged, there's a comfort in it, and I'm happy enough when I'm with Roger. But marriage is a bit of a step.' Polly twisted her glass round in her hands. 'He maintains I can't go on working once we're married. In fact, I think he expects me to give up my painting altogether. Which is all a bit of a wrench, I like what I do at the workshop.'

'I saw that coming, even if you didn't,' said Oliver. 'You do sound dreary, ducks. All this and the art not going too well.'

'Don't say that!' said Polly, roused out of her glumness by his unexpected attack.

'My dear Polly, your paintings are getting smaller and dingier by the week. Whoever is going to buy them? They're technically very good, but if you go on the way you are, you'll end up painting miniatures.'

'Canvases of a decent size cost money.'

'Come on, that's not the reason, and you know it. Life's boxing you in, that's what's happening to you. Time to burst out, Polly my dear.'

'Do you think one can do that? Change one's life? Leave the old one behind like a snake shedding its skin? I don't. I think however hard you tried, you'd still be the same old snake, hissing and coiling in the same old way. Even if you did have a shiny new shape, all green and gold and glistening . . .' The snake was there, in her mind's eye, or perhaps green and gold was more appropriate for a dragon. The creature morphed instantly into a beast with snorting, fiery breath and huge wings, and Polly laughed.

'That's better,' Oliver said. 'I've an idea. Come and spend a few weeks at my father's house in Cap Rodoard, in the south of France, where the light will dazzle your eyes, even in the depths of winter. It's a strange place, my father's house, but there's quite a community of artists in the village, plenty of kindred spirits for you. I think the dim dreariness of a bad London winter is seeping into your soul. Over there you can throw open the shutters in the morning, and there's the sun pouring in to lighten your life. Palm trees outside the window, colour everywhere to lighten your darkness.'

His father's house. Oliver never spoke about his family, he might have been an orphan or one of ten children for all Polly knew. 'Does your father spend much time in France?'

'He lives there.'

'Why? Doesn't he like England? Or is he French?'

Oliver looked amused. 'Good Lord, no. As English as they come, bad barons going back through the centuries.'

'So why France?'

Oliver went quiet, then lifted his glass and finished his whisky. 'He prefers it,' he said.

'Do you have other family over there? Is your mother . . . ?'

'My sister might be out there for the winter, with or without her husband, but she needn't bother you.'

Polly sighed. 'It's kind of you to ask, Oliver, and I should love to go to France, but it's impossible.'

Polly had suggested to Roger that they go to France for their honeymoon, Paris, she said, thinking of that city so redolent of artists, of galleries crammed with wonderful paintings, of *la vie bohème*. Then they could go down to the south for a few days, perhaps . . .

Roger had shaken his head. 'I don't care for France, and you wouldn't like the south of France, it's a frivolous place, if you mean the Riviera. No, mountains are better. Lots of clean, good air, and I might get some climbing in. Switzerland might be best, or Austria.'

'Why impossible?' said Oliver.

'Oh, too expensive, and no, before you offer, I won't let you fund me, and no, you don't want to buy one of my pictures. Come on, Oliver, you and I have always been honest with one another.'

'Have we?' said Oliver. 'I suppose so.'

One says these things, Polly told herself. But it isn't true. Oliver keeps most of his life to himself, I only ever get a glimpse here and there, when he comes out of his own world to come visiting in mine. And what about me? I haven't told him about Polyhymnia, and I don't know why not.

'Besides, Roger wouldn't care for my going. I've got to consider his feelings.'

'Surely he isn't jealous of me?'

'No, but . . .' Polly didn't want to tell Oliver that Roger disapproved of her friendship with him. He probably knew it already. Was that something else that would be cut out of her life, once she was Mrs Harrington? No, it wasn't. Her days would be her own, Roger couldn't keep tabs on her for every hour of the day, she wasn't entering a harem, for heaven's sake.

'Live a little, before you get shackled for the rest of your life, I can't see a woman like you ever leaving her husband. Shake the savings out of the piggy bank, and splurge it all on a ticket. Away with the gloom of an English winter, a month in the sun, what could be better for you? Bring some colour back into your cheeks.'

His words echoed those of Dr Parker, was she really so pallid? 'I don't believe it's sunny anywhere in January. I bet it rains there too.'

'Oh, it does, and snow has even been known to fall, every twenty years or so, but mostly it's far warmer, and always

54

brighter. It's the light, Polly, that's why artists love the south of France. Now, finish your lemonade, and I'll take you to Bertorelli's for supper.'

'I had a huge lunch.'

'Yes, but emotion is very draining, you need to keep your strength up.'

He said goodbye to the luscious Irene, the bosomy barmaid who presided over the bar at the Nag's Head, and they went outside.

'Touch of frost, tonight,' said Oliver. He lifted his hand as a cab came in sight, and opened the door for Polly.

Sitting in the dark, slightly smelly interior, Polly asked, 'How much does it cost to get to France? Oh, I suppose that's a silly question. You'd travel first class.'

'Third class would be about ten pounds,' Oliver said. 'Having second thoughts?'

'I haven't got ten pounds,' Polly said regretfully. 'Having ten shillings to spare at the end of the week would be a minor miracle.'

'Get some more of those book jackets you do.'

'And there's my work in Lion Yard to consider. I don't want Mr Padgett finding someone else to take my place.'

'It seems that you'll have to give it up in any case, so why not a month sooner?'

'No, Oliver. It's tempting, but I can't come, and that's that.'

SIX

Max Lytton arrived at the Feathers Inn before Inspector Pritchard. It was an old-fashioned pub, not so very different from when it was built in the seventeenth century, with its polished wooden boards and a warren of narrow passages and staircases that led into unexpected rooms or out into one of its several yards. It had been a haunt of highwaymen in its heyday, and it was easy to imagine booted and cloaked men lurking in dark corners or in the cobbled courtyard, where the stables had been turned into a bar.

Max went into the downstairs dining room, a discreet place, with the tables set against the walls and screened by high-backed wooden seats. A perfect place for private conversation, which was what Max wanted. A log fire burned in the wide stone fireplace, and there was sawdust on the floor. He found an empty table and sat down with a tankard of the pub's famous ale.

'I'm waiting for a friend,' he said to the waiter who was hovering to take his order, and as he spoke, he saw Pritchard standing at the door. Pritchard hesitated, looking round and then, as Max rose, lifted a hand in greeting and came over to join him.

A pint of bitter was brought for Inspector Pritchard, and the waiter came back to take their order. He could recommend a cut off the joint of Welsh lamb, excellent today or, of course, there was the inn's renowned steak and kidney pudding.

'They make it in the traditional way, with oysters,' Max told Pritchard.

'I'm not a great man for shellfish,' Pritchard said in his lilting Welsh voice. 'I'll have the lamb, since it comes from my country, and our sheep are the best in the kingdom.'

The waiter went away, and the two men regarded one another in silence. They had met two years before, when Inspector Pritchard was a detective sergeant, hoping for promotion. He had been working on a murder case, and Max, obtaining information that the police had no access to, had passed it on to the eager policeman. The case had been solved, a very unpleasant criminal brought to justice, and Pritchard had got his promotion.

'I take it this is a professional meeting,' said Max.

Pritchard's soft brown eyes were guileless, but Max knew better than to take the look of sleepy indifference at face value. Pritchard was a wily man, who possessed a strong moral sense coupled with a healthy cynicism as to the essential evil dwelling within his fellow beings.

'Professional, yes, but a matter best not tackled through the usual channels, do you see?'

'Unofficial business? That doesn't sound like your outfit.'

'Not precisely unofficial, just best if the details are kept between the two of us. You have your masters and I have mine. And yours are happy for me to talk to you about this. They, too, want to keep it unofficial for the time being.'

To his friends and relatives and to the closed world of London society, Max Lytton was no more than a man about town. An attractive man, surprisingly still a bachelor, despite the best efforts of debs and their mamas. He came from an old family, had considerable private means – a fortune inherited from a great aunt had come as a surprise to a younger son and a source of discontent to his father and older brothers. Because of this, he could live the life he wanted; a life to which his father took endless exception. 'Didn't fight for your country in the war, now you live an idle life, of no value to yourself nor anybody else. We weren't put upon this earth to be comfortable, but to leave it a better place, I don't see you doing that.'

Max knew there was no point in remonstrating or arguing with his father, who knew perfectly well that it was lameness from a childhood dose of polio that had prevented him being butchered in the trenches. The fact that he had spent a hard-working and successful war in Military Intelligence meant nothing to his father, a retired general. 'Desk job, waste of time, the place for cowards and men too old or effeminate to fight.'

Nor did his father have any idea that he had been one of the few men from his department kept on after the war ended, when the intelligence services were largely wound up, with the remnants tucked away in a forgotten corner of Whitehall, starved of funds. Although recently, things had begun to change, the situation in Russia was ringing alarm bells, and to the knowledgeable men who had experience of Germany, so were the repercussions of the Treaty of Versailles.

'Excuse me, sir.' The waiter put plates down in front of them, and then returned with a steaming pie which he set in front of Max. Another waiter arrived with a trolley, to cut thick slices of the succulent lamb for Pritchard. Dishes of potatoes, carrots and cabbage were placed on the table, and the waiters withdrew.

Pritchard spooned redcurrant jelly on to his plate beside his lamb. Max plunged a spoon into the golden crust of his pie and transferred a generous portion to his plate.

'If it's a police matter, I don't see what it has to do with us,' Max said.

'Then you haven't heard that I was transferred last year,' said Pritchard. 'To Special Branch.'

That surprised Max. The soft-spoken Welshman had a keen mind and that extra grain of intuition that singled out the exceptional policeman from the ordinary. But Special Branch? Perhaps it was a sign of the times, an indication of how alarmed the powers that be were about the rising anger and intensity of those who felt life hadn't offered them a fair deal. Which, in many cases it hadn't. Extremism was on the rise, certainly in continental Europe, possibly now even in England.

In which case, Special Branch would need capable officers like Pritchard. There was, after all, more to maintaining the peace of the realm than catching criminals.

Special Branch and the intelligence services worked in an uneasy alliance, with some bitter spats about territorial demarcations. If Pritchard's and Max's superiors were working together on this, it would mean that they were after someone who had dealings that went beyond the merely local and criminal.

'Out with it,' he said. 'What particular game is afoot?'

'I don't see you as Watson, nor myself as Sherlock Holmes,' said Pritchard, spearing a roast potato and chewing it carefully. He wiped his mouth with his napkin and took a draught of beer. 'I believe you know Sir Walter Malreward?'

'Ah,' said Max. 'Malreward. Yes.'

'By reputation, in the way of business, or personally?'

'He is a man much in the public eye, and I have a slight personal acquaintance with him. As to his business affairs, no, I have nothing to do with them.'

Pritchard was playing with him. Pritchard must know perfectly well who Sir Walter's constant companion was, to use the coy words of the lower kind of newspaper. Mrs Harkness. Cynthia Harkness, recent divorcée, and Max's sister.

'Surely he isn't up to any mischief? He runs what passes for a reputable publishing empire, gives money to the poor, is active in middle-of-the-road politics, keeps his nose perfectly clean.'

'Do you like him?'

Max took refuge in his tankard of beer. Like, dislike, what did that have to do with it? 'If your lot are interested in Malreward, it's hardly relevant how I may or may not feel about him. I don't go in for feelings.'

'I know that. But you're a fair judge of a man, for all that.'

'I wouldn't climb a mountain with Malreward on the other end of the rope, if that's what you mean.'

'I didn't know you went in for climbing,' said Pritchard, glancing down involuntarily to where he knew Max's bad leg would be stretched out beneath the table.

'I speak figuratively.'

'He is said to be tough but honest in his business dealings.'

'In which case you need to examine your sources more carefully,' said Max. 'No one gets to be as rich as Sir Walter is without being ruthless and sailing pretty close to the wind somewhere along the line. Risks are how fortunes are made. If you believe any businessman as successful as Malreward got there in any other way, I have some fairies at the bottom of my garden that I'm willing to sell to you for a reasonable sum.'

Pritchard smiled. 'Leave the fairies to us Celts, Mr Lytton. No, but Sir Walter's record appears to be cleaner than most. Which makes him a sensitive subject, which is why we're here and not in my or your office. Our lords and masters like Sir Walter. There's talk of him being offered a junior post in the government.'

60

Max frowned. It wasn't unusual for there to be some official vetting of a man's background before he was recommended for a difficult post or high honours, but it was hardly his line of work. 'Surely they went into his habits and antecedents before he got his knighthood.'

He fell silent as the waiter appeared to scoop up the empty plates and dishes.

'Very good, the lamb,' Pritchard said to him.

'Thank you, sir. Apple pie to follow? With cream or custard?'

The apple pie duly arrived, and Max poured cream over his portion. 'What's Sir Walter been up to that's caused these twinges of alarm? It can't just be the possibility of a government position.'

'We found out about it quite by chance. As you know, we take an interest these days in some of the smaller political groups. Both left-wing and right-wing outfits.'

'Trotskyists and Marxist Leninists on the one hand, and the blackshirts and others of a fascistic tendency on the other, you mean.'

'You'd know more about the fascists than I would, you've been in Italy recently, haven't you?'

'Yes, and although quite a few of the great and the good hold that fascism is our only bulwark against a Bolshevik takeover, my superiors are suspicious of any group that wants to overthrow society, challenge Parliament, or generally go in for rabble-rousing.'

'There's a group of anarchists we at the Special Branch are keeping our eye on, too, since we don't want to see any trouble from that direction, either.'

'You're hardly going to tell me that Malreward is a secret anarchist or Leninist?'

'No. It's stranger than that, and therefore possibly more sinister. He's given quite a substantial sum of money to the

Communist Party, but also to several groups of quite a different persuasion. And to the aforesaid anarchists.'

'It doesn't smack of intense political conviction.'

'It does not. And it doesn't fit in with the reasonable, moderate Conservative person he appears to be.'

'It sounds to me as though he's intent on stirring up trouble. Of one kind or another.'

'Exactly. And the sums involved are quite large, and we'd like to know where they're coming from.'

Max shook his head. 'That's no mystery. He's a very rich man.'

'Yes, and we have access to his accounts and to his bank, and these funds haven't passed through any of what you might call normal channels.'

'That just means he's had the sense and know-how to cover his tracks.'

'We have reasons to believe that Sir Walter has sources of income other than those arising from his perfectly open and respectable business dealings.'

Max's heart sank. He didn't like what he was hearing, not one bit. What had Cynthia got herself into? 'Out with it. Drugs?'

'It doesn't look like it, although that was our first thought. Yet he is up to something crooked, I'm convinced of it, and when you read the file, you'll come to the same conclusion.'

'It seems incredible to me. Why should a man who has built himself a large fortune and reached the position Sir Walter has feel a need to have any underhand or criminal dealings? Why jeopardize the chance of a post in the government?'

'Then tell me why, if he's an honest and upright citizen, does he pour large sums of money into subversive organizations?'

'Perhaps he feels this country needs a wider political base, so that matters are more thoroughly debated from both sides of the political divide.'

'And perhaps a flight of purple pigs are going to sail past the window,' said Pritchard.

Coffee was brought, and Pritchard lit a pipe. Max gazed into the fire, watching as flames licked round a new log and another log broke and fell into the grate in a shower of sparks.

Pritchard took a good draw on his pipe, then removed it from his mouth and let out a stream of smoke. 'This comes close to home for you. Your sister, now . . .'

'Yes.' If Sir Walter were revealed to be up to anything dangerous or crooked, the repercussions for Cynthia would not be pleasant. She had suffered a certain amount of vilification over her divorce, coming as it did after her flagrant flaunting of herself in Sir Walter's company, and among her set, her husband was very well liked.

He wasn't going to pass judgement; he had wished Cynthia would be more discreet, but it wasn't her way. On the other hand, it might turn out that Sir Walter was not up to anything illegal, let alone criminal. A man could choose to give money where he wanted, there was no law against handing over sums of money to any political movement that wasn't actually banned. It could be a quirk in his character, there could be a dozen reasons for such behaviour, although Max felt in his bones that there was more to it than the whim of a rich man.

'I took the liberty of mentioning the circumstances to my superiors,' said Pritchard. 'And—'

'If this is a job assigned to me, I'll do it,' said Max without hesitation. 'If my sister ends up made uncomfortable by it, well, that's too bad. One can't let emotional and personal ties get in the way of what has to be done. I take it my brief is to find out if Sir Walter is making money on the side, if he has ties to any foreign political groups – that's what your lot are really afraid of, isn't it? – and what else he might be doing with his money.'

'You're very brutal about it. Mrs Harkness—'

'Is a grown-up. If she plays with fire, she may get burnt. What background information do you have on Sir Walter?'

'I brought the file with me.' Pritchard dug into his brown leather briefcase and pulled out a buff folder, stamped Secret. He passed it to Max. 'Knighthood three years ago, member of the Conservative party, everything above board. He owns a house in London, another one in Wiltshire. There are gaps, however. He came to England before the war, from France, where he has another house.'

'As does my sister,' said Max. 'In the same place as Malreward, that's how they met. I wonder if she's going to France for Christmas . . .' His voice tailed off, and he was silent for a while, thinking about what Pritchard had told him, turning possible approaches over in his mind. 'If she is, I can invite myself to spend Christmas with her there. Although she might, of course, be staying at Malreward's villa.'

'Isn't that mixing your personal and professional lives rather too closely?'

'No, I don't think so. It could be useful in both ways.' Max gave Pritchard a direct look. 'I'm fond of my sister. She might not thank me for it, but if Malreward turns out to be a crook of some kind, the sooner she finds out the better.' He didn't add, preferably before she marries him and finds herself in God knows what kind of a mess.

'Is it a very strong attachment?' Pritchard asked. 'With society ladies, it's not always easy to tell.'

'Is that a polite way of asking if she likes his wealth rather than the man?'

Pritchard looked taken aback by the coldness in Max's

voice. 'It is not. It is only that women of her – of your – class live according to a different set of rules than those which apply where I come from.'

Max raised a hand to acknowledge the rebuke. 'True enough. However, I believe women generally find Sir Walter an attractive man. He has a masculine energy about him, and the aura of success has its own appeal.'

'A virile man,' Pritchard agreed. 'And a forceful one. I shouldn't like to cross him.'

'That's exactly what you're proposing I do, however.'

'He won't be aware that you have any interest in him, not the way you work. Your sister doesn't know what you are, what you do?'

'No,' said Max.

Which was probably true inasmuch as he had never told her; on the other hand, he had a suspicion that, unlike the rest of his family, she had a good idea that his apparently idle life wasn't entirely what it seemed.

Max paid the bill after a mild protest from Pritchard, and the two men walked out into the pale sunlight which was just filtering through scudding clouds. They stood on the corner of Kettle Street, watching the traffic in Holborn rushing past, red buses the only patches of colour among the cars and wagons and drably coated pedestrians.

'I may call in Lazarus,' Max said, as they parted.

Pritchard, about to head for a bus stop, paused. 'You take it that seriously?'

'Yes,' said Max, and watched his companion dive through the traffic and board his bus just as it was drawing away. Yes, he took it that seriously.

SEVEN

Every time she walked up the gangway of an ocean liner, crossing the symbolic boundary between land and sea, Cynthia Harkness felt she could happily spend all her days on board ship. Although in truth, it was the limited number of days that made a voyage so appealing. Five days lay ahead of her, five days when she wasn't·in England or in America, but caught in a floating world that had no existence beyond its railings, a ship that might, it seemed, sail for ever on the surging grey ocean.

'Perhaps we all have a bit of the Flying Dutchman in us,' she said to her neighbour at dinner on the first night out.

The man, a stolid American, looked at her in some surprise, and then smiled. 'I know you English people are renowned for your sense of humour,' he said. 'My business would surely fail if I were trapped on a vessel doomed to sail the seas for ever. And I guess the company on board wasn't any too good, didn't the guy lead a solitary life? For myself, I prefer company.'

The *Aquitania*, the Ship Beautiful as she was known, on account of the sumptuousness and extravagance of her fittings, was Cynthia's favourite ship on the Atlantic run.

This trip, she had made the booking herself, which meant that she could travel in a pleasant stateroom instead of in a suite, which would have been far too large for her needs, and which would have drawn the attention of everyone on board, exactly what she didn't want. Mrs Harkness, with a stateroom on B deck, was an anonymous creature. Whereas if Walter had made the booking, she would be sitting at the Captain's table, not where she was on the other side of the huge dining room, again quite anonymous, among less favoured passengers at a table hosted by a much more lowly officer. An attractive young man, dark and well groomed, but then the Cunard officers were in general a very creditable lot.

The man sitting beside her introduced himself as one Myron Watson, travelling to England on holiday with his wife, Lois. A woman of about her own age, with a smooth helmet of dark hair, and wearing a pale pink silk frock, smiled at Cynthia across the table

'I do like the way you make friends on board,' she said, her voice unexpectedly husky for one who had chosen pink. She wasn't pretty, nor even handsome, but she had sex appeal, Cynthia decided. There was something about the tilt of her head and her mouth that would interest more men than Myron, her big, bland, genial husband. No doubt a rich man; no doubt one of those who had been lucky enough not to see his business wiped out in the Depression.

A courteous enquiry brought a flood of information about ball bearings. Apparently, the world couldn't get enough of ball bearings, even in these sadly hard times.

'There are those, ma'am, I regret to say, who see War on the horizon.' Mr Watson was the kind of man who spoke in capital letters. 'And where's there's War, or threat of War, or even suspicion that one day there might be War, why, there is Opportunity.'

The dining room on the *Aquitania* was a glittering sea of mirrors and pillars and white napery and silver and crystal. It was an absurd great room, with its panelling and decorated ceiling and Louis-Seize furniture and paintings. The decor of the vessel always made Cynthia smile, the mad medley of English and French architectural styles: Grinling Gibbons carvings here, Palladian pillar there, Louise-Quinze sofas and mirrors, Elizabethan and Jacobean and Georgian features and fittings all represented in the public rooms.

'It's all so Olde Englande,' said Lois with enthusiasm. 'I just love everything old, and here on board, I feel I get an extra five days' worth of all the sights I'll be visiting when we get to London. The Tower of London, Tower Bridge, St Paul's Abbey . . .'

'Cathedral,' Cynthia couldn't help murmuring.

'Cathedral? Oh, yes. It's Westminster Abbey, and St Paul's Cathedral.'

'There is a Westminster Cathedral as well,' Cynthia said.

'Is that so?' Lois pursed her vivid lips. 'That wasn't on the list the travel bureau gave us.'

'It isn't very old. A lot of people think it's ugly, it's built of red brick. Victorian, you see, and then there are the smells and bells inside.'

'Pardon me?' said Lois, looking affronted.

'Incense and so on. It's a Roman Catholic cathedral. The others are Protestant. Anglican.'

'That's our Episcopalian, Lois,' said Myron. 'We're Baptists ourselves, Mrs Harkness, but I confess I'm looking forward to seeing some of your great English churches, which people say are most impressive edifices.'

Cynthia was beginning to feel that a little of Lois and Myron Watson would go a long way, but that was the joy of shipboard company; it was only five days, you could endure a lot worse than the Watsons for five days, and then, when you stepped ashore, you need never set eyes on them again.

She escaped from them after dinner, with some difficulty, and retreated to the garden lounge. It was deserted, not being a popular spot at this time of day on a winter crossing, with the glass flinging back dark reflections instead of the light that shone through to the trellis work and imitation stone in the daytime to give the illusion of being in a garden.

Cynthia sat in one of the wicker chairs, and an attentive steward appeared to offer more coffee, liqueurs, brandy.

Cynthia asked for another coffee, she was feeling so sleepy that it wouldn't keep her awake. It had been a busy couple of days, packing, paying farewell visits, writing letters. She had been in the States since the beginning of September, and she found she was looking forward to getting back to England. She hoped the fuss would have died down, it was ridiculous the interest the press and that amorphous thing, the public, took in divorce cases. At least they hadn't had the pleasure of any sensational details, indeed, her divorce would hardly have been noticed if it hadn't been bungled so that the first judge had thrown out the evidence from the hotel, knowing the lady in question and the chambermaid far too well. The next time, her husband had managed it better, paying more for a less well-known woman willing to spend the night in a hotel room with him. 'Playing cards all damn night,' he had told Cynthia irritably. 'And hopeless with it. When she suggested a round or two of snap, I nearly lost my temper. However, we came out of it all right, and thank God I wasn't up in front of that sarky old number of a judge like the one I had first time.'

Then it had been Cynthia who had put the divorce in jeopardy, when an eager press photographer, who had no business being at a private dance, had snapped her dancing very closely with Sir Walter Malreward – a man much in the news for his wealth and influence, a Member of Parliament, a man who didn't care to have scandal associated with his name. Whispers of collusion were heard.

Sir Walter was annoyed. 'If it comes to the judge's ears, there'll be the devil to pay, and of course those damn reporters are watching your husband like a hawk, he'll do well to keep away from that woman of his, what's her name?'

'Sally Lupin,' said Cynthia.

'Otherwise you'll have to start the whole damn process again. You'll have to go abroad for a while. We can't risk it. The decree nisi should be any day now, if you stay away until the decree absolute, they can't touch us. I suggest America. I shan't be going over myself until next year, no danger of any prying pressmen getting more illicit shots. And I'll deal with that bloody photographer, make sure of that, he won't be taking any more spiteful shots of us or anybody else. I shall miss you, of course, but it can't be helped.'

Cynthia had wanted to demur at this high-handed arrangement of her affairs, but it was Walter's way, and her husband accepted the news of her departure with some relief. 'Best thing. You're newsworthy, now your name's been publicly linked with Sir Walter, and it makes me look a bit of a fool, really, I'd be glad if you felt like going.'

Walter set to work, booking the best suite on the next boat to sail, rather to Cynthia's dismay, and all set to despatch telegrams and letters to his numerous acquaintances and business contacts in America.

'There's absolutely no need,' Cynthia said crossly. 'As it happens, I have family in America, my first cousin is married to an American and lives in Virginia, I can stay with them as long as I want. And I have a friend from my schooldays who lives in Boston, and friends in New York, I shall do perfectly well, thank you, Walter. Indeed, I don't suppose I'll have enough time to see all the people I want. I'll have some clothes made as well,' she added. 'I've seen some lovely designs by Mainbocher worn by American women in London, I plan to give him a try.'

'You could order your wedding dress. Blue, I like you in blue.'

That was going too far. She would choose her own dress for that ceremony, in a colour of her choosing, and it would come from Paris, not from America.

She stirred in her seat at the sound of voices. An English family had ventured into the garden lounge, a father and mother and two young women who must be their daughters. They were laughing and talking, but then one of the girls caught sight of Cynthia. Her clear young voice floated through the air.

'I say, Mummy, isn't that Mrs Harkness? The one who . . .'

Her mother sshed her.

'Don't you know them? Isn't she some kind of relation of Daddy's?'

The younger girl was staring with unabashed curiosity. 'I tell you what, she's Harriet Harkness's mother. Harriet was in my form at Rhindleys, but she had to leave the school last term, Mrs Youdall made her parents take her away, because of the divorce. They've sent her to St Monica's.'

And then the mother's voice rang out, with the sharp arrogant edge that marked the self-righteous, indignant Englishwoman of her class who knew she held the moral high ground.

'It's a shocking way to behave, and her husband a war hero . . .'

Cynthia remembered the woman's name. Gardner, that was it. Rosemary Gardner. Dreadful woman. She turned her head and smiled at the little party. 'Good evening, Mrs Gardner, isn't it? Won't you come and join me?'

Without replying, the woman gave Cynthia a furious look

and hustled her girls away, her husband following, after pausing briefly to give Cynthia a wry and apologetic smile.

The cut direct, Cynthia said to herself, as she settled back in her seat. Was that what she could expect when she was back in England? In which case it wouldn't be pleasant, either for her or for Harriet.

Her mind floated back to thoughts of her wedding dress. How different her wedding to Walter would be from her first one. With Walter it would be the Ritz, no doubt, with lavish refreshments, and guests summoned from his parliamentary colleagues and those who had too much to gain from his acquaintance to snub him on account of his marrying a rather notorious divorcée. The fuss would die down soon enough, Cynthia was old and wise enough in the ways of society to know that. The faint stigma would remain, but as the wife of an immensely rich and successful man she need care little for that.

As she looked out through the glass to the dark seas beyond, her mind took her back to the tiny, cold church, where she and Ronnie had plighted their troth. They had been married by special licence. She had scraped together the money for it from her Post Office savings, and told Ronnie how to set about getting the licence. He had no money at all, there was no question of a reception at the Ritz or Savoy or anywhere else. No guests to cheer the young couple – the very young couple, for they were both only sixteen – on their way to their new life. The witnesses were a friend of Ronnie's, a tongue-tied lad, a fellow soldier, ill at ease in his boots, who looked horrified at the whole affair, and, since the other witness who had promised to come never turned up, an obliging passer-by, who had consented to act as witness for the princely sum of half a crown.

'I had to tell such lies to get the licence,' Ronnie said as they came out of the church, the priest's unconvinced-sounding blessing ringing in their ears. No church bells, no kisses and congratulations, just a street with indifferent passers-by, never a glance for the newlyweds. Ronnie was in uniform, she had worn a grey woollen frock; she couldn't risk wearing anything less ordinary or she would have attracted the attention of her mother or her older sister.

They had gone straight back to Ronnie's digs. An attic room, where they had fallen into bed, hungry again for each other's bodies, lips, arms, hands legs entwining, desperate to lose themselves in one another.

What had brought all this back to mind? It wasn't just the thought of the wedding that lay ahead of her, no, there was more to it than that. These were memories that had been locked away in her mind, memories from half her lifetime ago. Why should they surface now?

It was that man going up the gangway. The tourist-class gangway. He was hatless, and halfway up, he had pushed his hair away from his forehead with the back of his hand, a gesture that brought back with extraordinary resonance the young Ronnie, who used to smooth his hair back in exactly that way. This man was rather like Ronnie, come to think of it, very much the same type. What a wonderful body Ronnie had had. Unscarred by the battles he was going off so blithely to face.

'I wouldn't have signed up if I'd known I was going to meet you,' he'd said. He lied about his age at the recruiting office, just as he had lied to obtain the special licence. But by that stage in the war, with a desperate need for men, and with Ronnie being big and tall and looking older than he was, no questions had been asked.

'If you hadn't been a soldier, we would never have met.'

Cynthia had been helping Helen, her much older sister, with her voluntary work, making and serving tea to the troops. Cynthia had poured out a mug of hot strong tea, stirred in two spoonfuls of sugar and handed it down to the handsome young soldier who'd told her that he liked his tea strong and very sweet.

Cynthia looked into a pair of the most astonishingly blue eyes, and was transfixed. The whole of her being vibrated with entirely unfamiliar sensations, and then the spell was broken, Helen sharply telling her to stop daydreaming, and another soldier jostling the blue-eyed man aside and demandingly holding out his hand for his mug of tea.

The blue-eyed soldier was waiting for her when she had finished for the day. Helen had wanted her to wait, she was only going to be another half hour or so, seeing everything was put away, and then they could go home together. But Cynthia, who was usually the most obedient of girls, had demurred. 'I want to get home,' she said. 'I've things to do. I can go on the Underground by myself, I'll be perfectly all right.'

A woman came up with news of a malfunctioning tea urn, distracting Helen's attention, and Cynthia had slipped away.

They walked to the Underground together, and he got on the train and sat beside her. They didn't speak much, but laughed together as a child in the seat opposite, cuddling a shabby toy rabbit, pulled faces at them.

Cynthia knew the minute he opened his mouth that Ronnie came from quite another world to hers. His was a London accent. 'Cockney, born and bred,' he told her. Common, her mother would have said, with infinite, dismissive scorn, but Cynthia liked it. Just as she liked everything about Ronnie.

She sat back in the wicker chair and lit a cigarette. The smoke drifted into the air. His young body. When they first went to bed together, she had been amazed by his lithe beauty. He was pale and smooth, with long limbs; she loved the small of his back, just above his muscular buttocks, and those, too, once she had got over her initial astonishment at seeing a man naked, she loved, holding them tightly to her after they had made love, lying her hands on them, soft and drowsy with pleasure. The weight and hardness of his penis had filled her with a kind of awe, such an astonishing thing, a man's penis, she had no idea, she said, brushing it with her lips. No idea at all.

She hadn't been Ronnie's first girl. He told her that, and she felt a stab of jealousy; who was this Ruby to roll under the hedge with Ronnie, the times he was staying on a Shropshire farm with his auntie's family?

He felt nothing for Ruby, it had been lust and curiosity, he told her, raising himself on one elbow so that he could kiss her.

He had run away from home two years earlier, scraping a living for himself in a hostile city. He signed up because he wanted to do his bit, and because you got three meals a day, he told her. His mother sounded, to Cynthia's innocent ears, a terrible woman, but Ronnie seemed to take the clouts and blows she and his less forceful father dealt out to him as just part of life.

'When I come back from the war, I'm going to make something of myself,' he had told her. 'You'll see. And we're going to have four kids at least, and be the happiest married couple in England.'

The steward was back, all attention. 'Are you warm enough, madam? Would you like me to bring you a rug?'

'No, thank you,' said Cynthia. 'I shall be going in shortly.'

He went away on light, silent feet. Cynthia slid back the door that led on to the open deck, and the bitter cold of a winter's night in the Atlantic hit her in the face. She tossed her cigarette over the side, the glowing tip almost immediately extinguished by the wind and rain. Then, shivering, she retreated back inside to the never-never land of soft lights and thick carpets and columns and gay chatter, shutting out the stormy weather.

She didn't feel inclined to play cards or gamble or dance or drink. She was too wrapped in her own thoughts to want company. So she made her way down the wide stairs to B deck, her reflection gleaming back at her from the mirrors, and went to her stateroom. The stewardess was surprised to see her, was she feeling seasick, could she bring her anything?

'No, thank you,' Cynthia said. 'I'll have breakfast at half past eight. Orange juice and a poached egg on toast. Coffee, and Cooper's marmalade, please, not jam.' She had grown to like the American habit of having orange juice at breakfast.

'You aren't travelling with your maid?'

'No.'

'Then I'll be back in a little while to collect your things.'

Cynthia's maid, Rose, was glad to be left behind. Not that she wouldn't have liked to see America, where the film stars came from, she told Cynthia, 'But I couldn't do with all those days at sea, madam, I really couldn't. Crossing to France is bad enough. I'm afraid if you'd asked it of me, I'd have to give in my notice.'

So Cynthia had lent her to an American friend who was spending a couple of months in London, and found that she rather liked doing without a maid; it gave her a sense of independence and a kind of freedom.

There was nothing of the ship's cabin about her stateroom, no narrow berth beneath a porthole and space-saving cupboards. It had a wide, comfortable bed with an ornate headboard, and elegant furniture of the velvet and boudoir kind. Ordinary, curtained sash windows looked out on to the deck, only used by the passengers in those staterooms. There was a marble basin, and a dressing table with three mirrors.

The stewardess had laid out a satin nightie and negligée, matching satin slippers tucked beside the bed. Cynthia undressed slowly, laying her dress over a chair and dropping her underwear into the linen basket. She put on the nightie and, sitting at the dressing table, began to cream her face, not looking at her reflection, but still thinking about her life. Her life then, when she had been no more than a girl and yet a wife, and her life now, an utterly adult woman, mother of a nearly grown-up daughter, divorced wife, fiancée – dreadful word – of a man who—

Who what? Compelled her admiration, suited her sexually, was more than her intellectual equal.

And of whom she was afraid.

The thought popped into her head unbidden, and so startled her that she dropped her hairbrush. How absurd, Walter could be overbearing, he was certainly a commanding man who expected to have his own way, but he was courteous and had never come near to threatening her – why should he?

So why had that unpleasant little idea popped into her mind? She shrugged and resumed brushing her hair with steady even strokes, a hundred a night, as her nanny had taught her.

The stewardess had unpacked for her, and had propped the one photograph in a leather frame that she had with her on the dressing table. Harriet's eyes looked out at her. She had her father's eyes. Then the words of the Gardner girl came back to her. It was hard on Harriet, having to leave her school.

'I do understand, Mummy, but it's a bit thick. I mean, you went there, you'd think they'd care about that kind of thing, instead of booting me out as though I'd been caught smoking in the lavs.'

'Darling, I do hope you don't . . .'

'Just a figure of speech,' said Harriet quickly. Then, seeing the look of distress on Cynthia's face, she had said. 'Actually, I don't mind so much, it isn't a very good school. It might have been once. It probably was when you were there, but it's all manners and flowers and things which are rather boring. The modern woman has more to her life than arranging flowers and knowing how to address a duchess or a bishop. I'd like to go to a school where you can learn something, properly. Languages, for example, the French teacher is hopeless, and Frau Passauer, who teaches German can't keep order, she gets dreadfully ragged, so we end up not learning to speak a word of German.'

'Why do they employ her if she's so hopeless?'

'I'll tell you why, it's because she's the impoverished cousin of some Princess whatsit *und* thingie, you know. That's why half the teachers are there, because they're fearfully well-bred or well-connected. Only most of them can't teach for toffee.'

'I had no idea. When I was there, the teachers were dull but competent.'

She had looked forward to the day when she would present Harriet at court, during her first season. Now she wouldn't ever travel up the Mall with her, dressed in a white dress with feathers, sitting for hours to reach the palace and then, finally, to make her curtsy to the King and Queen.

Divorced women weren't permitted to present anyone at court. Fuddy duddy, old-fashioned, but it was an absolute rule.

Her sister Helen would have to do it. It had been one of the facts Helen had thrown at her when she was trying to persuade Cynthia not to get a divorce. 'It may not be the happiest marriage on earth, but there's more to marriage than happiness.'

'Like what?'

'Duty and responsibility and shared interests. You have a daughter, you seem not to care about the effect all this will have on her. Divorce is a social stigma in our world, Cynthia. Humphrey's not at all happy about it.'

Humphrey, Helen's husband, was a distinguished lawyer. 'It affects us all.'

'Oh, come on, Helen, you aren't trying to say that Humphrey won't make the bench because I'm divorced? Good gracious, he was born to be a judge, I dare say he wore a little wig and a robe when he was in his cradle.'

'People like us . . .'

'Oh, bother people like us.' And then, 'I am sorry for Harriet, but she understands.'

'How can she understand? A girl of sixteen, I hope she doesn't understand. I suppose it's all about sex, and it would be shocking if a girl of that age knew anything at all about sex. I certainly didn't.'

No, thought Cynthia, and I bet your wedding night was a horrid shock, imagine knowing nothing about sex and having a naked Humphrey advancing on you.

She finished her strokes, and laid down the brush as the stewardess came back, to gather up her clothes. She smoothed down the wrinkleless sheet, and said that she hoped Cynthia would sleep well. 'You do look tired, madam,' she said. 'Would you like me to bring you a tisane? A warm drink can help you get a proper restful night's sleep.'

Cynthia accepted the tisane. She lay back on the pillows, sipping the hot drink, a book open on her knees, face down, unread. Harriet would be all right, she told herself. She was a sensible girl, resilient. Thank goodness the child had no idea. She moved restlessly, rustling the sheets. Should she tell Harriet the truth? No, she'd kept that secret all these years, and it would remain a secret.

Was Walter the best stepfather for a sixteen-year-old girl? Would he lay down the law, which would inevitably lead to dreadful rows, Harriet being a young lady with decided opinions of her own?

He had said Harriet should call him Uncle Walter, but she

told Cynthia that it was silly. 'He's not an uncle. If you marry him, I suppose I'll have to call him Father or something. Why can't I just call him Walter?'

'He thinks that's too informal, with your being only sixteen.'

Cynthia noticed that Harriet got round the problem by not addressing Walter at all, by any name.

Cynthia couldn't talk about Walter with Harriet, for the simple reason that Harriet refused to discuss the subject. 'You've got to do what you want. It's not as though I'm a child, I'm nearly grown up. Whether or not I like Walter isn't the point, really.'

Harriet had, on the surface at least, taken the divorce calmly. She didn't resent Walter for breaking up a happy marriage, that was one good thing. Her clear way of looking at life meant that she accepted that her parents had drifted irrevocably apart.

Although her honesty about her father startled Cynthia, when Harriet, watching her doing her face before going out for the evening, said, 'It's not as though I got on well with Daddy.'

'Harriet! How can you say such a thing? You know he loves you.'

'Yes, but that doesn't mean we like each other, does it? Love's obligatory, but liking's different. When I was little, I used to pretend I was a changeling. As one does, when one's reading nothing but fairy stories. I'd imagine that I wasn't Harriet Harkness at all, but an orphan baby left in a basket on the doorstep.' She grinned at her mother. 'Don't look so shocked, Mummy, children all tell themselves stories, I bet you did, too.' She wound an arm round her mother's neck, in a rare gesture of affection, and looked at their twin reflections in the mirror. 'Only it's not likely, given that I look so much like you, is it?'

Cynthia woke in the early hours, to find the bedside light

still on, and her book on the floor. She lay in a strangely peaceful state of neither being awake nor asleep. The man going up the gangway had brought back such a flood of memories, and now another memory came vividly into her mind.

Another dock, another ship, but this one wasn't an ocean liner sailing serenely across peaceful seas in comfort and ease. Ronnie's ship had been battle grey, battered-looking after three years of war, a troop-carrier, taking another batch of fresh-faced young men across to the killing grounds of France, to the misery of trenches and mud and barbed wire, to horrors unimaginable to the wives and girlfriends and sisters and mothers left behind.

Cynthia had driven Ronnie down, strictly against orders. He should have been on the train, but his mate had said he'd fix it with the sarge, pretend Ronnie was in the lavatory, stomach problems. Cynthia had borrowed her brother's car; he had taught her to drive when she was thirteen, on the quiet roads around Winsley, the house in the country where they had all grown up.

The sergeant, usually eagle-eyed, must have had other things on his mind, because the ruse worked, and by the time he was growing suspicious, there was Ronnie, mingling with the others in his platoon. 'Just a case of something I ate last night, Sarge, I'll be right as rain in a day or two.'

The sergeant didn't know the meaning of the word sympathy. 'A case of bleeding cold feet, more like it. Don't think you can get out of it that way, short of being dead, you're going on that boat, and if you was dead, you'd go just the same so's we could toss you overboard and save ourselves the bother of troubling the padre. Now, get a bleeding move on.'

And Cynthia, tears gracing her cheeks, had stood beside a bollard, a wan and wretched creature, wondering how

Ronnie could look so cheerful as he went up the gangway. He ran his fingers through his short hair, a habit from pre-army days, and then he saw her. His face broke into a broad smile, and he waved and gave her the thumbs up before he was lost in the tide of khaki.

Cynthia stayed on the dock to watch the ship until it was no more than a speck on the horizon. Then she drove slowly back to London, only stopping on the way to find a bush she could be sick behind.

She had been pregnant, of course, pregnant with Harriet, and feeling sick from the word go.

'Gastric flu,' Helen had pronounced, in her know-it-all fashion, and packed Cynthia down to Winsley, where Nurse would look after her.

Nurse had known what was wrong with her five minutes after she arrived, and Cynthia wept desperately on her comforting bosom, while the elderly woman stroked her hair and murmured soothing, meaningless words.

Before Cynthia slipped back into a deeper sleep, she thought of Harriet. Term would be over by the time she got back. She had been worried about what to do with Harriet. Helen said she would have her, she would enjoy being with her cousins; Cynthia knew that Harriet would rather stay on at school, alone, than have to spend time with her cousins.

Her brother Max, the brother closest to her in age and the one she felt the closest to, had come to her rescue.

'I'll pick Harriet up,' he'd said in his casual way. 'Tell me where and when, and I'll drive down and collect her. That is, if you haven't sent her to school in the Highlands of Scotland or anything like that.'

'Dorset,' said Cynthia. 'Would you really do that?' Urbane Max and a girl's boarding school didn't seem to go together.

'She's my goddaughter, didn't I say in church when she was christened that I would pick her and doubtless several trunks and a hockey stick up from whichever educational establishment she was at?'

Cynthia laughed. 'One trunk and an overnight case. I'm not sure about the hockey stick, I think it's a lacrosse school.'

'Nonsense,' cried Helen, breaking into their conversation. 'Harriet must catch the train. What, pray, would you do with her if you did collect her, Max? I know you've got nothing better to do than drive around the country, with the idle life you lead, but Harriet can't expect to be collected. She must come on the school train like everyone else, and I'll send Thrush to pick her up at the station – Waterloo, I suppose.'

'I'll drive her up to London and take her out for a good meal,' said Max, ignoring his elder sister's instructions and addressing Cynthia. 'She'll be all right at your house for a couple of days, surely. Won't that maid of yours be there, if she's not going with you? Surely Harriet will be better off in her own home.'

'A girl of that age, in London, on her own? I never heard of such a thing,' cried Helen. 'She'll be up to all kinds of mischief.'

'She won't be on her own if there's a house full of servants,' said Max.

'Quite unsuitable, nonetheless. I certainly wouldn't allow any of my girls to stay alone like that. In London!'

'If you can't trust your daughters, that's your problem,' Max said. 'I'll take her out to a show. Several shows if need be. What does she like, Cynthia?'

'Take her to the opera, and she'll be your friend for life.'

'Opera?'

'Quite unsuitable,' Helen said again.

'Wagner, for preference, I'm afraid,' said Cynthia.

'Good heavens,' said her brother. 'I'm more of a Mozart man myself, but I'll see what I can do.'

Max, thought Cynthia through a haze of sleep, was reliable, whatever Helen said about his frippery ways. And was he as frivolous as he seemed? Cynthia had long suspected there was a lot more to Max than met the eye, but he was a cagey man, slippery as an eel when it came to any questions about himself. Harriet would be all right with him, he'd take good care of her. And Cynthia realized, with a pang, that she was looking forward to seeing her daughter again. Almost more than I am to seeing Walter, she muttered to herself. Any problems with Harriet were practical, and time would resolve them. Whereas Walter . . .

EIGHT

Polly worked at the Rossetti Gallery workshop three days a week. It was a job that had started when she was still an art student on slender means, keen to earn any extra money she could. It had seemed heaven-sent, a job working with pictures, rather than waiting on tables or cleaning houses or collecting debts or any one of numerous jobs that she and her fellow students took to make ends meet.

Rossetti Gallery, with its entrance in Cork Street, was smart, but the premises behind it in Lion Yard were anything but smart. Lion Yard was a narrow, cobbled cul-de-sac, and few of the well-heeled customers who bought at the gallery ever ventured down it. The gallery itself and the main restoration studio, with a discreet entrance further down Cork Street, were forbidden territory to the students, and there was no way into them through their dingy yard. Dickensian, Sam called Lion Yard, and Polly could well imagine some of the novelist's grimmer characters lurking in the shadows there.

The workshop was a lofty, barn-like-place, redolent of linseed oil and turps and oil paint. Situated above a storage area, it was reached via a rickety wooden outside staircase. Students were taken on to touch up and improve unsaleable old pictures and canvases that the gallery had bought in job lots at country sales, or for a few shillings in the minor London auction rooms.

The truth was, Polly soon realized, that there was an awful lot of dull and downright bad art around. Yet even the most dismal picture, by a hopeless artist, could be made to look much more desirable with careful, skilled work and a sense of what was in fashion.

Polly was started on flower paintings, which always, so her boss, Mr Padgett, told her, found a steady market. Dreary collections of tired-looking blooms in frames that were often worth more than the paintings arrived at the back of the Rossetti Gallery premises, and were taken, minus their frames, up to the workshop to be stacked in daunting ranks on wooden pallets all along one wall.

Mr Padgett, who was quick to weed out those workers he considered would never make the grade, had watched Polly for a few days, and then told her that she would do. 'Unlike a lot of art students, you can paint. I don't know what they teach you at these colleges these days,' he grumbled. 'Some of you don't seem to know how to hold a brush or draw a curved line.'

'Modern art isn't about painting or drawing curves, Mr P,' retorted Sam Carter, a cheeky young student with a lock of hair falling over his forehead. 'Times have changed, you've got to keep up. Anything is art now, if you say it is.'

'Maybe to you it is, but it's not to our customers, so just you hurry up and finish that landscape before those cows there die of old age.'

Sam, a student at the Academy, could draw or paint almost anything, and Polly envied him his facility. Under his skilful hands, landscapes bloomed, animals looked as though they belonged to a known species, ships sailed and fought as though they meant it, and faces changed from blurred ugliness to beauty, which was why, despite the avant-garde nature

86

of his own work and his scorn for all old-fashioned representational art, he was kept on at the workshop while others came and went.

Mr Padgett, seeing Sam idly sketch a Quattrocento face, or draw a detail of a hand in the style of Rembrandt, had wanted him to move on to the main restoration studio, where the fine and valuable paintings were dealt with. 'You'd work on old masters there, national treasures even. Mr Dinsdale has a top reputation, you couldn't learn from a better man. It's a good, steady career for an artist of your talent.'

Sam had laughed and said he'd rather be poor and do his own work, thank you, and stayed on at the workshop.

Meanwhile, Polly's work turning dreary flowers into skilfully and pleasingly-coloured flower paintings such as would adorn any home, gave satisfaction. She did some work on landscapes, adding various animals on Mr Padgett's instructions. 'Buyers go for cats,' he would say. And he approved of her horses, which, added to another blank country scene, made an uninspired picture much more interesting.

Polly had her doubts as to the strict legality of what she was doing, but Mr Padgett assured her that since these works were almost all by unknown artists, and no pretence was made that they were anything else, where was the harm in making an unsaleable picture into one that a buyer was happy to hang on his wall?

'Artists don't always know best. If I had the painter of that landscape here, look at it, a few desultory hedges, a river going nowhere, a broken down bit of fence, I'd soon tell him what it needed to make a proper composition. And he'd be glad to learn, and wouldn't make the same mistake again.'

Polly had gradually been allowed to pep up some portraits, giving some worthy gentleman or prosperous paterfamilias more appeal and a touch of style lacking in the mostly very wooden portraits that came through her hands.

'People prefer not to have ugly or unpleasant faces looking down on them from their dining-room walls,' Mr Padgett told her. 'Of course, if they happen to be your ancestors, and your ancestors happen to be a lantern-jawed, disagreeable-looking lot, well, that's one thing. But if you're paying good money, then you want something more pleasing. A pretty woman will sell, where an ugly or even just a plain one won't. And of course, if one of our pictures turns out to be of someone well-known, an admiral or a statesman or an actress, so much the better.'

'Who buys these portraits?' Polly said to Sam. 'If you don't know the person, and it's not a wonderful painting, what's the point?'

Mr Padgett, who was passing behind her, paused to give her question his usual careful consideration.

'Sometimes a buyer wants to pass a painting off as an ancestor. Other buyers feel that having a few portraits hanging above the stairs adds a bit of class. And we sell a lot to hotels, of a certain kind, new places where they want to make foreign visitors feel they're staying in a bit of Old England.'

There were times, however, when a portrait or a flower painting would come into the workshop only to be whisked away before it was passed over to Sam or Polly.

'Hold on, Mr P,' she had cried on more than one occasion. 'That's a promising bowl of fruit and flowers, I can do something with that.'

To which Mr Padgett, frowning, had said, that, no, this picture was staying as it was.

These, Polly found out after a while, were the older canvases. Mr Padgett, in an expansive moment, showed her how, under close scrutiny of the back of the canvas, it was possible to see whether the canvas was hand-made, meaning it dated from the eighteenth century or earlier, or was machine-made.

'Machine-made canvases didn't come in until the very end of the eighteenth century,' Mr Padgett told her.

Of course if a picture had been ruined, then it was extremely difficult to judge whether the canvas had the irregularities that marked it out as hand-made, but Mr Padgett had an eye, and after putting his nose so close to the canvas that Polly thought he must make a dent in it, he would pronounce on its age and the picture would be handed over to her or her fellow assistants in the studio, or whisked away to the main studio.

Presumably Rossetti's had scruples about refurbishing genuinely old paintings; well, she respected them for it, although a bad painting was still a bad painting, whatever its age.

Polly liked the work, and it certainly allowed her to pay her rent at the times, more and more frequent, when she could make no other money from her drawings or paintings. She'd had a run of luck earlier in the year with book jackets, for which WH Smith paid two guineas apiece; these had recently dried up, and so the twelve shillings a day she earned at Rossetti's was a godsend.

That Monday was another wet day, the kind of day when the atmosphere became a grey cloud of drizzle, with the wetness creeping under collars and into shoes. Polly felt damp inside and out when she arrived in Lion Yard, she climbed the stairs with extra care, as the steps were always slippery in the rain, and pushed open the door to the workshop.

She was starting work on yet another flower painting, a small canvas, circa 1855, Mr Padgett had said. 'Believe it or not, the Victorians loved those vivid colours. So did the Georgians, but taste today won't stand for that kind of thing.'

So, under his watchful eye, Polly had applied his patent varnish-removing fluid, made up to a secret formula, and then the painting had been left out in the yard in the rain for a week, to fade the colours and leave a matt surface for her to work on.

It had dried over the weekend, and now her first task was to alter the colours to give a more realistic representation of the blooms in question. Then, she decided, looking at the picture through narrowed eyes, she would change the balance, to make the design less stiff and formal and give the flowers a more natural, relaxed look.

She took her tattered smock from the hook behind the door, and put some coffee on to brew, warming her fingers at the gas ring; she couldn't paint with fingers numb from cold.

Sam came up the stairs and into the room. 'Late again, Mr Carter,' said Mr Padgett, but without rancour.

'Sorry, Mr P,' Sam said, not sounding in the least apologetic.

Sam was working on what had been a battered seascape. He had a particular knowledge of ships which came from his belonging to a naval family; he had grown up in various ports around the world, and as a boy, he had spent hours out and about in boats. He pulled his easel round to get a better light, and, wiping a fine sable brush on an old rag, he set to work, painting delicate cotton wool puffs from the cannon he had added to an otherwise uninteresting sailing vessel. A man of war gave extra value to a painting, Mr Padgett said, and the more warlike violence a canvas contained, the more easily it would find a customer.

Sam was in a talkative mood when he and Polly were alone later that morning, Mr Padgett having gone off with a delivery of paintings.

'Of course,' Sam said, 'we should go into this business on our own account, make ourselves more than the miserly pay we get here.'

'What, set up on our own, touching up bad paintings?'

'Why not? We could buy them up at country house sales

and auctions just as Padgett and his scouts do. Cut out the middle man.'

'Would you want to?' said Polly, adding some blue dabs to a flat green leaf. 'What about your own work? What about all that stuff about preferring to be poor, when Mr Padgett wanted you to train properly as a restorer?'

'Oh, I don't know,' said Sam. 'One says these things, and one bangs on, in the name of art, but is one getting anywhere? I doubt it.'

'You're still studying.'

'Yes, but you aren't, and where's your own work going? Do you sell it? Do you think your painting is improving, are you getting down the visions in your head? Is anyone remotely interested? I sometimes think I'll end up painting Christmas cards, more jolly naval scenes. Robins, too, perhaps, I might have a go at robins.'

'Could one give it up, just like that?'

'Dunno. I suspect it gives you up, you wake up one morning and realize that you've nothing more to say. Look at you. Mr Padgett raves at your sense of colour, yet your own painting is all dreariness.'

Polly had invited Sam round for tea one Sunday and regretted it ever since. He, with all the braggadocio of a promising student, hadn't been able to hide his lack of enthusiasm for Polly's canvases. 'Why are they all so small?'

'Small canvases cost less and you use less paint.' Polly had replied, but it wasn't the entire truth.

'They all look as though you've been painting what you can see through a windowpane in the fog. I like this, though,' he had said, crossing the room to look at a canvas Polly had painted for her final show at college.

It was of three of her friends, students on the same course, a much larger picture than anything she had done recently. A red-haired, wild-eyed, hung-over young Irishman; she'd lost touch with him. Dark, sultry, soft-mouthed Fanny Powys, blowing rings of smoke into the air. The third grace, for that was how she had arranged her figures, was an ethereally fair and fragile girl, who was now living and working in New York. It was a good painting, and it was true, she hadn't done anything half so good since she left college. Polly hated Sam for being so breezy and gung-ho about losing one's artistic voice. Easy to talk about it when you hadn't lost your way and had utter confidence that you never would.

They went back to their easels, and worked steadily, until Sam drew back from his canvas, put down his palette and brushes, and pulled out a packet of cigarettes.

Smoking was forbidden in the studio, which was full of inflammable materials, not to mention the canvases stacked up against every surface of the room. But Sam squeezed himself up to the skylight and pried it open, so that he could blow the smoke out into the already smoky London atmosphere.

Sam pulled a magazine out of his pocket. He read all the gossipy papers he could get his hands on, and knew all about the goings-on of anyone in the public eye. 'My cousin in America sent this to me. Look, pictures of Mrs Cynthia Harkness, dancing at the Columbo Club. Don't you love that dress?'

Polly took her attention off a strange-looking flower that seemed to be a cross between a blowsy rose and a chrysanthemum. She'd make it a rose, it was a better shape, she decided. She wiped her fingers on a rag and took the magazine Sam was holding out to her, turned back to a page of photographs shot in a nightclub. She looked at the slim figure with the perfect hair and beautifully made-up face, then at the dramatic close-fitting dress, which billowed out in a froth at ankle level.

'I bet Sir Walter Malreward won't be pleased if he sees

that picture,' said Sam. 'He's going to marry her, you know. Do you think he has a press agency sending him any pictures of her that appear in the press?'

'Why would he do that?'

'Keeping tabs on her.'

Sam had followed every step of Cynthia Harkness's well-publicized divorce, and he followed the progress of Sir Walter's latest amour with keen attention. 'It won't last,' he had predicted. 'He rarely keeps his women for more than a year. Then he trades them in for a new model, randy chap that he is.'

Now Sam had changed his mind, and was inclined to think it might be different with Mrs Harkness. 'He wanted her to get the divorce, that's what it looks like. Mind you, is she wise? I think her husband looked rather a pet.'

'Well,' said Polly, as she squeezed a dollop of orange on to her palette, 'no one could call Sir Walter a pet.'

'No,' agreed Sam. He tossed his cigarette butt out of the window and closed it with a bang. Then he returned to his easel, looked at the picture with pursed lips, and painted a pennant on to the eighteenth-century man-of-war with a dramatic flourish. 'I've told Padgett that this is hopeless. There's a raging sea, lashing waves against the cliffs, and he wants this ship of the line to be coasting along – as if any captain in his right mind would be so close inshore in a blow like that.'

'Artistic licence,' said Polly, and then, 'oh, damn!'

'What?'

'I've used chrome orange, and this is a picture from the 1850s, it's a mite early for it.'

'As if anyone will notice. My ship caught on a lee shore is far more of a faux pas than a bit of anachronistic colour.'

'I like to get things right.'

They were paid on Mondays, and at five o'clock Polly

tucked into her purse the thirty-six shillings which Mr Padgett had counted out and given her. She'd pay her rent, which would take twenty-five shillings of it. Then, unless, miraculously, another book jacket came in, she'd have to last the rest of the week on the remaining eleven shillings. Which meant another raid on her almost empty piggy bank.

Sam walked beside her as they left Lion Yard. He'd noticed the way Polly had put her money away, and with sharp, inquisitive eyes, had seen the emptiness of the purse into which she had put it.

'Care for a flutter?' he said. 'I'm going to the races with Larry tomorrow, he's got a hot tip for the two-thirty.'

Sam's friend Larry was a bit of a wide boy, in Polly's view, and certainly not a likely companion for an admiral's son. But Sam had had some remarkably lucky bets through him, and imagine if she won! She shook her head. 'I'm broke, and they say if you're broke, never put any money on a horse, because it will always cross its legs and fall over, or come last, or both.'

'I don't think your two bob is likely to make Amarantha trip up. Larry knows one of the stable lads, he's sure she's a winner.'

'Oh, go on, then,' said Polly, recklessly handing over a precious half-crown coin.

Mrs Horton was at home when Polly went to pay her rent. Which was a pity; Polly preferred to put the money in an envelope and thrust it under the door. She didn't like Mrs Horton, who had hard eyes and was mean with everything to do with her tenants, from hot water to the cheap, low wattage lamps that so often burned out, leaving the staircase plunged into dangerous darkness.

'Oh, it's you, is it?' Mrs Horton said, drawing the shawl she always wore about her thin shoulders. 'I wanted to have a word with you. You'd better come in for a moment.'

Polly's heart sank. What had she done now? Left the front door ajar? Neglected to hang the bathmat over the bath?

Forgotten to avoid the creaking floorboard on the landing when she came in late? She stepped gingerly across the threshold, trying not to wrinkle her nose at the pervading aroma of tomcat and boiled cabbage.

Unlike the Spartan rooms she let out, Mrs Horton's quarters were almost sumptuous. Thick rugs were laid on the floor, overlapping in order to fit in. The sofa, a red velvet affair on stout legs, was piled high with plump cushions, and the lampshades always reminded Polly of a tart's knickers, since they were pink and black with lace trimmings. It had crossed her mind that scrawny Mrs Horton, who did so well out of the several properties she owned in Fitzroy Street, might have started her career in quite a different profession.

'I'm giving you notice,' said Mrs Horton.

'Notice?' Polly stared at her, hoping she had heard wrongly.

'Notice to quit. I want you out by the twenty-fourth of December.'

'Oh, but Mrs Horton, why? What have I done?'

'I'm not saying you're a bad tenant, because I've had worse, but I want the room. My son's coming home for a while, he's quitting the merchant service and wants to look about for some new line of work. So I'll be needing the room for him. His ship gets in on the second of January, and I want you out by Christmas, to give me time to clean the room. So you'll have to move all your stuff out, and don't go leaving it until the last minute.'

Polly opened her mouth to plead with her landlady. Why her? Why couldn't one of the other tenants be turfed out? But she knew the answer to that, and knew that there was no point arguing. Her room was the smallest and cheapest in the house, and naturally, Mrs Horton would want to keep her higher paying lodgers on for preference.

'That isn't much notice,' Polly said. 'Can't you give me time to find somewhere else?'

'No, dearie, that's the way it is. If I were you, I'd get your fiancé to name the day, you've been hanging about long enough, you'll lose him if you carry on that way. A man gets tired of waiting when he's decided to marry, even,' and she gave Polly a sly glance, 'even if he's doing a bit of anticipating on the bed front. You get hitched in January, that's my advice, and then you'll not have to worry about finding a new room for yourself, will you?'

Polly positively stamped up the three flights of stairs to her room, working herself into a thorough temper. Damn Mrs Horton. Damn everything. She looked around at her familiar room, and sank down on the bed. All right, it wasn't much, but to her it was home. She suddenly remembered the pictures Sam had shown her in a copy of *Country Life*, of the interiors of that Sir Walter Malreward's recently built country house, and she sighed. Then she laughed at herself. She didn't aspire to any such modern, chic opulence; she was content with her chilly and inconvenient attic room, which, compared to some of the places she had lived in before coming here, was almost luxurious.

With no money to pay a deposit, she'd be back in one of those dreadful places, like the room on the third floor of that house in Pimlico, which had peeling damp patches on the walls and where the nearest supply of water was down in the basement, and that a solitary tap. Moreover, the basement had had its own tenants, an impoverished, elderly artist and his wife – dear God, was that how she would end up, if she didn't marry Roger?

She shook herself into sense. It didn't arise. She was going to marry Roger, and besides, she wasn't the kind of person who ended up in a damp and dingy basement, painting rural scenes on stones as Joseph Forbes, the inhabitant of that dank region, had done.

She must be practical. How could she find a new room

96

at this time of year, one that she could move into before Christmas? Drat Mrs Horton and her son, she couldn't have sprung this on her at a worse time.

Roger would be pleased. He would point out that she didn't need to look for a new place to live, given that they would be married so soon. Why did that depress her so much? She looked at the ring on her finger, the neat hoop with a sapphire nestled between two diamonds. Not a flashy ring, but a good one, made from stones reset from one of his mother's brooches. 'No point splashing out on tawdry jewellery when you can have something decent,' he had said.

She loved Roger, she admired him, she knew that he was the perfect balance for her: his intellect as against her emotional approach to life – so why did the prospect of their marriage make her more and more dispirited as the actual day grew nearer? She'd welcomed the brief postponement, but the weeks would fly by, and that would be that. Hitched. It was such a big step, marriage. They had discussed living together; Roger was quite keen on that, since as a good socialist, he considered marriage by and large an outmoded and bourgeois institution. His parents, however, although modern in their outlook, weren't impressed by his idea of him and Polly living in sin. 'The hospital won't like it,' his father had said.

Polly had raised the subject with her mother, and been surprised at her response.

'No, dear, it would never do. It can work for some people, but Roger's people wouldn't like it, and there'd be all kinds of inconvenience. It's one thing to have an affair' – this with a sideways glance at Polly, what did she know about her and Jamie? – 'but living together, setting up home together without being married, it won't do, not for a man in Roger's position. He'd feel it in the end, and then there are always problems with the income tax and landlords and so on. I dare say he'd end up blaming you, men tend to do that.'

How could she know about that, for heaven's sake?

In the end, Polly knew, she would have to throw herself on Ma's mercy, and stay in Highgate while she waited for Roger to get back from America. The prospect filled her with dismay. Perhaps Oliver knew of some artist who was going to be away for a few weeks, who would be glad of someone who would look after their studio and in return pay a modest rent. Unlikely, and what most people considered a modest rent would probably still be beyond her present resources, but still, she would ask him.

That night her sleep was haunted with dreams. She was watching Mrs Horton, improbably attired in Cynthia Harkness's lovely frock, dancing with Sir Walter Malreward, who was wearing the brown overalls Mr Padgett put on while attending to the messier business of the workshop. Then the image faded, and she was standing on the doorstep of Sir Walter's white country house, at the bottom of a flight of steps flanked by two creatures out of ancient Egypt. She had a suitcase in her hand, and was explaining to a lofty personage dressed in a black uniform that she was Polyhymnia Tomkins, come about the room.

To which he had replied in a resonant voice that there was no such person as Polyhymnia Tomkins, and so certain had been his utterance, that Polly woke up in a cold sweat, to find herself exclaiming out loud that it was true, Polyhymnia Tomkins did exist, there was indeed such a person.

She sat up in bed, too unsettled to want to go back to sleep yet. Her eye fell on the table where she had left some sketches she had done before going to bed. She had drawn a caricature of Mrs Horton, complete with sequinned slippers and shawl and expression of long-suffering weariness, and, peeping out from a battlement of cushions and frilly lampshades, the heavy features of Eric Horton, her son, whom Polly had met on the stairs some months previously and taken an instant dislike to. She hated the thought of him taking possession of her room, and, by the dim light of the bedside lamp, she glared at his exaggerated features as though she could compel him to change his mind and go back to sea, preferably to be wrecked and cast up on a desert island on the other side of the world.

NINE

'They think you must be a war hero, limping like that,' Harriet said, as she slung her lacrosse stick into the back of Max's blue Delage.

'Hey, careful there, I don't want rips in the leather.'

'That's the trouble with a swish car, you can't just sling things in,' said Harriet. 'Daddy's old jalopy was much better in that way, although of course not nearly so smart.'

'Who thinks I'm a war hero?' her uncle said, as Harriet eased herself into the passenger seat and rolled the window down, the better to shout out incomprehensible messages to various nearby girls, all large and unattractive, to his eyes, in their shapeless grey gymslips.

'My friends. I told them you were horribly wounded holding the line against hundreds of ravening foes.'

'Don't they teach you not to lie at school these days?' Max asked. He tightened the strap on Harriet's bulging suit-case, stowed it in the boot and came round to get in the car. He settled himself behind the wheel, and looked along the drive to the handsome Palladian façade of the great house that formed the main part of the school.

'Inventing stories about war heroes isn't lies, it's fiction.

Like those horrible compositions we have to write, what is the point? My best day. A visit to the country. Well, buck up Uncle Max, let's get out of here.'

'Do we just drive off? You don't have to sign out or anything? Your mother will be annoyed if you or she are in bad odour because I didn't get it right.'

'Oh, I suppose I'd better go and say goodbye to Miss Ruthven, who's the headmistress, before you ask,' said Harriet ungraciously. She swung open the car door and jumped out. 'It's a complete waste of time, look, there she is with Leila, her mother's Lady Jonquil, and Miss Ruthven dearly loves a title. She won't have any time for me.'

Max lit a cigarette and watched with some amusement as his niece lolloped across the grass and then skidded to a halt in front of the tall, distinguished-looking woman with severely cut greying hair who stood, in an Oxford MA gown, on the steps of the house. To his further amusement, Harriet gave a kind of ungainly bob, and then shying like a horse, backed away from the headmistress and cantered back to the car.

'Was that creak at the knees meant to be a curtsy?'

'Yes, isn't it daft? She makes us do it whenever we want to talk to her. Oppression, I call it.'

'You'll have to do better than that when you're presented at court. Don't you have to sweep almost to the ground?'

'I expect I'll topple over and be carried off to the Tower through Traitor's Gate, like Princess Elizabeth. You go to classes, what a waste of time. Anyhow, I don't want to be presented. Mummy can't take me, not now she's a wicked divorced woman, and that'll mean Aunt Helen, and it'll be nag, nag, so by the time I get to be in front of the King I'll be so nervous, I'll be bound to fall over or trip over my feathers or something.'

Max put the car into gear and reversed with great care, not wanting to run down any of the numerous girls of all shapes and sizes who were milling around in the most alarming way, greeting parents, saying goodbye to friends, and all, it seemed, talking at the tops of their voices.

'Do they always make this much noise?' he enquired. He braked, quickly, to avoid a flying child, her plaits streaming behind her as she shot across the drive to join another girl.

'No, which is why it's so loud when we're let out. In a moment old Ruthven will abandon her place on the steps and come down into the throng looking cross and everyone will quieten down. Most of the time we are hardly allowed to open our mouths, it's no talking in the corridors and no talking here and no talking there and walk on the left and no running, and what's happened to the ribbon for your hair, Harriet Harkness?'

Harriet twisted her head round to look back at the receding school. She tore off her grey pudding basin hat and shook her hair free. 'Thank goodness,' she said. 'Are we going to London? Thank you for coming to pick me up, Uncle Max. It's fun on the coach and the school train, but this has more style.' She sat back with a luxuriant sigh. 'I do like your car. I'm going to have a car like this when I'm grown up. Only mine's going to be red.'

Max drove through the enormous school gates and concentrated on steering the car along the twisting country road that led to the main road.

'Is Mummy back? She wrote from Virginia, but that was some time ago, and she said she wasn't sure about dates and sailings.'

'Didn't you get a letter from your Aunt Helen?'

'Oh, yes. But I never read her letters, she's always so stuffy, am I behaving well, and try to make sure I get a good report. I bet she didn't get good reports when she was at school.'

'I believe she did,' said Max. 'Helen has always done what's expected of her.'

'What about Mummy?'

'Not so good. Poor attitude, I seem to remember.'

'Schools go on and on about attitude. It's all rubbish.'

'Nonetheless, you should have read Helen's letter, since it contained useful information. Your mother's back on Friday, and until then you're staying in the London house. Rose will be there, and she'll look after you, and if you behave yourself, I'll take you out.'

'Oh, goodie. Will you take me to a nightclub? I can wear one of Mummy's evening dresses.'

'Certainly not. Your mother told me you like opera.'

'I do, as long as it's Wagner. But I've been to see Wagner, and I've never been to a nightclub.'

'I should think not, at your age. Frightfully vulgar places, nightclubs,' he added. 'I never go near them if I can help it. Full of desperate people pretending they're having a good time.'

'I thought that you were the kind of person who went to nightclubs every night of the week,' said Harriet, sounding disappointed. 'Aunt Helen says you do nothing except enjoy yourself, she disapproves of your way of life. That's not telling tales, by the way, she says it to everybody. Oh well, if you won't take me to a nightclub, you won't. How I long to be grown up so that I can go wherever I want. Which opera?'

What an obliging child Harriet was. '*The Mastersingers* is on.'

'Ah.' The word came out as a satisfied sigh. 'Could we go to the flicks as well?'

'We might.'

Harriet hung her head out of the window, nose forward, like a dog. The wind sent her hair blowing about her face. 'Daddy wrote,' she said bringing her head back in. She brushed the hair out of her eyes. 'He wants me to go out to Kenya in the summer.'

Harriet's voice was tight. She clearly didn't want to go. Did she mind her father going to live in Africa? Max had thought, over the past two or three years when her parents' marriage had been under obvious strain, with Cynthia living in Walter's pocket and her father spending so much time with Sally Lupin, that Harriet was a most adapting young person.

'Does he? I expect you'd like that.'

'No, I wouldn't. Why do people always suppose one's eager to rush off to places on the other side of the world? France is bad enough. I don't want to go to Kenya. It'll be full of people pretending to farm and drinking every evening and laughing in that way grown-ups do when they're full of whisky. Ugh. And don't say it would be interesting to see lions and so on. If I want to see a lion, I can go to the zoo. I grant you that if I went to Kenya I'd have something more interesting to write when they set you that pointless composition: write about an incident in your holidays, but that's not much compensation for having to spend all that time somewhere I don't want to be. I do hope Mummy doesn't insist, she might say I ought to go, that I mustn't lose touch with my father. But if he doesn't want to lose touch, he should stay in England. Perhaps Mummy would like me to go, so that she can be alone with Walter, although she's got all term for that. It'll be funny when she marries him, and we'll be living in his houses, not ours.'

Max heard the courage in the words, the courage of a temperament like his own, that preferred not to pretend that things were other than they were, but he also caught the forlorn note in her voice.

'You get on well with Sir Walter, don't you?'

'He's sort of kind to me. A bit patronizing, but then people do patronize you when you're my age. He goes on about how much fun I'll have when I leave school and do the season.'

'He has a point.'

'Do keep up, I told you that means Aunt Helen. I'll come out at the same time as Joyce, won't that be nice for me?'

And she gave Max a wicked look from under her eyelashes. Harriet's cousin Joyce was Max's least favourite niece. He found all Helen's children dull, but Joyce was sanctimonious with it.

'You won't be going to any nightclubs if Joyce is detailed to keep an eye on you.'

'No, that's rather what I thought. But I expect I'll be able to slip away, she's rather dim, you know. Do you like Walter?'

'You are one for direct questions, aren't you? As it happens, I hardly know him.'

'He's too good to be true,' Harriet said. 'He has all the virtues, of course: good-looking, if you like that type, stinking rich, Member of Parliament, gives to charities, no scandals attached to his name – if you don't count Mummy. A girl at school says he won't marry Mummy, that he has one mistress after another, and then he gets tired of them. I wouldn't like Mummy to be cast off exactly, because she might be upset, but I'd be quite pleased if he took up with someone else. Before they got married, of course. I don't think Mummy could bear to go through all that divorce stuff again, it really got her down.'

Max could think of nothing to say. He could hardly tell her that a girl of her age shouldn't be talking about mistresses, and what a naughty thing to suggest about her own mother. That would be hypocritical. Girls these days knew too much. Either that, or they were kept in a state of appalling igno- rance – innocence, their well-meaning but foolish mothers would call it – which was certainly more harmful.

'Are you shocked?' Harriet asked. 'My talking about mistresses? Or my knowing that Mummy and Walter – well, you know?'

'Nothing shocks me. However, I think your mother is the kind of woman who is happier married than not. And if Sir Walter is going to marry her, then I dare say he plans to settle down and lead a more regular life himself. Men do that, you know.'

'Get bored with being rakes and long for the charms of domesticity?'

'Good God!'

'It's a quotation,' said Harriet. 'Watch out, you nearly went into the ditch. Will you teach me to drive? Mummy says I can't learn until I'm older, but that's all rot. Are you going to get bored with the single state and get married?'

'In a moment I shall regret coming to collect you, and I shall deposit you and your luggage at the nearest station to make your own way home. You really mustn't ask such questions.'

'I hope if you do, you marry someone nice, that I like. I suppose she'd have to be terrifically smart and sophisticated, though, to appeal to you. Like Thelma Warden.'

Max stood on the brakes. He took his hands off the wheel and raised them in a gesture of submission. 'I am a bachelor, and I intend to stay one. Now, Harriet, if you don't stop dissecting the lives of your nearest and dearest, there will be no opera, no flicks, and I shall never teach you to drive.'

'There's a tractor coming up behind us, and you're blocking the road,' said Harriet, unrepentant.

TEN

'Twelve pounds and ten shillings!' cried Polly. 'Sam, this can't be right.'

'It can. It is. The nag came in at a hundred to one. I put your half-crown on to win, Larry said each way was a waste of money, Amarantha was going to win by a length, and she did. Pretty filly, chestnut with white socks, would look good in a painting, pity you didn't get to see the race.'

'Watch my half-crown galloping down the course? I'd have had my eyes tight shut. Oh, Sam, I don't believe it.'

'Quick, put it away, here comes Padgett, and you know how he is about betting.'

Mr Padgett was a pillar of the Salvation Army in his off-duty hours, and held strong views on gambling and drinking and other sins of an indulgent nature.

Polly hastily stuffed the notes in the pocket of her smock, and took up her brush. Mr Padgett, normally an amiable and relaxed-looking man had a harassed expression on his face, and it looked as though betting was the last thing on his mind. He was brusque when Sam asked him which canvas he wanted him to work on next; Sam and Polly exchanged glances – what was up?

Polly picked up her palette, and looked at the painting on her easel. A desolate scene, of a water mill and a broken-down bridge, a badly-drawn broken-down bridge, moreover, and a depressed-looking, rather lumpy horse grazing disconsolately on what looked like damp and unwholesome ground.

Chestnut, Sam had said. With white socks. 'Did the filly have any white markings on her face' she asked Sam, *sotto voce*.

'Long white blaze,' Sam whispered back.

Polly paused to make a sketch of a horse, a far cry from the dejected creature in the painting. This was a lively horse, with a bold eye, standing with head up, looking expectantly out on the world. She passed it to Sam.

He put his finger and thumb together in a circle indicating, 'Perfect,' and Polly set to work.

As she applied an opaque layer of paint to cover up the bridge before she repainted it, her mind was busy. Twelve pounds ten shillings. That would pay the rent for January, but it would also pay a fare to France. Had Oliver been serious, was it just the kind of remark you make in passing, not expecting the invitation to be taken up? He knew that Polly was always hard-up, and that she wouldn't borrow from him. No, Oliver didn't play games like that, not with her. If he'd made the invitation, he meant it.

Roger. What would Roger say if she told him that she was going to France, a guest of the Fraddons? She hadn't yet told him about having to leave her room before Christmas. She knew exactly what he'd say about that: 'It's nothing to make a fuss about. It's perfectly simple, go home to Highgate, stay with your mother. You'd have to give in your notice soon in any case, don't let it bother you.'

She knew that he wouldn't want her to accept Oliver's invitation. Too bad. If he could sail off to America, postponing their wedding without consultation or hesitation, then she could go to France. Sauce for the goose, after all, and she had a spanking new passport. Thank goodness she had got it, and no, she wasn't going to let him put her on his passport when they were married. He might think it a good idea; she didn't.

Mr Padgett received a phone call in the little booth that served him for an office, and after he hung up, he hurried out of the workshop, telling Sam that he would be away for about an hour, and to take any calls. The door swung to behind him, and Sam and Polly waited for a minute to see if he would come back, as he was inclined to do, to pick up some piece of paper or a docket that he had left behind on his desk, and then, when Sam could see him walking out of the yard, they downed tools and looked at one another.

'Coffee?' said Polly.

'Yes,' said Sam. 'And then we can discuss what you're going to do with your windfall.'

Polly told him about Oliver's invitation, and Sam whistled. 'Good God, Polly, you've got to go. A month in the south of France, all found? And I bet Oliver's dad does himself proud. He lives out there, you know, he did something frightfully wicked a few years ago, I don't know what, it only gets hinted at, but he seems to be *persona non grata* among his own set. What I mean is, it'll be a luxury billet, not a house that's only used for a month or so a year, or rented for the season. Think of the light, think of the painting you can do.'

Polly handed him a mug of coffee, her face glum.

'Ah,' said Sam. 'I was forgetting. Roger.'

'Roger can go hang,' said Polly with a vehemence that surprised herself. 'I know he won't like it, not one bit.'

'Don't tell him. Doesn't he sail on Saturday? Wave him a fond farewell, and then board the train for France.'

'That would be underhand.'

'True, but you can't be a Girl Guide all the time, Polly.'

109

'I do long to go. It would be my last fling of freedom, before I turn into Mrs Harrington. Do you think Padgett would give me any extra hours next week? To make up for my not being here in January?'

'Ask him. January's always a bit slack, anyhow. No skin off his nose.'

Polly went back to her perky horse. Go? Not go? She was turning into a thoroughly indecisive person. Perhaps she was in reality two people, and Polly Smith could stay in London, put in the hours at the workshop, go back to Highgate and live the small existence Roger wanted for her, while the wilder, more adventurous Polyhymnia set off for foreign shores.

She laughed at the absurdity of it, and when Sam enquired what she was grinning at, said, 'Nothing, just a bizarre thought that crossed my mind.'

'Get on with your horse if you want to keep on the right side of Padgett.'

'Where's the book on Stubbs? Oh, there it is, on the table beside you. Pass it over.'

Mr Padgett returned to find his two painters hard at work. Polly put down her brush. 'Mr Padgett, I was wondering. I can't work in January, and so if I could do any extra hours in December . . .'

Mr Padgett looked at Polly as though his thoughts were elsewhere. 'January? Extra hours? Ah, I see what you mean.' He stroked his chin. 'I don't see why not. Things are slack in January, whereas in the run-up to Christmas. Yes, yes, what a good idea. In fact—'

He looked at Polly as though seeing her for the first time. 'Miss Smith, do you possess any clothes other than those you come to work in? A frock. Mmm? Something neat?'

A frock? What was he talking about?

'Because there's rather a crisis at the gallery. Miss Norton, the receptionist, has flu. She's quite poorly, and won't be back for at least a fortnight. Doctor's orders. It would be better if we were to have a young lady who is familiar with the paintings. That is, I am sure you would be able to answer clients' questions, just initially, find out what they are looking for, and judge whether to pass them on to Mr Grandison or Mr Folliott. They would fill you in. However, it is necessary for someone at the desk to look – mmm. To look more like a receptionist.'

'What about pay, Mr P?' Sam said. 'What does Miss Norton get a week? Bet it works out at more per day than Polly gets doing this. It should be taken into account. Especially if Polly's got to update her wardrobe.'

'Surely not. Surely all you young ladies have suitable frocks, for when you're not painting.'

'I can find the right kind of thing,' said Polly at once. She knew perfectly well she possessed nothing remotely suitable for greeting clients to the Rossetti Gallery, but that was a minor problem, all problems had a solution if you knew how to go about it.

'And the pay?'

'Of course, Miss Norton is highly skilled at her work. She has experience, it is quite different, you would be a fill-in, no more.'

'Rate for the job,' said Sam. 'Fair's fair. I happen to know that Miss Norton is paid four pounds a week.'

'It is not my decision, but I will put it to the management,' said Mr Padgett. 'Can you start tomorrow, Miss Smith? What are you working on now?'

He came and looked over her shoulder at the canvas. 'Very nice, very nice indeed. The horse is excellent, the customers like a fine mettlesome beast in a picture. And the bridge, yes, derelict fences and bridges aren't viewed with much favour. Can you finish that today? Mmm? Then you can start in the gallery tomorrow. Nine o'clock sharp.'

111

'If I've got to finish this today, and then find some clothes – how can I possibly do it?' she hissed at Sam.

'Finish the horse, I can do the bridge. Hop off as early as you can. Where will you go, Swan and Edgar? Aren't they open until six?'

'I can't afford Swan and Edgar. I've got a better idea.'

Mr Padgett's eye was on them, and she set to work with swift, even strokes, filling in the elegant, shining rump of the horse.

Polly's friend Tina Uppershaw was an actress, good enough for small West End roles, and still with time to make her way to more important parts. Polly nipped into the booth and dialled Tina's number.

'Tina? Listen, I need something to wear. No, I know I can't borrow anything of yours,' Tina was four inches shorter than Polly. 'Where can I get what I need? I'm going to be a receptionist.'

'Good part?' said Tina. 'Let me think. What time do you get off work? You can leave at five? Meet me at the corner of Mercer Street, off Shaftesbury Avenue.'

Tina was waiting, a chic figure in a green coat and a coquettish hat. 'The idea of you as a receptionist is ridiculous,' she said. 'Oh, it's at the gallery. I suppose you have to know about art, while still looking right for the part. In we go.'

In turned out to be backstage at the Florian Theatre. 'Mattie runs the wardrobe here, she's a chum,' said Tina. 'She's bound to have something you can borrow. I thought of her at once, because they do a lot of contemporary plays. No good trying to fix you up in a bustle or crinoline.'

Mattie turned out to be a gaunt female of uncertain years, with unexpectedly humorous eyes. 'Gallery receptionist? Quite restrained then, dark grey, dark purple. Size, let me think.' She vanished through a door and Polly heard a clinking noise.

'Hangers,' said Tina.

Mattie emerged with an armful of garments. 'Take off your skirt and jumper. Oh, Lord, what a dreadful brassière. That won't do at all. And no corset! I can't provide those, I really can't, but you won't look right in anything without decent underthings.'

And two minutes later, Polly was being propelled out of the theatre by Tina, buttoning up her jumper as she went. 'Where are we going?'

'Round the corner, Madam Hortense, if only she hasn't gone home.'

Madame Hortense hadn't, although she was letting down the blinds as Tina and Polly arrived panting on her doorstep. 'Miss Uppershaw,' she said. 'This is no time to come shopping. I open at half past nine in the morning.'

'Too late,' said Tina. 'This is an emergency.'

And when Polly, by now feeling severely embarrassed about her undergarments, had taken off her skirt and jumper again, and heard the sharp indrawn breath of the *corsetière*, she was regretting she'd ever agreed to take the job at the gallery.

'An emergency indeed! *Quelle horreur*! Have you no lover, have you no pride?'

'No money,' said Polly, adding hastily. 'I mean, I have enough now, but usually I don't spend it on clothes. I'm not much bothered what I wear.'

'That I can see.'

As to the lover, Roger had never commented on her underwear, being mostly engaged in removing it as swiftly as possible. Perhaps he didn't expect a woman to have pretty undies, perhaps he just had a mind above all that.

Madame, whose accent was becoming less French and more South London with every word she uttered, was tweaking

113

boxes down from the shelves. Satin brassières were produced, a slip, a corset. 'Two brassières, and this one I put in the bin,' said Madame, acting the deed to the word. 'No, you shall not have it back. You wear one, and you wash the other. For all this, I make a substantial reduction, because you will find yourself a rich and charming lover or, who knows, even a husband, and then you will return here and buy more corsets and slips and brassières. You will please the young or older man who sees you undressed, and men who are pleased are generous. Perhaps your mother never told you this, but you can believe I speak the truth.'

Polly, dashing back to the theatre could not believe that she had just spent so much money on underwear. Ten shillings and sixpence for a brassière! 'I can't believe I spent so much money. What's the point of earning extra doing this job if it all goes on clothes?'

'It's about time someone took you in hand,' said Tina. 'I've been longing to do it. I know, I know, you have a mind above such mundane matters as how you look. It beats me how you ever got Roger to look at you.'

'Roger does have a mind above clothes,' said Polly. 'He cares about the inner me, not how I look.'

'Then you're a fool to marry him, where's the fun in that? Oh, I know, it's love and love is blind. Has to be, with the shapeless clothes you wear, and there you are, when you strip down, you've got a really good figure. Perhaps Roger just shuts his eyes until everything's off.'

'Don't be vulgar.'

Mattie was waiting for them. 'Hurry up,' she said. 'They'll be arriving at the theatre for tonight's performance at any minute. How long is this job for, dear?' she said to Polly.

'Only two weeks,' said Polly, twisting herself round to squint at the back view in the long mirror. 'I don't recognize myself. I feel an awful ass.'

114

'You would pay for good dressing,' said Mattie. 'Colours, though, you could wear colours. Or black, not many young people look their best in black, but it would suit you.'

'Well, it's grey and navy for the next couple of weeks,' said Tina. 'Mattie, thanks a million.'

'Hope it goes well, dear,' Mattie said to Polly. 'Break a leg.'

ELEVEN

'Six no trumps.'

Myron, sitting on Cynthia's right, passed, and she laid out her cards, her partner smiling approval and relief as she revealed two useful kings, a queen and two jacks, one of them heading a long line of clubs.

She didn't care greatly for cards, but had been roped in to make a fourth at the bridge table when Mrs Butler cried off. The Butlers were travelling with their two young children, and their little girl had developed a nasty cough. Mrs Butler, now that dinner was over, wanted to go down to the cabin to make sure she was all right.

'My wife likes to fuss,' said Mr Butler indulgently, as they had sat down at the table. 'We have an excellent nurse travelling with us, but it's a mother's lot to be concerned about her young. Will you cut, Mrs Harkness? I am grateful to you for taking Betty's place, I do enjoy a hand or two of bridge on board. One so seldom has time at home, I find.'

Now that she was dummy, Cynthia rose from the table, quite uninterested in whether her partner made the contract or not. She had been dragooned into making up the four by

Lois Watson, who, on the strength of the dinner-table acquaintance, was becoming alarmingly proprietorial.

'It's so hard for a woman travelling on her own,' she cooed.

'No, it isn't, not at all,' Cynthia almost snapped back, but good manners forbade anything so uncivil, and she merely smiled and did her best to keep out of the Watsons' way. This evening, however, she hadn't been quick enough, she had been cornered and put in a position where she could hardly refuse to play at cards.

She went over to one of the small sofas, and lit a cigarette. She sat back, listening to the quiet voices around her of the other card players, considering what she could do about Walter, forcing herself to think clearly and rationally about whether she truly wanted to marry him. Each day she ran round and round the same questions, and every day brought her a different answer. Max would laugh at her, tell her she didn't know her own mind. No, he wouldn't. He didn't know Walter well, they had only met once, but they hadn't hit it off. Walter commented on it, afterwards.

'I'm sure you're mistaken. He hardly knows you.'

'Maybe he disapproves of my courting his sister.'

'Courting! What a lovely old-fashioned word, Walter.'

Courting didn't begin to describe the impetuous course of their affair, a passionate attraction at first meeting, then a visit to his magnificent house, which ended inevitably in his large bed. Adultery, an unpleasant word for something that had brought Cynthia to life again.

Her husband had commented on it. 'Found yourself someone, have you?' he'd said in his laconic way. 'Bound to happen, I suppose. We're all washed up, you don't want to come to Africa, I suppose you want a divorce?'

Which had caused Cynthia to do some long, hard thinking. She had no regrets about her marriage. It had been something of a sham from the beginning, given the circumstances, but did she want it to end like this?

'There's Harriet to consider,' she said.

'She's old enough now to understand. Got to grow up, she'll be off into the world soon, can't live in a world of make-believe, you know. Malreward won't want his name dragged through the divorce courts, I dare say, and he can make life damn difficult for people who get in his way, so I've heard. I'll see my man and get it fixed up, you only have to say the word.'

It was too soon, it was too risky. It wasn't entirely altruism on his part. He'd been seeing a lot of Sally Lupin, and she was just the type to go off to Africa to make a new life. But as Mrs Harkness, her position, and that of Harriet, was unassailable. As the ex-Mrs Harkness, a divorcée, life might be very different. And she had no illusions about the likely outcome of her relationship with Walter. Men like Walter spent time with a woman, then grew tired and moved on.

There she had done him an injustice. They had been making love, in the afternoon, that was the special thing about adulterous lovemaking, it happened at such odd hours of the day. Sex with Walter was a world away from the fumbling efforts of her married life, and she felt languorous from the pleasure of it. Walter had the sheets tucked under his arms, only the top of his decidedly hirsute chest showing. He was smoking a cigar.

'You'd better get a divorce and marry me,' he said abruptly.

'Marry you?' Cynthia rolled on to her side, and looked up at him from the crook of his arm. 'Is this a proposal?'

'I'm not going to get down on one knee and produce a ring in a box, if that's what you mean. That would be absurd, given the way things are. Yes, I want to marry you. I'll make you into the most dazzling hostess in London. Paris, too, if you want. New York. You name it. You can twist that husband of yours round your little finger, tell him what you want. And,' he added after a reflective pause, 'tell him I'll cover the costs.'

'Walter, are you buying me?'

'If I have to, yes.'

'As it happens, he wants to divorce me. Only it means we'd have to be awfully careful, you know how judges are these days.'

Easily said, and now it was a year later, with the decree absolute in the bag, and nothing standing between her and her marriage to Walter except her doubts about marrying again. And now? Now that niggling worry was fretting her, making her more wary than ever.

Walter had it all planned. She would land on Saturday, and the following Friday they were due to be married at the Chelsea Register Office. 'I've arranged everything,' he had cabled her.

He would have to unarrange it, but what reason could she give? Too soon after the divorce? Unseemly haste, more items in the gossip columns? Concern for Harriet? Real excuses, all of them, and he would brush them aside with the contempt they deserved.

She could tell him the truth.

No, she couldn't. For one thing, what was the truth? For another . . . Well, she couldn't stand the prospect of having all Walter's forceful attention brought to the problem. Perhaps she could throw a tantrum about the very fact that it was all arranged: reception, flowers, food, guests. How could he know whom she wanted to invite?

Our friends, he'd say, but how many of their friends were also her friends, from pre-Walter days? He had clear-cut ideas about acceptable and not acceptable; it had rung warning bells in her ears when her friends were frank about him, warning bells that she had ignored.

'Sexy as hell, darling, but not the stuff of which good husbands are made.'

'Sweetie, are you sure he's entirely pukka? He seems too good to be true.'

'There's an aura about a man who's reached his age and not married. Of course, he's not queer, not with his randy past, but will you ever be able to trust him?'

'Exchange your husband for him? You're mad. And what about Harriet? A girl of that age is so impressionable, what kind of view of marriage will she end up with?'

Her husband – her ex-husband – with his melancholy and his edginess, was hardly the man people imagined. At least she'd been able to protect him to the extent that very few people ever saw that side of him.

'Walter Malreward's madly virile, darling, but such a bull, men like that always are. He's filthy rich, though, isn't he? Just you bide your time, be chaste as ice and pure as whatever it is, that won't be difficult for you, because you're such a monogamist. Then, when he strays, you can move in for the kill, get a tremendous settlement, you'll live in luxury ever after.'

Cynthia had been startled by this cynicism. What an attitude to take into a marriage. 'Besides, divorce is disagreeable, it leaves a ghastly taste behind.'

'Tell me about it. But it's like everything else, the first time is tricky, only think of the first time you went to bed with a man, yet one gets used to it. You incur all the odium re divorce first time round, so a second divorce isn't going to raise any eyebrows. They say it's only the first murder that's hard, and then that gets easier, too. I wonder if that's true. I could see Walter Malreward committing murder without turning a hair.'

'In which case,' put in another friend who had been listening to the conversation, 'Cynthia had much better mind her p's and q's and turn a blind eye to any roaming propensities Walter may have.'

Mr Butler let out a satisfied grunt as he finessed west's queen. 'Home and dry,' he muttered under his breath as he took the trick and arranged the cards neatly in front of him.

The Watsons were a strange pair. Such a perfect married couple, and yet . . . Tolstoy's aphorism about happy marriages came to her mind. How could you possibly tell what kind of a marriage anyone had, whether it was a happy one or not? Since one couldn't judge one's own marriage, then it was a certainty that other people's marriages would be a mystery.

There was something missing in the relationship between the Watsons. An absence of sexual chemistry, perhaps that was it. Despite the caressing words and affectionate gestures, there was no erotic charge. Perhaps they'd been married for too long for there to be that kind of sexual tension, perhaps they'd been childhood sweethearts and were simply too familiar. One never knew with Americans.

Were they just too typical of American travellers, with their wholehearted and childish delight in the treats in store for them in little old England? A pair of confidence tricksters? She didn't think so, and what was there to be got out of her, or the Butlers? Perhaps Lois had married Myron for his money, that was the simplest explanation. Money could be far more binding than passion. Now she was becoming as cynical as her friends. She stubbed out her cigarette and went back to the table where Mr Butler, with swift efficiency, was collecting his last two tricks.

He jotted down the score. 'That's game and rubber to us, partner. Shall we have another rubber?'

'No,' said Cynthia. Myron had his wallet out and was counting out money.

'I don't think I'll ever get used to your British coinage,'

he said. 'I'm good at mental arithmetic, but how you cope with these twelves and twenties beats me.'

'Give Mrs Harkness that ten-shilling note – that's a ten-shilling note you've got there,' Mr Butler said helpfully. 'Then I'll give you a florin, and we're straight.'

Cynthia tucked the note away in her beaded evening bag. It wasn't late, but she'd had enough of cards, and the atmosphere in the card room was becoming too smoky and stuffy for her. She'd like to go out on deck and breathe some fresh air, but she was wearing an evening dress which left her back bare to below her waist, and her wrap was in her cabin.

So she drifted back to the saloon, where some couples were circling on the polished dance floor. A young officer at once asked her to dance, a handsome boy in his early twenties, and a surprisingly good dancer.

And that brought back a memory of Ronnie, red in the face with the effort of it, in his rough uniform, guiding her around the floor at a *palais de danse*. Dreadful place, garish and over large, and full of people who didn't have access to hot baths or clean clothes, and she, drunk with love, had thought it wonderful and romantic.

'These are your dancing years,' she told the officer, who gave her a surprised look. 'Make the most of them, before life crowds in on you.'

He led her back to a table, but she didn't sit down. One dance with an officer was all very well, but if she sat alone at a table, other men would come and ask her to dance, eyeing her up, a woman looking for company, easy meat, prey for a shipboard fling. She had warded off several offers on the voyage, not with the slightest regret. Besides not having any inclination for such encounters, she had a feeling that eyes were watching, that Walter had a way of knowing what she was doing. She had letters from him mentioning places she had been to in the States, people she had visited, which she had never told him about in her regular letters to him.

There it was, back to Walter. Tomorrow she must decide. No, she had already decided. Nothing final, but a postponement. A delay.

They were due to spend Christmas at his country house, she and Harriet. Harriet had never been there and Cynthia didn't think she would like it. But it would be Harriet's home, one of her homes, at least until she was married; she would have to get used to it.

The room was full, voices, music, a liveliness in the air. Outside, couples walked up and down the grand staircase, or stood at the top, watching the coming and going. A dazzling crowd, the women in evening frocks, the men's black and white evening dress setting off the colours of their companions' silks and satins and lamés.

She was apart from them, as though she were watching them in a film, or seeing them through a glass, shadowy reflections. Perhaps each and every one of them felt the same, each trapped in his or her own bubble of life and interests, fears, hopes, desires.

The notion of bubbles coming and going about the ship amused her, and she went to her cabin with a smile on her lips, to find her stewardess laying out her night things and exclaiming at how early she had retired from the delights on offer.

'There's a package for you,' she said. 'I put it on your dressing table.'

Cynthia hated her for the knowing look in the stewardess's eyes as the woman opened the door. 'Goodnight, madam. I hope you sleep well.'

'Goodnight,' said Cynthia mechanically.

The package was a slender one, sealed with a label. Tiffany, New York.

Cynthia turned it over in her hands. Another present from Walter. Gifts for a mistress, presents for a future wife. She slid the edge of her scissors under the label and took off the wrapping. Inside was a velvet box, inside that, nestling in a bed of scarlet silk was a slender diamond watch. Pink diamonds, a lovely thing. Cynthia held it looped on a finger. She didn't try it on. It would be exactly right for her wrist, Walter never erred in details like that.

She put it back in the box, shut it and slid it into her drawer. Then she sat down at the mirror and looked at herself. Mystery woman, she said aloud. A mystery to myself, moreover. If one doesn't know oneself, how can one begin to make sense of other people?

TWELVE

Mr Grandison and Mr Folliott turned out to be a pair of exquisites. Mr Folliott was short and bespectacled. Glossy brown curls were cut tight to his small round head, and he rocked to and fro on small feet as he pursed a rosebud mouth and flashed a quick glance at his colleague. Mr Grandison was the chief here, Polly guessed, a suave and confident man in pale grey, with smooth black hair and a pale skin, a whiff of cologne hanging about him. The two men looked Polly up and down.

'Miss Smith?' said Mr Folliott, in a fussy voice. 'Mr Padgett told us you were filling in for Miss Norton. I only hope you're up to the job. We're extremely busy just now.'

'You know something about art, I suppose, if you work for Mr Padgett,' said Mr Grandison. 'Not that it's necessary for you to do so, because Mr Folliott and I do all the selling. You will simply welcome clients, and look after them if I and Mr Folliott are already engaged. You will take notes of any sales that are made, Mr Folliott will show you the book, with details of delivery and payment and so on. Please do not pretend to be an expert, there is nothing more embarrassing than ignorance masquerading as expertise. Now,

I will show you round the gallery, and then you can begin your day's work by brewing coffee, which is to be made exactly as we like it, Mr Folliott will show you how.'

Polly had never been in the gallery before, although she often paused to look at a picture or sculpture displayed in its solitary glory in the main window on her way home. Inside, everything from the thick carpet to the silk wallpaper was pearly grey and shades of oyster; a perfect match for Mr Grandison. Elegant chairs were covered in silvery velvet, and the paintwork was another shade of grey.

All of which provided a perfect backdrop to the works of art.

'We have four principal rooms,' said Mr Grandison. 'While here, in the reception area, we hang a selection of small engravings and objects d'art. These allow a waiting client to have something to look at without really wearying his eye. At this time of year we find many clients also buy one of these small and minor works for themselves as a treat, or to give as a present. Come this way.'

This way was through an arch.

Through into a room of nineteenth and twentieth-century paintings. Polly's eye was at once caught by a fine Paul Nash, an autumn landscape with rocks and trees.

Mr Grandison waved a languid hand. 'You'll recognize several of these artists, I dare say. I assume you are an art student, where are you training?'

'I was,' said Polly. Did he think she looked young enough to still be a student? 'I left art school three years ago.'

'I thought Mr Padgett only used impecunious art students. That's tautologous, of course, when was any art student ever not in a state of parlous impecuniousness? You've given up art, then?' he went on.

'I paint,' said Polly. 'The money from the workshop helps pay for a studio.'

'Mr Padgett told me you have a deft way with the paintbrush. Useful work, useful work. Now, in here' – through another arch – 'we have prints. Always popular at this time of year, the perfect gift for a husband or wife, or,' he hemmed behind a polite, well-manicured hand, 'a mistress or lover. This way. These paintings are traditional, we always put on a show of them in December for the same reason. They fly off the walls, positively fly.'

Among these levitating paintings, Polly noticed an arrangement of flowers in a Delft bowl. Very like the one— She went over to it. It was the very one she had finished last week. The label read 'Flowers in a Bowl, by Willem van Elst, c. 1850.'

'But—' she began.

'Rather nice, don't you think? A fine if minor painter, one can detect his hand in the exquisite shading of the leaves there.'

Polly nearly said, Thank you, but restrained herself. She'd noticed the tiny price sticker beside the painting. Fifty guineas! Fifty guineas for a painting that was most certainly not by any van Elst, whoever he was, but some Victorian dabbler, improved and turned into a half-decent painting by none other than Polly Smith. She doubted if it had cost more than five bob, and then two days of her work at twelve shillings a day, that was a huge profit. She told herself to take it lightly, to imagine telling Sam about it, and laughing about it, but she wasn't sure she was amused.

All her uneasiness vanished, everything in her head vanished, when she stepped through the arch into the final room.

Facing her was an enormous painting. A portrait of a woman, larger than life, a woman with a long, long neck, impossibly slender hands, and an extraordinary presence. In a low-cut dress of black velvet, every slight crease accentuating her form, her fair hair dressed up in a swathe of curls, her vitality and sensuality burst out of the frame.

Polly stepped back, letting out a little cry of disbelief.

'Rather overwhelming, isn't she?' said Mr Folliott, his soft mouth taking on a disapproving moue. 'A major painting, naturally. Do you know the artist?'

'I think – I've never seen one in the flesh—'

'Flesh being the operative word, my dear, look at that cleavage,' said Mr Grandison. 'It's a Cortoni. Paris, about 1919. He was an Italian, from Siena, hardly quite in the traditional style of that city. He went to Paris when he was about 30, in 1875, and never returned to his native land. Rather mannerist, I don't care for mannerism, myself.'

Polly wasn't listening to a word he said. She went up to the canvas, overwhelmed by the dynamic brushwork that dissolved into chaotic swirls and lines as she drew nearer; yet, viewed at a proper distance, there was nothing chaotic or wild about the painting at all. It was the brushwork that gave the picture its extraordinary energy.

Folliott was burbling on. 'It's a portrait of Lady Strachan, who is still alive, living in Canada, I believe. Cortoni painted a great many society beauties, and they rarely come on the market, the owners usually prefer to keep such portraits in the family. But of course, in the case of Lady Strachan . . .' He restrained himself with a little cough.

'However, that is neither here nor there,' said Mr Grandison, a note of reproof in his voice. 'Since Lord Strachan wanted to sell the painting, we are, of course privileged to have it on our walls. It is a notable portrait. Now, Miss Smith, if you can tear your eyes away from it we have our duties to attend to, we aren't here for our pleasure. You will hardly need to come into this room, only Mr Folliott and myself will bring clients in here. It is the inner sanctum, as it were.'

Mr Folliott hustled Polly back through the other rooms to the desk. The intricacies of the telephone were explained to her.

'"Good morning, this is the Rossetti Gallery", is what you say when you pick up the instrument,' Mr Folliott told her. 'Keep your voice low and speak in a pleasant way, nothing brisk, but you mustn't sound bored or indifferent, either.' Here was the pad to make a note of every call, here were the cards, which were to be presented to every visitor to the gallery, here, behind the desk, cleverly hidden in an almost invisible cupboard in the wall, were further supplies of stationery.

Downstairs was a storeroom, the bathroom and a small kitchen. 'Now you can make the coffee, Miss Smith. I have cream and no sugar, Mr Grandison takes his black, with one sugar. We open our doors at ten, so off you go.'

Polly made the coffee in a daze, filled with a kind of delight at the portrait in the room above. Perhaps she could sneak in and have another, longer look, while the two men were otherwise engaged.

She racked her brains, trying to remember what she had heard about Cortoni. No, it was hardly more than a name to her, a recollection of small photographs in a reference book. Of course, if all she had seen were reproductions, they wouldn't give even a hint of the power of an actual painting. Such an outsize canvas, and the colours; there was no way that could be reproduced in black and white on the page of a book.

The gallery opened and Polly smoothed her cuffs, trying to look alert and composed, a stranger to herself in her new role and the navy frock.

The morning was quiet. At lunchtime, Mr Folliott went out first, deep in conversation with a client who had bought a small engraving, casting instructions over his shoulder to have the item packed up and ready for their return.

Mr Grandison pointed her to packing materials down in the basement, and told her to make sure to polish the glass before wrapping the engraving.

The picture was parcelled in brown paper and sat on her desk, and still Mr Folliott had not returned. Mr Grandison was checking a silver watch which he kept pulling out from his waistcoat pocket.

'It's too bad,' he said. 'However, this is generally a quiet time. I shall leave you in charge, you may expect Mr Folliott back within a very short while.'

I hope not, Polly said to herself, hardly able to wait for the door to shut behind Mr Grandison so that she could get back to that astonishing portrait.

Damn. The discreet buzzer that indicated the door was opening sounded. Mr Folliott back, no doubt.

She was wrong. A tall, very fair man was standing at the desk. He had a long face, a mask of a face, with supercilious eyebrows and chilly eyes above a haughty nose; she took an immediate and irrational dislike to him.

'Can I help you?' she said.

He looked at her in silence for a few moments and then, 'I understand you have a drawing by Martin Johann Schmidt. A pen-and-wash, of a cherub. I should like to see it.'

Polly hadn't noticed any such thing, but presumably it would be among the other drawings, engravings and prints in the first room. She took him in there, and flashed a glance around the room. There, near the corner, that must be the one he wanted: a plump, frolicsome, dissolute cherub, reaching for a bunch of grapes.

The man stood in front of it, screwing in a monocle to have a better look.

Charming, in its way, but she couldn't imagine this man liking it. Or perhaps beneath that icy façade was a sentimental and soft heart, with a taste for rococo cherubs and angels. Maybe his house or flat was full of baroque excess, of cavorting figures and pouting lips. Boucher ladies, with luscious behinds, draped in next to nothing. Her mouth twitched.

'What are you laughing at?'

She was instantly scarlet, as though he had looked into her head and seen the Boucher ladies.

'I, laughing? I was just admiring the drawing.'

'Were you? It's more than I can bring myself to do. However, I shall buy it.'

'Will you take it with you, or would you like us to deliver it?'

'I shall take it.'

'Perhaps you'd like to look in the other rooms,' Polly said. Where were Grandison and Folliott, did she just pluck it down from the wall and wrap it up? What about payment?

'There's a wonderful Cortoni through there,' she added.

She couldn't keep the note of enthusiasm out of her voice.

'I am hardly in the market for a Cortoni if I have come in to buy a small drawing.'

'Oh, no, I wasn't suggesting . . . It's just that it's a magnificent painting.'

He strolled away, stopping in front of a sketch of a spirited horse and man. Then he let his monocle drop and went into the room of contemporary artists.

'There's a lovely Paul Nash in there,' she called out to his retreating back. 'If you like Nash,' she added lamely, and turned around to find herself face to face with an outraged Mr Folliott. 'Never, never let me hear you speaking to a client like that,' he hissed, hurrying after the man.

Damn it, Polly said to herself, as she swathed the cherub in tissue paper. She wrapped it all in more brown paper, tied it neatly with string and ran back up the stairs.

Mr Folliott was a different man, his face wreathed in obsequious smiles. 'Of course, Mr Lytton. No trouble at all. Miss Smith, take down an address, Mr Lytton has decided to have the Schmidt delivered.'

Polly had her pencil ready.

'Then Hon. Mrs Thelma Warden, 19 Buckingham Mansions, SW,' he said.

'And the Nash to your address, sir?'

Polly looked up in surprise. The man gave her a minimal smile. 'I bought the Nash.'

Polly was about to ask for his address, but Mr Folliott waved at her to put her pencil away. 'We have Mr Lytton's address. A boy will bring it round later this afternoon, if that is convenient for you, Mr Lytton.'

'My man will be there.' He went towards the door, with Mr Folliott nodding and becking beside him. At the door, he turned to Polly. 'You were quite right. The Cortoni is a remarkable painting. Good afternoon.'

'Goodness,' said Polly, sitting down with a thump on the chair behind the desk, making its spindly frame shake. 'He must be a decisive man, buying the Nash just like that.'

'That,' said Mr Folliott importantly, 'is Mr Maximilian Lytton. A very rich gentleman, with a good eye for a painting. Now, I will make out the bill for those paintings myself. Mr Grandison,' he went on, as the door opened. 'We have sold the Nash, Mr Lytton was in. He also bought the Schmidt cherub. For Mrs Warden,' he added, with a knowing look.

'Who is Mrs Warden?' Polly ventured to ask, since the sales had clearly put him in a good mood.

'A well-known society lady,' said Mr Grandison.

'A particular friend of Mr Lytton's,' said Mr Folliott, with the emphasis on 'particular'.

'Mr Lytton is a bachelor,' said Mr Grandison. 'A gentleman of means, a man about town.'

'Does he do anything?' said Polly, intrigued despite herself by the chilly specimen of humanity who had blown through the gallery with such decision.

Mr Grandison was shocked. 'When I say a gentleman of means, I imply that he has a substantial private income. He is not a man of business. He has no need of a profession.'

'Heavens, how boring for him,' said Polly, and was dismissed downstairs to make tea.

'Earl Grey for Mr Folliott, with a thin slice of lemon, and I have Darjeeling, with just a teensy drop of milk. No sugar for either of us.'

The two men were in the room supervising the taking down of the Nash, and squabbling about what to put in its place.

'The tray on that table there, Miss Smith.' Another look at the silver watch on its chain, 'Then you may go for today.'

Polly paused in front of a canvas of a river scene, painted at sunrise, with the first rays glittering through the still water, a masterpiece of reflected light and shadows. 'That's a Kolyov, isn't it?'

'Yes, indeed,' Mr Folliott said approvingly. 'I am glad you are not as ignorant as most young artists today.'

Polly looked more closely, peering into the corners. 'Odd, though, that it's signed there in the bottom right-hand corner.'

'What do you mean? Where else should he sign it?'

'He usually signed his paintings in the left-hand bottom corner. He was left-handed, I believe that's why he did it.'

'Well, clearly he wanted a change. There is no doubt that it is his signature, we do check that kind of thing most carefully.'

'Oh, please, I wasn't suggesting— I merely noticed it,' she said hastily.

'One can have too much of an eye for detail, Miss Smith,' said Mr Grandison in frigid tones. 'Please close the door behind you as you leave.'

THIRTEEN

Max Lytton's house in Lantern Street dated from the eighteenth century, a slender town house nestling between two more imposing mansions. His sitting room and study were on the first floor, a surprising mixture of comfort and austere good taste. Polished floors, fine Turkish carpets, two deep armchairs and a sofa. Pale walls, covered with pictures from the seventeenth century to the moderns. A small grand piano. His study was lined with books, and his roll-top desk was at the moment covered in papers, arranged in neat piles.

He sat in one of the armchairs and Lazarus Farmer sat opposite him, on the other side of the fire that burned in the original grate. Above the fireplace a delicately-faced clock gave out a pleasing and sonorous tick-tock. Heavy curtains shut out a dirty night and muffled the sound of London's steady roar of traffic. Max's manservant served drinks to the two men and then left the room on silent feet, closing the door behind him with a soft click.

Max regarded Lazarus with a look almost of affection. The two men went back a long way and had worked together during the long hard years of the war when Lazarus, a mathematician, had been seconded to Max's department. Cynthia, with her idea of detectives as sleazy types, would have been astonished to learn that he was now a freelance investigator; he didn't at all fit the popular idea of a private inquiry agent. Short, already half-bald, although not yet forty, with soft dark eyes magnified by thick, round spectacles, he was dressed in a well-tailored suit, and his accent was that of Max's own class.

Max knew that Lazarus could speak English with any accent he chose, and, moreover, could do the same in four other languages. Not even Max was sure where he came from, but since he spoke fluent Hungarian as well as German, French and Italian, he suspected that he might have hailed from Budapest.

After the war, Lazarus had returned to his university department at Cambridge, but finding it dull in comparison to his wartime exploits, and realizing he had no desire to drum the higher mathematics into youthful minds mostly much less brilliant than his own, he had abandoned the academic life and set up as an investigator. Not for him, however, the mundane jobs of divorce and tracing missing persons. The information he provided for his clients was of a more rarefied kind. He understood business and finance, and could follow a money trail with swift and efficient ease. He had a knowledge of human nature combined with an instinct for his subject's shadowy side that was invaluable. When asked to provide background on an individual, he would come up with details that the person himself had probably forgotten.

'So, Max, this is like old times,' he said, settling his rotund form more comfortably into the armchair. 'You've had nothing for me to do for a couple of years, and now it's urgent and political and financial and maybe personal.'

Max's outfit had its own ferrets, but none of them was a patch on Lazarus. Each of them had a speciality, a region or an area of expertise in which they shone, but Lazarus's skills crossed all borders, especially international ones.

'I dare say you've heard of a man called Malreward,' Max said.

Lazarus sat up, his relaxed slouch gone in an instant. 'Max, there are some people it's wisest to have nothing to do with. Let me put it to you that Sir Walter Malreward is one of them.'

Max took no notice. 'He seems to have kept out of trouble, given his line of business. I think he's too good to be true.'

'Don't you think he will have been given a clean bill of health before he was offered that safe Parliamentary seat?'

'There are plenty of crooks in the House, as you well know.'

'Yes, but they come with family connections and the right schools or from the right part of the Labour movement. Predictable, and by the time they get there, the party – whichever party – knows their little weaknesses. With newcomers like Sir Walter, it's different, and the party bigwigs do ask some questions, take it from me.'

'Which, obviously, were answered to their satisfaction. What if Sir Walter is cleverer than they are?'

Lazarus snorted. 'Hardly difficult, I grant you. But they bring the police in, you know. Who may be unimaginative, but they do a solid job.'

'Do you remember Pritchard of the Yard?'

'I do. Now with Special Branch. Good man. Intelligent. Persistent.'

'He's got his doubts about Malreward.'

'Has he just?'

'And I don't need to say that his and my suspicions are for your ears only.'

Lazarus put the tips of his fingers together and looked at Max over the top of his glasses.

'Pritchard, hmm, yes.' Then he shook his head. 'Malreward is a powerful and influential man, not a man to cross. I do advise you to drop it, Max.'

'I can't. Special Branch and my big chief have put their heads together on this one and dumped it in my lap.'

'You can't give me any clues as to what kind of naughtiness your client might have been up to?'

Max grinned at him. It took him back to the old days, when the subject of an investigation was always a client, and wrongdoing ranging from treachery to murder was always called naughtiness by Lazarus.

'If it's Special Branch, you don't have to ask, you old fox. Political. Financial, yes: we would like to know exactly how he made – and makes – his money, and how he spends it.'

'Wine, women and song, one hears. I see him at the opera, he likes Italian opera. And there is the matter of his being engaged, as it were, to Mrs Harkness. How is your sister, by the way?'

'Bit jumpy, since you ask. And yes, that is personal. It's her own business whom she marries, of course, but I shouldn't care to see her tied to a . . .'

'Naughty boy,' Lazarus finished for him.

'You won't ask, but I'll tell you anyhow that I shall foot your bill for this, because it's partly a personal matter, and because if you do the legwork, it'll save me a heap of time. It is urgent.'

'Give me a week, and I'll be back to you. At least by then I'll know how clean Malreward is or is not, even if I don't have the details.'

'Take care, Lazarus. Heed your own warnings, there's a good fellow. Of course,' he added reflectively, 'it may all turn out to be a mare's nest.'

Lazarus cocked an eyebrow at Max. 'You don't have any

doubts about the man, do you? You know he's up to naughtiness. Your nose quivered when you met him. Let's hope your instinct, which is rarely wrong, hasn't in this case been distorted by protective feelings for your sister. Who is, if I recall, the only woman you have real affection for. Such feelings may warp the judgement. I do not include Mrs Warden, of course. That involves a different part of the anatomy, not the heart.'

'To the devil with you, Lazarus,' said Max, torn between exasperation and amusement.

'I expect he, too, will turn up in my order book one fine day. Until next week, old friend.'

FOURTEEN

Very few people knew that Mr Rossetti, the founder of the Rossetti Gallery, was no longer the owner of the business he had built up patiently and diligently over the years. He had earned for himself a reputation for honest dealing – rare among picture dealers – and would always and without question take back any purchase by a client if there appeared to be any later problem about its authenticity. People bought from Rossetti knowing that if he weren't sure about a painting or drawing, he said so. He had a good eye, was perfectly willing to pick up bargains when and where he could, but didn't make a habit of cheating either his sellers or buyers.

He still had his office on the top floor of the building which housed the gallery, a fine room, with a view over London on clear days. He came in two or three days a week, advised on acquisitions if asked, but spent most of his time on his great love, the drawings and engravings of Piranesi. He had been working on a book about Piranesi for years, and now could indulge himself with all the hours he wanted. This was because, privately and almost secretly, he had, three years previously, sold the gallery, retaining only a ten per cent share.

The buyer was Sir Walter Malreward, who had had his eye on the gallery for some time. He knew a good business when he saw one, and for his purposes, the excellent reputation of the gallery was worth every penny of the high price Rossetti asked.

Sir Walter had intended to knock him down; every man had his weak spots, details of amours and business that he would rather weren't known to the world at large, and no one had better ways of discovering these weaknesses than Malreward. However, Rossetti had him beaten. Happily married for nearly fifty years to a graceful and formidable Italian matron, with a thriving family of sons and daughters, the sons with sound professional careers, the daughters all well-married, there was nothing Sir Walter could discover about Rossetti's personal life to give him leverage. No strange sexual proclivities, no misdemeanours committed by sons or daughters.

And professionally; although he was sure that Rossetti, while more honest than most, must have had some wily dealings in his long career, his researches similarly threw up nothing that could be of any use to him. There were some sales of pictures to private American collectors that might not be quite what they seemed – but to have tried to put pressure on Rossetti for those would be to damage the very reputation of the Rossetti Gallery that he was buying. He did bring one or two of these sales up with Mr Rossetti, who simply smiled and shrugged.

Sir Walter paid the price Rossetti wanted, on the condition that Rossetti continued his association with the gallery, a living symbol of continuity and probity.

Mr Folliott and Mr Grandison knew the truth, but they, too had to keep up appearances. Which was why, when the blinds were drawn down on the windows, and the door was locked for the day, Mr Grandison rang up Mr Rossetti on the internal telephone and explained the situation.

Mr Rossetti wanted nothing to do with it. He had no idea who the young person in question was, nor did he wish to. He would get in touch with Sir Walter.

Which he did. Five minutes after he had replaced the receiver, the instrument on the desk in the gallery rang, making Mr Grandison and Mr Folliott jump, despite both of them standing in expectation of that very call.

'Malreward here. What's the matter?'

Mr Grandison told him.

Sir Walter had no time to waste. 'What's the young woman's name? Miss Smith? And she's been working for Padgett? Leave it to me. Get on to an agency and find a replacement receptionist, and for God's sake make sure she knows nothing whatever about art.'

Mr Padgett was just putting on his coat to go home when the telephone rang in the workshop. With a click of impatience, he went over and picked up the receiver, holding it slightly away from his ear as the instructions came booming down the line. He was apologetic, as he knew he had to be. 'I am very sorry to hear that. Yes, she has a keen eye. Her work for me is first rate. Well, if you say so, but I'll be sorry to lose her.'

'Get rid of her. At once. She's not to set foot on the premises again, make that quite clear to her.'

'She's been a good, reliable worker, and it is just before Christmas.'

'She can have a day's pay for the gallery and that's that. As for Christmas, what's that got to do with it? I can't have anyone like that in my employ. Make it clear that if she talks to anyone, it'll be the worse for her – I'll see she's blacklisted and will never work in the art world again.'

The unfairness of this roused Mr Padgett to protest. 'She has to make a living. She's an artist.'

'Well, she won't be selling to anyone in London in the

near future. I don't suppose she's any good in any case, or she wouldn't be doing this kind of work. Forget her, Padgett. Find someone else, there are plenty more impoverished artists out there. And tell that young man, what's his name, Mr Carter, to keep his head down and his mouth shut, or he'll be out of a job, and worse.'

'I was trying to persuade him to move over to the main restoration workshop,' Mr Padgett said. 'He'd do well, he has real flair for the work.'

'Don't do it, not if he's been working with this Miss Smith. Watch him for a bit, and then we'll see. Pity, if he's as good as you say, but I'm not taking any risks. He's a queer, isn't he? Remind him just what the penalties are for homosexuality.'

Mr Padgett's wince was almost audible. He was a prim man, and while his Christian upbringing had taught him that Sam's ways were sinful, he liked the lad, and in his view, sins such as envy and avarice were far more destructive of the soul than those of the affections.

'He is more or less open about it,' he said. 'In his world—'

'Yes, and in the world of all the public school oafs. I know. And I know that unless a man is caught soliciting or with his trousers down in a public lavatory in the company of a naked guardsman, the police turn a blind eye.'

Mr Padgett winced again, hating the vulgarity, and having to make an effort to keep his tone respectful. Miss Smith might survive if booted out from Rossetti's; Mr Padgett had no wish to find himself in the same position.

Sir Walter hadn't finished. 'I have a personal friend at the Yard, Superintendent Kingsley, and a word in his ear will bring a policeman to young Mr Carter's door within hours. Mr Carter may take it lightly, but you could remind him what the inside of a prison cell looks like. Artists hate prison, so I'm told.'

Mr Padgett put the telephone down with a sigh of relief. He appreciated the good salary that Sir Walter paid him, but felt he earned every shilling of it. Sir Walter, a personal friend of Superintendent Kingsley? He wasn't surprised.

Sir Walter, sitting at his desk in his study in his handsome town house in Berkeley Square, thumped the receiver down. Perhaps he'd have a word with Kingsley about Miss Smith. No, better to let it go. If Miss Smith turned out to be a troublemaker, which he doubted, these women artists were a wishy-washy lot, then he could get in touch with Kingsley, report something missing from the gallery or workshop, get her hauled in for questioning and a warning, or, if she were too dim to get the message, see how she'd like finding herself up before the magistrate.

FIFTEEN

The next day, Polly arrived early, neatly turned out in the grey frock with a row of buttons down the front. I look like Jane Eyre, she'd told herself, craning to check her appearance in the small oblong mirror that hung above her washbasin in her room in Fitzroy Street.

As she walked down Cork Street, she saw a man coming out from Rossetti's. She put on a spurt, checking her watch, surely she couldn't have mistaken the time, surely the gallery couldn't be open yet.

She arrived breathless at the gallery entrance, and looked more closely at the man who'd come out. He was wearing flannel trousers and a frayed jacket, not at all the type to be buying pictures from Rossetti's.

He was taking his leave of someone inside: 'Bye, Mrs Frith. Ta for the cuppa.'

She had an impression of vivid blue eyes, saw he had a short beard, noticed a slight American accent. Who was he? Certainly not a client. An artist, perhaps, delivering a painting or drawing to the gallery. She glanced at his ungloved hands and saw that his fingers were stained in a way she knew well.

He walked quickly away down the street, and Polly jumped to the door before it closed. A middle-aged woman in a wrap-round pinny looked enquiringly at Polly and said in a strong Cockney accent, 'The gallery isn't open yet.'

'I know,' said Polly. 'I work here, while Miss Norton's away. Can I come in?'

'Course you can, ducks. I thought you didn't look like one of the customers. Fancy a cup of tea? I've a pot brewed downstairs.'

'I'd love one,' said Polly, pulling off her woolly gloves and blowing on frozen fingers.

'The gents aren't in yet,' Mrs Frith went on as she pattered down the stairs to the basement. 'That was Mr Ivo, come to do something to a painting. My word, you look chilled to the bone, you need a thicker coat in this weather. I've lit the gas fire, you get warm while I finish upstairs. Then you'll want to get the coffee on for Mr Grandison and Mr Folliott, they like it the minute they come in.'

'I started yesterday,' said Polly, glad to talk. 'You weren't here.'

'Tuesdays and Fridays I do evenings here. Mondays, Wednesdays and Thursdays I do it early, then I'm off to me other daytime job.'

'It sounds like hard work.'

'Got to keep going. Me old man's out of work, hasn't brought more than a few quid in all year, poor thing. And four kids to feed and clothe, if I don't work, what'll happen to them? Sugar?'

Refreshed and warmer, Polly ran up the stairs. She wanted to have another look at the Cortoni portrait while she had the gallery to herself. She sniffed, there was a familiar tang of oil paint on the air. It must come in from the restoration workshop that abutted the gallery at the back.

Mrs Frith had switched the lights on, very necessary on

another grey day, and the portrait glowed from its lofty position.

Then she heard the door open and close, voices. Mr Grandison and Mr Folliott were here. She hurried back to her desk, glancing around the other room as she went through, just to see if they had put up another painting in place of the Nash. There was what looked like a small Augustus John there. Quite nice, and then Mr Grandison was calling her name in peremptory tones. 'Miss Smith? At once, if you please.'

The smile died on her lips as she looked at the two frowning faces. 'Good morning,' she said doubtfully. Goodness, what had happened to make them look at her like that?

'Collect your things, Miss Smith. From here, and Mr Padgett is waiting at the studio with any possessions you may have left there. At once, please.'

'What?'

'You're fired, Miss Smith. In this envelope is your pay for yesterday.'

'But why? What have I done?'

'We do not have time to discuss it. I am requested by the owner of the gallery to inform you that if you ever set foot on any of the premises here or in the studio again, he will call the police to have you summarily removed.'

And there was Mrs Frith, holding out her coat and gloves and scarf, shaking her head as Polly scuttled behind the desk to retrieve her handbag.

Then, with a surprisingly firm hand on her elbow, she was hustled out of the door by Mr Folliott. 'I am to take you round to the studio,' he said, marching her along the pavement towards the alley that led into Lion Yard.

She wasn't allowed to set foot inside the studio, but was obliged to call instructions up to Sam as to what she had left there. A shabby smock. Her brushes, which Mr Padgett

147

made some comment about, only to recoil as Sam retorted with what Polly concluded was an unusually rude remark. Her palette. A mug. A headscarf, which Sam found wrapped round the leg of an easel.

'That's enough,' said Mr Folliott. 'Come along,' he said to Polly, who was clutching her few possessions to her chest. Like something out of a Victorian melodrama, she told herself, as she moved quickly to leave Lion Yard; she would scream if Mr Folliott touched her again. As she went, she turned her head for a last look, and there, looking out of the skylight, was Sam, his finger in the air. A rude gesture? Possibly, but just as likely . . .

At one o'clock, Polly was sitting in the Wagoner's Arms, at the table where she and Sam and many of the students at the Academy who formed part of their circle were in the habit of gathering. Today she was alone, had she been mistaken in the meaning of that finger? No, here was Sam, in a temper by the look of him.

'Temper! I should think so. I've had a right old one and two with Mr P, my blood's boiling.'

'Sam, do be careful, or you'll get the heave-ho as well.'

'Not I. They can't sack their two most productive and competent workers, not at the same time.' He took the beer which Polly had bought him and glugged it down, before putting the empty tankard on the table and wiping the foam off his mouth with the back of his hand. 'That's better,' he said. 'Now, Polly, out with it. What have you been up to? Goosing the prim Mr Folliott? Making eyes at stuffy old Grandison, which in itself would cast Mr Folliott into a tantrum?'

'I've done nothing, and I've been racking my brains all morning, trying to work out why I was booted out like that. Quite brutally, and it was very humiliating.'

'Tell Uncle Sam all about it. Every detail, leave nothing out, I want to get to the bottom of this.'

So Polly did.

'Honestly, Sam, it's wicked. I knew we were improving those old canvases which Mr Padgett and his helpers bring in. He told me they buy them in country house sales and provincial auctions, they pay next to nothing for them, five bob or just a few shillings more if the frame's in fairly decent order. And then to sell it like that.'

'What did you think happened to them?'

'Well, Mr Padgett always implied they sold them to hotels, or put them back in minor sales. I knew they'd sell them with a mark-up, but fifty guineas, Sam, fifty guineas! For a painting they paid five bob for and then paid me a quid or so for improving.'

'There's the cost of the paint, don't forget that,' said Sam, straight-faced.

'Cost of the paint! Well, that's pence, not even shillings, the amount it takes. Oh, you're being sarcastic.'

'It's a crooked old business we work in, Polly. You must have known that what we were doing was on the shady side.'

'I suppose so. But I never dreamed they'd pretend that one of my improvements would mysteriously acquire a painter's name, and I dare say provenance of some kind.'

'That is rather naughty. At least we make good art out of bad art, which you could say was honest endeavour. Who is this Dutchman whose brush you have apparently been wielding?'

'I went to the library and looked him up. A minor Dutch artist of the nineteenth century, worked in Amsterdam, flower painter. It fits, only of course he never went near that canvas. Even at his worst, he couldn't have produced a daub of the kind that canvas was before I got to work on it.'

'Did you say anything?'

'About the flower painting? Not a word. I was being canny and careful.'

'So it probably wasn't that. Then you sold a drawing and painting to a rich customer, I can't see any harm in that. It's not as though you were going to get Folliott's or Grandison's commission, was it?'

'Nobody mentioned it, at all accounts.'

'Whole-hearted admiration for the Cortoni. I suppose it's genuine? Yes, I know of the picture, it has a genuine, copper-bottomed provenance. The lady's ex-husband is short of cash, times are hard for the landed gentry, and he needs to raise cash to keep his acres from disappearing under the hammer. He's been estranged from his wife for years, probably perfectly happy to have a space on the wall instead of her compelling gaze. No, she's the real McCoy. Actually, as dealers go, Rossetti's are considered squeaky clean.'

'What about my van Elst, then?'

'Yes, it does raise the tiniest doubt in one's mind. Come on, Polly, there's got to be something else. Who came into the gallery? What sold?'

'Various people came and went. I mostly sat at the desk trying to look occupied. Very boring, really, not half so much fun as the studio. Oh dear, I can't bear to think I won't be going back there.'

'Stop moaning and concentrate. Anything special about any of the customers?'

'I'm not moaning. Just regretting. As I say, I was mostly part of the furniture. Mr Folliott and Mr Grandison dealt with the clients, as they call them. Except for one man, a supercilious person, very fair and grand and Mayfair, with a monocle, would you believe it? He came in while the two of them were out at lunch.'

'What did he want?'

Polly made a face. 'A drawing. A pretty enough thing, a cherub. Not for himself, he had it sent to some woman.'

'More details, please Polly. What was his name?'

Polly told him, and he whistled. 'Maximilian Lytton? Of course, you know who that is, don't you?'

'Not a clue, except that he lives in Lantern Street, W1, and sends expensive presents to his mistress. I suppose she's his mistress, unless it's an aunt he's buttering up for his inheritance.'

'Not an aunt. Listen, his sister is Cynthia Harkness. Oh, do sharpen up, Polly. I showed you a photograph of her only a few days ago, dancing the night away in New York. Very glam, very *soignée*. And rumoured to be about to tie the knot with Walter Malreward.' He shook his head. 'No, that's all interesting enough, I do love making connections between people, but I can't see there's anything strange about him or his purchase.'

'Why on earth should it be? He came in, found a drawing he liked. Then he saw the Nash and decided to buy it for himself.'

'Was the Nash OK?'

'Very much OK. And you'd be a fool to try and palm a dodgy Nash off on a good customer, or on any customer, not while the artist is still around and able to say, "Hey, that's not one of mine."'

'Anything else?'

'No. I pointed him at the Nash, and by that time the experts were back and took over. All I did after that was look pleasant and write down the details for delivery.'

Sam rolled a beer mat to and fro, catching it every time it was about to dive to the ground. 'Nothing else?'

'Oh,' said Polly, sitting up very straight. 'Of course. I do believe I know— Listen, they've got a Kolyov. A river scene at sunrise. Nice.'

'Fashionable, the Americans can't get enough of him. What about it?'

'The signature was in the bottom right-hand corner.'

'So?'

'He usually signed in the opposite corner. Bottom left. I mentioned that to Mr Folliott. I said that Kolyov did it that way because he was left-handed.'

'And?'

'He just said that artists weren't the most consistent of men, in that prissy way he has.'

'And?'

'I've only just realized. Before they saw me off the prems so swiftly this morning, I'd been having another dekko at the paintings.' She shut her eyes. 'Shut up, Sam, let me see . . .' Her eyes flew open. 'This morning, the signature had moved. To the left-hand side, where you'd expect it to be.'

'Come off it. You're mistaken, you got it wrong, either this morning or yesterday.'

'No, I don't make mistakes like that. Yesterday it was in the right-hand corner, this morning in the left. And, when I got to the gallery this morning, there was a man just coming out. An artist.'

'How do you know he was an artist? Was he wearing a smock and carrying a palette hooked over his finger?'

'He had smudges of paint on his fingers, and besides, one can tell. He was one of us, Sam. And when I went into the gallery, I noticed there was a lingering smell of turps.'

'Describe the man who came out.'

'A bit taller than you. Brownish sort of hair and beard. Blue, blue eyes. Lean. American accent, or could be Canadian, I can't tell the difference.'

'Well, well, well,' said Sam. 'That's the man Mr Padgett calls Mr Ivo.'

'Yes, yes. Mrs Frith, she's the char, said he was Mr Ivo.'

'He was in the studio yesterday, picking up a goodish canvas from Mr P. Handmade, early eighteenth century. Flaking landscape, asking for a horse or sheep or two – but we only get the machine-made canvases, as you know.'

'Earlier paintings are more valuable. Too valuable to entrust to us amateurs.'

Sam made a derisory noise. 'Believe me, there was nothing to restore on the picture Mr Ivo took away with him. And there he is this morning, on the spot when signatures on expensive paintings mysteriously start moving around. Maybe I should ask for a pay rise.'

'If you give any hint that you think the Rossetti Gallery isn't as respectable as it's made out to be, you won't get a pay rise, you'll be out on your nose.'

'Perhaps you're right.

'Oh, I don't believe it,' Polly cried, stung by the injustice of her speedy removal. 'Can they really sack me just because of a signature? All they had to do was tell me I was mistaken, I wouldn't have said anything to anyone – why should I?'

'They can and they have. You'd better find a few more book jackets to do, Polly. Or get hitched quick to your quack.'

'Don't call him that.'

'Better still, why not paint a decent picture or two on your own account?'

SIXTEEN

'You look different,' Roger said, putting down his cup of tea and looking closely at Polly over the half-glasses he used in the hospital, but rarely outside it; Polly suspected he found spectacles an unacceptable sign of weakness.

'Have you been listening to a word I've said?'

'Of course. I know, it's that frock. Have you been splashing out on new clothes? I do like it, grey suits you. It's your colour, goes with your eyes.'

'My eyes aren't grey.'

They were sitting in Lyons, having afternoon tea. He leaned across the table and looked at her more closely. 'Perhaps not. Flecks of hazel in them. Still, you should buy more clothes in grey.'

Grey wasn't anyone's colour. Grey was a non-colour. How could grey suit her or anyone else, unless you were a ghost, a wraith whispering through the marshes, a creature of the mist and the imagination? Mist was grey, early morning, before the sun had risen could be grey. Pigeons were grey, cats in the dark were grey, London skies in December were grey.

'I'm still here,' said Roger.

Polly blinked and abandoned her thread of grey thoughts. 'I didn't buy it, I borrowed it. For work. Don't you mind that they gave me the sack?'

'Polly, what does it matter? You tripped up, that's all. Put a foot wrong, trod on someone's toes. It happens, out there in the real world. Of course, if you relied on the job to keep yourself, then being turned off without a reference, because I don't suppose any word Mr Padgett put in for you would cut much ice for any other employment, could be a disaster. As it is, since you were going to give up the job anyhow, it's of no importance.'

'Not to you, but it is to me.'

'Are you very short of money?'

That was like Roger. Not understanding, seemingly callous, then, in a swift burst of perceptive kindness, going to what might be the real heart of the problem.

'I've got a little put by.'

'I thought you said you were scraping the bottom of the savings jar.'

'China pig, actually.' She wasn't going to tell him about the horse, Roger was fearfully down on all forms of gambling and had an almost Calvinist streak when it came to horse racing. 'I had some in my savings book at the Post Office that I'd forgotten about.' There she went, lying again. Fluently, easily and believably, what had come over her?

'Because otherwise – now, don't take it in the wrong spirit, I know you'll never let me help you, and I admire your independence, but since we're to be married so soon, I wish you'd let me help.'

'No, thank you, Roger.'

'Borrowed, did you say? The frock, I mean. Can you hang on to it a bit longer? You could wear it to be married in. Just the thing for the Register Office. Neat but not gaudy. Celia and Mother are seeing to some other things for you, undies and so on. They told me, it's their wedding present to you. No frills and furbelows, of course, but you can't be a doctor's wife without having some suitable clothes.'

Neat but not gaudy. That might turn out to be a motto for their married life. If she and Roger could go to bed every night together, no danger of his landlady rapping her knuckles on the door, no question of Roger having to dress in a hurry and go back to the hospital, then even their lovemaking, which had at least had the stimulation of urgency and a certain riskiness, might become neat but not gaudy.

Roger paid for their tea, and they went out into the chill twilight of the December day.

'Let's walk,' said Polly. 'While we can still see the river. Arm in arm, along the Embankment.'

Polly loved the Thames, even in its bleak wintry state of sluggish muddy waters, the tide on the ebb, revealing edges of grey-black sludge, with the detritus of all the river traffic washed up on it. Some boys were wading at the edge, their bare legs blue and red from cold, fishing out objects with long poles: bottles, battered crates.

'Poor little blighters,' said Roger. 'What kind of a country is this where kids have to do that to earn a penny or two?'

'I expect they'd do it, even if they didn't need the coppers they get for what they fish out,' said Polly. 'Isn't that what London boys do and always have done? Isn't that the way boys are, mud and grubbing about?'

Roger stopped and leaned on the stone parapet. Overhead, a pair of gulls wheeled, letting out their mournful mewing sounds as they floated on a surge of wind. 'It shouldn't be like this. We've got to build a better world.'

'Yes, Roger.' It wasn't that he wasn't right, it was that she'd heard it all before. Roger's socialism, although admirable in its way, had become monotonous. It was at its best when he put in long hours of his free time at a clinic in the East

156

End, for no money; at its worst when he proposed an equal Britain, with no man earning more nor less than his neighbour, a Britain of state control ensuring fairness for all. Such fairness to be determined by committees of people doubtless rather like Roger. It all sounded too communistic for Polly, but when on one occasion she had ventured to say so, Roger had been first angry and then hurt, so now she just listened. Thank goodness, his mind was on personal matters, now, not putting the world to rights.

'You've got to be out of that room of yours by Christmas, you said. Well then. Take a few weeks to yourself, the rest of December and January. Let Celia and Mother take you out a bit, do some shopping. And there's plenty to do on the flat, I expect.'

'Like what?' Polly muttered under her breath.

She had loved the attic flat at the top of the house in Bryanston Square when Roger first took her up there. He told her that Edmund and Celia had lived there when they first married. 'It helps no end with the budget, not having to pay much rent for a nice flat. When I've finished my exams and I'm earning a bit more, we can look around for a place of our own.'

Polly had been pleased with the pleasant view, the good sized rooms – and as to sloping ceilings, she was quite used to those.

'There's nothing for me to do, it's all furnished and ready to move in.'

'Well, womanly touches of your own. Cushions. That sort of thing.'

A string of barges went by, the man at the tiller a huddled figure in oilskins and a woolly hat with a bobble on it. Polly waved and, catching sight of her, he lifted a hand in greeting.

'What did you do that for?' said Roger.

'What?'

'Wave at the bargeman.'

'He looked so chilly sitting there.'

'Honestly, Polly, you're like a child sometimes. Come on, I've got to go on duty in half an hour. We've lingered long enough.'

Polly ran to keep up with him as he walked away. 'Roger, Oliver's asked me to go to France. To stay at his father's house. For Christmas, and I can stay all January if I want to,' she said in a rush.

Roger stopped in his tracks and turned on her.

'Fraddon's done what? Did I hear you aright? He's invited you to his father's place in France? What a cheek that man's got!'

'Why is it a cheek? He knows I'm homeless, and it's in the South of France, lots of artists live around there, he says. I could paint, and . . .'

'You're your own mistress, Polly. I can't stop you. I can't even stop you considering that you might accept. You have to see for yourself why the thing's impossible. Go to France, indeed.'

'Well, why not?' Polly yelled at his retreating back as he strode away from her. 'Why shouldn't I? I'm homeless, and he's offering me a roof over my head.'

Roger stopped and waited for her to catch up. 'Don't be dramatic, Polly. You've got a home, with your mother. And as for painting, what painting? If it's those book covers, going to the South of France is unnecessary. Now, not another word, I'm going to catch this bus.' He brushed her cheek with his lips and gave her shoulders a quick squeeze. 'I'm not cross with you Polly. I know you get these crazy ideas in your head. I am sorry about the job, but honestly, don't dwell on it, in the circumstances, it's not a problem. I'll see you on Saturday morning at the station, eight o'clock sharp, don't be late.'

And with a wave, he jumped on the platform of the bus as it moved away from the stop.

'Now what do I do?' Polly said to a gull perched on the parapet. She turned her gaze back to the river, taking comfort in the steady flow, the timeless London skyline, the smooth curves of the bridges. A train rattled across on its way to Charing Cross. A tug gave out a loud hoot, answered by another, and voices called across the water.

She dug her hands into her coat pockets and walked slowly back towards the way they had come. You couldn't argue with Roger. He didn't listen. He was right and she was wrong, and that was the beginning and end of it.

How could she marry him?

How could she not marry him? He was the answer to loneliness, he was her family, her future.

SEVENTEEN

'Balls to that,' said Tina.

Polly had carefully folded the two frocks and wrapped them up in the tissue paper and put them back in the brown shopping bag Mattie had given her.

'Do you think I need to take them to the dry-cleaners?' she asked Tina. 'I wore the navy one for a day, and the grey one for less time. I've sponged them.'

'They're fine,' said Tina. 'Not a speck on them, and Mattie will freshen them up if they need it. Your job ended? That was quick. What happened?'

Polly told her.

'And Roger doesn't think it matters, and he doesn't want you to go to France with Oliver. I can understand that, I expect he thinks Oliver's in love with you.'

'How ridiculous. Are you saying Roger's jealous of Oliver? He isn't, he doesn't have a jealous nature.'

'All men have jealous natures, some of them just hide it better than others.'

'In the words of the old line, Oliver and I are just good friends, and I mean that literally, since—'

Tina gave her a knowing look.

'No one more discreet than Oliver, I will say that for him, and I know Roger hasn't anything to worry about on that front. Trouble is, you and Oliver do seem rather a pair.'

'Rather a pair?' said Polly.

'When you're together. You kind of belong. Like people do who know one another awfully well. People who are close. Which is odd, because you aren't that close to Oliver, are you? No one is. But as to marrying Roger, you really have got to stop shilly-shallying. It isn't fair on the man and it's going to muck up your life if you make the wrong decision.'

'I've made the decision. I've got engaged to him.'

And Polly waved her engagement ring at Tina.

'Funny how you only wear that when you're seeing Roger.'

'I don't want to get paint on it.'

'Freud would have a different explanation. For heaven's sake, Polly, do one of three things. Marry him, in February. Give him back the ring and tell him the engagement's off, you love him, but you aren't ready to get married yet.'

'But I do want to get married.'

'I dare say. So do most of us, deep down. But perhaps not to him.'

'What's the third option?'

'What you'll do. Procrastinate, just as you've done quite successfully all this year. It's never the right time, there's always a reason. Then every Sunday you go along and share the Sunday roast with the Harringtons, and rejoice in that heavenly feeling of belonging to a family which you've never had, and then you go to bed with Roger, and that's more or less all right – or isn't it?'

'Damn you, Tina, I'm not discussing my going to bed with Roger.'

'Thank you, I don't want a blow-by-blow account. Good as Jamie?'

161

Polly was silent.

'Thought not.'

'Jamie . . . Jamie isn't the kind of man you marry.'

'Why did you break up with him? We all thought you were a perfect pair.'

'I stopped him painting,' Polly said, her voice suddenly bleak. 'That's what his friends said. That I was moving on and he wasn't, because of me. They said I inhibited him.'

'Who's laughing now?' said Tina. 'I heard he's going down a wow in the States, big exhibition in New York. When's your show, Polly?'

Polly flinched.

Tina got up from the sofabed on which she'd been sitting with her elegant legs tucked up under her. She went to a cupboard and got out two glasses and a bottle of vermouth. 'All I've got at the moment,' she said, pouring out two generous measures. 'Go to France, Polly. It's a once-in-a-lifetime opportunity, and besides, you can come back and give us the low-down on the scandalous Lord Fraddon.'

'Scandalous?'

'Oh, my dear, yes. I don't know the details, but he did something perfectly dreadful. You'd never think it, would you, knowing Oliver. You can't imagine him getting in that kind of trouble.'

'What kind?'

'Oh, sex, unexplained death, something nasty at the bottom of the garden. Or on the lake, I believe it was. Never mind, just go. The light's wonderful, it'll banish those winter blues, and how could you not enjoy being in the South of France? And staying in some style, I would imagine, I don't think Lord Fraddon spends his time in a seaside apartment.'

'I don't think Roger would forgive me.'

'Tell Roger he can lay down the law when you're married, but until then, you're your own woman.'

'There are practical problems. I've got a little money, but there's the fare. And clothes, I've nothing suitable. Not even for a seaside apartment, let alone anywhere grand.'

'Money I can't help you with. I'm broke as usual. Clothes I can do something about. Or rather, let's see if Mattie can.'

Mattie accepted the frocks back with a surprise lift of her eyebrows. 'Back already?'

'I got the sack,' said Polly, perching on a tall stool in Mattie's den. 'The frocks were perfect though. I just didn't suit.'

'Polly's been invited to the South of France for Christmas and most of January,' Tina said. 'She's absolutely nothing to wear. Her host's Lord Fraddon, she can't sit down to dinner with him night after night in her one velvet frock. Which has seen better days.'

'I should think not.'

'Mattie's a terrific snob,' Tina whispered in Polly's ear. 'She loves a lord.'

'I was thinking about you after you left the other evening,' said Mattie, diving behind her curtains and then popping her head back round like a figure in a Punch and Judy show. 'It occurred to me then that Miss Smith has a figure and height very much the same as Miss Joliffe.'

'Georgia Joliffe,' Tina said helpfully. 'That's a compliment, because Georgia is a stunner. I do believe you're right, Mattie. Go on.'

'When the costumes for this show came in, there was a red dress for Miss Joliffe for the second act. Only she's superstitious, and red's her unlucky colour. So she says. Wine, I'd call it, but she got quite het up about it, and so we had the frock made up in blue. The red's still here, she's never worn it, and never will. She told me that if anything happened to the blue dress, I was to get her something else, "For I won't wear red, Mattie," she said, and that's that. There's no point

163

keeping it for her understudy, Miss Desmond is a head shorter and quite a different shape.'

Tina winked at Polly.

'Here it is,' Mattie said, coming out with an armful of red silk. 'And I don't see why you shouldn't borrow it.'

Polly had never worn such a dress, such a subtly cut, sleek glory of a frock, that moved with every step she took and rustled in shimmering, silky folds around her legs.

'It's only a start,' said Mattie. 'I had another thought, seeing it's this time of year. Hatchet and Feltz sell off some of their stock around this time.' And, seeing Polly's blank expression. 'Theatrical costumiers, dearie. They hire out, for productions and to individuals for fancy dress, amateur theatricals and so on. Of course, they all come up from the provincial venues, but they'll be getting ready for the sale now. If I was to give you a note to my friend Gertrude who works there, well, she might be able to oblige. And at a fraction of the price you'd pay for half the quality up the West End. Given that you're the sort that pays for dressing. No grey and navy, though, not for the Riviera, not unless you're playing a dowdy companion or the secretary. If you're staying somewhere grand, you want oomph.'

'That's fate at work,' said Tina, pleased, as they ended the evening in Polly's room, with her new acquisitions hanging on her hat stand. 'Have you enough money left for your fare?'

'These clothes are wonderful, but it still doesn't mean I'm going.'

'It does,' said Tina. 'No woman ever had clothes to wear and then cried off. Good thing you haven't bought your wedding dress, if you ask me. And no, you couldn't wear any of these frocks to be married to Roger, he'd be horrified.'

EIGHTEEN

Lazarus was waiting for Max in the Temple church. Deserted on a cold winter afternoon, the stone exhaled the smell and chill peculiar to ancient sacred buildings.

'Of all the places to meet,' said Max, who had walked along from Charing Cross Underground station under dripping trees, and now brushed the wet from his shoulders. 'It's freezing in here, apart from anything else, I swear the temperature is several degrees lower than outside.'

'If I, a Jew, can stand the cold of Christianity, you, a Christian, most certainly can,' said Lazarus. 'Walls have ears, that's why I wanted to come here. Those Templar knights are long past hearing or caring what I have to say, and it's not the kind of place the people I'm worried about would ever expect to find me. Were you followed?'

'Followed? Why should I be followed?'

Lazarus shook his head. He was wearing a voluminous tweed overcoat, with a brown trilby. Max was more soberly dressed in a long dark coat and a bowler, with a red muffler around his neck adding a touch of unexpected colour. His hands were cold in their leather gloves, his breath made little clouds as he spoke. 'At least let's walk up and down, keep the blood moving,' he said. 'What's up?'

'What's up is that you've set me not on to a mare's nest, but a nightmare's nest, a veritable hornet's nest, and with a chief hornet of a most vicious and dangerous kind.'

Max waited, knowing that Lazarus would make his report in his own way and in his own good time.

'Malreward's no good, Max. He's definitely not the kind of man you want in the family. He's been up to wicked mischief for years and years, and is, if I'm any judge, embarking on his most ambitious scheme yet.'

'Money?'

'Politics. Nasty, unpleasant politics. He's using his money, legitimate and not so legitimate, to further his political ends. And these ends are not, as Special Branch has discovered, raising the status and standing of the Conservative Party.'

'Tell me more.'

'No. First I'll go back, because it's a story that begins a long time ago.'

'Is it a long story?'

'Long enough that with what I've got to say and the cold here, our balls will have frozen off by the time I've finished. Walk faster, stamp a bit.'

Max drew his scarf tighter round his neck. 'Out with it.' They had left the Norman part of the church, with its curved walls and effigies of long-gone knights, and moved into the long Gothic nave.

'To begin with, there is no Walter Malreward.'

Max stopped, and stared at Lazarus. 'What?'

'Walter Malreward does not exist. He's a name, an identity, but not a real person. There was once a Walter Malreward, the only son of Angus and Purity Malreward. Angus was a Scot who went to America and married an American. The couple opened a draper's shop in Illinois and did well, until their son, young Walter, died in 1895. Typhoid. They sold up, left Illinois, and moved to New York where they opened another draper's shop. In 1887, they were both killed in a fire. A grieving son came forward to claim his inheritance. He had all the right papers, there were no other relatives, and the new Walter Malreward was on his way. He had inherited a business, which he promptly sold, had money in the bank, including the insurance money, and a choice of British or American citizenship.'

'Good God!'

'He wisely decided to leave New York and America. There was always the chance that someone would turn up who remembered the real Walter Malreward, these coincidences do occur, as we know. So in the early part of the century he turns up in Paris, where he falls in love with the city, the arty life, and, so it is said, with an artist's model. She rejected him, preferring another protector, and Walter left Paris for London. His money was nearly all gone, but he brought some pictures with him, which he sold for a good price. He had a nose for business from the beginning. He liked to acquire what appeared valueless and sell it for a great deal of money.'

Max took off his gloves and blew on his fingers. 'You're a marvel, Lazarus. America, Paris, how did you find out all this so quickly?'

'You'll know when you see my bill. Transatlantic wires don't come cheap. As for Paris, it's what, a few hours away? That part I did myself.'

'Go on.'

'From now on, the whereabouts and overt activities of Malreward become easier to trace. He continued to make money, buying low, selling high, anything that people wanted he was willing to provide. More or less within the law. I can find no sign of him dealing in drugs, for example. Which is in itself interesting. Tangible criminal activity of that kind

167

has a tendency to surface at inconvenient moments later in life, when one needs to be seen to be squeaky clean.'

'As when standing for Parliament.'

'Exactly. Malreward isn't a man of the moment. He doesn't have an impulsive bone in his body. He plans, thinks ahead, his schemes and ambitions are long-term, he understands consequences and acts accordingly.' Lazarus stopped to look up at a stained-glass window, glowing with the light of the wintry sun. 'Your sister is undoubtedly part of his long-term plan. He needs a wife like her.'

'Even though she is a divorcée? She's excluded from Court circles, for example, if he's aiming high.'

Lazarus shrugged. 'The Court doesn't interest him. It has no real influence, and that joker, the Prince of Wales, is none too fussy about his companions, divorce won't matter to him. Consider. For the kind of wife Malreward wants, he has to marry a divorced woman or a widow. A debutante is of no use to him. Any charming, beautiful, well-connected woman of the right age will inevitably have a husband.'

'Let's get back to Malreward. How did he get into publishing?'

'He worked as an art critic and writer for one or two newspapers when he first came to England. Then one of the editors discovered that the man had a nose for gossip and he started writing a gossip column. We need to bear this in mind, Max, because I think it's at the heart of the man's success: he's an outstanding collector and assessor of information. He would have excelled in our field, he is almost as good as I am.'

Max was astonished. Lazarus took a justifiable pride in his skills, and he'd never heard him suggest anyone came near him in his ability to gather information and put two and two together from what he'd found out. 'That's praise indeed.'

'Ha, surprised you there, haven't I? There is a difference between us, however. I don't do what I do to harm and destroy

168

what's good, in people or in society. Unlike our man, who chose the dark path, the road to the left, the devil's way. To Malreward, information is power, and he uses it for his own purposes. Once you know something about a person, about his or her private life, about what they have done which is illegal or bad for a reputation, then you can use that in various ways. You can extract further information about other people. You can persuade someone to do this or that, which benefits you. You can ask them for words in the right ears, in the right places. I don't need to spell it out to you.'

'Blackmail is a harsh word.'

'Blackmail is evil, in my book. Malreward would never use the word. He would say he has influence, can exert pressure, encourages people to help him. By the way, he has a very senior policeman in his pocket. Superintendent Kingsley.'

'Does he just?'

'It's a symbiotic relationship. He discovered that a young police officer was corruptible. He corrupts him, then threatens him with exposure unless . . .' Lazarus waved a hand in the air. 'In return, he feeds him useful titbits and so the officer succeeds in his profession and rises through the ranks with remarkable speed. And then again, when there's someone whom Malreward wants punished or removed from circulation, the superintendent will oblige. We'll probably discover more such arrangements as we dig deeper into the doings of Malreward. Money, knowledge and the ability to inspire fear take a man to great heights.'

'Still, from gossip writer to proprietor of several flourishing publications is quite a step.'

'And the war intervened. Now, a man like Malreward isn't going to risk his skin in the trenches. So he arranges for himself to become a war correspondent. He dots about in the arena of war, and disappears in Italy in 1917.'

'Italy?'

'That's where he learned Italian, so he says. I think he spoke Italian already, and that's why he went to ground in Italy. Captured by the Germans was his story, escaped, a usual tale.'

'And he reappeared after the war was over, fit and well, at a time when our lot were disbanding, and no one was in the least interested in the wartime activities or non activities of a war correspondent.'

'Exactly. We'll find he was holed up in Rome or elsewhere in Italy, I suspect he has relations there. He certainly knows Mussolini and that crowd.'

'Does he? That's not on our files.'

'No, because Malreward knows all about keeping out of official files. Take it from me, he dines with Il Duce.'

'Let's hope he uses a long spoon,' Max said.

'He's not the devil in this play,' Lazarus said, very sombre. 'There's a man with far more fire and brimstone about him than Mussolini putting his head above the parapet in Germany. I dare say we shall find Malreward visits him, too.'

'You depress me more and more. Go on. After the war, apart from hobnobbing with various unsavoury foreign politicians, what else? Whence the fortune?'

'He acquired the first of his magazines ten years ago. It was a failing rag, he bought it for next to nothing, turned it into *The Garden of Fashion*, and in no time at all it has a startling circulation, a stable of sister publications and Malreward has in his employ an army of journalists whose talent lies not in writing, but in investigation. Some juicy bits hit the columns of the press, others are stored away for future use. One has to admire the man.'

'He's vulnerable, though,' said Max. 'A blackmailer is always vulnerable, all it needs is one person to say, publish and be damned, and to tell the world what Malreward's threatened him or her with, and he's rumbled.'

'He works at one remove, and remember, he isn't doing it for the money. In the end, if people are paying endless sums of money to a blackmailer, they get desperate. No, he's subtle and safe.'

'Did he get his knighthood and seat through blackmail?'

'He's too clever for that. He bought his knighthood, hardly difficult these days. Money to the party also played a large part in his getting his safe seat, but he has friends in high places, who doubtless think he's a good man to have on their side. They'd like him to have a wife, however, that's the message I got, which is where Mrs Harkness comes into the picture. Of course, he is genuinely fond of her. He's a man of strong passions, has had a string of mistresses, but his only real former attachment seems to have been to the artist's model I mentioned. And now your sister.'

'That makes it worse,' said Max. 'Self interest can be shown up for what it is, but if the man's in love with her, then it's going to be harder to make her understand what kind of a man he really is.'

'And bear in mind that Malreward has a ruthless streak beyond the killer instinct of business and putting pressure on his victims. He almost certainly removed Angus and Purity Malreward from this world, and there have been other convenient accidents along the way. No, don't look so alarmed, he wouldn't try anything like that with your sister, she's too prominent, she has family to kick up a fuss, he wouldn't risk it. He goes for the smaller fry, whom it's easier to remove entirely than neutralize or threaten into silence.'

Max's eyes showed his distaste. 'I dislike this man more and more. Let's get back to the money. The magazines are successful, and I expect all the accounts are in order and so on, since he's evidently keen to be above suspicion.'

'They are successful, but they're expensive to run, not least because of the army of snoops he employs. They aren't producing

171

enough to keep Sir Walter in the style to which he is accustomed, nor to provide the sums that Pritchard suspects he's feeding into various political movements. So he must have other lines on the side. One such is art. He owns the Rossetti Gallery, did you know that?'

'I did not. Good Lord, I buy from there myself. I had no idea, I thought old Rossetti was still in charge. He's always had an excellent reputation in a world not known for honesty.'

'Malreward may be having some very profitable dealings with pictures and other works of art. There's a lot of money to be made in the art market, if you know your way around it, aren't too scrupulous, and have connections in America, where, despite the Depression, there are a lot of eager buyers for their private collections.'

Max blew out a long breath. 'Let's get out of here, Lazarus. The evening's drawing in, and with what you've said and these shadowy figures at our feet, I don't find the atmosphere encouraging.'

'I'm sorry to be the bearer of bad news,' Lazarus said.

The lamplighter was doing his rounds with his long pole, the gas lamps popping as they began to glow with a soft light. They walked along the embankment to the Underground.

'On the other hand, I'm grateful to you, I haven't had such an interesting case in years. Watch your back, though, Max. Malreward has you in his sights. He knows you don't want Mrs Harkness to become his wife. Just be discreet, indifferent and keep up the façade.'

'Façade?'

'Play the role of the entertaining man-about-town. No threat to anyone.'

NINETEEN

Polly arrived at Waterloo Station, breathless, at ten to eight. A grim-faced Roger was waiting at the head of the platform.

'I would have had to go without you,' he said, striding down the platform where the boat train for Southampton was waiting. 'And I bought your ticket, I knew you wouldn't leave yourself enough time to get one.'

Ticket! Polly had forgotten all about a ticket in her rush to catch the train. She jumped as the engine let off steam with a wild whistle and a hiss of steam. It was a long train, the line of green carriages stretching into the distance.

Roger was wearing a greatcoat and carrying a brown leather suitcase in one hand and his medical bag in the other – too precious to be entrusted to the porter, who was trundling the rest of his luggage along the platform.

'Here you are, sir,' the porter said, stopping beside an open door. 'Coach D. I'll put this lot in the van, it will be taken out to the customs shed for you at the docks.'

Roger helped Polly aboard, and led the way to their seats, facing each other beside a window. There was a little lamp on the table, and a menu. 'Breakfast,' he said, examining it. 'Good.

I didn't have time to do more than snatch a piece of toast this morning.'

The train was full. A waiter in a white jacket hurried past with a tray, and informed Roger that breakfast would be served as soon as the train pulled out of the station.

Polly wasn't hungry, but she made a valiant effort, toying with a poached egg and chewing on a piece of toast. Roger ate a hearty meal of eggs and bacon, sausages, fried bread, grilled tomatoes, mushrooms and a lot of toast. Polly poured him another cup of coffee.

There might have been constraint between them, after the sharp words at their last meeting, but Roger wasn't a man to bear a grudge. He talked in his normal way, about the hospital work he was leaving behind in England, and what he wanted to achieve while he was in America, and Polly tried to listen, tried to be interested, yet, looking out at the sodden fields and forlorn desolation of an English winter landscape, all she could think of was France.

'Don't look so wretched, old thing,' he said, laying a hand over hers. 'It isn't long, only a few weeks, the time will pass in a flash. I wish you'd reconsider and spend Christmas day with my family. You're one of us now, you know.'

Polly shook her head, trying to produce a convincing smile. She wasn't one of them, that was the trouble. Without Roger, she would feel out of place; what did she have in common with the alarmingly clever and reasonable Harringtons?

It was a mystery why Roger had ever fallen for her. He had told her it was when he saw a drawing she had made of a child. A friend of his had bought it, he had admired it, and the friend had said, 'Come along one evening and meet the artist.'

And Roger hadn't seemed out of place in that noisy gathering of artists and musicians and writers. He was a civilized man of sense and taste. He turned out to know quite a lot about art, particularly modern art, and Polly was fascinated by him. It was only later that she realized that art to him was an interesting part of a cultured man's existence, as were newspapers, sport, the latest political theories, wine . . .

She had been flattered by his evident attraction to her, and he had made her feel happy and safe, and then one thing led to another, as it did, and they'd ended up in bed, smothering their laughter under the bedclothes and trying to make love silently so as not to attract the attention of Roger's landlady.

Recently there'd been less laughter and Roger's conversation had taken on a more serious tone. Could a man change so much in the space of a year?

Men are May when they woo and December when they wed. Who said that? Shakespeare, probably, Shakespeare said it all when it came to love.

'I don't think you're paying attention, Polly,' said Roger.

'I am, of course I am. I shall miss you,' she added, and she would, she would miss Sunday lunch and warm stolen hours in bed with Roger, and batting around London in his ridiculous car.

'You need to grow up, Polly,' he said. 'That's your trouble. Not having a job, nor any purpose in life, has kept you too young. Yes, I know you're nearly twenty-five, but years passed on this earth have nothing to do with it. I grew up when I was about fourteen, and I know people in their forties who are really only in the teens. Make a New Year's resolution not to be so impetuous, to approach everything with sense, not feeling. You'll find life much easier if you do.'

'But so much duller,' she cried.

'No, Polly, darling, you could never be dull,' he said, with such fondness in his voice that her heart turned over. 'People who live life ardently, as you do, end up unhappy. I've seen it over and over again. My father agrees with me, and you'll admit he knows what he's talking about when it comes to our nervous make-up. Emotion takes a terrible toll on those who overindulge in it. Of course, it's part of the artistic nature, and it's partly why I love you, but for your own good you must try to keep your feet a little more firmly on the ground. No, I'm not lecturing you, it's just that I want you to be happy.'

He crunched another piece of toast. 'And besides, you've got the wrong name for the kind of temperament you have. Polly Smith is a name for a sensible young woman; moments of frivolity, yes, but deep down a Polly Smith is a person who sees life as it is, not as she'd like it to be, or as she imagines it is. And Polly Harrington will be a dignified woman, don't you think? No place for freaks and fancies in the daily doings of a Mrs Harrington. I often think we underestimate the effect our names have on how we and others view ourselves.'

Harrington. A brown name, with sombre shades of dark grey, no brilliant colours there. It suited Roger. Would it suit her?

The train was slowing down, and around them people were retrieving possessions and taking bags and coats down from the overhead racks.

'Now, here's the return half of your ticket,' said Roger. 'You won't be travelling in quite such comfort, but it isn't a long journey. And don't worry, you'll find yourself quite busy, you'll have no time to brood.'

Brood? Why should she brood? And busy with what? No job, one book cover to finish, then what?

Polly's feeling of apprehension and melancholy vanished as the train drew into Ocean Terminal. She had seen the liners at Tilbury, but the vast array of shipping in Southampton Water took her breath away. Roger pointed out some of the famous vessels moored nearby. 'That's the *Aquitania*, the waiter said she'd docked earlier today, her passengers are just disembarking.'

Polly watched the figures coming in a steady stream down the gangways, huddling into coats against the stiff, icy wind that blew even these sheltered waters into foamy grey ruffles.

'Time to say goodbye,' said Roger, enveloping her in a bear hug. He wouldn't want to kiss her in public, but she caught his face in both her hands and planted her mouth on his. He tensed, then kissed her back.

Then he held her at arm's length and looked into her eyes. 'I want a promise from you, Polly darling. Promise me you won't be silly and go to France. Do you promise?'

'Promise?'

It was a question, but he took it as agreement, and swept her up in another tight hug. He released her, looking over her shoulder. 'There are my fellow medics,' he said, waving.

'Is the woman a doctor?' said Polly, turning round.

'That's Veronica Hilton, we trained together. She's a paediatrician. And the man she's with is Dick Abercrombie, I'm sure you've met him. Goodbye, darling, take care of yourself.'

She watched him heading for the customs shed. He caught up with the other doctors, and then moved off to join the queue standing in line under the huge letter H. Dr Hilton stood beside him, deep in conversation, a serious-looking woman in a matching tweed skirt and coat, with her hair drawn up under a severe green felt hat.

It was nice for him to have friends on board, she told herself. He and Dick and Veronica could talk medicine and swap anecdotes of their student days.

If she were going, she wouldn't be waiting in the line as S for Smith, but T for Tomkins, and wouldn't that surprise Roger. What would he say to her other name, her real name? Would he regard Polyhymnia Tomkins as a sensible name, the name of a woman destined for a rational and seemly life?

The *United States* towered above her. She had no idea liners were so immense, it seemed impossible that it could stay afloat. Tugs were busying themselves all around the huge ship. Bunting flapped, a band was playing. And there was Roger going up the gangway. He turned to wave at Polly.

'You're not to wait once I'm on board,' he'd told her. 'I shan't expect you to be on the dock when the boat sails, you can't wait that long, or you'll miss your train. I shan't be out on deck in any case, for as soon as I find my cabin, I shall settle down to catch up on some work.'

If I were on board ship, Polly said to herself, I shouldn't shut myself away in my cabin. I'd want to explore it all, it's sumptuous on board, Sam showed me those pictures, luxury run riot. It did look wonderful, she wished she could have gone on board and seen it. People did, only leaving the boat just before it sailed, but Roger had said that was a waste of time.

She felt suddenly lonely, bereft. How ridiculous, as though Roger were sailing away to the other end of the earth, instead of across the Atlantic and due to come back in a matter of weeks.

She looked at her watch. She had half an hour before her train left. She walked along the quay, sniffing the tarry, fishy smells, looking down into the oily water.

Several cars were drawn up outside the Ocean Terminal, one of them a magnificent Rolls Royce. As she watched, a woman in a fur coat, a sheaf of flowers in her arms, came out of the Terminal, she hesitated, and then a man got out of the Rolls Royce. He didn't walk towards the woman, but stood beside the car. She gave a little wave, and, followed by a porter with a mountain of luggage, went over to the man. He embraced her. A lover, not a husband, Polly told herself, as he gave directions to his chauffeur and the porter about the luggage. The woman climbed into the car.

She knew who that woman was, it was the one in the photograph in Sam's magazine. Mrs Cynthia something. And the man must be Sir Walter Malreward. The chauffeur shut the door on Sir Walter, went round to the driver's side, got in, and started the car. It purred away.

Two figures were standing at a window in the Ocean Terminal, watching the dock below. Lois Watson handed the binoculars to Myron. 'That's him, all right. I'd know him anywhere from the photos.'

TWENTY

Walter was angry. He was a controlled as well as a controlling man, but Cynthia was familiar enough with his moods to know that his formal, courteous words of greeting were no more than a veneer on his anger.

He leaned forward to speak a few words to the chauffeur, then slid the glass screen across and sank back into the leather seat.

'What is all this, Cynthia?' he demanded.

'All what?'

'Don't play games. You know exactly what I'm talking about. We agreed before you left for the States that we should be married as soon as you returned to England. Before the ship has even entered Southampton Water I get a garbled wire from you, saying you want to postpone the wedding until the New Year. What is all this about?'

Cynthia looked at him, and then out of the window at the dreary Southampton streets. She turned back to him.

'Don't try to bully me, Walter. It's a number of things. Harriet for one. Christmas for another.'

'Harriet? Christmas? What have Harriet and Christmas got to do with it?'

'I haven't told Harriet we're going to be married.'

'For God's sake, you don't have to tell her. She can read the papers, can't she? Everybody in London, in England, knows we are going to be married.'

'Nonetheless, I haven't told her when, I can't set a date until I've talked to her. I'm not springing it on her, I can't say, "Hullo darling, how was school, and by the way I'm getting married next week." And,' her voice grew more positive, 'I want to go to France for Christmas.'

'Why didn't you say so? Where's the problem? I'll wire Beaupré straight away, tell him to make sure everything's in order at the Villa. We can fly over, but there's absolutely no reason why we can't go as man and wife.'

'I want to spend Christmas at my own house, at Le Béjaune. With Harriet.'

Walter was silent for a few moments, apparently studying the gasworks outside the window of the car, which had stopped at traffic lights. 'I've already put the word about that the house is up for sale, I see no reason why you shouldn't get a reasonable price for it, although I don't understand why you've had all that work done, waste of time and money.'

'You've what? Walter, I never said I was going to sell Le Béjaune.'

'It's pointless hanging on to a house you won't use. If we're in France, naturally we'll be at the Villa Trophie.'

'Harriet loves the house, and even if I weren't using it, she wouldn't forgive me if I sold it.'

'Harriet, Harriet, that's all you ever think about. You've spoiled that girl, and now you pay the price for it. And I'm not having my plans upset by the tantrums of a schoolgirl. She needs to learn to do as she's told, time enough for her to have opinions and wishes when she's older and married and living her own life.'

Cynthia glanced at Walter's set face. She knew why he

was hitting out at Harriet, he was hurt, and it wasn't in his nature not to hit where it hurt others. Harriet wasn't the real issue here – well, she was to a degree, Walter wasn't a man who was prepared to share a woman's affections. That was too bad. Harriet was her daughter, and no amount of ranting or raging on Walter's part was going to change that. 'Listen, Walter,' she laid a hand on his arm, 'I've had some letters from her while I've been away.'

'If she's been . . .'

'Be careful what you say about Harriet, Walter. Reading between the lines, it's clear that Harriet isn't entirely happy at school. She's been philosophical about the divorce, but it has brought a great deal of unpleasantness on the girl, and left her anxious and not sure where she stands. That's something I don't think you appreciate.'

'I don't appreciate the anxieties of an adolescent girl? Quite right, I don't, nor do I sympathize with it. If you think she's taking it all too much to heart, then I suggest you take her to a doctor, one of these nerve men. I can find out a good man for you, he'll get her sorted out.'

'She doesn't need sorting out. She needs a little time to get accustomed to it all. And that's what I propose to give her. I don't intend to arrive back and rush straight to the Register Office. Nor do I want to spend Christmas in your house with Harriet knowing I'm your mistress.'

Walter gave her a sardonic look. 'As if she didn't know already. Girls these days aren't that naïve. If we're married, you aren't a mistress any more, there's no immorality in our sharing a room.'

'I've told you, I'm not getting married this side of Christmas and the New Year. I'm sorry, but my mind is made up, it's not going to happen.'

'Very well, then you can have a separate room.'

'And she'll know or suspect I'm sneaking along the passage

to your room or vice versa. That kind of thing is terribly bad for a young girl. No, Walter, I won't be steam-rollered on this. We can be married in January, and then of course I'll be where you are, and I'm sure Harriet will accept it.' She sounded so convincing, she almost convinced herself.

'She'd damn well better.'

'It will be easier for her if we spend Christmas in our own house.'

There was more than an element of truth in what she was saying. Harriet wasn't exactly unhappy at school, but nor was she happy. Cynthia saw no need to tell Walter that Harriet had never quite settled down at boarding school. She was a home bird, and had asked Cynthia, when the divorce meant she had to leave her school and go to another one, whether she couldn't stay at home and go to a day school. Cynthia had been firm, sure that the routine and companionship, not to say isolation, of a girls' boarding school might be a better place for her at such a time. Apart from the Walter situation.

Even so, this was all sophistry. She was lying to Walter because she couldn't tell him the truth.

Last night, her mind was quite made up. She would marry Walter, as soon as he liked, and the devil take the consequences. She had fallen asleep planning her *toilette* for the wedding, only to be haunted by dark disturbing images and memories. So much so, that with the first light of dawn she had sat up, knowing that she must cable Walter, now, at once, telling him that no, they couldn't be married next week as planned.

As soon as the *Aquitania* docked, Walter's flowers had been brought to her cabin, earning her another knowing look from the stewardess, whom Cynthia had tipped unreasonably well, as though in an attempt to win her better opinion. Why? What was it to her what a Cunard stewardess thought of flowers and jewellers' boxes?

She looked at her reflection in the mirror on the dressing table, noticing the dark rings under her eyes. She had imagined herself arriving back in England with a spring in her step, with the past behind her, her marriage and divorce receding into history, looking forward to a new life as Lady Malreward.

Her bleak mood had persisted as she attended to the last of her luggage, and went out on deck, holding her furs tightly around her against the bitter wind. And there, as though to confirm her decision, was that man going down the gangplank, the man who reminded her so much of Ronnie.

Walter was talking about the arrangements he had made, his displeasure seeping out of him. She'd forgotten how bad-tempered he became when he was thwarted in any way. And it was with some relief that she heard him direct his chauffeur to drive first to her house in Henry Street. She had expected a passionate reunion with him in his huge bed, but somehow, now, it didn't hold much appeal.

He helped her out of the car, told his chauffeur to see to her luggage, and then accepted the chaste kiss on the cheek which she gave him with an unsmiling countenance. 'I'll ring you up later on,' he said. 'We'll dine together.'

The front door opened, and there was Harriet bounding down the steps. Walter completely forgotten, Cynthia held out her arms, only protesting when Harriet's hug squeezed the breath out of her lungs and knocked her hat askew.

TWENTY-ONE

Sam helped Polly with her move from Fitzroy Street, shattering the silence of Sunday morning with the roar from the damaged exhaust of Larry's disreputable little van.

Polly eyed it doubtfully. 'Will it make it up Archway? It's a steep hill.'

'Lord, yes, she'll make nothing of it,' Larry said, patting a side panel as though the vehicle were a horse. The two men clattered upstairs, Polly opening her mouth to warn them to be quiet on the stairs and then saying to herself, to hell with it, let Mrs Horton complain, there's nothing she can do about it.

She'd sent Ma a postcard, warning her that she and her possessions would be arriving for a stay of several weeks, and Dora Smith was standing on the doorstep as they drove up – Larry had been right about the van making it up the hill, even though Polly and Sam had had to decant themselves and walk, while the van crawled up at a snail's pace.

What did her possessions amount to? Polly watched Sam and Larry carry in two boxes that contained her books, shoes and a few ornaments; an old brown leather suitcase; a rolled up rug; a mirror; a cane chair, an easel and the rest of her painting stuff. The easel and sketchbooks and paints went into the small spare room that she had used while she was an art student, and the rest of her things were swiftly stowed away in her bedroom.

'Wouldn't be hard for you to take off, would it?' said Sam, as he came back down the stairs two at a time. 'Travel light through life, that's the way.'

Polly thought of the passengers off the *Aquitania*, with their trunks and hatboxes and well-made suitcases and laughed. 'It's not the way if you travel first class.'

'And that's the way to do it,' said Larry. 'Minimalism is for the birds, I intend to be immensely rich one of these days, houses full of glorious objects, everything of the best.'

'Meanwhile,' said Dora, 'would you care for some refreshment after your efforts?'

They sat in the kitchen eating bread and dripping and drinking cups of tea. The cat, with an infallible nose for food, sauntered in and jumped on Sam's lap.

'Don't shoo him off, Mrs Smith, I like cats,' he said, offering the animal an unctuous morsel from his plate. And then, 'What do you think of Polly's invitation to France, Mrs Smith?'

'Sam,' began Polly.

'I knew you hadn't told her. Nor about losing the job. I thought, here's a mother who isn't too sure she wants her grown-up daughter hanging about the place at a loose end over Christmas and the New Year.'

Dora exclaimed at the very idea that Polly wasn't always welcome, and then looked at her with concern. 'France? What invitation? And you've lost your job at the gallery? You never said.'

Sam, not letting Polly get a word in edgeways, told her the whole story, while Larry, who had heard it all from Sam at the time, nodded his head and accepted another thick slice of bread and dripping.

'It sounds to me as though that gallery isn't what it ought to be,' Dora said severely. 'In which case, I'm glad you won't be working there any more, Polly. And you, Sam, you want to be careful. It doesn't do to get mixed up in that kind of business, or before you know where you are, you'll find yourself in much deeper than you know. The art world's always been a doubtful one, you know that as well as I do. It'll end in tears, one way or the other.'

'I'll be out of there before it does,' said Sam. 'I've been given a warning by Mr Padgett, speaking under orders I reckon, since he's basically a nice man. You could call it a threat, but I think it's more noise than substance. Hope so, anyhow,' he said, with a quick look at Larry from under his long lashes.

Dora turned to Polly. 'As to this turning down an invitation to go to France, what are you thinking of? You'll regret it for the rest of your life if you don't go.'

'Hang on, it's only a few days ago you were saying I shouldn't go abroad, what's changed?' said Polly indignantly.

'A honeymoon in the Alps is quite different. This is an opportunity not to be missed.'

'What Sam hasn't mentioned is that Roger doesn't see it in quite that light. He wanted me to promise before he went to America that I wouldn't go and stay with Oliver.'

'While he swans off across the Atlantic?' said Larry. 'What a nerve. Is this Oliver another boyfriend, an ex, or what?'

'A kind friend, that's all. He's keen on art, and helps a lot of young artists one way or another. And no, there's no kind of romantic attachment between us. There never has been and never will be.' The finality of her voice closed the subject. 'Apart from going against Roger's wishes, there's the matter of money.'

'You haven't got rent to pay,' pointed out Sam.

'Just as well, given that my prospective earnings amount to two guineas for a book jacket. That won't get me to France.'

'How about your winnings? Not enough, I suppose,' said Sam.

Polly flashed him a warning glance, but too late. Ma wasn't letting that past. 'Have you been betting, Polly? That's most unwise, in your circumstances.'

'It was a sure bet, Mrs Smith,' Larry said. 'The nag came in at a hundred to one, I knew she would.'

'And I made twelve pounds ten,' said Polly. 'Only I've spent some of it on clothes.'

After Sam and Larry had clanked away in the old van, Dora came back into the kitchen, an envelope in her hand. She gave it to Polly. 'This is for you. I put it aside so you could buy some clothes for when you get married, but it seems to me that this is a much better use for it.'

Surprised, Polly opened the envelope and took out five large black and white notes. 'Twenty-five pounds! Ma, you can't spare this.'

'I can. I've been setting a little aside every week, from the housekeeping and my winnings at cards—'

'Ah ha, and there's you raising your eyebrows at my little flutter.'

'It's for you. You can choose what to do with it, but what I hope you'll spend it on is going to France.'

'And what about Roger?'

'Time enough to worry about Roger when he gets back from America. If he minds sufficiently to break off the engagement – no, don't cry out in horror, he might do that – then you're better off not marrying him. You of all people, Polly, can't live under a man's thumb. Did you give your word you wouldn't go?'

'He thinks I did, but I didn't really. Oh, Ma, I'm not sure. It's only France, it's not as though I was setting off for the wilds of South America or anything like that, but even so . . .'

'Go. Go and enjoy the sunshine, it's beautiful in the South

of France, everyone knows that. Go and spend a happy Christmas with your friend, and make sure you take your paint box with you. It's an adventure, and who knows what may come of it?'

TWENTY-TWO

Cynthia Harkness was on the telephone, sitting in the drawing room of her pretty London house, twisting the cord of the phone around and between her slender fingers. With the other hand she was tapping the end of a cigarette on the table, longing to finish the conversation and light the cigarette. She looked up as Max was shown in, and held out her hand to draw him to the sofa.

'Darling,' she said into the phone, 'I simply must go. A visitor. No, no one you know, just a man from the solicitors with papers for me to sign. Bye.'

She put the receiver back on its hook with a thankful sigh, and put up her face for her brother to kiss.

'Who was that?' he enquired, shaking his head as she offered him the silver cigarette box. He produced a lighter, lit her cigarette and sat down on the sofa opposite her. 'When did I become a solicitor's clerk?'

She smiled at him. 'Sorry about that, but it was Lois Watson on the phone, you won't know her, she's recently arrived in London. From America. I met her and her husband on the *Aquitania*, and I thought that I could bear them for five days and then that would be that. No such thing. Lois dogs my

190

footsteps, and seems to turn up in the most unlikely places, wanting, moreover, to be introduced to everyone. I think she must secretly work for a newspaper, for I never knew anyone to pick up gossip so fast, old and new; she probably knows more about all of us than we do ourselves. If I'd told her it was you, she'd have counted that as an introduction and come bang up to you at the next cocktail party you were at, claiming acquaintance with you.'

'No she wouldn't, since I never go to them.'

They were alike, the brother and sister, in their ash blond colouring, but Cynthia's eyes sparkled and her smile radiated warmth, while everything about Max was reserved and his eyes were both wary and world-weary. 'It's a weak lie,' he observed. He adjusted a cushion behind his back. 'I don't know why you have these sofas, they're damned uncomfortable.'

'Only because you've got long legs. Why is it a weak lie?'

'Lawyers are surely a thing of the past, now the decree absolute is through.'

She pulled a face. 'Unfortunately not. Divorce doesn't just wreck your social life, you should see how all the dowagers cut me, but there are all kinds of loose ends that have to be tied up.'

'Like Harriet having to change schools.'

'Yes. Her ghastly headmistress wrote me a faux polite letter saying she felt Harriet would be happier elsewhere, that it would give her a chance to make a fresh start.'

'Perhaps the headmistress saw a chance to be rid of a troublesome pupil,' said Max. 'Harriet strikes me as being rather too outspoken for her own good.'

'It was kind of you to drive down and pick her up. Did she rattle on at you? She does speak her mind, rather,' said Cynthia. 'And now I've had a letter from the school saying that one of the girls went down with measles the day she went home. I have to write to Nanny, because I know Harriet had something when she was quite tiny, only I can't remember whether it was measles or German measles. Do you remember when we had the measles? All five of us at the same time, the nursery like a hospital wing, and Nanny practically having a nervous breakdown.' She sighed. 'It all seems a long time ago.'

'Don't go maudlin on me, for heaven's sake. If that's what divorce does to you, perhaps you'd better find yourself another husband quickly.'

'Don't mention Walter, Max,' she said, quickly.

'Are you going to marry him?'

'I expect so, but not until next year.'

'Are you going to France for Christmas and the New Year?'

'Yes, I am.'

'Will you be with Walter?'

Cynthia was playing with a tassel. A thread caught on her nail and snagged it, and she bit it irritably. 'Not exactly, no, although he's planning to go to Rodoard. I shall be staying at Le Béjaune.'

'Excellent. May I invite myself?'

Cynthia straightened and looked at him with suspicion. 'You? Why? I don't remember you ever going abroad at Christmas. You usually go to those friends of yours near Cambridge, don't you?'

'I do, only it happens that they are out of England until the spring. It would suit me very well to come to Rodoard. Shall I drive you and Harriet down?'

'We were going by train, but yes, it would be fun to drive, as long as the weather isn't too beastly. I don't fancy ending up in a snowdrift. Rose and your man can go ahead by train, with the luggage.'

He got up and bent over to kiss her. 'Let me know which day you want to leave.'

She watched him walk towards the door, suddenly concerned. 'Is your leg bothering you?' she said. 'You look a bit stiff.'

'I took a fall from my horse yesterday when I was riding in the Row, very shaming. He shied, I came off, and I landed badly, that's all.'

'I suppose you landed on your bad leg.'

'Don't worry, nothing really makes it better or worse, you know that. Just a few bruises, that's all.'

'Can you drive with your leg like that?'

'Good Lord, yes.'

The door closed behind him, leaving Cynthia, her face grave, looking at it. She had been the one who had given Max the polio that had left him lame. She'd suffered nothing more than a few flu-like symptoms, but he had had it more severely, and it had left the calf muscles of his left leg permanently damaged. She still felt an obscure guilt about it, although as she pointed out to him, she had probably saved his life, since it meant that his war had been a deskbound one. This had infuriated his father, who felt that sons, especially younger sons, were born for no purpose other than to fight and die for their country.

Even if he hadn't been lame, his mind would have been of more use to the war effort than his physical presence in the trenches, but that wasn't a decision that anyone would have made, he'd have ended up in the trenches regardless. As it was, he'd been drafted into Intelligence, and had emerged with the rank of major and, unlike so many of his contemporaries, alive and as fit as he had ever been.

'I wonder,' Cynthia said to herself, as she glanced at the gloomy news in the morning's paper. She didn't take much interest in politics, but Walter did, and expected her to have at least a superficial knowledge of what was going on in Parliament and internationally. Personally, she'd rather not know about possible rearmament nor about the increasing tensions in Germany, which always got Walter worked up.

Some people said it would end in another war. Dear God, she prayed not, and found herself feeling profoundly thankful that Harriet was a girl. If there were a war, Max would be back in his old job in a flash. If, that was, he had ever left it. Her father, the General and her eldest brother were always going on at Max about his useless and purposeless and indolent life – and she'd seen an amused look in his eyes which made her wonder. She turned the pages of the newspaper and found an article about hemlines for next spring.

TWENTY-THREE

The rain had turned to sleet, and Max hunched his shoulders as he walked across the centre of Trafalgar Square. Landseer's lions were shiny grey in the wet, and pigeons huddled for some protection under the rim of the fountains. He went up the steps to the National Gallery, and as the warm smell of polished wood greeted him, he brushed the cold drops off the shoulders of his coat and loosened his scarf. He walked through the galleries to the large room where Inspector Pritchard was standing by the huge Uccello painting, gazing at the dragon.

'Life in the olden days was a lot easier,' he said, waving at the mêlée of horses and riders. 'You knew where you were with a dragon and a captive maiden. These days, the dragons are all invisible, and you never know whose side the knights are on.'

They sat on the wooden bench in the centre of the room, alone except for the uniformed gallery official snoozing on a stool in the doorway.

Max told Pritchard what he had learned from Lazarus about the Rossetti Gallery.

'Owns it, does he?'

'He bought Mr Rossetti out three years ago, although that's a well-kept secret.' He got up and went over to inspect a medieval Madonna holding a stiff infant Jesus in her arms. He addressed Pritchard over his shoulder. 'I'm a regular customer, and I had no idea the gallery had changed hands. I bought a picture there a few days ago.'

'A profitable concern, I take it?'

'Very. Of more relevance to us is its reputation. An outfit like that is worth a fortune to anyone involved in, shall we say, the less honourable trading in the field of art.'

'And there's money in art, is that what you're saying? Buying and selling pictures, is that how he's getting his extra cash?'

'It's part of it, yet I'm not convinced that's the whole story. Profit margins are good on the genuine article, but much, much higher if you paid next to nothing for what you're selling, because it isn't the genuine article.'

'That's criminal,' said Pritchard with some satisfaction. 'We could get him for that.'

'You have to prove it. And a bit of improvement to paintings here and there might be dishonest, but if it's done carefully, and the descriptions of the works are carefully phrased, you'd have the devil of a job getting a conviction. The gallery does restoration work, I've been into their workshop, which is behind the gallery. All apparently above board, top quality work, so the experts tell me. Paintings smartened up for their owners, or to sell, valuable works of art properly restored with loving attention and skill. Yes, it's making a profit, but not enough to fund a movement, and there's no foreign connection, bar the overseas clients who buy at the gallery.'

'Does there need to be a foreign connection?'

'Lazarus says so.'

'And we've not known him to be wrong on that kind of thing.' Pritchard loosened his coat. 'They keep it warm in here.'

'It has to be the right temperature for the paintings.'

'I wish you'd stop prowling, you're making me jumpy, stalking up and down like that.'

Max returned to the bench. 'I'm going to France for Christmas and the New Year. It turns out that my sister and niece will be at Rodoard for the festive season.'

'Staying with Malreward?'

'Actually, no. Cynthia says she prefers to be in her own house. So I shall accompany them there, and see what I can glean about their rich and reclusive neighbour at the imposingly named Villa Trophie.'

'Rodoard,' said Pritehard thoughtfully. 'That would be Cap Rodoard, would it not?'

'Yes. The main town – well, more a village really – which is where my sister has her house, is called Rodoard.'

'Don't make yourself conspicuous, will you. Given what Lazarus says . . . However, you can look after yourself.'

'Don't worry. I'll watch my back. My hope is that when Malreward's in France he may be more relaxed than in England, I may get a hint of what's making him tick. And, more importantly, what he's up to.'

Pritchard pursed his lips. 'He's a clever man, a very clever man.' And then, with a smile. 'Fortunately for us, so are you.'

They retraced their steps to the entrance, Pritchard turning up his collar and jamming his hat back on his head as they pulled open the doors.

'One other thing,' said Pritchard, pausing at the top of the steps.

Below them, Trafalgar Square was practically deserted. A few figures hurried across, heads down and umbrellas up. By the church of St Martin in the Fields, a newspaper vendor called out mournfully, 'Unemployment rises'. The placard under his stand was flapping damply, making the words, 'Britain to rearm' almost unreadable.

197

'Yes?' said Max.

'There's another neighbour of Sir Walter's and your sister's at Cap Rodoard. A Lord Fraddon.'

'Fraddon? Yes, He has a house there. I don't know him. I remember Cynthia telling me that he lives in France all year round.'

'He does indeed, he can't come back to England. He's an exile, that's what he is. He made this country too hot to hold him.'

Max stopped and looked at Pritchard, catching the note of anger in his voice. 'There was some kind of scandal, wasn't there? I was out of the country at the time, and as I say, I don't know him, so I never learned what it was about.'

'Scandal! You could say that, but in my mind, it was more than a scandal. It was a case I worked on, when I was a wet-behind-the-ears constable. But his lordship got away, and there was never quite enough evidence . . .' His voice faded, as he looked into the past, his pleasant face unusually severe. 'I went over there to Rodoard to interview him, oh, four or five years ago. When Delsey was made Super and he went over all the unsolved cases, keen to show what he could do. I could have told him that was a dead end, there was nothing to be got out of that one, but I got a trip across to France on the strength of it. Can't say I took to France. Interesting to visit, travel broadens the mind, as they say, but I wouldn't want to live there. Hot, it was, very hot. His lordship was courteous enough, but it was like talking to a brick wall. He knew nothing, had nothing more to say. He lives in a remark-able house, although not at all what I expected, not after Fraddon Park.'

'Fraddon Park is one of the great Palladian houses, isn't it?'

'Magnificent,' said Pritchard without enthusiasm. 'His daughter lives there now, with her husband. A banker, he is.

Lady Fraddon left soon after Fraddon fled the country. Divorced him, not surprising, given what he'd been up to.'

'Which was what, exactly?'

Pritchard handed him the envelope he'd been carrying. 'I had a hunch you might be off to Rodoard. These are my notes on the case. Read them for yourself. It's unlikely anything will come up, especially if you aren't acquainted with Lord Fraddon, but if you should chance to learn anything . . . It was a deeply unpleasant business, and I don't like to see a man get away scot-free just because he has the money and friends and influence to do so.'

'What a moral soul you are.'

'It goes with being Welsh. And I'd say you walk on the right side of the moral path yourself.'

Max raised his brows at this unexpected encomium. 'Talking of right and wrong, there was one other thing Lazarus told me. He's not the only one looking into Malreward's life and achievements. There's definitely someone else on the trail, someone skilful, he says. You haven't put anyone on the job have you?'

'Without telling you? I have not. Besides, I've no one to touch Mr Lazarus.'

TWENTY-FOUR

The ring of the doorbell transfixed Harriet, who was seated at Cynthia's dressing table, carefully refining the line of her eyebrows. The soft crayon was suspended in midair as she listened to the voices. Hell, not Mummy back already; no, it couldn't be. She was dining with Walter Malreward and then going on to the opera. Besides, it was a man's voice. Uncle Max? No, his voice was deeper.

A knock on the dressing-room door. Harriet put down the eyebrow pencil, and tried to look as though it were the most natural thing in the world for her to be there, dressed in one of her mother's most elegant evening dresses, with her face made up and her hair arranged in a style quite unsuitable for her years.

The maid opened the door. She was new, and rather shy; Rose had the evening off, which was why Harriet had ventured into the exciting realms of her mother's dressing room; Rose would never have allowed her near her mother's cupboards, which she guarded over with a dragon-like sense of possession.

'Please, miss, there's a Mr McIntyre called. He asked for madam, but I said she was gone out and only you were here, and he says he'd like to see you.'

Harriet's face brightened. She slipped out of the high-heeled evening shoes, not trusting herself on them, and ran down the stairs in her stockinged feet.

Archie was standing by the fireplace, gazing into the flames.

'Archie!' cried Harriet. 'What are you doing here? Mummy said you were in Paris.'

Archie turned around, his jovial words of greeting fading on his lips as he saw Harriet. 'I'm sorry,' he began. 'Good God, it's Harriet!'

'Of course it is,' she said, giving him a hug. 'Mummy's off at the opera, I'm afraid.'

'The maid told me she was out. Good Lord, Harriet, you are grown up. I had no idea you'd come out, surely you aren't . . .' His voice tailed off.

'I'm not old enough? No, I'm not out, you idiot. You should know how old I am, seeing that you're my godfather.'

Archie smoothed back his red hair, its flaming colour somewhat subdued by hair cream. His face was pink with embarrassment. Then the colour faded, and returned to the pallor natural to him.

'For a moment I didn't recognize you. I know exactly how old you are. You were sixteen a few weeks ago, because I sent you a present. You're still at school, unless St Monica's is a convent and Cynthia sent you there for safekeeping.'

'Yes, a super wristwatch and a box of chocs, of course you did, and I wrote you a long thank-you letter, and of course St Monica's a school.'

'Well, if you're only sixteen and still at school, you certainly aren't out, so why are you dressed up like that? Ah, Cynthia's out on the town, that dragon of a maid of hers has been given time off, and you're peacocking about in some of her clothes. Am I right?'

'You always were quick on the uptake. You won't tell Mummy, will you?'

'Do I have the countenance of a sneak?'

Harriet arranged herself on the sofa. 'Honestly, Archie, you don't have any idea how boring it is being sixteen. Either I'm at school, bells and lacrosse and lessons and deportment, or it's the holidays when I just sit about at home. I mean, I quite like school, and I want to go on and take my Highers and everything, not like some of the girls who do nothing but talk about finishing school and when they're married. But I do long to see a bit of life. Uncle Max took me to *The Mastersingers*, only horrible Rose made me wear my velvet frock, the one I have for Sunday evenings at school, and it isn't even long. I do think when one is sixteen one should be able to wear a long frock, don't you?'

'What I think doesn't count. When I was sixteen I was swotting away at Latin and Greek and trying to get out of games at a school in a cold and remote part of Scotland, so you see, things could be worse.'

Harriet pulled a face. 'I know about those schools. Kilts and freezing legs and cold baths and hearties everywhere. I bet you were glad to get away.'

'Yes, people who say that your schooldays are the happiest days of life are either lying or moronic. The happiest day of my schooldays was the day I left the wretched place for ever.'

'What I really hate is the way one's parents and in my case my uncle and aunt, go on at you to work hard and play the game and get good reports and all that.'

'Don't tell me Max says any such thing.'

'Not Uncle Max, no. I mean Uncle Humphrey, and Aunt Helen, who's always lecturing me about pulling my socks up and showing more team spirit. I loathe games. Cousin Joyce is captain of hockey and cricket at her school.'

'Is that the sallow girl with big teeth and a booming voice?'

'Yes. Now Mummy's divorced, she can't present me, so Aunt Helen's bringing me out, and I'll be lumbered with

Joyce. I don't mind doing a season, although I know it's friv-olous. But it could be fun, just for a few weeks. After that I want to go to university, Aunt Helen's very disapproving about that as well, says education is a waste of time and money for gels, as she calls us. Only if I've got Joyce keeping an eye on me, I won't get to do any of the exciting things that debs do, like going off to nightclubs, and fighting off suitors in taxis.'

'I can't see your cousin Joyce doing much fending off.'

'Exactly, just my point.'

Harriet recollected that she was chattering away like a schoolgirl, not at all in keeping with the finery she had on. She sat up and put on her most polite voice. 'I'm sorry that Mummy's out, Archie.'

'Don't you come the great aunt on me,' he said. 'It isn't convincing, not with you sitting there in your stockings. Don't your mother's shoes fit you?'

'Actually, they do, but I felt a bit unsafe on them. I'm not allowed to wear high heels.'

'It was a long shot, coming round,' said Archie. 'I got in from Paris this afternoon, so I thought I might just drop in on the off chance that Cynthia was at home.'

'No, she's gone swanning off with Sir Walter, dinner and then Puccini. I think Puccini's music is awfully vulgar, don't you?'

'Quite jolly tunes.'

'Mmm. Sir Walter loves all that Italian stuff. He speaks Italian, so I suppose that helps. Only when you read the libretto in English, it seems to me better that you don't under-stand what they're saying, it's mostly awful rubbish.'

'So they've left you here on your own.'

'Sir Walter did say there might be another seat in his box, but Mummy didn't approve, and I could see he wasn't keen to have me tagging along.'

Harriet, with a moment of perception unusual for one of her years, knew that Archie was pained by the thought of Sir Walter and her mother out together. She wasn't supposed to know that Archie had been carrying a torch for Cynthia for years. Perhaps, with the divorce, he'd thought he was in with a chance. She'd much rather have him for a stepfather, but she couldn't really tell him that, and what was the use? Her mother wasn't going to marry to please anyone except herself, although Harriet suspected that if she behaved really badly and made enough of a fuss, Cynthia might hesitate.

'Is she going to marry that man?' said Archie, his face giving nothing away.

Harriet approved of his self-control. 'You'll have to ask her. I'm not exactly in on their plans. I just go where I'm told and do what people tell me, not much choice at sixteen, unless I run away from home, and that wouldn't solve anything. And it would put me in Sir Walter's bad books, where I fear I am already, and I may be quite a baby in the eyes of all you lot, but I can tell Sir W isn't a man to cross. So I'll keep my lips buttoned, and my powder dry.'

'How about not mixing your metaphors while you're about it? Harriet, you've got a look in your eye that I recognize and mistrust. I've known you for long enough – sixteen years to be precise – and when you've got that expression on your face, you're always up to mischief.'

'It's not mischief. It's just – oh, please, Archie, there you are, all dressed up in your evening clothes, and so am I; please, please, would you take me to a nightclub?'

'My instinct for danger never fails me. No, it's out of the question.'

'Why? Please. I'm old enough, I know for a fact that Ellie Garsington was going to nightclubs when she was sixteen.'

'Yes, and she was married and with a sprog at sixteen,

too, which possibly had something to do with going to night-clubs.'

'Don't be silly. I know all about the facts of life, what has that to do with nightclubs?'

'Quite a lot, as it happens. Anyhow, you can't cite the Garsingtons, all those girls are as wild as can be.'

'What I mean is, they won't turn me away at the door because I'm too young. Besides, I don't think I look sixteen, do you?'

'Twenty-five is more like it, it's frightening how grown-up you look in that frock.'

'Please, Archie. We could go to the Blue Monkey, there won't be anyone we know there. And we can sit in the darkest corner.'

'Damn your brilliant blue eyes, Harriet Harkness. Your mother would never forgive me.'

'She won't mind, not really,' said Harriet blithely. 'Mummy doesn't believe in girls launching into a season wet behind the ears. She said she'd take me about as soon as I was sixteen, only that was before Walter came into her life and messed everything up. And what's the harm? I'm with you, you're one of the family, really. I asked Uncle Max to take me, but he went all stuffy.'

'If Max doesn't think you should go . . .'

'It wasn't that,' Harriet said hastily. 'He doesn't like night-clubs, that's all.'

Archie hesitated. 'I wish you hadn't asked, Harriet. I have a feeling your mother wouldn't approve at all.'

'Does she need to know? I mean, if she doesn't ask, why don't I simply keep quiet about it? That wouldn't exactly be lying.'

'No, but deceitful would cover it.'

'I suppose so.' Harriet let out a huge sigh. 'Oh, well, if you won't, you won't. But I think it's jolly mean of you.'

'I know,' Archie said. 'I'll take you out to dinner. Then we'll see.'

'We'll see is no,' said Harriet. Still, going out to dine was better than being in the house. 'Can I stay dressed like this? You don't want to take me out in my school best, not with your being all togged up.'

'Do you know where Sir Walter is taking your mother for dinner?'

'Coward! I do, actually. Boulestin's. Where are we going?'

'To a French restaurant I know. Are you hungry?'

'I'm always hungry.'

Max put down the telephone, a feeling of annoyance, rare for him, creeping over him. Thelma's voice was still ringing in his ears. 'So you see, darling, here I am, all dressed up and nowhere to go, it's so like Bobbie to cry off at the last moment, and I can't tell you how much I'm in the mood for dancing.'

In vain Max pointed out that she should phone another of her numerous friends if it was dancing she wanted, she knew perfectly well that he didn't dance. And that he loathed nightclubs.

'It won't hurt you for once. Now, Max, don't be disobliging. I had a fearful row with Bobbie, my nerves are shattered. He promised to take me, it's too bad. And I know you can't dance, but there'll be heaps of people there one knows who can dance with me.'

How like Thelma to row with her husband because he couldn't take her to a nightclub. He might be a complaisant husband – you couldn't be anything else if you were married to Thelma – but she surely understood, after more than ten years of marriage, that when your husband was a member of the government, he would have greater calls upon his time than going to nightclubs.

'Stupid politics,' Thelma said, when Max collected her from her flat in Westminster – which was a further source of grievance to her. 'All this division bell stuff, having to live so close to the House, it's a bit much. I'd far rather live in Mayfair or anywhere smart. And our dreary place in the country, no one would choose to live in Essex, I keep on at Bobbie to try and swap his seat for one in a better county, but he won't listen. He's so unreasonable.'

Thelma's exquisite mouth drooped with self-pity, and Max's feeling of annoyance returned with greater force.

'Where are we going?' he inquired.

'The Blue Monkey. Haven't you heard about it? It's new, all the rage.'

Cynthia and Sir Walter dined *à deux* in a discreet corner of Boulestin's.

'I've invited the Watsons to join us for the opera,' he said. 'Since they're friends of yours. Lois says she's keen on Italian opera.'

Friends of hers! Hardly, but they had dogged her footsteps ever since she was back in London. They seemed to have an uncanny knowledge of where she was, and each time she saw Myron's stately form, or heard Lois's husky voice – at a cocktail party, at a show, at an exhibition – she knew with a sense of inevitability, that they would appear at her side, making it necessary for her to introduce them to whoever she was with.

It hadn't taken them long to wangle an introduction to Sir Walter, and it was clearly an acquaintance they wanted to foster. For his part, Walter seemed to like them. Cynthia had warned him that they'd cling.

Walter shrugged. 'Knowledgeable chap, Myron. Talks a lot of sense about what's happening in America, knows some key politicians. He could be useful. And Lois is charming.'

Cynthia was about to say she didn't entirely trust them; could any American tourists be so entirely stereotypical? Then she decided that Walter was well able to judge the Watsons for what they were.

She and Walter arrived at the Opera House some ten minutes before the curtain was due to go up, to find the Watsons, always punctual, waiting for them.

'Such a pity,' Lois said. 'Lanfranchi has had to cancel, apparently he has a sore throat. They say he's very temperamental.'

Sir Walter frowned, and beckoned to an attendant, gorgeous in the breeched livery of the Opera House. 'Who's singing instead of Signor Lanfranchi?' he demanded.

'A young English singer, sir, Mr Ledbetter.'

'Ledbetter? Never heard of him. And English? English singers can't sing Puccini.' He turned to Cynthia. 'We won't stay,' he said. It wasn't a question, but a simple statement of fact. Myron and Lois were making noises of dismay and concern. 'You stay if you'd care to,' Walter told them. 'My box is at your disposal.'

No, they didn't feel at all inclined to hear Mr Ledbetter.

Cynthia fiddled with the clasp of her fur stole, while the words flowed around her. What Lois would love to do was to go to a nightclub, they hadn't been to a nightclub, she was sure Sir Walter would know just the place, somewhere really smart.

'How about the Blue Monkey?' Walter said to Cynthia. 'New, it wasn't open when you went to America. Good music, you'll like it.'

Oliver watched with a critical eye as Polly emerged from behind the screen and twirled round in front of him.

'The colour's good on you,' he said. 'I like the cut.'

Polly had met Oliver in Fitzroy Street when she came back

from the theatre, carrying the dress with great care. He had at once said he would come in and give his opinion on it.

'Changed your mind about France yet?' he said. 'Just the place to wear that dress.'

'I don't think Roger would like me in it,' Polly said.

'We were talking about France, not about Roger. Well, the offer stands. Meanwhile, with you looking so elegant, why don't we go out on the town? Dinner and then dancing. I feel in the mood for dancing.'

Polly was surprised by this suggestion.

'I promised a chum I'd look in on Ricky's new place,' Oliver said. 'Did you ever meet Ricky? No? He's an old university chum of mine, and he's opened this nightclub, all the rage right now. It's called the Blue Monkey. First-rate music, if what he tells me is true. It'll be better if I go with a partner, though. Single men are apt to get a reputation, you know how it is. You'd be doing me a favour.'

'Of course I'll come,' said Polly. 'Only you have to know the dreadful truth: I'm a rotten dancer. Two left feet.'

'We can sit and watch and listen,' said Oliver. 'Come on then. We'll have to go via my flat, so I can change. Have you got a wrap?'

Polly bit her lip. 'Nothing, I'll have to go as I am, or wear my mac over my shoulders. Oh, dear, I can see from your face that won't do, you couldn't bear to turn up at a smart nightclub with me in my mac, I do realize that.'

'Put on your mac for now, and we'll see what we can find in my wardrobe.'

Which turned out to be a most satisfactory solution, since hanging in splendour in Oliver's dressing room was a velvet cloak. 'I bought it for a masked ball a couple of years ago,' he said. 'I'd forgotten I had it. Rather long for you, but I expect you'll manage.'

Dressed in rustling silk and swathed in soft velvet, Polly

felt a completely different person from her usual self. Perhaps Polyhymnia was a silk and velvet kind of person, perhaps the shabby skirts and shapeless jumpers were an integral part of Polly Smith, and in some magical way the revelation of her real identity would trigger a change that went beyond a mere name. Then she laughed at the absurdity of the idea.

'Share the joke?' said Oliver.

'Only a ridiculous thought that crossed my mind,' Polly said.

Oliver leaned forward to address the driver. 'Drop us here.'

The blue neon sign flashed on and off, and a jerky monkey appeared to swing from the branches of an impossible palm tree. Beneath it glowed the words 'Blue Monkey'.

The man on duty at the door let the party through without asking for their membership; he bowed a greeting to Sir Walter and that was that.

Lois was in gushing mode. 'My, Sir Walter is obviously quite somebody around here,' she said. 'I'm not so used to nightclubs, what's the form? Oh, I guess this is where we check our coats,' she continued, as Cynthia stopped in front of a window where a woman in a neat black dress stood waiting with hangers.

The proprietor of the club, in immaculate evening dress, greeted Sir Walter with imperturbable suavity. 'I have a perfect table for you,' he said, threading them past the small round tables, each with a central light shaded in silk of red and blue and purple. The walls were hung with the same colour fabric, giving an impression of both richness and intimacy. He stopped by a table set in a circle of buttoned plush seating. Sir Walter stared round at the crowded room and nodded.

Despite the dim lighting, Cynthia could see several people she knew. Clearly this was the place of the moment. There was a pianist playing a white piano; in a little while, the waiter told them, there would be a jazz band, from Paris.

There was a time when the rhythm of the music, the smoky atmosphere, the buzz of conversation, the erotic charge between couples, would have set her spine tingling and heightened all her senses. As it was, she felt a slight weariness, a headache coming on, and yes, a hint of boredom.

The American couple were drinking in the atmosphere, exclaiming, thank God not too loudly, when they recognized a famous face.

'They say the Prince of Wales comes here,' Lois whispered to Cynthia. 'Do you think that's so?'

'It's his kind of place,' Cynthia replied, but forbore to add that it was sufficiently vulgar to appeal to the Prince's tastes.

Walter was on his feet as soon as he had ordered champagne, wanting to dance with Cynthia. He should have asked Lois, she thought, as she took his hand, and swayed into his arms.

The masculinity of him was appealing as always. The faint smell of cologne; Sir Walter was a man who believed in grooming, and she appreciated that. Her husband had tried, but he looked his best and felt most comfortable in flannels and an old jumper, never in a town suit or evening clothes. She wondered how he was liking Kenya, she hadn't heard from him since she got back from America. She must ask Harriet if she'd had a letter.

They circled the floor. Walter was talking about some plans he had for alterations to his villa in France, and she listened with half an ear. It was dull for Harriet, at home on her own. She'd been good about it, merely looking resigned and saying she had a book she wanted to finish. Tomorrow, she'd take Harriet out, to a film or a show. Too bad if Walter didn't like it. He was too possessive of her time, almost as though they were already married, and he assumed that she was at his disposal.

It was his way of ignoring her delaying tactics, she supposed. If he behaved as though they were married, then the fact of their wedding being postponed would seem no more than a wrinkle in his plans. For a man who had such an instinct for business and for the weakness of other people, he was being obtuse about her uncertainty over naming a day. She was half afraid of his realizing there was more to it than a reluctance to tie the knot. Almost, like biting on a sore tooth, she wanted him to throw his weight around and demand to know what was up, and then, in his ruthless way, to solve the problem swiftly and efficiently.

As it was, he was still angry with her, there was no question about it. He wouldn't be open about it, but he would find his own way of making it clear that she had upset and disappointed him. Such behaviour would be a feature of their marriage, she had to accept that. For herself, she could cope with it; after her husband's moodiness, Walter's ways wouldn't be too hard to take. Unless he hit at her through Harriet. That was her underlying, increasing worry. He didn't like Harriet, and the sooner she was out of his life, except as a visitor, a stranger in her mother's house, the better as far as he was concerned. He wanted children of his own. A son, of course a son, to follow in his footsteps. And then a daughter, for him to dote on.

Did she want more children? At her age? That wasn't an issue, her own mother had been nearly forty when she was born, the youngest of her brood. And Helen, her sister-in-law, had astonished everyone by having a fourth baby only two years ago, at the age of forty-two. People had shaken their heads over that, a late pregnancy, so dangerous, but Helen had sailed through both pregnancy and delivery without turning a hair.

212

There was a pause in the music, and Walter, laying a possessive hand on her elbow, escorted her back to their table. Lois and Myron had been dancing, and they came back, Lois flushed and laughing and ready for another glass of champagne.

'I'm flying over to France,' Walter announced, with a swift glance at Cynthia. 'Taking Lois and Myron with me, I've invited them to the Villa Trophie for Christmas, they've never been to France.'

So that was it. Intended as a dual punishment, for Cynthia loathed flying, would do anything to avoid it, and he knew that she would find the company of the Watsons disagreeable. As surely, would he; what was he doing, inviting strangers to his house?

'What a good idea,' she said, managing to sound calm and unbothered. 'When are you leaving?'

That brought a frown to Walter's broad forehead.

'We'll fly out on Tuesday. Across to Paris and then down to Nice. Ferdie Sarler is flying us, it's all fixed up.'

Cynthia smiled. 'Far too long a flight for me, Walter. I'll go by boat and train.' She turned to Lois and Myron. 'I have my own house at Rodoard, you know, you must dine with me while you're staying at Walter's place.'

'Nonsense,' said Walter. 'You'll be staying at the Villa Trophie as well, for Christmas and New Year.'

Lois and Myron exchanged uncomfortable glances; the edge in Walter's voice was unmistakable. 'I can't wait to see Cap Rodoard,' bubbled Lois. 'I hear all the smartest aristocrats have places there.'

'No, Walter,' Cynthia said, her voice bright and clear. 'I won't be bullied. I shan't fly, you know how much I hate it. And I shall be spending Christmas and New Year at Le Béjaune. It's what Harriet wants, and I've promised her that's what we'll do.'

Walter got to his feet again, and said to Lois, 'Shall we dance?'

Myron lit a cigar and looked reflectively at Cynthia. 'You annoyed Sir Walter there.'

Cynthia smiled. 'He likes to be in charge, but Christmas is a family time, don't you agree? Do you mind being away from your own family over Christmas?'

'Lois and I were never blessed with little ones,' he said. 'And we have only ourselves to please. Lois is looking forward to an old-fashioned Christmas, a European Christmas. Although I gather it can be pretty warm in the South of France, so I guess it won't be log fires and snow outside.'

'I have log fires in my house,' Cynthia said. 'Walter's villa is centrally heated, he goes in for modernity.'

'Then it sounds as though we'll be comfortable, whatever the weather. My, that's a pretty girl there in the dark blue dress, dancing with the man with red hair, Judas hair we call it where I come from.'

Cynthia looked without interest across the floor, and then stiffened.

'You look like one of those creatures at the zoo, all eyes,' said Oliver, as he guided Polly around the floor.

'Sorry,' said Polly, as she stumbled over Oliver's toes. 'I told you I was a hopeless dancer.'

'Stop looking round in wide-eyed wonder and concentrate on your feet. Don't pretend you haven't been to clubs before, Polly.'

'I have, but never anywhere like this. My God, do you see the jewels that woman is wearing?'

'That's Lady Lingford,' Oliver said. 'If you mean the one with improbably dark hair and festooned with glitter like a Christmas tree.'

Polly wasn't listening. She had spotted a famous actor, deep

214

in conversation with a film star, and wasn't that Irene Fox, the singer? And there was that Sir Walter Malreward, dancing with Mrs Cynthia Harkness, who was wearing the same dress as in the photo in the magazine, backless, with a kind of long kick pleat at the back. Lovely, but not as striking as her own red frock.

'Do you know Sir Walter Malreward and Mrs Harkness?' Polly asked Oliver. The music had changed into a slow waltz, and she was doing better.

'He has a house near us in France. The Villa Trophie. We don't see much of him, he and my father don't get on. Cynthia and her ex-husband also have a house nearby, in the little town of Rodoard.'

'Villa Trophie, what an extraordinary name.'

'There's a Roman ruin near Rodoard, a vast edifice put up by Augustus in his usual overweening way. It's called the Trophy of the Alps. You can see it from Malreward's villa. I think Malreward sees himself as something of a new Augustus, ruling over his empire of magazines and God knows what else.'

'You don't like him.'

Oliver shrugged, and moved Polly out of the way of a revolving couple. 'I don't care for his type much. I like Cynthia, though. They say she's going to marry him; she's a fool if she does. Plenty of money, of course, but apart from that . . .'

Polly, as the gyrations of the dance brought her closer to where Sir Walter and Mrs Harkness were sitting with another couple, saw just why a woman might marry Sir Walter Malreward. He had bags of sex appeal, anyone could tell that. Not her type, but you couldn't deny the energy and the masculinity. Mrs Harkness didn't look happy, she had a faraway look in her eyes that Polly recognized as the look of one detaching herself from her immediate surroundings in order to get away from an unpleasantness.

At that moment, Mrs Harkness's expression changed abruptly, as though she had suddenly seen a ghost. What was up?

Harriet's colour was up as she and Archie made their way through the tables. She was flushed with the excitement of a very good dinner at the French restaurant, with the thrill of a guilty conscience and the satisfaction of knowing that she had crossed a forbidden boundary.

Archie's red hair was subdued in the dim lighting, but they made a noticeable pair as they went on to the floor, and several heads turned as they went past. 'I am enjoying this dance, Archie,' Harriet was saying, when like an arrow soaring over the hum of conversation she heard her name, called in a clear, precise, all too familiar voice.

'Hell,' she said, the colour draining from her face. 'Hell and damnation. Mummy! Whatever is she doing here? Archie, can we pretend we haven't seen her and just slide out?'

'Hell and damnation is right,' said Archie ruefully. 'No, we can't. Got to face the music, I'm afraid, Harriet. Still, one thing, your mother won't make a scene here.'

'Bottled up and saved it'll be much worse,' said Harriet, as Archie virtually pushed her to the table, where Cynthia was on her feet. Sir Walter was, too, and the large man beside Cynthia got up as they reached the table.

'Harriet!' Cynthia said again. And then, 'Archie!'

Archie, with great aplomb, kissed Cynthia on both cheeks. 'Good evening, Cynthia, I've just got back from Paris. Looked in at Wentworth Street and found Harriet on her own.'

Cynthia wasn't wasting time on Archie. 'Harriet, please sit down and close your mouth and try to look normal. People are staring.'

Sir Walter was one of them. Harriet hadn't ever seen him put out, but judging by his expression, he was now. He recovered swiftly. 'Harriet, how charming,' he said with perfect insincerity. 'And this is?'

He doesn't like the look of Archie, Harriet said to herself, as the waiter brought two more chairs and she sat down. I wonder if he knows he's a suitor.

Cynthia was making introductions. 'I'm sure you've heard me mention Mr McIntyre, Walter, an old family friend, and Harriet's godfather.'

'Kind of you to take the girl out,' said Walter. 'Only I thought that she . . .'

Myron and Lois burst out into exclamations of delight at meeting Miss Harkness, and Mr McIntyre, Scottish of course, Lois's grandfather was a Scot, a McTavish, did they come from Mr McIntyre's part of Scotland?

Cynthia was speaking to Archie in a low, venomous whisper that made his ears burn. 'How could you, Archie? I know you're far too kind for your own good, but this isn't kindness at all. Word will get about, and she'll have a reputation for being fast before she ever becomes a deb. People will say, like mother, like daughter.'

Archie was horrified. 'Cynthia, that's ridiculous.'

'You have no idea how stuffy the mothers are, no idea at all. It could ruin Harriet's season if she's cold-shouldered by the mothers and dowagers. And if Humphrey and Helen learn she's set foot in a nightclub, I'll never hear the end of it.'

'Blow Humphrey and Helen,' said Archie. 'When have you ever paid any attention to what they say?'

'And my blue silk dress, Harriet, how could you?'

Harriet shot her mother a glance from lowered eyes, didn't at all like what she saw, and muttered, 'I'm sorry, Mummy.'

'Walter, get them to call a taxi. Archie must take Harriet home at once.'

Walter shook his head. 'Not a good idea, Cynthia. It would

simply draw attention to her. Let her stay for at least half an hour. One thing, got up like that, I doubt if anyone will recognize her. I didn't at first.'

Lois and Myron looked interested. 'Say, are you out on the town without permission?' said Lois. 'That's just what I used to do when I was a girl, and my, didn't my mother get mad at me!'

More glasses appeared. 'No, Harriet,' Cynthia said sharply. 'You are not having champagne.'

That was a voice Harriet knew well, and she didn't protest when a fruit cocktail was ordered for her. She cheered up when it arrived, as it came in an elegant glass with a glacé cherry spiked through with a little stick, topped by a miniature blue monkey; no one would know it wasn't a real cocktail.

Sir Walter rose and was about to take Lois on to the floor. Now Myron was opening his mouth, he was going to ask Cynthia to dance, and Harriet could see that she didn't want to dance at all. Just wants to sit and keep an eye on me and brood on my sins, she told herself. Goodness, there was going to be a row in the morning.

Her gloomy thoughts were interrupted by the arrival of a tall, very graceful man, accompanied by a young woman all big dark eyes, wearing a stunning red frock. 'Archie,' the man said. 'I'd no idea you were in London. Sorry to butt in, Mrs Harkness, how are you? Good evening, Sir Walter.'

More introductions, the girl was called Polly Smith, not much of a name, not the right sort of name for someone who looked like that, Harriet said to herself. And of course, the man was Oliver Fraddon, Lord Fraddon's son. Harriet had seen him at Rodoard. He was bowing over her hand. 'Miss Harkness! Now, I remember you as a schoolgirl, all legs and eyes and plaits.'

'Harriet is still at school,' said Cynthia, unforgivably.

Another table was brought, more chairs. Sir Walter and Lois went off to dance, Myron glanced at Cynthia, but she was deep in conversation with Oliver and Archie. 'Would you care to dance?' he asked Harriet.

'I'd better not,' she said.

'Miss Smith?'

Polly gave him a grin. 'You wouldn't ask if you'd seen me dancing. Oliver's feet must be a mass of bruises. I'll sit out for a few numbers, I think.'

Harriet liked the look of Polly. 'I say, I love your frock. Who made it?'

'No one famous, it was made for Georgia Joliffe, the actress, for a play, only she didn't care for the colour, so I got it through a friend.'

'Are you an actress?'

'I'm an artist, a painter.'

'Goodness, how exciting. Can you make a living from that? I mean . . . ?' Harriet broke off her sentence abruptly, and she half stood, flapping her napkin in a most unlady-like way. 'Uncle Max! Uncle Max.'

The man turned his head, and gave Harriet a long, unsmiling look.

Polly recognized him at once. It was the man from the gallery, the tall, very fair man with the limp and the monocle. So he was Harriet Harkness's uncle, and therefore – yes, he must be Cynthia Harkness's brother, the likeness was striking.

He had reached their table now, accompanied by a beau-tiful woman, perfectly turned out, with hard eyes. She didn't look at all pleased.

'Harriet, what on earth are you doing here?'

'Hullo, Uncle Max. You told me you never went to night-clubs.'

'I don't, if I can help it. More to the point, you most certainly don't go to nightclubs. Does Cynthia know you're here?'

'She's just this minute gone to dance with Mr Watson,' said Harriet, nodding to the corner where her mother was doing a rather staid foxtrot with the American.

'Archie, I didn't know you were in London,' said Max. 'You know Mrs Warden?'

'This is Miss Smith,' Archie said.

Introductions, handshakes, the return of Sir Walter and Mrs Watson, more chairs, more talk.

Myron Watson finally took Harriet off for a dance. 'Please allow me the pleasure,' he said in his grave way to Cynthia. 'It will do her no harm to dance with me, she reminds me of my own niece, and it's hard on a girl if she can't party a little.'

Sir Walter and Mrs Warden joined them on the floor, Oliver bore Lois off, and Archie almost pulled a reluctant Cynthia up from the table.

'No, you dashed well don't want to sit and talk to Max. Your brother, in a nightclub, it's outrageous.'

Which left Polly, rather tongue-tied, with Mr Lytton.

'I apologize,' he said. 'I never dance.'

'No, you're lame,' said Polly. 'Was it in the war?'

'Nothing so heroic. A childhood illness.'

'Poliomyelitis? A boy at school died of that, you were lucky. Oh, I'm sorry, that sounds rude.'

'Not at all. You are quite right. A limp is nothing compared to a life in an iron lung, or not surviving at all.'

Polly wished Oliver would come back. She felt safe with Oliver there, and he could talk art with Mr Lytton. Yet at the same time, she didn't want him to come back. There was something fascinating about Mr Lytton, although she couldn't put a finger on it. She would like to paint him, that lean face and high bridged nose and – most of all, those chilly eyes. Not chilly in the same way as Mrs Warden, hers were cold and predatory. Snake's eyes. Was he in love with her?

Presumably, if he'd bought her that drawing and went to nightclubs with her, they must be close. His eyes were shuttered, there was feeling there, but filtered from the world. An observant man, a watcher, as she was, but he was watchful in a different way from her, those weren't the eyes of a painter.

All this from flew through her mind, until her own eyes were caught by Sir Walter and Mrs Watson. Without thinking, she felt inside her shabby velvet bag and extracted her pen. There was a little mat under her glass, and it was blank on the other side. In a few quick lines, she had captured Sir Walter, his stance, his confidence – and something else.

'May I?' said Mr Lytton, and without waiting for permission, he picked up the mat. 'Ah,' he said. 'You have a talent for caricature, I see.'

'Please,' Polly began, but before she could take it back, Harriet was at her side, with a smiling Myron.

'Sir Walter!' exclaimed Harriet. 'To the life. That's awfully clever. Look, Uncle Max, look Mr Watson.'

Myron looked at the sketch and then gave a quick glance to where Sir Walter was dancing with his wife. 'I'd say you'd got him to a T,' he said slowly.

'Oh, you must show it to him, how he'll laugh,' said Harriet. 'He might give you a job on one of his magazines, they have caricatures of people.'

Max removed the mat from Harriet and passed it back to Polly. 'No, Harriet,' he said in a authoritative tone that startled her. 'You are not to mention it or try to show it to Sir Walter. He is not a man possessed of a sense of humour, I'm sure he won't appreciate it, clever as it is.'

Polly was red with embarrassment. 'For heaven's sake, it's just a doodle.'

'Your doodles may have more power than you realize,' Max said. 'Do you only do caricatures, or do you do portraits?'

'Actually at the moment I mostly do book covers,' said Polly with defiant honesty.

Harriet slid another mat in front of her. 'Do me, please. Then I'll have a memento of tonight, for I've a feeling it'll be a long time before I go to another nightclub.'

Polly relaxed, and five strokes later, there was Harriet.

Harriet doesn't see that Miss Smith has portrayed her exactly as she is, a girl in her mother's dress, thought Max. She's got a real gift there, far too much perception, the insight to see what most people wouldn't notice or even suspect. A friend of Oliver Fraddon's, that's an odd kind of friendship, but of course the art would be a bond. Dramatic dress, but I expect it's borrowed. Is Oliver Fraddon the kind of man who collects artistic waifs and strays? Surprising, if so; the man had a reputation for a devastating tongue where artists' work was concerned.

He noticed the ring on her finger, at the same moment as Harriet did. He felt a moment's disappointment, which took him by surprise.

'Are you engaged to Mr Fraddon?' Harriet asked.

Polly laughed. 'No, he's just a friend. I'm engaged to a doctor.'

'Doesn't he mind you going off to nightclubs with another man?'

'I'll tell you a secret: he doesn't know. He's gone to America, you see, for a few weeks.'

'So are you a mouse, playing while the cat's away?'

Polly seemed struck by this question. 'Do you know, I suppose I am. He isn't at all a nightclub sort of person. Nor am I, I've never been to anywhere like this before.'

'When are you getting married?'

Cynthia should teach Harriet not to ask so many direct questions, but give her credit, Miss Smith, what was her name?

Polly. Polly was taking it all in good part. Although there was a guarded look in Miss Smith's eyes when she replied, 'Early next year. As soon as he's back from America.' A look that was gone as quickly as it had come.

The pianist finished his stint in a ripple of chords, stood up, his forehead gleaming with beads of perspiration, and bowed. He went off, wiping his forehead with a large white handkerchief, talking to the proprietor as he went.

'Ricky seems to be making a good thing of this,' said Oliver, watching his friend and looking pleased.

Thelma Warden had taken out a diamond encrusted compact, and was powdering her nose. 'It won't last,' she said. 'These places are all the same, wildly fashionable one week and empty the next.'

'He has good musicians,' said Oliver. 'That's always a draw.'

A small band was assembling: a saxophonist, a man with a trombone in one hand and a mute in the other, a clarinet-tist, who sat down and sucked at his reed. They were joined by a different pianist, a stately black man, who flexed his hands before running his fingers over the keys. Finally a tall man with lank hair came on, carrying a double bass in one hand. He had a cigarette drooping from his lips, he sat himself on his high stool, looked round for an ashtray, stubbed out the cigarette, twanged a string, tightened it, then, with a nod to the others, tapped his foot three times for the beat, and they swung into action.

'They are good,' said Cynthia.

'I heard them in Paris,' said Archie. 'He's lucky to get them, they're very hot at the moment.'

Max sat slightly drawn back from the rest of the party. It was a disparate group, on the surface having a good time, but with too many undercurrents for real merriment. Sir Walter was engaged in animated conversation with Thelma, who was always attracted by wealth and power; of course, he would be bound to know her husband from the House of Commons, if not from her wide social network.

Thelma was a flirt, and at her best when sexually charged as she was now, responding to Sir Walter's evident admiration. How did Cynthia take to that? He watched his sister for a few minutes. She was listening to Myron telling a story about Chicago in the days of Prohibition, but Max saw her eyes flicker over to Walter and Thelma more than once. It was impossible to gauge what she was thinking.

Sir Walter didn't improve with further acquaintance. There was an arrogant brutality about him, and Max didn't care for the way he'd run pasha's eyes over Polly Smith, as though measuring her up for his bed, then dismissing her for the moment as beneath his notice. And he didn't care for Harriet, that was blindingly obvious.

Max was irritated; he disliked it when normally intelligent people behaved stupidly, and to his mind, Cynthia even thinking of marrying Walter was stupid. Sex, no doubt, that will o'the wisp that led ninety percent of humanity astray. Lust and desire and passion took away all reason – but why wasn't Cynthia's sense asserting itself? Or maternal instinct? Sir Walter wouldn't make Harriet a good stepfather, although here she was, looking far older than her years, perhaps already spreading her wings and venturing into her own life, apart from her mother.

After all, Cynthia had married at sixteen, putting herself out of reach of a domineering mother and older sister in that swift ceremony. Her family had prophesied then that it would end in tears, but it had lasted longer than many marriages. Had she got divorced just in order to marry Walter? He suspected the marriage had been rocky for a lot longer than Cynthia had known Malreward.

Polly Smith was sitting with a smile on her face and her hands hidden under the table. Harriet was glancing down and trying not to laugh. He knew just what Polly Smith was up to, and he found himself wishing he could see what she had drawn. Odd that one so dextrous with her hands should be clumsy on her feet.

'Are you really a bad dancer?' he asked her. 'Or was that politeness because I can't dance?'

'It's perfectly true. I can follow the music in my head, it's not that I don't catch the beat, I do; listen to this now, it pulses through one. Only my brain doesn't send the right messages to my toes, that's all. I expect it comes of not being very musical. I'm the despair of my mother, who's a piano teacher.'

Thelma heard that, and sent Max a moue of disdain. He liked Polly Smith the better for speaking of her mother with evident pride and affection. 'Has she always taught the piano, or did she play professionally?'

'No, never, she doesn't have a performer's temperament, is what she says. She was at the Royal Academy, and I think she'd like to have been an accompanist. Only she got married, and then my,' she hesitated only for a second, but he noted it, 'then my father died. In the war. So she had to work, and she loves teaching.'

'Your brain seems able to send messages to your hands well enough,' he said.

She wrinkled her brow. 'That's different. It's partly years of practice, like with music, I suppose, but I don't have to think about it at all.'

'Tell me, when you draw a caricature, as you've done this evening, do you assess the subject in your mind and then draw them as you see them?'

She understood at once what he meant. 'How odd you should say that. I never really thought about it. No. My fingers draw them, and then I think, Oh, yes, that's what he or she is like.'

He twitched the hidden drawings from her fingers before she realized what he was doing. 'May I?'

Thelma, as predatory as a cat. Archie, with a look of desperate affection on his face as he looked at Cynthia – so Archie hadn't got over Cynthia yet. Cynthia with worry in her eyes – how did Polly Smith manage that, when the eyes were no more than two dots with two brief lines above them? Himself, all monocle and detachment. And, intriguingly, the Watsons each with a mask of their features held on a stick in front of totally blank faces, like revellers in Venice at carnival time.

She snatched them back, as he apologized for being so inquisitive.

'You aren't sorry at all,' she said.

He lowered his voice. 'The Watsons, masked. Why?'

She shook her head. 'I don't have the least idea. It's how it came out. Perhaps they aren't quite what they seem.'

The party was breaking up. Sir Walter offered to send Harriet home in his car, 'She'll be all right with my chauffeur,' but Cynthia said she was tired and would take Harriet home herself.

Oliver was deep in conversation with his friend Ricky, and the Watsons had drifted over to another table to greet some acquaintances.

Thelma's eyes were shining. 'You've got that bored look on your face, Max. It's too bad, the night is young, we're having a good time. Walter suggests we go on to the Motley for supper.'

Max stood up. 'You go,' he said, his eyes on Polly, who was watching the dancers and the people at the table with an absorbed expression. Taking mental snapshots, he wouldn't be surprised. Thelma gave him a long, hard look.

'I want you to come, Max.'

'No.'

She turned a thin, brusque shoulder on him. 'Don't trouble yoursef to call me, Max.'

'No,' he said. 'I shan't.' And then, to Polly, who was waiting for Oliver, 'I'm sure we'll meet again.'

'Do you think so?' she said, giving him a direct look with those stunning eyes. 'It's hardly likely, we don't move in the same circles, after all.'

'Ah, but we've bumped into each other twice, don't you believe in the rule of three?'

PART TWO

TWENTY-FIVE

Polly leaned on the railing of the second-class section of the ferry and watched a car being winched on board. A sleek, powerful car, with beautiful lines and enormous headlamps. What must it be like to be rich and to travel with your car when you went abroad? And a car like that. Roger's car broke down with depressing regularity; Polly had spent hours sitting in the car or out on a bank, sketching, while Roger did mysterious things to the engine, or disappeared under the car to emerge with streaks of oil on his face. He was a dab hand at changing a tyre, Polly had to admit. She couldn't imagine the owner of that blue car poking his head under the bonnet or being smudged by oil.

She felt in her bag for her sketchbook, her attention caught by an old tar sitting on a capstan, a battered cap on his head, huge boots on his feet and a pipe in his mouth.

She was so engrossed in her drawing, that she hardly noticed a man standing further along the deck, who was also recording the scene on the dock in a sketchbook. And, sketching the sturdy shape of a fishing boat, and the men on board with nets across their laps – she would show that to Sam when she got back, he would appreciate it – she hardly noticed the ropes being cast off, until the change in the sound of the engines and the receding sea wall made her realize they were on their way, making steady progress across the smooth water of the harbour towards the open sea.

Beyond the harbour wall, the sea was choppy, with white crests to the waves. Was she going to be seasick? Were you invariably seasick the first time you went to sea, before you got used to it? Hadn't she read that some people were always seasick, however often they travelled, and other people never were? Nelson suffered from seasickness, she'd learned that at school, but it must have worn off after a while, otherwise how could he ever have fought any battles?

She'd soon find out. Pink-cheeked, her nose getting colder by the minute, she rubbed her gloved hands together and watched the turbulent waters draw nearer. Then they were through, and the boat gave a lurch as it headed into the waves.

'Best go inside, miss,' called a steward, hurrying past. 'There's a bit of a blow.'

Inside was stuffy and bleak. She walked past the door to a restaurant, the tables laid with white linen; that wasn't for her. She needed to find somewhere she could sit and eat the sandwiches she had brought with her.

A woman, looking very green, with a handkerchief pressed to her lips, hurried by. She must be seasick. Polly felt cheered, she didn't have a trace of queasiness, and if it hit that quickly, perhaps she was going to be all right.

Her slight qualms about seasickness allayed, she settled down to enjoy the crossing. There had been an excitement to catching the boat train at Victoria. The sign for the *Golden Arrow*, Dover–Calais–Paris, carried the magic of foreign travel. All those other people catching their trains to Dorking and Littlehampton; there was nothing adventurous about that. Paris! She was on her way to Paris.

Only I've been there before, she reminded herself. I was born there. I'm going back to the city of my birth. What a pity that you weren't magically endowed with the language of where you happened to be born. Polly had bought a second-hand phrase-book, and had borrowed gramophone records from the public library, but neither seemed to teach the kind of French that might be useful. The phrase-book was one issued to the troops in 1917, in France, and was full of strange military phrases: *Where is the front line? The baggage horses are arriving tomorrow. Call a medical orderly. We need a stretcher.*

And the gramophone record had taken you into what sounded like the very dull life of the Dubois family, Monsieur and Madame Dubois, and their tiresome children Pierre *et* Chantal. If that was *la vie française*, then she'd stick with the good old English variety. The high spot of the Dubois year was their summer holiday, spent at Le Havre, with much careful repetition of how to ask for a room with two beds, and complaints about the bathroom facilities.

The *boulangerie* sounded fun, although Madame Dubois did rather argue with the baker. And she wasn't sure what Madame was buying. She knew about croissants, but what exactly was *une baguette*? Her pocket dictionary offered no enlightenment, not with its simple translation into 'loaf of bread'.

Perhaps, staying in Oliver's house, she wouldn't ever go near the *boulangerie* or the *boucherie* or any of those interesting-sounding shops. She was sure that none of Oliver's family ever did the shopping.

She hadn't given a thought to what Oliver's father's house might be like, until Dora had reminded her about tipping the servants when she left.

'Tip the servants?' Polly stared at her.

Dora sighed. 'I don't suppose Oliver's father lives in a small apartment on the seafront. He'll live in a big house, with a horde of servants.'

Polly didn't like the sound of that, but of course it was true, after all, the Fraddons had a huge house in England. Oliver didn't talk about his family home, except for saying that he never went there, but another friend had told Polly that Fraddon Park was one of the grandest houses in England. And Oliver lived the life of a rich man. He had a valet, a manservant just to look after him, in his elegant flat, and there was a housemaid who came in every day as well.

She'd only been to Oliver's flat a few times. She suspected that he deliberately kept the two sides of his life quite separate, his artistic friends being a different set from those of his school and university days. Like Bertram.

She remembered going to his flat when he had a friend from France there, who had arrived with drawings he wanted Oliver to buy. The valet let Polly in, and although his face gave nothing away, his stance reeked of disapproval. She had been looking a bit rough that day, straight from the workshop, with paint on her fingers and an aroma of linseed oil clinging to her clothes.

Polly wasn't impressed by the drawings. They were German, Oliver told her, from the last century. Whatever nationality they were, she didn't like them: the artist didn't draw well enough. 'Look at this, and this. The shading's not right and this tree stump is awkward, the composition is poor.'

'He's an artist with quite a reputation.'

'Then I expect they're a good buy, but would you want to look at them?' And then, as she caught sight of a final picture, 'Oh, I like this. Surely the same man didn't draw this?'

It was a simple drawing of a small fishing boat tied with a slack rope to a tree on a river bank.

'Not the same artist,' said Oliver's friend. 'He doesn't have a reputation.'

'I'll buy that one,' Oliver had said, and then his man came in with a tray of cocktails, and at Christmas, a small flat parcel arrived for Polly, which, when she unwrapped it, turned out to be the sketch.

Yes, of course there would be servants at his father's house.

'Does Oliver's mother live in France as well?'

'Oliver hasn't mentioned her. I don't think she does.'

'Well, even so, there'll be his father's manservant, and two or three maids at least. A cook, well, chef in France, with assistants in the kitchen, and if they've a garden, there'll be outdoor staff as well. One of the maids will look after your things, you'll have to tip her, and he'll have a butler, I dare say, or whatever they call them in France.'

Polly couldn't for a moment imagine pressing coins into the hand of a butler. Still, such embarrassments lay in the future, she wasn't going to worry about that now.

'They aren't going to get rich on what you give them, but they'll count on the extra from tips, I don't suppose wages are high in that part of the world,' Dora said. 'And keep enough money to buy yourself paints and so on while you're there, French materials are very good.'

How did Dora know that? She hadn't thought about it at the time, but Dora had spoken with a casual conviction as though it was something everyone knew.

Polly found a quiet spot in the corner of the saloon to eat the sandwiches Dora had prepared for her. Was it all right to eat sandwiches? Perhaps they didn't like you bringing your own food, perhaps everyone was expected to eat in one of the dining rooms. Not that there were many people on board, certainly not enough to fill all those tables. She felt relieved when a middle-aged couple near her put a vacuum flask on the table and produced a basket of food. They exchanged smiles, and Polly, reassured, tucked into her egg and cress sandwiches.

She wanted to be on deck when the ferry arrived in France, weather or no weather. With her coat belted tightly, her collar up and her hat pulled firmly down over her ears, she pushed the door open and went out on deck. It didn't look so different from England: scudding, lowering clouds, gulls swooping and calling, and a line of misty coast.

Polly was fascinated by the whole procedure of coming into the harbour and docking. She leaned over the rail to watch the men on the quayside, Frenchmen, dressed in dark blue, many of them with berets, just as she had imagined, calling out to one another in incomprehensible phrases.

The mooring ropes were thrown down, twisted round capstans, the boat nudged its way closer to the dock, and then, with a final blast of the whistle, the throb of the engines faded into silence.

She was here, in France, and in a minute, she would walk down the gangplank and set foot on French soil, be in the land of her birth. Greetings to France from Polyhymnia Tomkins, she wanted to shout.

She didn't linger at the customs shed. She was carrying a single suitcase, a battered, square-edged leather one, which had belonged to Ted Smith and had his initials on it: E F S for Edward Frederick Smith. She laid it on the long table and the bored looking customs official in his peaked cap gestured to her to open it. Her fingers itched to draw him, but she'd probably be arrested if she took out her sketchbook. He cast an indifferent look at the contents of her suitcase, said something in French, which she supposed meant for her to shut it, and shrugged his shoulders. She closed it, and he slapped a chalk mark on it before sauntering away to join a colleague who was interrogating a harassed-looking man in a dark coat.

Now where? Where did she catch the train to Paris? A sign with a childish outline of a railway engine and a large arrow pointed the way, and she walked across a mishmash of lines sunk into cobbles, past crates piled high with fish, judging by the smell, to where a train stood waiting. There didn't seem to be any proper platform, which was odd. Another man in a peaked hat bustled up to her. '*Paris? Votre billet, s'il vous plaît.* Ticket,' he added.

Polly produced it, he inspected it, holding it up to his eyes; he should wear spectacles. He handed it back to her, and directed her to the next coach along.

Polly climbed on board the train and found her seat. The compartment smelled of smoke, un-English smoke with an exotic touch to it. She heaved her suitcase on to the rack above her head and sat down. She reached into her shoulder bag and took out her sketchbook. A few rapid lines, and there was the ticket inspector, holding her ticket up to myopic eyes.

The door opened, and she tucked the sketchbook away as the middle-aged couple from the boat came in, both acknowledging her with little nods and smiles. She was pleased to see them, it was ridiculous how a shared glance and packets of sandwiches could give you a sense of familiarity.

The woman took out a handkerchief and brushed her seat before settling herself into it. 'You never know who's been sitting here,' she said darkly. 'First time in France, dear?'

'Yes, it is, actually,' Polly said. 'Is it so obvious?'

'Oh, you looked a bit apprehensive, that's all. We come over twice a year to visit my husband's sister, who lives in Paris, and we can always tell when a fellow traveller's new to the country, can't we, Bill?' and she gave her husband a nudge.

'That's right,' he said.

'That's right,' was all he ever said, while his wife kept up a flow of conversation. Was she going to talk all the way to Paris? Polly hoped not, she wanted to savour the journey, to keep her nose pressed to the window, not to miss a thing.

The words lapped over her, the woman's sister-in-law had been in service, a good position, with an English family who had come to live in France. Then the sister-in-law had married a Frenchman, which wasn't what she held with, foreigners being so different from English people, but she seemed happy enough and he was in a good way of business, a coal merchant. With Bill now retired, they came over to France for two weeks at Christmas and for a month in the summer every year.

How could they afford it? It seemed that they were in easy circumstances, comparatively, with the inarticulate Bill having quite a flair for picking winners, and the woman having her own small business as a tobacconist. 'We leave Jenny in charge, that's my youngest, when we come away.'

The locomotive was making the hissing, snorting noises of a train that was about to start. Polly turned to look out, and saw the blue car bumping over the cobbles. She couldn't see the faces of the occupants. Were they driving to Paris? The train started with a jolt. Polly found it odd that the train at first ran along what seemed to be a general thoroughfare, but in a few minutes it had left the docks behind and was steaming on a railway line in the normal way.

The woman stopped talking at last, and gave a little yawn behind her raised hand. 'I think I'll just take a little nap if you don't mind.'

Her husband was already asleep, although sitting bolt upright. He didn't look at all relaxed, only his shut eyes and occasional little snuffling sounds confirmed that he was in fact asleep.

Polly sat back and concentrated on the view from the window. The houses looked quite different from English ones. No stucco terraces here, as there were in Dover, no neat redbrick streets or thatched cottages, and most of the houses had shutters. Was that instead of curtains, or to keep them warm? Or perhaps to keep out the sun, not that you needed that on a grey winter's day like this one.

The carriage was heated, and it quickly became hot and stuffy. Polly wriggled carefully out of her coat, anxious not to wake her sleeping fellow passengers, and she tucked it on the empty seat beside her. She supposed that not many people were travelling to France in December.

They were out in the open country now, running beside sodden-looking fields. A squat church tower flashed past and the train rattled over a crossing where a man stood propped against his bicycle, waiting for the gate to open again. Cows, cream-coloured cows with swooping horns, straggly-looking sheep. A flat, dull landscape, not at all the France of Polly's imagination.

The man and woman didn't wake up until the train was drawing into the Gare du Nord. They yawned, and apologized for being such poor company, 'It's nice to have someone to talk to on a train journey, I always think,' and asked Polly where she was staying in Paris. 'I hope it's somewhere quiet and respectable, a young lady on her own can't be too careful.'

'I'm not sure, I have one or two addresses,' Polly said. 'Probably near the Gare de Lyon, that's where I catch my next train. It's only for a day or two, and then I'm catching another train down to Nice.'

'Nice? Oh, that's nice,' she said, with a laugh. 'It'll be warm down there. Nice and warm,' she added, laughing loudly at her joke. 'And while you're in Paris, use the Metro, dear. It's not a patch on the London Underground, quite basic, really, and confusing, they don't have a proper map like we do, but keep your wits about you, and you'll get there all right. Of course, you could always take a taxi.'

'No, I want to travel on the Metro,' Polly said.

'And the taxi drivers cheat you, being foreign. No, you're better on the Metro. Watch your bags, though, there are pickpockets everywhere these days.'

Bill hauled Polly's suitcase down from the rack for her, and, while they were sorting out their own possessions, Polly seized her opportunity, and with a quick 'Thank you and goodbye,' she slipped out of the carriage and made her way down the corridor and so down on to the platform.

She stood there for a moment, taking it all in, and then she picked up her suitcase and headed for the barrier.

The parting words of the couple in the train as she'd left the compartment had been a warning, Polly was to be careful, no one in Paris was to be trusted, she mustn't talk to strangers, particularly strange men.

She couldn't resist pointing out that they were strangers.

'Not the same, dear,' the woman said. 'We're English. We come from Carshalton, it's not the same. A pretty young woman like you, well, these French men have quite the wrong idea about women in most cases. You have to be very careful.'

'Miss Smith!'

She stopped and looked around. There must be another Miss Smith, well, probably dozens of Miss Smiths went to and from Paris on the train. She walked on.

'I say, do stop. It is Polly Smith, isn't it? Yes, I'd know you anywhere.'

TWENTY-SIX

From the stern of the ferry, Ivo watched the foaming wake, white froth mingling with the grey water of the English Channel. It was cold on deck, the wind stirring up choppy waves under scudding grey clouds. Grey skies, grey sea; grey was the colour of England. Forget England's green and pleasant land. He had never found it pleasant, and never felt anything but relief and a lightening of his spirits when he left its shores and saw the white cliffs diminish and vanish into a gloomy horizon.

Ahead of him lay France, a country which he loved for its light, its art and its food; France was where he worked, where he painted, where he lived his artistic life. Whereas America, an ocean away, was where he lived his domestic life. He didn't think even for a moment about the wife and children busy about their various daily occupations on the other side of the Atlantic. When he moved between his two worlds, the States and Europe, doors shut behind him, and only the present time and place occupied his thoughts. Which thoughts were, at the moment, entirely of painting. He had notebooks filled with sketches and preliminary drawings; two or three days in Paris, visiting galleries, refreshing his artistic eye, and then he would be on his way to the south, to the brilliant light and weeks of intense work in his attic studio.

He wrapped his arms round himself to keep the warmth in, withdrew into the pictures inhabiting his mind, oblivious to the muttered recommendation of a member of the crew to 'Get inside, sir, we're in for a roughish crossing.'

He stayed there, a chilly, motionless figure, for another half hour, and then he went inside to where he had left the hefty leather portmanteau that was his only luggage apart from the canvas bag with his immediate painting equipment. A glare scared away a man who looked like a commercial traveller, a man who, to Ivo's experienced eye, was the talkative sort. Then he arranged his long limbs along the bench and lay motionless until the sound of the engine changed from its steady throb, the sound of gulls intensified, voices called out in French, and the boat was edging alongside the dock.

Interesting bones, thought Ivo, as he watched Polly, face alight with excitement, gazing down from the rail. An artist, he'd seen her sketching. And he remembered bumping into her as he came out of Rossetti's a few days ago. Amateur or pro? It didn't make much difference for a woman, not, at any rate, one who looked like that. In two or three years she'd be married with kids, art pushed into the background of her life. Waste of time training women, in his opinion. They passed through art school, some of them quite talented, but few of them stuck with it or made any kind of a name for themselves.

Well, he had stuck with it, and what kind of a name had he made for himself? Funny old world, he said to himself, as he loped down the gangway.

TWENTY-SEVEN

The man who was hurrying towards her, his hand outstretched, repeating, 'Miss Smith, Miss Polly Smith?' was surely a stranger. Or was he?

'Archie McIntyre,' he said, extending a hand. 'We met at the Blue Monkey, if you remember.'

Of course she did, but for a moment she hadn't recognized him. Men's evening clothes changed them, here in a flannel suit, his red hair its natural unslicked colour, he looked quite different.

'I'm a friend of Oliver's, oh, good, you do remember me. I thought you were standing there wondering whether to call the police to stop this mad man pestering you. I am glad I caught you, Oliver was most insistent that I must meet the train, but the traffic's pretty awful today, and I was afraid I'd be too late.' He picked up her suitcase. 'Is this all your luggage? Surely not?'

'I'm afraid it is.'

'Congratulations! I never knew a woman who didn't think she had to travel with most of her wardrobe, and most of the contents of the bathroom cupboard to boot.'

As they spoke, he took her by the elbow, and was guiding

her through the crowd of people standing under the departure board. 'Can't think why there are always so many people at stations. Where have they come from, where are they going? Very odd. Now, the car's parked outside, better whiz along, or an *agent* will start asking questions. This way.'

'Hold on,' said Polly, breathless, but wanting to get things straight. 'Why a car? I mean, why are you here?'

He stopped abruptly, then swung round to apologize to the besuited Frenchman who had cannoned into him as a result. 'Instructions from Oliver. I was to gather you up, take you to wherever you're staying, he said you wanted to spend a day or two in Paris, and would I show you the sights. It's your first time to Paris, isn't it? Then in due course I'm to see you catch the train to Nice all right.'

'It's very kind of you, but—'

'Oh, I hate buts. Don't worry that you're keeping me from anything; you aren't. I'm supposed to be working on a book, you know – well, of course, you won't know the first thing about me. Anyhow, I write books, travel stuff mostly, and I live half the year here and half the year in London.'

They had arrived at a rakish, low-slung sports car, parked at an erratic angle between a large black Citroën and a little three-wheeler van. 'One thing, I've had a spot of bother with the roof, which doesn't in fact work. Are you going to be all right in the open?'

'Oh, I'd rather,' said Polly. It was warmer than London, although just as grey, with gleaming wet pavements reflecting the lights from the café tables set out under awnings on the pavements. 'I want to see as much as I possibly can.'

He shut the tiny door which reached up to her waist, and went round to the driver's side. He jumped in without opening the door and wrapped himself around the steering wheel. 'Let's hope she starts, she doesn't like the wet.' There were some spluttering noises and a dull whirring before the car fired into life. 'Jolly good, I thought for a moment there I'd be out with the crank handle.' He laid his arm across the back of the seat as he turned his head to reverse into the traffic, causing honking horns and loud Gallic cries to rend the air.

'Noisy lot, the Parisians,' he said, swerving past a lorry and out into the stream of traffic. 'OK, let's take the scenic route to wherever you're staying. Be my guest. What do you want to see? The Eiffel Tower? Notre Dame? Les Invalides?'

'Montmartre,' said Polly, although she was hardly attending to Archie, so enthralling was the scene flashing past. In her mind's eye, the streets and cafés were those of Toulouse-Lautrec and Utrillo and Cheret. At any moment she expected a glass door decorated with gold curlicues to swing open, and a woman in a bustled dress and a saucy hat to emerge into the street, perhaps accompanied by a dashing young officer with moustaches and a wide stripe down an elegant uniformed leg, or a distinguished-looking man in a cutaway coat and a shiny top hat. She half shut her eyes, taking in the lights and colours of the pavement cafés and the steady flow of people.

The modern world impinged. 'How smart the women are,' she exclaimed.

Archie glanced down at her. 'You look very nice,' he said. 'I like the beret.'

Polly smiled. 'You complimented me for not bringing half my wardrobe, little did you know that there is about half my wardrobe in there. I'm an impoverished artist, as Oliver probably told you, so, much as I'd love to have suitcases crammed with entrancing little suits, I don't.'

'Oh, no one expects Englishwomen to dress like that,' he said.

'Nor Scotswomen?'

'You should see my mother, I think she was born wearing

245

a hairy tweed suit. Once or twice a year, for the Highland balls, she emerges upholstered in white satin and a tartan sash. She considers French fashions nothing but wicked frippery.'

'I think they look wonderful,' Polly said, twisting round to get a backward look at a round kiosk. 'It's covered in posters, just like in the pictures. And a *pissoir*! Oh, and look, a Métro sign.'

They crossed the river on one of the broad arched bridges, and Polly pulled herself up to sit on the back of her seat, so that she could see over the parapet and down along the Seine.

'Don't fall out,' Archie shouted. 'More bridges to come, we're taking the scenic route.'

'I won't, I won't, oh, I can't believe it; it's all so heavenly.'

Archie parked the car and they climbed up the steep streets and steps to the top of Montmartre. An artist sat at an easel, working on a street scene and Polly stopped to look at the painting.

'Any good?' said Archie as they moved on.

She shook her head. 'No. Definitely not a budding Monet or Lautrec.' And then, 'Do you know about art?'

'Nothing at all. Oliver calls me a philistine, but words and music are more my thing. He didn't call you an impoverished artist, by the way. He said you were a young painter who might one day be very good.'

Polly's heart missed a beat, and she stopped, looking directly at Archie. 'Did he say that? Did he really say that?'

'Yes, I wouldn't lie, fellow creative spirits and all that, you know.'

Polly plunged her hands into her coat pockets. 'I can't tell you what that means. Oliver's got an eye, you know, and he never says anything to flatter.'

'No, he wouldn't need to, would he? He also said that you and he were kindred spirits.'

'I wonder what he meant by that. Are we kindred spirits? I know I like him a lot, and we – well, we understand each other.'

'You aren't in love with him?' he asked, his voice taking on an anxious note. 'Sorry, scrub that, total impertinence, forget I spoke.'

'No, we're friends.' She gave him a direct look. 'You're an old friend of his, aren't you? A much older friend than I am.'

'Lord, yes, I've known him for ever. School, university, all that kind of thing.'

'Then you'll know that Oliver doesn't have much time for women, not romantically. And I'm engaged. To a doctor.'

'A doctor? Oh, jolly good.' He paused. 'Do doctors like wives who are artists?'

Polly felt a cold chill, and she pulled her coat more tightly to her body. 'Why not? Anyhow, I'll find out, won't I.'

'Useful if he's one of those successful medical chappies, brass plate up in Harley Street and all that. They earn a bundle, I believe. He can make money, and you can paint. Science supporting the arts, I'm all for that.'

It sounded noble, put like that, but Polly had an idea that Roger wouldn't look at it in the same light.

'Penny for them?' said Archie. 'You look uncommonly glum for a moment.'

Polly looked out over the city, beginning to twinkle with lights as dusk descended. 'Oh, I was just wondering why any of us become artists. It's such a stupid thing to do, when you think about it.'

'Can't help ourselves,' said Archie cheerfully. 'Like going to become a monk, I can't understand that, but men – and women – do get the urge, and there you are.'

'I can't imagine wanting to be a nun. It isn't quite the same thing, art isn't religion.'

Or was it the same? A vocation, the voice of God calling to someone with a religious nature, the voice of the muses whispering relentlessly into the mind of an artist.

Roger understood vocation. He had a vocation for medicine. Yet would he ever accept or understand that her wish to paint was as fierce as his desire to practise medicine? 'Being a doctor is useful in a way that art isn't,' she said. 'In a social sense, or if you break a leg.'

Archie gave her an understanding look. 'Got yourself engaged to a philistine, have you?'

'A philistine? No, of course not.'

Polly hated disloyalty, and felt she was being disloyal to Roger.

'He doesn't look at the world in the way I do, that's all. He's practical. He likes a purpose to everything. Paintings have a purpose, he knows that. Colour doesn't matter to him very much, so . . .'

'It's like a musician marrying someone who's tone deaf, then. Could work, could give you lots of space, could be disastrous. But then marriages so often are disastrous, at least they are in my opinion. Doesn't stop us hankering after the state, does it? No, we all rush to fall in love and long to spend a life of bliss with our chosen partner.'

'Are you going to get married?'

'Oh, some day, I expect,' said Archie, turning it off lightly.

Polly, her senses more than usually acute from the rush of new sensations that had been crowding in on her, heard the underlying note of bitterness.

'I love the word Montmartre,' she said, as Archie held out a hand to steady her over an uneven patch of steeply cobbled street. 'It has rich colour to it, red shading into purple with a dash of warm light in it.' She laughed, and apologized. 'There you are, it sounds as though I'm talking nonsense. I'm not, because I see letters and words – and numbers if it comes to that – in colour.'

Archie stopped and looked at her, his face alive with interest and curiosity. 'Do you? I know a writer who does the same. He writes poetry, so he has to have a heightened sense of the world. It must be rather jolly, seeing all those black and white characters in a blaze of colour. Are they always the same colours, or do they change?'

When she had told Roger about this trick of her mind, he had frowned. 'Aren't you being rather fanciful? You do let your imagination run away with you.'

And she had protested that it wasn't imagination, that she really did see letters in colour, 'Each letter has a separate colour and then in words they kind of blend together,' she explained. He merely said that she must have had coloured letters on bricks when she was a child, and this was where she had got the idea from.

It was true. She had had a set of alphabet bricks, with the letters on them in bright painted colours. Which had worried her, because the colours weren't the right ones. It wasn't until she went to school that she discovered that other children didn't have the same colourful vision of words.

'That's probably one of the reasons you became a painter,' said Archie. 'If you've an unusually strong perception and awareness of colour.'

'Only my work is mostly monochrome,' she said.

Archie had pulled out the watch from his pocket. 'It's getting late. Where are you staying? We can go there and leave your suitcase, and then we'll toddle out for a spot of dinner.'

Polly bit her lip and gave Archie a rueful look. 'I've had such a joyful time, I completely forgot I need to find somewhere to stay. Do you suppose there'd be a room somewhere here?'

'Yes, only I wouldn't advise it.' He hesitated. 'Look, please don't think I'm getting fresh, but would you care to stay with me?'

A wariness came over Polly's face, and he hurried on. 'I've got an apartment, and it has a room for a *bonne*, that's a maid. Which is quite separate from the flat, I'm on the second floor and the room is right up at the top of the building. I don't have a live-in maid, so I use it for odds and ends. But there's a bed, and you can use my bathroom. And,' he finished temptingly, 'it won't cost you a sou.'

'You've gone to so much trouble on my account already,' Polly said, although she was longing to say, 'Done'. It had been a long day, and the prospect of finding a place to stay at this time of the evening was daunting.

'Oliver would have my guts for garters if I didn't help. I mean there are dozens of hotels, if you'd rather . . .'

'Let's go,' said Polly.

'Sensible girl. There's a lock on the door and all that, and nobody goes up there. Peaceful, and a frightfully good view, even if the window is on the smallish side.'

The restaurant Archie took her to was just as she had imagined a Parisian restaurant would be. Soft lights, white tablecloths, warmth and comfort, waiters in black with long white aprons, a exquisite aroma hanging on the air. As she sat down on the buttoned velvet seat, she sighed.

'Everything all right?' asked Archie. 'If you don't like it here . . .'

She was quick to reassure him. 'It's perfect. Quite perfect. It was a sigh of contentment, it's been such a day! And here I am in this blissful restaurant, I'm so hungry, I can't tell you.'

'We'll start with champagne, to celebrate your first visit to a magical city,' he said, summoning the hovering waiter. 'And I know what you're thinking, which is, what extravagance, and does this mean he won't eat for a week? I know I'm a writer, but fortunately, I do rather well out of it, so I can certainly run to a glass of champagne or two.'

'I sometimes wish I could,' said Polly sniffing at the wine, and wrinkling her nose as a bubble reached it. 'I've never had any money, and I don't suppose I ever will, but I do occasionally wonder what it would be like not to have to count every penny.'

And then, when they had read the menu, most of which was incomprehensible to Polly, and Archie had ordered for them both, she asked abruptly, 'Please tell me about Oliver's father. I'm not sure what I'm letting myself in for, you see, accepting Oliver's invitation to stay at Lord Fraddon's house. He said there's a group of artists working down there, that his father is a patron of the arts, which sounds awfully grand. I'm not sure that I'll fit in. Tell me about his family.'

Archie lifted his wineglass and inspected the sparkling wine held against the light.

'Fraddon won't like it if you feel uncomfortable. Don't worry about him, he's a charming man, if formidable in his way. Just be yourself. The house isn't exactly grand, it's an extraordinary place, no, I'm not going to tell you anything more about it. If Oliver hasn't, it's because he wants you to be astonished by it as every one else is.'

'Why does Lord Fraddon spend all his time in France? Doesn't he like England? Or is it tax?'

'Tax? No. It's just that, well things were difficult for him in England, and he can't go back.'

'I don't mean to pry,' said Polly quickly.

'It's an old story, bit of a scandal in its time, no point in raking it all up now. But Rodoard is his home now. It's a lively place, you'll like it there, I promise you. The only one you have to watch out for is Oliver's sister, have you met her?'

'No. What's she like?'

Archie thought before he answered. 'She – well, she isn't always very kind to people she doesn't know. Come to that, she's sharp with her friends and family, too. She's got a tongue on her, that's all.'

Polly gave him a speaking look. 'You mean she's a bitch.'

'I wouldn't use the word myself. Don't let it worry you. It's always a bit awkward, going to stay with strangers, but you know Oliver, and you'll get on like a house on fire with all the artists and writers who drift in and out. Now, try the red wine, that'll put the roses in your cheeks. You're pale with fright, quite unnecessarily, I do assure you.'

Polly made herself concentrate on the food, which was of a kind she had never tasted before, and so good she wanted to savour every mouthful. Archie seemed to know a good deal about food, explaining to her how the *Daurade à la Dugléré* was prepared, and urging her to try the *Île Flottante*. 'Floating Island in English, nothing but froth and flummery, yes, you do have room for it. And then a cognac, and you'll sleep like a log and wake up fresh as a daisy.'

TWENTY-EIGHT

Polly woke with a start; where was she? Then she remembered.
Paris.

In the maid's room, sleeping on a bed amid such of Archie's possessions as he felt no daily need for: leather suitcases, a hamper, fishing rods, a pile of old *Strand* magazines, skates and boots – where would he skate in Paris? Polly wondered. She yawned and stretched languorously before climbing out of bed and going to window. It was small, as Archie had said, and the view was obstructed by a parapet, but she could see roofs, the roofs of Paris, with curls of smoke rising into the air.

Archie had given her a key to his flat. 'That's my bedroom there. Bathroom at the end, kitchen to the left. If you wake up before me, come down and bang on the door. If I'm dead to the world, we'll meet for lunch. Brasserie Fouquet, here, I'll show you where it is on the map.'

From something Archie had let drop, Polly guessed that he was a night owl, the sort who worked into the small hours and then slept until late the next morning. She had several friends like that. She had no intention of waking him up, but tiptoed silently to the bathroom before running back upstairs to dress. She would have a French breakfast at a café, her first *petit déjeuner*. Then, she was going to explore.

Out into the early-morning street. It was a grey day, but dry, with a lightness in the sky that gave a promise of later sunshine. A wagon loaded with cabbages rumbled past, a man on a bicycle swerving round it and then riding on the pavement to avoid an oncoming car. A policeman, dapper in his uniform, was standing at the corner, talking to a woman who held a small dog on a leash. Their vigorous French filled Polly with pleasure, and she almost danced along the street, so full of life and happiness that the shopkeepers taking up their shutters smiled at her, and a man leaning out of his window whistled at her.

Archie's flat on the Left Bank was central, and Polly abandoned her map for the serendipity of simply going where her feet led her. She did have one place she was determined to visit, but that could wait. For now, she was simply going to let the spirit of Paris wash over her.

She had her sketchbook with her, and when she'd had enough of walking, and the sun had duly made its appearance, she applied herself to the map and set off for the Brasserie Fouquet, fortunately not too far away. No sign of Archie, so she sat down at a table on the pavement – amazing that one could sit outside in December – and watched the world go by.

The waiters were sleek and brisk and attentive, the customers elegantly dressed and carrying themselves with the air of people who had both leisure and money at their command.

Polly's pen flashed across the page, capturing a delightful couple. He caught her eye first, a man in his late fifties, with a high brow, Roman nose and humorous mouth. His companion was younger, perhaps in her forties, with an expressive, lively face and a Latin way of speaking with her hands.

254

It was evident that they were in love. The man was over-flowing with affection, and the woman responded with warm smiles and the occasional caress of his cheek or hand. Lucky them, to have such a glow of happiness in each other's company. Were they married, or lovers?

Would she, twenty years from now, be gazing into Roger's eyes with such ardent and amused attention as this woman was?

Thirty years from now, would Roger sit outside at a café table in the sunshine? Somehow, she doubted it. Roger at that age would be full of dignity and gravitas, a top man in his profession, not given to frivolity and flirtation in the unexpected sunlight of a December day. The man summoned a waiter and paid him. Then, arm in arm, the two of them walked away, heads close, still talking to each other.

She didn't notice Archie until he slid into the chair opposite her. 'I never heard you come and go, you must have trodden on cat-like feet,' he said.

'Were you working late last night?'

'Yes, but even so, it's devilish rude to sleep on when one has a guest.'

'I like to get up early, other people come to life and want to work at the end of the day. If you've got writing to do, why should you be put out because I'm here?'

'You take it uncommonly well,' he said. 'Let's have lunch. And after that, I'm entirely at your disposal.'

Over a delicious *soupe a l'oignon* and a melting beef-steak, she took out the map and told him where she wanted to go.

'Rue Villon,' he said. 'Can't say I've ever been there, but I expect we'll find it.'

When they got there, he looked up and down the short, narrow street in surprise. 'Are you sure this is where you

255

wanted to come? You must have a reason, I don't want to pry, but I'm intrigued, why a convent?'

Polly was reading the polished brass plate attached to the side of the large, pointed entrance, which was firmly closed. 'Soeurs du Sacré-Coeur,' she read out.

'Nuns of the Sacred Heart,' said Archie helpfully. 'Were you at school with the nuns, something like that?'

'No,' said Polly, as puzzled as he was. A convent? It must be a mistake, but Dora had written the address down quite clearly. She looked up at the blank façade and then turned to Archie. 'I was born here.'

'Good heavens, I had no idea. Are you French, then?'

'My mother was living in Paris when I was born,' Polly said evasively; she might well be half French. Or half Russian or German or American, for that matter; she would never know.

'In that case,' said Archie, 'I expect the nuns are a nursing order, it's probably a clinic, a maternity hospital as it were. Do you want me to ring the bell and ask?'

'No,' said Polly quickly. 'No, don't. I've come to see where I was born, and it was here in this street. That's enough. Don't let's linger, I'm longing to walk along the Seine, could we do that?'

Polly took Archie to the Louvre, where to her delight she found two portraits by Cortoni – 'Bit of a stunner, her grace,' Archie commented, as he gazed up at the huge portrait of an English duchess. Then, surfeited with paintings, he took her forcibly out and made her drink an illegal glass of absinthe – 'All artists have to try absinthe at least once.'

The bright green liqueur made her sneeze. 'I didn't know it tasted of aniseed. Those artists must have had a sweet tooth,' she said. 'Will I start hallucinating, do you think? Not that it matters, since now we have to go to that Dalí exhibition I saw the poster for.'

He groaned. 'Must I come? They say Paris is crazy for Surrealists, and as far as I'm concerned, crazy is the operative word.'

'It's good for you to stretch your horizons,' she told him, but in the end, she found the art empty and disappointing. 'Dazzle and technique and fashion,' she said as they came out.

'What would you like to do this evening?' he asked her. 'Do you want to go to a nightclub?'

Polly shook her head.

'I just thought, since we met at the Blue Monkey, you might go in for that kind of place.'

'Not at all. I did enjoy the Blue Monkey, it was fun to see what a fashionable nightclub is like, but I don't think I'm a nightclub sort of person.' And she laughed at herself. 'That makes me sound like a Puritan, which I'm not. I love going out, only I'm a hopeless dancer, and so it would be rather a waste of my time here. I'd much rather go to a show, could we do that?'

So Archie took her to a cabaret in the Rue Fromentin, at the foot of Montmartre, where she understood one word in five, but nonetheless managed to grasp, with Archie's whispered translation in her ear, quite a lot of what was going on.

She asked him about Harriet. 'It looked as though Mrs Harkness wasn't pleased to see her at the Blue Monkey that evening.'

'I should say not.' Archie was rueful. 'I got a ticking off, and as for Harriet, poor kid, she was almost in tears. Still, she'll get over it, she has a stoical streak, like her Uncle Max.'

Polly's ears pricked up, she was interested to hear what Archie had to say about Max. 'Is he a good friend of yours?'

'The Lyttons and the McIntyres have strong ties, family connections and so on, and the general has a place in Scotland near us.'

'The general?'

'Cynthia's father. And Max's, of course. The Lyttons are a military family, going back for generations. Crimea, Waterloo, Malplaquet, Hastings I dare say.'

'Not Mr Lytton though?'

'His leg, you noticed he was lame?'

'Polio, he told me.'

'Yes. People always think he was wounded, not surprisingly when you think of the halt and the lame and the blind the war left behind. And those were the lucky ones. War's ghastly, and now some people say it's all going to come rolling back again.'

'I don't,' said Polly. They were walking over the Pont Neuf, and she stopped to lean on the stone wall and look at the line of bridges, and the teeming, brilliant city life all around them. 'I can't imagine war ever coming to Paris, it's so full of life and gaiety. Were you too young to fight in the last war?'

'I went into the army right at the end, and spent several weeks on the Isle of Wight. No actual fighting, for which I am profoundly thankful. Max was behind a desk in the war, doing brilliant things, and his father has never forgiven him for it. He lost his favourite son, Max's eldest brother, who died gallantly in France. Max is well aware that his father would far rather it had been he who carried the family tradition to an early grave on the battlefield.'

'That's awful. What about his mother?'

'She's cut from the same cloth, daughter and sister of army men. She said that it was a disgrace Max being allowed to wear uniform, and she was livid when he was promoted to major.'

258

'How sad that he doesn't get on with his family. At least Mr Lytton and his sister seem fond of one another.'

'They're very close, those two, always have been. Cynthia, Mrs Harkness that is, doesn't get on well with the rest of her family either.'

What a waste, Polly said inwardly. A complete family: mother, father, brothers, sisters, and yet the bonds of affection stretched no further than one brother to his sister.

'She's going to marry Sir Walter Malreward, isn't she?'

'So it seems,' Archie said, tossing the stub of his cigar into the river and watching it glow for a second before the dark waters extinguished the last sparks. 'Bloody man.'

'You don't like him.'

'I like Cynthia too well to want to see her married to a man who's going to make her damned unhappy.'

Paris, city of love, city for lovers, Polly said to herself. Love was in the air, from the pair in the café that morning to the lovers entwined on benches by the river, and the elegant couple walking past them now, heads close, bodies in harmony, voices low and intimate.

The darkness made her bold. 'You're in love with her. With Mrs Harkness. Aren't you?'

Archie leant his back against the bridge. 'Is it that obvious? I'm making a fool of myself, I dare say. Since you ask, yes, I am in love with her and have been for years.' He lowered his eyelids, shutting out the pain. 'Love's the devil, Polly Smith, and don't let anyone tell you otherwise.' Then he opened his eyes and looked at her with a wry smile. 'You know all about love, with your doctor waiting for you.'

'Do I?' said Polly. 'Actually, I don't know the first thing about love. I get it wrong, every time.'

They walked on, in silence, until Polly said, 'Englishmen don't talk about love much.'

'I'm not an Englishman, I'm a Scot.'

'Does that make a difference?'

'No. Put it down to my being a writer and having a professional interest in violent emotions.'

Violent emotions? What was he talking about?

TWENTY-NINE

They arrived in a soft, chilly darkness lightened by a sky thick with sparkling stars. Harriet rolled the window of the car down and let in the scent of cypress, Cynthia closed her eyes and let the smells waft over her.

Le Béjaune was set back from the main square of the small town of Rodoard. Its wrought-iron gates were closed, and the house beyond was barely visible.

'Sound the horn,' Cynthia said to Max. 'Someone will come out to do the gates.'

'That's silly,' said Harriet, getting out of the car and stretching. She gulped the air, 'You can almost taste it,' she called out, and then went to the gates, lit by the powerful beam of Max's headlamps. 'They aren't locked,' she said, heaving at the handle and swinging one gate open. She hauled the other clear, and stood back as the car rolled through, and then she shut the gates with a bang, and ran along behind the car.

The Delage drew up in the oval of sand and gravel in front of the house. The shutters were all closed, and for a moment Cynthia thought that there had been a mistake, that there was no one there, that Rose and Max's man, Ketton, hadn't arrived. Then the front door opened, spilling light down the shallow steps, and there they were, Ketton hurrying forward to see to the luggage, Rose running round to help Cynthia out of the car.

'Don't stand around outside, madam, it isn't at all warm.'

'Goodness, it does look different,' Harriet exclaimed as they went inside. 'Clean, and painted, look at the panelling, it was all dingy before.'

'You never came before, so you didn't see it in its original state,' Cynthia said to her brother, as she stood for Rose to remove her fur jacket and Max handed his driving coat to Ketton. 'Come into the sitting room, you can't call it a drawing room in France. I can smell a wood fire.'

'And hear it, too,' said Harriet. 'Snap, crackle and pop. Heavenly.'

The long, beamed room was lit only by a sidelight and the glow from the fire, burning merrily in the huge arched stone fireplace.

It was the fireplace that her husband had fallen in love with. 'Look at that,' he said, when they came to view the house. 'Big enough to roast an ox. That's what I call a fireplace, a man could feel at home here.'

Except that he hadn't. Cynthia doubted if he would ever feel at home again, anywhere. The war, in which he had fought for three terrible years with courage and gallantry, had destroyed some essential part of him, the part that would otherwise have settled down to a quiet hard-working life of his English contemporaries. 'God,' he'd said when he came back from the war. 'I never thought a word could sound as beautiful as peace. Peace is all I want. Peace, and a green and tranquil place to live.'

That remained his dream, and when he caught a glimpse of it, as he'd done in the serene and peaceful surroundings of this house in France, he had been enchanted. Then, as with a mirage, the reality always fell short of the dream.

'That's why I'm going to give Kenya a go,' he'd said to Cynthia, standing moodily in front of the gas fire in their London house. 'Break with the past, a clean break, cut it off. Like a leg with gangrene,' and his face had clouded for a moment, as bitter memories crowded back.

Perhaps he would come back together again, in an African landscape.

'I thought I'd find myself again in England, or in France,' he'd said. 'It hasn't worked out that way, that's all.'

Cynthia held out her hands to the fire, feeling suddenly weary after the long drive. 'Of course, once we'd bought the house, we discovered that Rodoard is something of an artist's colony. Houses are cheap to buy or rent, and once one or two came here, others followed. Some of them quite well known.'

'What's wrong with artists?' Harriet demanded.

'Nothing, but the painters and writers and musicians here weren't your father's sort of people, and they irritated him. Poor lamb,' she added. A stray spark landed on the stone flag and she extinguished it with her foot. 'Everything irritated him.'

'Including me,' said Harriet cheerfully. 'He told me that he liked Le Béjaune, but not the village or the neighbours – he said he'd come to the conclusion it was the French he couldn't get on with. Too foreign. So don't start fretting, Mummy, and thinking you're one of those grasping women who grab everything and leave their ex-husbands poor and homeless.'

Max went over to the tray of drinks placed on an old oak chest in the corner. 'I must say, it looks a charming house to me. Dry Martini, Cynthia?'

'Can I have one, too?' said Harriet, sensing an opportunity.

'No, you can't,' Cynthia said automatically, but relented when Max raised his eyebrows at her. 'Oh, very well.'

Harriet beamed.

'A very weak one,' Cynthia mouthed at her brother.

'You can't see, because it's dark, but there's a terrific view,' said Harriet. 'Down over woods to the sea. You can walk to the beach in about half an hour, but it's longer coming back, uphill all the way.' She yawned, setting her mother off, and Max laughed at the pair of them.

Rose put her head round the door. 'Dinner will be served in fifteen minutes, madam.'

'I'm almost too tired to eat,' said Cynthia, who for a moment wished she could simply go to bed.

'Oh, Mummy, don't be so dreary,' said Harriet. 'I'm starving, which isn't surprising when certain people didn't let us stop for a proper lunch,' – this with a baleful look at her uncle.

Cynthia was surprised to find how hungry she was herself, when she sat at the oval table in the small dining room, and a plate of leek soup was set in front of her. Harriet attacked her food with enthusiasm. Still a schoolgirl in her appetite, despite the wish for a dry Martini.

Max read her mind. 'One year to the next, you know how it is.'

Indeed she did. She remembered herself, awkward, pudgy and shy at fourteen, and then, butterfly from chrysalis, a young lady at fifteen. And a wife at sixteen. Thank goodness Harriet wasn't growing up in wartime, thank God she was holding on to her childhood for longer than she had. Despite the Blue Monkey incident.

Max was full of praise for the grilled red mullet. 'With fennel, butter, olive oil and lemon juice, simple and perfect. Fish always tastes different in this part of the world. I can see,' he went on, 'that an artistic community wouldn't be everyone's cup of tea, but it suits you. I dare say. You always got on well with the Bohemian set, who was that girl you were at school with, the daughter of some celebrated composer, a delightful family? I remember Mother was quite desperate at the company you preferred, and when you left school, she was always lamenting the fact that you couldn't go to be finished in France or Switzerland and had such a liking for what she called the arty set.'

'Why not Switzerland?' said Harriet, speaking through a mouthful of fish. 'I mean, Switzerland wasn't at war with anybody.'

'No, but it's hardly patriotic to send a daughter off to finishing school when your country's at war.'

'I know,' said Harriet. 'You had to do your bit. If there's another war, I think I'll scud to America and get away from it all.'

'Don't say it,' said Cynthia with a shudder. 'Don't joke about it. It must never happen again.'

'What arty people did you know?' said Harriet, irritatingly. 'Anyone famous?'

'No. And most of the artists went into uniform and off to the front to be killed along with all the other young men. Those who didn't end up in prison as conscientious objectors. Meanwhile, we young women went to work as VADs, or did voluntary work. By the time we knew the war wasn't going to finish in a few months, there was a feeling that we must all do our bit, as you put it. A finishing school would have been out of the question.'

'Besides, you got married practically the minute you left school,' Harriet said.

'Eric Gibbons, do you remember him?' Cynthia asked Max. 'He lived near us. He was going to be a sculptor, people said he was remarkably talented. He died the day after he got out there, what a waste of a life.'

'Not if he died to save his country,' said Harriet. '*Dulce et decorum* and all that. Pay attention, Uncle Max, that's the

265

only Latin I know, you're supposed to be impressed. It's Horace.'

'*Dulce et decorum est pro patria mori*,' Max recited, and then, at once. 'Wretched girl, goading me into showing off my scraps of Latin.'

'Anyhow, it's all lies, there's nothing *dulce et decorum* about getting shot to pieces in a muddy field in Flanders. I think all war's hateful, whoever's fighting.'

That was the vision that had tormented Cynthia's imagination through the war years, of Ronnie blown to pieces, in a second that took him from existence to non-existence. At night she had seen him strung up on barbed wire like a crow hung out to warn predators away. Lying in some lonely field hospital, a German hospital, not understanding, no laughter left, thinking of his own country as he lapsed into a final, fatal coma. How many had died like that, anonymously, without a soul to care for them, or mind, or mourn?

And it had been all just in her imagination, for he had survived, physically unharmed, although mentally – who could say? That was another story for most of the war's survivors. Gassed lungs, nerves shot to pieces. 'Yes, it's all very sad, but being mournful won't bring any of them back. Why are you looking at your food like that, Harriet?'

'How was I looking? And mayn't I look, am I supposed to keep my eyes shut, is that the new etiquette?'

'What a dreadful word, where did you pick it up?'

'Our deportment teacher at school is always going on about etiquette.'

'Well, all the same, don't let me hear you saying it. Manners will do nicely, thank you.'

'I was thinking, apart from how French puddings are so light and frivolous that it's almost not like eating at all, about what I'd do if I was in a war.'

'You just told us you'd hotfoot it to America,' Max said.

He waited for a hovering Ketton to fill his glass and sat back in his seat.

'You didn't fight, but you didn't hotfoot it, either. Didn't you do frightfully clever hush-hush stuff?'

'Do you know, Harriet, it was all a long while ago, almost before you were born, and the past isn't a good place to spend much time.'

'Miss Spottiswood at school says you have to watch every step you take and every decision you make because then in a second it's done and finished and you can't change it. Irrevocable.'

Irrevocable, what a terrible word, Cynthia said to herself.

'And,' she said, 'when you think you've done with the past, then it looms up into the present and causes all kinds of problems. She teaches us history, jolly interesting in fact, how people in the olden days made mistakes, thinking it was all for the best and then they learned later that they'd sealed their own fate. Or somebody else's. Bloody Mary, for example, marrying a Spanish king. That was a big, big mistake, and I expect lots of people told her so.'

'It's time you went to bed, Harriet,' Cynthia said.

THIRTY

Polly loved stations at night, with the smoky darkness, the sounds of the looming steam locomotives, the eerie out-of-time quality that a great terminus always had. And this was a station full of excitement and promise. The blue carriages of *Wagons-Lits* trains with the boards on the side, Warsaw, Istanbul, Vienna.

'Have you got your ticket?' said Archie. 'The sleeping cars are at the other end.'

'Sleeper! Good gracious, I couldn't possibly afford a sleeper. I've just got a seat.'

Now she had shocked Archie. He stood staring at her.

'Dearest Polly, you can't seriously say you're planning to sit up all night! In a train.'

'Of course I am. I've done it before, when I've been to the north of England and Scotland. I'm quite used to it.'

'No, I say, you must let me sub you.'

Polly was adamant. 'Archie, you've been amazingly kind, taking me about and giving me all that delicious food. I can't afford a sleeper, and I'm not letting anyone else pay for it. I won't let Oliver pay for me, and you're not going to either. I don't mind, honestly I don't. And I'm so full of food, I shall sleep soundly wherever I am. Like a python.'

'Python? What python? Oh, I see.' Archie shook his head. 'I don't like it, I don't like it at all . . .' His voice broke off.

'What's the matter?' asked Polly.

Archie had ducked behind a fluted metal column, dragging her with him, as an extremely elegant woman, dark, with a beautiful face marred by the coldness of her expression, went past, accompanied by what was obviously her maid, a porter with a trolley piled high with a large trunk, hatboxes and several leather suitcases, and a railway official, smiling and bowing as he hurried along.

'That's Katriona, Oliver's sister,' said Archie. 'I don't feel up to facing her right now.'

'She doesn't look like Oliver, not a bit.' Polly found herself whispering; how absurd. The woman couldn't possibly hear them.

'Katriona takes after their mother,' said Archie in a normal voice; the woman was climbing up into the train. 'Come on, let's find your seat.'

They walked alongside the train, carriage after carriage. Did so many people go to Nice? Every night?

'Of course, the train won't be full, not at this time of year. You may be lucky, you may be able to stretch out and get a bit of sleep. Give me your ticket, I'll ask the conductor where your coach is.' He deposited her suitcase at her feet. 'Wait here. I shan't be long. Don't move.'

He vanished into the gloom, leaving Polly for a moment, with a sense of abandonment. Then she laughed at herself, she had been going to do all of this by herself, how quickly you could come to rely on someone else. Then Archie was back. 'Come on.'

The compartment they entered was empty, and cold, with

a strong smell of Gauloises lingering in the air. Archie put her suitcase up on the rack.

'Please don't wait,' Polly said. 'You left your car double-parked outside the station, there's probably a furious Frenchman jumping up and down and cursing you.'

'Well, if you're sure, I will take myself off. I hate seeing people off, actually, waving as the train goes out. It always makes me melancholy.'

'Oh, Archie, how can I thank you for these last three days?'

'I've enjoyed every minute, we've had a splendid time.'

Polly stood on tiptoe with her hands on his shoulders and kissed him soundly on both cheeks. Pleased, he gave her a warm hug in return, and, with instructions to look after her suitcase, left, only to put his head back into the compartment a moment later. 'We'll meet again. I'll be down at Cap Rodoard later in the month.'

Polly took off her coat, folded it and put it on the rack. She sat down in a corner, felt the slats of the wooden seat beneath her, retrieved her coat and sat on it.

Ten minutes later, the compartment was filled with a French family, garrulous, aromatic and prepared to make a night of it. An extraordinary number of parcels were piled on the rack, her suitcase was subjected to intense scrutiny, with the father of the family openly looking at the labels, and the tribe, consisting of three or four generations, from an old man who could be touching ninety to a silent baby wrapped up like a cocoon, settled into their seats.

They addressed her in loud, voluble French; she smiled and shook her head, and managed to convey that she was English and spoke no French. They exclaimed among themselves, and then the train slowly began to move, with a loud whistle and a blast of steam from the engine. Madame opened the basket she had on her knee and began to hand round garlic sausage and cups of red wine.

Polly felt obliged to accept some, although she was full to bursting from her dinner with Archie, and she chewed a mouthful of the pungent sausage, watching the platform rush past as the train gathered speed.

She sat for a while, looking out of the window at the lights of the city. She caught glimpses of interiors, a couple sitting at a table, a child at a window, waving, a maid on a little balcony shaking out a cloth. She had a sense of separation, of being out of the stream of normal life that a long journey brings; one world had shut behind her, and a new one lay ahead. For the moment she was both in transit and in a state of transition.

The French people wanted the blinds down, and she smiled and nodded her agreement, although she'd rather have left them open. The atmosphere was growing hotter and smokier and more garlicky by the minute, and the lights had been reduced to a dim glow. Polly peered at her watch, it was nearly midnight. She propped herself up against the corner and shut her eyes.

The door slid open, and a shadowy shape filled the doorway. The newcomer said something in French, then came in and sat in the corner by the door, a pack resting on his knees. Polly stole a sideways glance, but couldn't see his face, which was covered by the hat he'd pulled right down over it.

For a few moments, she sat with her eyes open, listening to the clicking rhythm of the train, and then she was asleep.

Polly woke to darkness, with a jolt, confused, wondering where she was. She had slept soundly and dreamlessly, and although she sat still for a while, she knew she wouldn't go back to sleep. She ran a hand through her rumpled hair. Six o'clock. And the compartment was empty, where had everyone gone? Had she dreamed them? With sudden panic, she looked up at the rack, but her suitcase was still there, and her handbag was where she'd put it last night, wedged between herself and the wall. A quick inspection proved that her purse and its contents were still there, and so was her passport.

She put up the blind and peered out, as a bell clanged and the train ran through a station: a light, a name that came and went, fencing, and then it was far behind them.

She took her sponge-bag out of her suitcase, and transferred toothbrush and toothpowder, face flannel and soap to her handbag. Then she slid back the door, looked up and down the empty corridor, and set off along the corridor.

When she came back, she watched the sky take on a pearly glow that turned into palest pink and yellow, which gave way to turquoise and then to broad daylight.

A different world indeed. The train flashed past stone farmhouses, villages nestling in valleys, a ruin on a hill. Polly saw a church tower, and then it was gone, and there was a winding river glittering in the early sunlight of a new day, set between green banks with overhanging trees. She saw a large house in the distance, exactly like a picture in a fairy tale, with round turrets and shutters. Two huge farm horses cavorted in a field, and a boy hustled a flock of goats along a track.

Those must be vineyards, she knew that from seeing them in paintings and photographs, and those gnarled and fascinatingly-shaped trees were olives. With gnarled women all in black, doing mysterious things to the ground around the trees with ancient-looking implements.

The blue hills, the silvery green olives, the red earth; Polly felt light-headed, and let out a long breath of pure delight, entranced by the colours crowding in on her senses. Now they were surging past a small town with higgledy-piggledy houses with terracotta-tiled roofs, a pretty church, and, towering above it all, a fortress.

272

Despite having eaten so much the night before, she was very hungry. Not that she could afford to eat anything on the train. She'd provided herself with an apple and some squares of chocolate, and she ate those and thought longingly of coffee. They were no longer travelling through the countryside, but were in suburbs, and slowing down. Washing was hanging outside the windows and balconies of the houses that backed on to the railway line, and she was amazed to see geraniums, still flowering, in window boxes and in pots. She hugged herself as she saw palm trees, majestically larger than she had imagined them, actually palm trees.

The train slowed, and a voice rang out. 'Nice! Nice!'

Quick, quick; she didn't want to waste a minute, she wanted to be out in the light and the sunshine. Bother, her sketchbook had fallen out of her handbag. She wouldn't need it for the moment, better put it somewhere safer if it was going to fall out. She opened her suitcase, thrust the pad down the side and closed the locks with a snap.

THIRTY-ONE

Sir Walter was pointing out the features and beauty of the landscape beneath them as though he owned the country: here was the Seine – craning to look through the tiny window of the plane and past the wing struts, Lois could see a train of barges making its placid way along the wide river – there was a chateau that had belonged to the kings of France, here was a ruined castle left over from some war of the Middle Ages . . .

Lois had long ago developed the art of appearing to listen with interest to what people were saying while her mind was busy with something quite different. Life brought her into contact with an astonishing range of personalities, but Sir Walter was of a type she had rarely encountered. On the surface, he was easily readable, a confident, dynamic self-made man – well, Americans respected that, unlike the Europeans, who still clung to old values of inherited money and land and ancient names.

Yet he was more complex than at first appeared, and one thing she was sure of: he was both uncannily shrewd and untrustworthy. She and Myron would have to watch their step. To become as successful and rich as Sir Walter a man had to be ruthless, and it was clear that Sir Walter's ruthlessness wasn't limited to his business dealings but extended into his private life. That was why she and Myron were here in the air above France, simply because Malreward had wanted to annoy his mistress and soon-to-be wife.

Lois couldn't quite make out what Mrs Harkness was up to. She'd had her down at first as a woman on the make, happy to be the mistress of a man like Malreward, and even happier to marry him and secure both position and fortune.

Yet there was an aloofness about her, an unwillingness to please Sir Walter at any cost to herself, and that was unusual among gold diggers. Perhaps she genuinely liked the man; Lois knew too much about him to find him at all attractive, but she could see that he was a type to appeal to many women.

Had Mrs Harkness been put out at Sir Walter's invitation to her and Myron? Lois smiled. Not all the famed English good manners could disguise the look on Cynthia Harkness's face when she learned that she'd have to put up with the voluble Americans over Christmas. Had she, alone with Sir Walter, remonstrated with him, argued, made a scene?

Lois doubted it. And not from any fear of the man, or reluctance to make her views known. Myron, who was a good judge of human nature, had given it as his opinion that Cynthia was concerned for her kid. 'Would you want that guy as a stepfather to your daughter? He'll find her nothing but a nuisance, and he'll resent any attention she gets from her mother.'

Time would solve that problem for mother and daughter. English girls of her class married young, and once Harriet had a husband and home of her own, Mrs Harkness, or Lady Malreward as she'd be, could devote herself to her husband, which was certainly what he wanted and expected.

They would land shortly for lunch and for the plane to

refuel, Sir Walter called across to her. Then another three hours flying time to the aerodrome near Nice; they'd land on the sands there, the Fox Moth pilot had told her when she asked about the flight. For herself, she preferred the comfort and warmth of a train journey, but, as Myron said, business was business, and personal preferences didn't come into it. She huddled further into her fur jacket and hoped their lunch would be a good one. Knowing Sir Walter's tastes, she doubted they'd be eating sandwiches and drinking coffee from a vacuum flask while the plane was attended to.

The note of the engine changed, and the ground was closer. She could see the buildings of the aerodrome, and, yes, there was a large car, with a chauffeur in uniform standing beside it, shading his eyes as he looked up at the descending aircraft.

'My car and my man,' Sir Walter said with satisfaction. 'Waiting to take us to lunch.'

THIRTY-TWO

With her mind full of palm trees and flowers, suitcase in hand and her beret – clearly quite unsuitable headgear for this sunny place – crammed inelegantly on her head, Polly got off the train. Once at ground level, she put her suitcase down at her feet and gazed around her. Palm trees here, too, growing in tubs, and baskets of greenery and flowers. She looked for the exit; Oliver had said someone would meet her, but who, and where? How would they know who she was?

And then she heard Oliver's familiar voice. He hadn't seen her, he was talking to his sister, surrounded by her luggage, whose cut-glass voice floated over the noises of the station: 'Are you serious, one of your scrubby artists? And you've asked her for at least a month. Oh, really, Oliver, you are impossible. Why must you inflict these ghastly people on us?'

For a moment, Polly felt as though the breath had been knocked out of her. She stood there, her shabby suitcase in her hand, unwashed, unkempt, looking exactly as though she had spent many hours in the company of a good deal of smoke and garlic sausage. She shouldn't have come, this whole thing was a terrible mistake. She would go back at once now on the very next train.

Oliver spotted her, and came striding over. 'Polly, there you are! I was looking all along the platform for you, which carriage were you in?'

'Further along,' Polly said, glad to see him, but uncertain as to the genuineness of his welcome. What if that Katriona woman – Archie never mentioned her surname, blast him – was only voicing the general Fraddon opinion?

'Further along? Polly, please tell me you didn't travel all the way from Paris third class.'

'I did,' she said defiantly. 'Sitting up on a wooden seat in the company of a garlicky French family.'

They had caught up with Katriona, who was standing beside a porter tapping her beautifully shod foot impatiently.

'Polly sat up all the way,' Oliver said.

'She looks like it,' said Katriona, with a cold glance. Polly had held out her hand, but Katriona ignored it, telling Oliver to buck up, she was tired of hanging around in the station.

'Pay no attention to my sister,' said Oliver. 'She's the rudest woman in England, you'll get used to it.'

I doubt it, Polly said to herself, knowing that her face was crimson, and not sure whether that was from fury or embarrassment.

A gleaming motor was waiting, complete with liveried chauffeur, who leapt forward to attend to the stowing of Katriona's luggage.

'The trunk will have to come later,' said Oliver. 'I can't think why you need so much luggage, Katriona. And where's Rory? I thought he was coming with you.'

'Hamish is bringing him down. He wants to stop off at a couple of places, educational, I gather. It's a nuisance travelling with a child, anyhow, and Rory can't sleep on trains, it makes him sick.'

Rory, Polly guessed, must be Katriona's son. 'They may be here by the weekend, but I should think it will be nearer Christmas. You know how busy he always says he is.'

Polly's heart sank. Oliver was fine, and she thought she could cope with his father, however grand – after all she could probably keep out of his way. Katriona changed this cosy picture, and moreover at a big house, and at this season of the year, with Christmas and New Year, there would probably be crowds of people, all like Katriona, all making her feel as out of place as she undoubtedly would be.

'Hap in,' said Oliver. 'Is that all you've got, just the one suitcase? Attagirl, I do admire anyone who travels light.'

Oliver sat in front beside the chauffeur, and Polly got in beside Katriona. She looked as though some undesirable insect had just landed beside her, and wrinkled her nose in an ostentatious way.

Polly wasn't going to show that she minded. And, two seconds later, Katriona was forgotten, as she saw the sea, an impossible blue, and the full strength of the winter sun hit her dazzled eyes. 'Oh, how beautiful,' she exclaimed. Oliver turned round to smile at her, Katriona winced at the gaucherie, and Polly sat bolt upright on the edge of the seat, craning her head to see everything, the great sweep of the bay, the tall palms, the hillside rising steeply behind the town. 'Mountains! Peaks covered in snow.'

'Oh, really,' said Katriona.

'I've never seen proper mountains before,' Polly said. 'Only the ones in Scotland, and they aren't like these. Look at the colours, the mauves and greys and the light and shadow.'

Oliver laughed at her enthusiasm. 'I still stare and stare at the mountains,' he said. 'They're never the same, like clouds, they are full of moods and differences.'

'Clouds,' said Polly, glancing up at the blue sky. 'Are there ever clouds here?'

'In fact,' said Katriona, 'it rains a good deal, especially in the winter.'

Katriona was a cloud all by herself, one of those spiky, ominously steely clouds that surge up behind fluffier numbers presaging storms and evil weather.

How could Oliver have a sister like this? Yes, he had a sharp tongue when it came to art that didn't please him, but Katriona seemed to be the kind of person who was pleased by nothing.

She was talking to Oliver, 'I do trust there are going to be some interesting people here.'

'Oh, the usual crowd, I expect,' said Oliver easily. 'Don't look so alarmed, Polly, my father likes artists, you'll have a lot in common with his friends.'

'They're established artists,' said Katriona. 'Hardly likely to want to have anything to do with a student.'

'I am not a student,' said Polly, goaded too far. 'I earn my living by my painting, as it happens. It may not be a very good living, but I count as a professional.'

Katriona wasn't listening, she had her face turned away.

Polly watched a leggy boy in shorts and a too-small jersey with a long loaf of bread under his arm, running along the pavement. They were out of the town now, driving along a road that twisted and turned, following the line of the coast. Each time they rounded a bend a new vista opened, and her eyes were riveted on enchanting little beaches, and now and then a harbour, with brightly-painted fishing boats, a river snaking down a valley into the sea, a longer beach with a white hotel above it, and out to sea, yachts swooping after each other in effortless perfection of movement.

After a while they left the main road, and the car, taking the bends of a white, dusty road at what seemed to Polly alarming and casual speed, began to descend towards the sea. She hoped they wouldn't meet anyone coming the other way, as there was no room for anything bigger than a bicycle to pass.

The car braked and swung through a pair of gates and then drove along a sandy drive. Oliver, turning round, said, 'Here we are, Polly. Welcome to the Domus Romana.'

Polly was obscurely disappointed. She had questioned Oliver about his house in France, and when he replied vaguely, had summoned up mental images: it might be a gleaming modern structure, all balconies and glass and white curves, a beacon of modernity. Or, if old, something along the lines of the chateaux she had seen in photographs, like those she had glimpsed from the train, with towers or turrets. Or it could be a house in the classical style, with a regular, formal appearance.

This wasn't like any of her imaginings. It was rectangular, with pale ochre walls, very plain, its roof tiled in those rounded clay tiles which she had noticed as soon as she arrived in France, so different from the flat tiles she was used to in England. There were shutters at the windows, but they were plain wood, not painted in the enchanting blues and greens she had seen on other houses.

Oliver was holding the door open for her to get out, 'Do stop looking around like a cat in a strange place,' he said, laughing at her.

People were milling around the car, servants in morning uniform, men in long aprons, maids in print dresses. One of these took her suitcase. 'Go with Marie,' Oliver said. 'She'll take you to your room, you'll want to wash and change after your night on the train.'

He spoke to the maid in rapid French. Katriona was already inside the house, her loud voice echoing as she called back to Oliver, 'I suppose Fraddon is in his library?'

Fraddon? How odd to call your father by his surname like that. It sounded so cold.

Polly went through the door and stopped so abruptly that Marie, close on her footsteps, nearly fell over her. What kind of a house was this? She looked down at a mosaic with the outline of a growling dog, and then blinked as her eyes took in the columns with their flutes picked out in gold.

Ignoring the servants, Oliver and Katriona, she walked through a marbled, becolumned hall into an area with more columns set around a small central pool, graced by an exquisite bronze of a naked boy balanced on one foot. He was holding a horn, from which water cascaded into the pool. More mosaics underfoot, and through another chamber she could glimpse a garden. A garden indoors? She walked round the pool and through into what was indeed a colonnaded garden, with plants, and trees, trees heavy with oranges and lemons.

Behind the colonnade were painted panels, depicting all kinds of creatures against a deep red background.

She took a deep breath of astonishment. Oliver had come up beside her. 'It's pure Hollywood,' she said impetuously. 'I don't believe a place like this exists outside the talkies. The colour, the columns, the marble, the mosaics, the water . . .'

'Sensational in its way, don't you agree? And there's more to it than this. However, I'll postpone the guided tour for the moment, since Marie wants to take you to your room. If you'd like to go with her, she'll show you the way.'

Polly came out of the dazed state this extraordinary house had induced, how could anyone actually live in a place like this?

At Marie's urging, Polly went up a flight of stairs that led off from the left of these rooms, still wondering at a house that had a garden inside, let alone one with oranges and lemons on the tree – were they real? – and followed the maid along a gallery which ran around above the garden, From this vantage point she could see that the garden was a formal one, divided into four quarters, with a statue in the centre.

Marie opened a door, and stood back for Polly to go in. It was a square room, with a plain wooden bed, a table under a window, and a lamp on a tall stand. Polly went straight to the window and looked out over the gardens, lush even at this time of year. Turning her head, she saw the sea. The house must be right on the shore, and that sucking, hissing sound was the susurration of waves against rocks.

She withdrew her head, the maid was talking to her. Polly smiled, and made it clear in a few desperate and, she was sure ungrammatical, phrases, that her French was almost non-existent.

Marie had laid her suitcase on a stand and was holding out her hand. Did she expect a tip?

'*Les clefs, s'il vous plaît,*' she said.

Clef. Key, of course. Polly fumbled in her bag and drew out not keys, but a solitary key, tied to a bootlace. Marie took it, knelt down, put in the key and opened the suitcase.

No, this was too much, she wasn't going to have this maid in her neat dress rummaging around in her things.

'*Non,*' she said, the word coming out in a much more peremptory way than she had intended. Marie looked around, startled.

'*Merci, moi,*' she added, pointing to the suitcase.

A puzzled Marie departed, and Polly heaved a sigh of relief. She sat down on the bed, which hardly gave at all. She examined the mattress, which was very dense and thin, and set not on springs but on leather webbing. The bed frame was set on four legs which ended in what looked like paws. She bounced up and down. In fact, it would probably be quite comfortable.

Goodness, she was hungry. No, she mustn't think about food, there'd probably be nothing to eat until lunch, which would be hours away. She needed to change. Bother, Marie had gone without showing her where the bathroom was. She took out her sponge bag and looked around the room for a towel. There wasn't one. She opened the door which the departing Marie had closed behind her, and looked out. Could she just set off and explore? Hardly, if she were to start opening doors, she could end up anywhere, and knowing her luck, probably in Katriona's bedroom, heaven forbid.

She was spared this embarrassment by the appearance of Katriona, who came briskly along the galley.

'Well?' she said. 'Do you need something?'

'I was looking for the bathroom.'

'Bathroom? Where's Marie? Honestly, these girls are impossible.'

Polly could see she was about to ring the bell that was positioned in the corridor, and she said hastily, 'I sent her away.'

'Oh, really,' and Katriona stalked past Polly and into her room. She opened the door opposite the bed, which Polly had taken for a cupboard. 'Here's your bathroom.'

Polly could barely get out a thank-you before Katriona had gone, shutting the door behind her with what was only just not a bang. Polly went through the door, which didn't lead directly into the bathroom, but into a space with hanging rails on one side, and shelves and drawers on the other. Beyond was the bathroom, a bathroom to herself, Polly had never had such a luxury before.

It had an enormous bath, on lion's feet, a lavatory, and what looked like another lavatory but with no seat – Polly felt a certain pride in knowing that was a bidet – and a round basin set on a fluted pillar. The whole bathroom was tiled, floor to ceiling, in white, with a key pattern running around at dado height.

Here was her towel, towels in the plural, set on a rack,

thick white towels, why ever would they think she'd want so many? At the end of the bathroom was a huge headed brass shower, set above and separated from the rest of the bathroom by a lip set into the tiles. On a shelf near the shower were bottles of various shapes and sizes, and cakes of soap in the shape of nautilus shells. What a pity to use them, but she needed soap and a good deal of it to wash away the grime of the journey, shell or no shell.

She took off her clothes, reached towards the large handle beneath the shower and turned it rather gingerly. The wide-headed shower burst into life, and Polly, after testing and adjusting the temperature, stepped under it.

She shut her eyes, rejoicing in the bliss of the stinging water. She soaped herself all over, and since her hair was wet – it was only after she'd started showering that she noticed the bath cap on a hook by the basin – she might as well wash her hair; here was a large bottle marked shampoo.

Invigorated and refreshed, if still hungry, she dried herself on an immense towel, grinning to herself at the difference between this and the washing arrangements in Fitzroy Street, where the bathroom was a narrow, high-ceilinged room with peeling paint, a large and temperamental geyser and a bath with the enamel chipped and greying where the tap dripped. And the lavatory was next door, no gleaming porcelain there, just cold lino underfoot and an old wooden seat, and a tricky chain that you had to tug in exactly the right way to make it flush.

She picked up her tweed skirt and took it into the bedroom. Katriona had been wearing a silk frock with a little jacket, in clear blue with a yellow pattern; something told her that tweed was wrong for the South of France.

Since she possessed nothing even remotely like Katriona's silk frock, she would simply put on a fresh cotton blouse – crumpled, but at least clean, with another skirt. She put on a clean pair of lisle stockings, wishing they were silk, and pulled a comb through her damp hair.

Now what? Well, first of all, she'd wash out the clothes she'd been wearing. Then they might be dry for tomorrow. She'd have to use the shell soap, even if Marie came back, she had no idea how to ask for a bar of washing soap. As she ran hot water into the basin and was about to plunge the shirt and underwear in, Marie appeared at the door.

'*Mademoiselle*!' she cried, sounding in real anguish, and Polly looked up, startled, what on earth was the matter?

With further cries of horror, Marie whipped the clothes away from her, and bundled them up in the damp towel.

Polly tried to summon the words to protest, but Marie, with a last look of dismay, scurried out of the room.

Polly sat down on the bed again. When would she ever see her clothes? How was she going to explain to Marie . . . Her thoughts were interrupted by a tap on the door, and to her relief, she heard Oliver's voice. 'Polly?'

'Yes,' she called, standing up. 'Come in.'

He put his head round the door. 'Is everything all right. Do you like your room?'

'It's perfect,' said Polly. 'Lovely.'

'I bet you didn't have anything to eat on the train. Am I right, no breakfast?'

'I had some chocolate and an apple.'

'Thought as much. I've told them to bring coffee and something for you to eat down by the pool, come on.'

'Pool? Do you have a swimming pool?' She might have guessed.

'Of course. You're a bit overwhelmed by the house, aren't you? It isn't to everyone's taste, but you get used to it. That's why I wouldn't tell you anything about it, it's a house to be experienced, not described. You need to see it for the first time with no expectations, then it hits you in all its glory.'

He was leading the way downstairs as he spoke, and now he took her through the garden. She followed him through the pillars at the other end of the garden and across a lobby, which had a richly-decorated floor and more panels on the walls. She saw a shimmer of water, and they came out beside a pool, marble-edged, with plain marble pillars set round it in another colonnade. The walls here were painted in greens and blues, and all over them frolicked an exuberant swarm of marine life, from octopuses and seahorses to dolphins.

Polly couldn't speak, but just stood and stared. On the other side of the pool, behind where shallow steps led down into the turquoise water, was a wall and an open door through which she could see luscious green plants and trees set against the blues of sea and sky.

The pool was open to the heavens, with a tiled gallery running round it above the colonnades.

'It's extraordinary, to bring the outside inside.'

'It's what the Romans did.'

'Romans? Oh, of course, how stupid I am. That's why it's the Domus Romana.'

'Exactly. Built, reconstructed, I should say, by my grand-mother, who was a passionate classicist and archaeologist. It's accurate in all its details, as far as one knows. Based on houses in Pompeii and elsewhere, although the final design was my grandmother's own work. Father has made some changes, which she would have disapproved of, such as modern plumbing and bathrooms. When she lived here, there was only the Roman bath, used by everyone, I'll show it to you later. And she had to draw the line at the lav in the kitchen, that was one area where her admiration for Rome had to give way to modern science.'

'Lav in the kitchen?' said Polly.

'Oh, yes. That's what the Romans did, so they could use

287

the waste water to clean it. Don't think about it. Didn't you do Latin at school?'

'Of course,' said Polly with dignity, then she laughed and said, 'but I was hopeless at it. And it was all *mensa, mensam* and dull books with no pictures except diagrams of Caesar's ditches. Nothing about lavatories in the kitchen, and certainly nothing that gave you any idea of what a Roman house looked like.'

A maid brought a tray, and set down a coffee pot on one of the tables by the pool. Cups, plates, and a basket of rolls, croissants and brioche. A dish of pale butter, a silver dish with three compartments, each with a silver spoon.

Oliver inspected the jam. 'Plum, peach and lemon marmalade,' he said. 'All from our own fruit trees.'

Polly was lost in the smell of the warm rolls and coffee. 'Peach jam? I've never had that.'

She spread a roll, crusty on the outside, magically soft and slightly warm inside, with butter and then with jam. Oliver poured her coffee, added cream and passed her the cup.

'I never tasted anything so good,' she said, wiping her mouth with her napkin and eyeing the other contents of the basket. 'What's this?'

'Brioche.'

'Which is?'

'Try it and see.'

'Delicious,' said Polly.

'These have chocolate in them,' said Oliver, helping himself. 'I adore them.'

'Is the pool heated?' Polly asked, watching the play of light on water and the hint of a mist on it.

'At this time of year, yes. It's sea water, pumped up here, and heated by a system of pipes. My grandmother installed a hypocaust system, hot coals and all that, but of course it was a fire hazard, and besides, although labour may be cheap in this part of the world, it isn't the same as having bath house slaves as in antique times, which is, she discovered, an essential part of a hypocaust. So it was modernized, with a closed furnace, but the under-floor heating on the ground floor and the water for the pool remain.'

Under-floor heating: Polly slipped a foot out of her shoe and laid her stockinged foot on the tile. 'It is warm, what a luxury, better than carpets.'

Katriona's voice sounded in the distance, then grew louder, she was coming this way.

Oliver was sitting nearer to the pool than Polly, who was hidden from view by the pillars at the entrance to that part of the house.

It was clear that Katriona hadn't seen her. 'Oh, there you are, Oliver. Listen, what on earth possessed you to invite that frumpy scrap of humanity to stay? My dear, where did you find her? She's impossible. Marie tells me she found her trying to wash out her clothes in the basin of her bathroom, what does she think this is, a youth hostel? Oh, you're there,' she added coolly as she caught sight of Polly's indignant face.

The last remnants of the brioche turned to ashes in Polly's mouth. Frumpy, indeed.

Oliver, looking and sounding annoyed, laid a hand on her arm.

'Polly has one thing you don't possess, Katriona, which is perfect manners. One would think you'd been born and reared in a slum, the things you say. Haven't you ever heard what terribly bad form it is to be rude to a guest? Or, in fact, any other human being?'

'Don't moralize, Oliver. Now, Miss Smith, we must get one or two things straight. Have you brought evening clothes with you? Marie says there are only the two long frocks, and neither of them sounds at all suitable. And two cock-tails, very smart I dare say, but outré, not the thing for here.'

Suitable for what? Polly thought, but didn't say.

'Polly has youth and looks and good humour on her side,' said Oliver. 'What the hell does it matter what frocks she wears? Besides, Polly, if one of them is that red affair you wore to the Blue Monkey, you look wonderful in it, whether it's in fashion or not.'

'The red dress is like something for the stage, and her other frock, according to Marie, can never have had anything to do with any known fashion. Where did you get it? At the jumble sale?'

'I don't remember,' said Polly, who did, but she wasn't going to say it had been passed on to her by a friend. 'And I like it, even if it is a bit shabby.'

Katriona ignored her, and went on speaking to Oliver. 'We've quite a few people coming to dinner tonight.'

'Perhaps I could have a tray in my room,' said Polly, speaking to Oliver. 'If I don't have the right clothes.'

Oliver was on his feet. He took his sister by the elbow and propelled her back towards the inner garden. He was speaking to her in a low, determined voice, and Polly could only catch a few words, but it was clear he was telling Katriona to back off, to try and behave better, to curb her rude tongue, 'It wins you no friends. No, I know you don't want Polly for a . . .'

Polly sat beside the remains of the breakfast that such a short while ago had brought her such pleasure, and looked gloomily at the shimmering water.

Oliver was back, looking down at her. 'Buck up, duckie, I've told you, you just have to ignore Katriona, that's what everyone else does.'

'You could have warned me how you lived, Oliver. I'm not suited to all this. I don't belong here, with maids and dinner parties and all that. I'm uncomfortable and I make your sister uncomfortable.'

'More coffee?' he said, sitting down and lifting the lid of the coffee pot. 'You don't, I only wish you could. Nothing makes Katriona uncomfortable, she has the most supreme disregard for other people's feelings or ideas. The fairies of kindness and courtesy were not there at her christening, handing out their gifts. She's always been like this, it's really nothing personal.'

Footsteps, and Oliver stood up as a man came through the pillars. 'Good morning, sir,' he said, in quite a different voice. 'Polly, may I introduce my father. Lord Fraddon?'

Polly rose, catching the edge of the basket as she did so, and sending it flying. It slid across the tiles and slipped into the pool, where it floated towards the other side.

'Oh, I'm so sorry, how clumsy . . .' Her voice faded. It couldn't be, surely – yes, it was! It was the man with the imperious nose that she'd sketched in Paris.

THIRTY-THREE

Lord Fraddon was holding out a hand. 'Good morning, Miss Smith,' he said. He was about the same height as Oliver, and had the same graceful figure. He spoke with a slight drawl, in a deeper voice than Oliver's; it was a curiously attractive voice.

'Don't concern yourself about the bread basket bobbing there like a ship of fools. Oliver, get the pole and retrieve it.'

Oliver had already gone round to the other side of the pool, and taken up a long pole with a net at the end from its stand against the wall. He swished it across the pool, scooped up the basket, netted a roll which had escaped and was drifting down into the water, and deposited the soggy remains at his father's feet.

'Thank you, Oliver. Ring for a maid to come and clear it away.'

Polly's awkwardness and temper had both vanished in laughter at Oliver's neat fishing. Then she caught Lord Fraddon's heavy-lidded eyes watching her.

'I like the sound of laughter. And you have a pretty laugh, Miss Smith.'

'You'd better call her Polly,' said Oliver. 'I do, Miss Smith is so very Jane Austen.'

'Oh, please do,' said Polly, still wondering if she could be right – or so wrong, she trusted her memory for faces absolutely. And she had become slightly uneasy about using the name Smith; even though she had sworn to herself that she would never use the Tomkins name. What if someone asked to see her passport, and there she was, passing herself off as Miss Smith? Not that there was anything wrong with Smith, or with people called Smith, only it might not be wise to use it in a foreign country.

'You're miles away, Polly,' Oliver said. 'Wake up, there's a whole day ahead of you.' And to his father, 'Polly sat up in the train all last night.'

Lord Fraddon looked at her with raised brows. 'Did you? How uncomfortable. Was this done because you had run out of francs, or because you were expressing your solidarity with the workers, who rarely travel in the Wagons-Lits compartments.'

'To save money,' said Polly. And adding, 'I'm all for the workers, but I don't see that my being uncomfortable would help any of them one bit; if I had the money, I'd certainly have taken a berth.'

'Thus showing sound common sense,' said Lord Fraddon. 'A rare attribute among Oliver's friends. Do you read Latin?'

Polly was so taken aback, that she simply goggled at him. 'Latin?' she repeated, looking desperately at Oliver, who came quickly to her aid.

'Polly's an artist, Fraddon,' he said with some severity. 'You know that, because I told you. Artists spend their formative years drawing and painting, not studying the classical languages.'

'Then I will provide a translation of the passage that I think might appeal to Polly. From Horace, a man who knew how to live and, one is sure, how to laugh. I will see you at lunch,' he said to Polly. 'And I advise you not to take very much notice of Katriona's sharp tongue, I am sure you won't, you look like a sensible young lady. My daughter can make guests feel ill at ease, and I regret that.'

He walked away; he had a walk very like Oliver's, Polly noticed.

'I would like to paint him,' she said to Oliver. 'I admire that nose.'

'I am sure you would do him justice.'

'Does he live here all the time? I know you said he never goes back to England, but does he travel at all? To Paris, for instance?'

'Oh, yes, he's up and down from Paris several times a year. He just got back from there yesterday, in fact.'

Oliver showed her all over the house, including Lord Fraddon's huge bedroom, with views of the sea on three sides, and some astonishing wall paintings. 'Done in the Pompeian style,' Oliver said. 'Rather too lewd for the public rooms, and it shocks the staff, but apparently it's correct for a Roman bedroom. It dates from my grandmother's time, I think she must have had a saucy soul. It suits Fraddon, he has a touch of the old Roman in him, I always think.'

Polly was amazed by the attention to details, which Oliver pointed out to her, the lights, the style of the banister, the shape of a basin, the clawed feet on a table, the handle on the doors.

'All perfectly authentic,' Oliver said. 'My grandmother was a stickler for getting details right.'

'There aren't many paintings or modern works of art,' Polly said, who had been busy admiring the frescos of people, and rural garden scenes. 'I thought you said that your father owned a lot of paintings and sculptures.'

'He does. This part of the house is very much as it was

originally, but he's built a section on, still in the classical style, and that's where his pictures are. And he hangs two or three favourites in the library, did you notice the Picasso?'

'Does he know Picasso?'

'Lord, yes, he knows most of the artists working down here.'

'It's the light, isn't it,' said Polly, shading her eyes as she looked out to sea. 'It's as though you could reach out and touch it, and it gives a quality to the most ordinary objects.'

'Ah, yes, the light,' he said, watching her with amused affection. 'Blowing away the melancholy is it? I thought it would.'

'Is that why you asked me? Doesn't everybody feel a bit down in the winter, in England?'

'Some more than others. Besides, you need more colour in your life, I defy you to remain monochrome here.'

Polly wasn't having that. 'It isn't that I don't see the colour. I just don't choose to put it into my work.'

'Afraid it might make you run mad, a riot of colour?'

'Well, it was kind of you to invite me.' And, a voice in her head whispered, I wish you hadn't, because the colours and the sea and the mountains are tremendous and make my soul stir, but this house isn't welcoming or like a home at all, and your sister is a bitch.

'Homesick?'

'Of course not, I've only been away from England for a day. I'm not unadventurous, it's just I haven't had much opportunity to travel. Not like you, I expect you've been to all kinds of different countries, all over Europe, Switzerland for the winter sports and mountain air, Germany for the night life, Italy for – I don't know what, why do people go to Italy?'

'Spaghetti,' he said promptly. 'And opera, and, these days, to watch soldiers strutting up and down. To call on the Pope.'

'Or Mussolini.'

'Now, I have had an audience with the Pope, but I can't say I've met Mussolini. For which I am profoundly thankful.'

'Audience with the Pope? Why?'

'The Fraddons are Catholic, from way back. My mother took me to Rome when I was still at school, and we went to the Vatican.'

New social horrors rose in Polly's mind. 'I don't go to church.'

'Don't let that worry you. Katriona will go, I do sometimes, Fraddon doesn't.'

Polly longed to ask why, if the Fraddons were Catholic, Lord Fraddon didn't go to church, weren't you obliged to if you were a Catholic? Didn't you have to confess your sins every week?

'Now, I've one last room to show you, I'm sure Fraddon won't mind, I can see he's taken a liking to you. This is his study, his sanctum. It's another library, but a smaller one, supposedly based on Cicero's.'

He opened a door into a room with cream walls and floor, with a rectangular table in the centre, inlaid with an intricate pattern of shells and fish. A marble bench ran down each side of the room, beneath shelves of books. The marble benches had sumptuous cushions on them, red velvet and gold silk. A chair was pulled up to a smaller table, set against the far wall, which was obviously used as a desk.

Polly noticed none of this; oblivious to her surroundings she let out a long sound of ecstatic incredulity. On the wall opposite hung a huge canvas, a painting of a woman, more than life size. An elongated figure, a slender neck, and compelling dark eyes. The explosive energy, the dynamic brushwork, the chaotic whirls and slashes of colour which had so stunned her in the portrait of Lady Strachan were in this picture, the artist's vitality matching that of his subject. 'It's a Cortoni,' she cried. 'He's a painter that's come bursting into my life, in London, in Paris, and now here! I love it, oh, it's wonderful.'

Oliver shook his head at her enthusiasm. 'I've never seen you like this, Polly. It is a good portrait, isn't it? Fraddon and Cortoni were friends, and he cherishes this painting.'

'I simply want to gaze and gaze, how does he do it? She's there, looking at us, and not looking at us, just about to step into the room, so alive, every inch of her.'

'I don't know her name, Fraddon will never let on. He only says that she was the most beautiful woman he ever met. Not conventionally beautiful, of course, but there's a tremendous glamour to her. He'll be pleased you admire her. He hangs the painting in here to keep her from vulgar and curious eyes, as he puts it. This is where he writes and composes; he claims she inspires him.'

THIRTY-FOUR

After lunch, a meal which was served in a room filled with rippling light from windows overlooking the sea, and a meal from which Katriona mercifully absented herself, Oliver said he was going to abandon Polly for an hour or so, as he had some business to attend to. 'Will you be all right?'

'I'll take my sketchbook into the garden and find a sunny spot.'

Which she did, sitting on a rock at the base of the house, overlooking the tranquil sea. The sun was amazingly hot, and there was a breeze just ruffling the branches of the pines above her. Sailing boats were zigzagging to and fro, making a charming scene, although not one she wanted to draw. So she opened her sketchbook and drew a caricature of Katriona, portraying her as a witch. Not in the likeness of a big-nosed crone with a besom, but as a wicked witch, sultry, elongated, a bitchy witch with long spiky nails and a sinuous figure slinking in a skin-hugging gown.

Which, Polly was startled to see, was exactly what Katriona looked like that evening. Polly had changed into her old velvet evening dress. It was a dusky pink, with no sleeves and a cowl neck, and it was a frock she had always loved, but now, seeing it through the eyes of the pitying Marie, she looked at her reflection and saw it as shabby and dowdy.

Well, she told her mirror image. I like it, even so. She had black suede shoes, bought from another, richer friend, who said that they pinched her. They pinched Polly's feet, too, but at least they had a touch of elegance about them.

Shutting the door behind her, she didn't turn right to go down the stairs, but instead walked on silent feet along the gallery and looked down. A buzz of voices came up to her from the square room below. She saw that glass doors now closed off the garden, gay with lights suspended between the pillars and the trees.

And there was Katriona, a pure, sleek creature in silver lamé, in a dress that plunged in a perfect dip at the back and flared out over her bottom into a fishtail train. Paris, Polly guessed, and despite herself, she envied Katriona her dress and her confidence.

She told herself she would be perfectly content to stay up in the gallery, a watcher in the shadows. It wouldn't do, however, she must gather her courage and make her way down, in her unfashionable dress, which probably cost less than the silver cigarette lighter a man was just flicking open beneath her. He moved to one side, and Polly got a good view of the woman whose cigarette he had been lighting. The cigarette was, remarkably, purple; Polly had no idea you could get purple cigarettes. And the woman now blowing tiny circles of smoke into the air was wearing a purple dress, swathes of chiffon over satin. Tina could have told her the dress was by Vionnet, but Polly just admired the way it shifted and moved with every step and gesture the woman made.

If she'd been younger, she would have looked as though she were dressing up as a fairy; if stout, like a dowager trying to make the best of herself, but being slim and not too tall and with a tremendous air, she looked perfect.

There seemed to Polly to be a crowd of people, so she counted. The Fraddons, three of them, Oliver moving with his usual grace among the guests, a cocktail in one hand, a cigarette in the other. Then three strange men. A dark man, not tall, bouncing on the balls of his feet as, gesticulating a good deal, he talked with enthusiasm to a younger man with springy brown hair that all the right smoothing creams had failed to quell. He was smiling, a pleasant enough smile, in as much as you could tell from Polly's vantage point. And there, at the purple woman's elbow was an extremely handsome young man, a suave delight, who was wearing a purple cummerbund. For a moment, Polly thought of him as the purple woman's accessory, perhaps he was her son.

Lord Fraddon was a dandy in an embroidered waistcoat with glittering strands of gold woven into the rich red damask pattern. Very flamboyant, very dashing, very un-English. Could you describe him as an eccentric, one of those rich English eccentrics beloved of the press and foreigners, and no doubt a nuisance to their nearest and dearest? Polly wasn't sure. Eccentric carried a hint of effeteness, and there was nothing effete about Lord Fraddon. Although, of course, if you were a rich eccentric, you could be anything you liked, dandy, rake, lunatic, lover, poet; your eccentricities would merely be considered charming, and you could pursue them without causing any bother to those around you.

Was he eccentric in his dinner gatherings, or would he go for matched numbers? In which case, they were two women short down there, and, if she didn't pluck up her courage sufficiently to take that long walk down the stairs and across the hall, they'd be three short.

No, here were more people arriving. Two men and a woman; no, she was wrong. Two women, surely, but how very dashing for the taller of the women to wear trousers, to wear in fact, a feminine version of a man's evening suit.

Polly stared down, quite fascinated by the new arrival, and hardly noticing the second of the women, merely seeing a pretty woman who must be in her late twenties, although with her kind of fragile fairness, she could pass for much younger.

At that moment Oliver, who was talking to the man with springy hair, looked up and waved at her.

'There you are,' he called up to her. 'I was wondering what had become of you.'

To Polly's horror, this drew the attention of all those assembled below, and she felt herself scrutinized by a dozen eyes.

She shrank back, and then Oliver compounded his sins by continuing, in the same ringing tones, 'Time to come down, Cinders. If not to the ball, then at least to dinner.'

He left the others, and in a minute was springing up the stairs.

'I wish I could eat in my room,' said Polly, and then was immediately cross with herself for sounding petulant and childish.

Oliver looked at her. 'Do you want to? I was forgetting how tired you must be, sitting up all night, how very thoughtless, of course you don't have to join us, I shall send a maid up.'

'No,' Polly cried. 'No, of course not, I'm not so feeble, but these are your friends, and I—'

'Don't know anyone,' Oliver finished for her. 'Don't worry, I'll introduce you, and then you will know us all, and find us the most amiable company.' He drew her back to the edge of the balcony. Down below, people had resumed their conversation, the girl looking down on them from above quite forgotten.

'I'll give you a quick run-down on them, and then you

can meet them all on equal terms. Let's start with your fellow artists, the last arrivals. The mannish woman in evening dress is Miss Saxe, Jo to her friends, who is a Neo-solidist.'

'A what?'

'I shan't explain; I don't think I could. Let Jo reveal all. Maud, Mrs Elgin, is the fair pretty one, she does illustrations for children's books, fairies and elves and other skipping, flitting characters. Charming.'

'Her or the fairies?'

'Both. The roly-poly man with the stupendous moustaches is Augusto, known as Gus, Ibanez, a Chilean painter. He's a Surrealist, a friend of Dali's. Inclined to become amorous when the wine is upon him, so watch out. I'm sure you're used to fending off unwanted attentions, so don't worry about him.'

That was true enough; you didn't go through art college and live in Bloomsbury without having numerous passes and pounces made at or on you, and Polly, disinclined to go in for the sexual experimentation of some of her contemporaries, had become adept at extricating herself from tricky situations.

'What about the woman in purple?'

'Ah, that's Mrs Wolf, Mrs Daphne Wolf. A cousin on my mother's side, although I have to say she and my mother cordially dislike one another. She gets on very well with Fraddon, though. She's extremely rich, and likes the colour purple, you never see her in another colour, and all her servants wear purple livery. Those cigarettes are made specially for her in Paris. The exquisite in the purple cummerbund is Ettore, a French-Italian, and, as you will have guessed, her particular friend.'

'Particular friend?'

'Lover, sweetie. Daphne likes them young, and having bags of sex appeal and a great deal of money, she can take her pick.'

'She's quite old, she must be over sixty, and he can't be much over thirty, half her age!'

'It's a wicked world we live in, but you'd think nothing of a man of that age with a popsie on his arm, now would you? Don't be suburban, Polly, that's not the genuine you.'

The colour rushed to her cheeks. How she hated to be called suburban. Or naïve. Or an innocent.

'He's so good-looking, why doesn't he get a girlfriend of his own age?'

'She wouldn't have the shekels. Besides, some young men like older women. Fact, don't look so unbelieving.'

'Who's the other young man?'

'An American, Tulliver Penn. Son of a banker ruined in the Wall Street crash, or so he says. He lives in Rodoard, is apparently writing the great American novel, acquiring any number of female admirers. I don't believe he ever gets near his typewriter, far too busy with other more physical pleasures.'

'Don't you like him?'

'Like? Polly, you have to get out of this like, dislike business. One's fellow human beings are far too complex for facile judgements. The myriad nature . . .'

'Stop it. I'm right, you don't like him, so you don't need to smother me with words. Besides, his name is pale and malevolent in colour.'

'I couldn't comment on that, but let's just say I'm not sure I trust him.'

As in that he might pinch a wallet, betray a friend, be less than honest as an artist? You could never tell with Oliver.

'I want to introduce you to everyone,' Oliver said. 'Enough of the lurking. Perhaps your velvety eyes will seduce the handsome Ettore, and yes, he certainly is a looker, away from the divine Daphne.'

'Not my type, actually,' Polly said, but Oliver didn't hear.

Lord Fraddon greeted her, waved a hand for a servant to bring her a cocktail, and said, 'Let me introduce Gus, who's in your line of business.'

Two intense, deep brown eyes gazed at Polly, sad eyes, she thought. 'An artist? You have my sympathy, it is a terrible life, nothing but anguish and poverty. Find yourself a rich husband, my dear, and then you will be happy, as artists are not.'

'Did anyone ever tell you to find yourself a rich wife, so that you could be happy?'

His hands flew up in a dramatic gesture. 'Oh, yes, but all the time. My mother, my grandmother, my sisters, even my wife, who in fact has no money at all. Don't make the mistake I did, escape while you can.' He arched his eyebrows in a tragic gesture, and resumed his conversation with Lord Fraddon.

Oliver rescued Polly, and took her across to where Miss Saxe and Mrs Elgin were laughing at something that Tulliver had just said. He turned and took her hand, his eyes looking into hers with warm intensity. Polly smiled back at him, then stiffened as Katriona, talking to Daphne, said in a clear, hard voice. 'Don't ask me, Daphne, where you can buy a frock like that? Or do you buy it? Surely you find it at the vicarage fête, cast off by the vicar's wife.'

'Pay no attention to her,' Miss Saxe said swiftly, giving Katriona's elegant back a contemptuous look. 'No manners, that woman. I like your dress, and besides, at your age and with your figure, you can wear anything and look splendid, don't you agree, Maud?'

'Tell us about yourself,' said Mrs Elgin, with a smile. 'What are you working on? Have you come to paint? Oliver told us you were a painter.'

Confession time; how banal covers for WH Smith sounded.

'Good money, though,' said Mrs Elgin. 'Do they still pay two guineas?'

'Yes.'

'I did a lot when I was starting out,' said Mrs Elgin. 'Is illustration what you want to do? Where did you train?'

And Polly relaxed for a moment, as the familiar talk, gossip about fellow artists, teachers, dealers, common friends, washed over her.

'We're out of touch in Rodoard, much as we love it here,' said Miss Saxe.

Polly began to be more at ease, only to stiffen as a bell began to toll, the clangour resonating through the room.

Oliver saw her face and laughed. 'I should have warned you. It rings at five past nine every night. It's a recording, very well done, don't you think? Tom Bell, from the House.'

Polly stared at him, uncomprehending. 'What house?'

'Fraddon's old college, at Oxford. Christ Church.'

'Why the house?'

'The Latin name of Christ Church is Aedes Christi. Which, translated, is the House of Christ.'

'Arcane nonsense,' said Miss Saxe.

'How long will it go on?' said Polly, covering her ears with her hands.

'A hundred and one dongs,' said Mrs Elgin. 'It's very loud, he has it amplified, you can hear it for miles around.'

'Don't the neighbours object?'

Oliver shrugged. 'We don't have many neighbours. It is also the signal for dinner,' he added, as the last toll died away, leaving a blessed silence. 'Come along, Polly.'

Polly was pleased to find herself sitting at a distance from Katriona, and Tulliver Penn, who was seated to her left, seemed, on acquaintance, to belie the sinister colours of his name. He made light conversation, setting her at her ease, although her momentary sense of pleasure vanished when she saw the array of silver on the table, ranks of knives and forks on either side of her plate, three glasses set out above the knives, good God, what did you do with them all?

More of Dora's warning words flashed into her dismayed mind. 'I expect Oliver's father dines in a formal way. Lots of cutlery, don't worry, start at the outside and work inwards. And there'll be more than one glass, just watch what the others drink and do as they do.'

'A wineglass, you mean.'

'One for white wine, one for red, one for dessert wine. There could be another one if they serve champagne. And a glass for water.'

How did Dora know about glasses and knives and forks? And, a more present concern, however many courses were there going to be?

Tulliver confided in a private whisper that he adored dining at Fraddon's house.

'Wonderful food, he has a first-rate chef. Here comes the soup, *consommé Grimaldi*, how delicious.'

Fish followed the soup, and then a portion of a dark meat Polly didn't recognize was placed deftly in the centre of her plate. It had a gamey smell, what could it be?

'Partridge,' said Tulliver, with his mouth full. 'Watch out for lead shot.'

Lead shot? Oliver had taken Polly out to restaurants in London, which had considerably widened her knowledge of food, but being asked to eat a bird with lead pellets in it was a new experience. She rolled every mouthful carefully round her mouth before biting, encountered nothing untoward, but was still thankful when the plate was removed, and pink slices of lamb arrived. Pink? Polly was used to roast mutton or to lamb chops; although neither formed a regular part of her diet when she was cooking for herself, it was the kind of food that Roger enjoyed. But pink?

306

'Lamb's eaten underdone in France,' Tulliver said. 'Try it, you'll like it.'

Polly didn't, and she managed to hide what was left on her plate under the heavy silver knife and fork.

The next course was a green water ice. Polly blinked. This meal was turning out to be like something out of *Alice in Wonderland*, did Oliver's family eat like this every evening?

'Seven courses if it's a big do,' Tulliver said, seeing her expression. 'Five tonight, since we're quite an informal gathering.'

Polly made up her mind that she would never sit down to dine with the Fraddons on any formal occasion, not if she could help it. She gingerly spooned a small scoop of the ice into her mouth, and found it tasted surprisingly good.

'Basil,' said Tulliver. 'It clears the palate.'

Cheese was handed round, soft creamy cheeses, some of them with a very strong smell; thank goodness, the meal must be almost at an end. But no, the ice was not, as she had supposed, a pudding, for here was a slice of tart laid in front of her, a mercifully small slice, with glazed fruit shining up at her. Berries, black and red, beautifully arranged. She had to appreciate the artistry of whoever did the cooking, which was intended to please the eye as well as the taste buds. People spoke of cooking as an art, and she could see why.

Finally, the meal was at an end. Polly looked at her wristwatch, her plain, schoolgirl's watch, which was the only one she had ever possessed; she had noticed the diamond-studded one on Daphne's wrist, and the slim gold one round Katriona's slender wrist.

Miss Saxe, she noticed as she went out, was wearing a man's watch, and Mrs Elgin didn't have one on at all. It was past eleven, Polly's eyelids were drooping, and she felt extremely full.

The men rose to their feet as Katriona led the mere females out; how barbaric how old-fashioned, Polly muttered, with all the indignation her sleepy self could manage.

Coffee was waiting in the drawing room. Polly refused the petits fours and chocolates. Luscious though they looked, she couldn't eat another thing. She stood by the deep window, where the curtains were drawn back to give a view of the sea, now a glimmer of shifting water and flecks of whiteness as waves broke gently against the rocks below. She shivered.

Maud Elgin came to stand beside her. 'Ominous, the sea at night, isn't it? Huge and dark and restless, as though it's waiting to gobble you up. I quite like the sound of the waves, though I'm not sure I would want to hear the sound of them all night long. Fraddon says it soothes him to sleep, his bedroom is above here, you know.'

'Is the sea dangerous around here?'

'The sea is always dangerous,' said Miss Saxe, who'd come over to join them. Katriona and Daphne were deep in conversation in the corner. 'There's a small private beach on the other side, very pleasant in the summer for bathing.'

Polly had little experience of the sea. She had gone once on holiday to Clacton, before the war; after Ted Smith died, there had been little money for holidays, and a day trip to Brighton with some artist friends had been her only other experience of the seaside. She yawned, unable to help herself, earning another contemptuous look from Katriona.

'You'd better slip off to bed,' said Miss Saxe. 'You look all in, didn't you sleep on the train?'

'Not much,' said Polly.

Miss Saxe took matters into her own hands, going up to Katriona, and saying in a firm voice. 'Miss Smith is going to bed, she's exhausted, poor girl.'

'Of course,' said Katriona, returning to her conversation with Daphne. At least Daphne had the grace to wish her goodnight with a wave of her hand, and with Jo's assurances that she'd say everything that was necessary to Lord Fraddon and Oliver, Polly escaped.

To lie in her strange Roman bed, with the sound of the sea in her ears, looking back over a twenty-four hours that seemed to have lasted for days. The final image in her mind before she slipped into a deep sleep was the brilliant, vivacious, wilful face of the woman in the Cortoni painting.

THIRTY-FIVE

Ivo was an early riser, whether in France or in America, the two countries in which he spent most of his year. It was his habit, as soon as the first fragile light of dawn appeared in the sky, to open his eyes, immediately wide awake, and ten seconds later, he would roll out of bed, go over to the window, fling it open it and throw back the shutters. This morning, he stood by the window for a few moments, breathing in deeply and letting out the breaths with a shuddering ah-ah-ah sound, which startled a sleepy pigeon above his head into almost falling off its perch under the eaves.

After that, standing in front of the open window, he carried out a series of physical jerks, with a smooth, practised ease that showed how familiar they were to his body.

He had done the exercises for years, it was a system entirely personal to him, devised in the cramped and appalling conditions of the trenches in France in the war, and developed further in the unpleasant conditions of a German prisoner of war camp.

Next, he stripped and washed himself from top to toe using the jug of cold water he had brought up the night before to the attic where he slept. That was an essential part of his routine, washing away symbolically the wastes of the night, cleansing his dreams and chasing the phantasmagoria back into the shadows.

Then it was on with a pair of shabby corduroy trousers, held up with a tie instead of a belt looped round his waist. A shirt, frayed at cuffs and collar, and a Fair Isle sweater with faded, loopy threads completed his outfit.

He didn't bother with socks, despite his lean and lanky frame, he was more or less impervious to cold, and he just thrust his feet into an ancient pair of Oxford brogues. He scooped coffee into an old Italian coffee-maker and placed it on the stove, a temperamental black affair, with a long black pipe leading from it up to the roof and into the chimney.

His rooms, a tiny bedroom and a spacious studio, were on the top floor of the baker's house. He went down the narrow stairs to the next floor, where Tulliver Penn had a large room; he would still be asleep two hours from now, not being inclined to rise with the lark. From there an outside staircase led down to the inside courtyard of the baker's shop, and he bounded down the stone steps with the speed of familiarity. He went into the back of the shop, where the ovens were still warm from the morning's baking. Lucille, plump cheeks rosy from the heat, handed over a *pain au chocolat*, still warm. Back upstairs, where the coffee was ready; the timing was perfect, as it was every morning. He liked routine, saying it put him in the right frame of mind for his day's work.

Tulliver frequently pointed out that Ivo could have a baguette for the cost of a *pain au chocolat*, but since Ivo liked chocolate, liked the rich pastry, and furthermore knew that if he had a baguette, quite apart from having to bother himself with buying and keeping butter and jam, he would end up sharing it with Tulliver. Who could damn well get his own breakfast.

311

It took Ivo precisely ten minutes to eat his breakfast and drink his inky coffee. He used a painting rag as a plate, and when he had finished, flapped the crumbs out of the window. Then he picked up the faded khaki bag which held his painting equipment and, with an easel in his other hand, went back down the steps and out into the square.

He looked afresh at the pollarded trees that formed an edge to the neat rectangle of the sandy square; the light on them was always different, at this time of the year, with only a few leaves clinging disconsolately to the branches, the interest was in the bark and the shapes of the trees. He glanced at the gates of Le Béjaune. He had heard people arriving late last night, which meant no more roaming in the grounds until they left. Which he regretted; he'd done some good painting there, making himself free of the house and gardens all through a mellow late summer, while the gates were left open by the builders and decorators who were working while the owners were away in England.

He had strolled into the house one August day, and the workmen had looked at him, nodded, called out friendly *bonjours*, and when he installed himself and his easel on the terrace, facing the olives and the sea, had shrugged and left him alone. What harm was he doing? Artists were different, and he was English, the owners of the house were English, let them look after their property and possessions for themselves, they could have words with the intense painter who spoke such excellent French if they felt so inclined. Besides, he was happy to lend a hand if asked, holding a ladder, helping to carry stones and beams.

The workmen gossiped about the owners of the house. Monsieur Johnson wasn't acquainted with them? He had arrived in Rodoard after the family had departed for

England. They were heathens, heretics, there had been a divorce. Not that monsieur and madame quarrelled, one of them added regretfully. They weren't like a married couple at all. Very polite to one another, no angry words, no signs of anything being thrown, no slammed doors, no telltale tears on madame's face. But that boded ill. A marriage might flourish on heat, raised tempers, rows, but never on courteous indifference. Jules, the plasterer, knew at first hand about the politeness and the indifference, for his affianced, Anna, had worked for the family. She had been greatly upset when the news became known in Rodoard that the marriage was at an end. Monsieur and madame had gone home after their last visit, with their daughter – a very English type, but *très jeune fille* – seemingly perfectly in harmony with one another. But then word had got around, lawyers had been involved, said Martin, whose cousin, rising in the world, worked as a clerk for the *notaire*. No, even after the break it was all civility, no complications, no contesting of ownership, just an assignment of the property to madame's name.

Monsieur had, it was said, gone to Africa, to shoot lions. Doubtless he would be eaten, in which case, the couple need not have gone through the disgrace of a divorce, for madame would be a widow, which was far more respectable and much cheaper.

At this all the men nodded their heads in agreement, except for young Pierre, who was a socialist and held advanced views about bourgeois institutions. 'If there were no marriages, then none of this would arise. And no one should own property, why should madame own this house, a single woman with a daughter? Such a house could provide a home for five poor families.'

The others were used to Pierre and his wild ideas. 'Tell your uncle that,' suggested Jules. 'The one who lives in that house with five bedrooms and all those hectares of good land, tell him he should hand it over to the poor.'

Pierre said they would see, that the world was changing.

'And not for the better,' said Martin, cramming a disreputable beret on his head as a signal that it was time to break for a long and leisurely lunch.

Ivo had lunched off fresh bread and a chunk of garlic sausage, keen to finish the sketch he'd made of Pierre, a drawing which proved very useful in his next canvas when he needed a tense figure of a young man watching his girl approaching along by the river.

On fine mornings he usually worked out of doors; that was his time for sketching and improvising and painting quick scenes for future use. Then it was back to his studio, where, to the accompaniment of the desultory patterings of Tulliver's typewriter from downstairs, he worked on his meticulous canvases, with books, photographs and his own sketches spread open beside him. He worked fast, with the expertise of years of practice layered on top of huge native skill.

He kept working hours, long hours, and then, on Saturday afternoons and Sundays, he painted for himself, the figurative paintings that were all anyone ever saw of his work, which were considered by all the artistic members of his little community to be old-fashioned, representational and therefore banal and without merit.

This morning, after a satisfactory couple of hours sitting by the fountain, drawing the women doing their washing, he went back to his studio to pick up a new sketchbook. He decided he would go up the hill for the rest of the morning, he liked working in the little square by the church, where he could sit on the stone bench attached to the church. It was a pleasant spot, warm and sheltered and full of light, and he hadn't been up there since he'd got back from America. He might even bump into *Père* Joubert, the village priest, who knew nothing about art, and so could be allowed to see and admire whatever he was working on.

THIRTY-SIX

The sound of the sea had echoed in her ears as she fell asleep, and now, as Polly stirred into wakefulness, the resonance of the waves was the first thing she noticed. The room was dim, with tiny patterns of sunlight on the ceiling, filtered through the closed shutters.

She had fallen asleep the minute she turned the light out, and hadn't, judging by a cramped arm, stirred all night. She sat up abruptly, as a knock sounded at the door. It opened and Marie came in, carrying a tray with little legs, which she set down on Polly's knees.

Breakfast in bed? Was that normal? She reached out for her watch, as Marie opened the shutters, letting sunlight flood in. Ten o'clock! Good heavens, how awful, she must have missed breakfast, and so they'd had to send it up.

However, Marie seemed in a more amiable mood this morning, she almost had a smile on her face as she wished Polly *bon appétit* before going into the bathroom. Polly watched her with alarm as she came back, the dress and her underwear from the night before over her arm, but before Polly could protest, she was gone, the door closing with a click behind her.

Polly hitched the pillows behind her. Oh well, she couldn't remonstrate with her, she didn't have the French, and besides, the coffee smelt so enticing, and there were some more of those mouth-wateringly good rolls and croissants. A pot of jam, another one of honey. How could she possibly be hungry after eating such an enormous meal the night before? She found she was, even scraping the last of the jam on to the last piece of a roll.

She pushed the tray to the end of the bed, and thrust the covers back, wanting to go and stand at the window and absorb all that light and make sure that the sky was still that extraordinary blue. She craned round to look at the sea, and then the other way, where the craggy hill towered above the house. A path wound its way up, and two riders were coming down it, the horses' hooves making a gentle clip-clop on the dry track. Oliver and Katriona. How assured they looked, on their glossy brown horses. Katriona was in jodhpurs and a tweed jacket, with a silk scarf tied under her chin. Oliver wore breeches and long brown boots, and the inevitable wide-brimmed hat.

They belonged here, well, of course they did, it was their home, or one of their homes, but there was more to it than that. They took all this for granted, it was how people of their sort lived, to them the substantial meals, the luxury of the house, the groomed horses, the well-cut clothes, just right for whatever activity or idleness they might be under-taking, were perfectly normal, everyday, taken absolutely for granted.

It was another world. Polly drew back from the window, not wanting to be seen. And one in which she didn't have a place, what was she doing here in this house that looked as though it belonged on a film set. Extravagant, she told herself. Bordering on the vulgar, scholarship or no scholarship. Just because the Romans went in for exuberant excess didn't mean

317

you needed to reproduce it two thousand years later on and expect people to like it.

Her suitcase had vanished. Which probably meant that Marie had unpacked it. In which case, her clothes, that odd collection of the shabby and the theatrical, would be hanging up outside the bathroom, where they would make a poor show in an area that was doubtless meant to accommodate the garments of more suitable guests, who would arrive with outfits for every occasion, from tennis, golf and riding to morning frocks, tea gowns, cocktail dresses, and numerous *toilettes* for the evening. Not to mention furs, wraps, shoes, handbags and silk underwear.

She was going to put on one of her shapeless skirts, teamed with a threadbare jumper, and if the Fraddons didn't like it, they could lump it. Katriona could raise scornful, incredulous eyebrows, she, Polly Smith—

That deflated her defiant mood. She, Polyhymnia Tomkins – no, it didn't sound right at all. It made no difference. As Smith or Tomkins, she couldn't stay here. It was impossible, a huge mistake, she had no business to be here. And where was she supposed to work? She couldn't lay out her paints and materials here in this neat-as-a-pin bedroom. She'd told Oliver she'd need to bring work with her, and he'd said, 'Oh, of course, if you want to,' as though he were surprised.

Decision time: another shower, or a bath? While she was here, she might as well sample the perfumed contents of the jars ranged beside the bathtub. She opened one and sniffed. It smelt of pine trees, and she tipped some into the bath. Another jar held crystals with a chestnutty tang, and she recklessly tipped some under the tap, and watched the water foam in a most inviting way.

Baths to Polly hadn't hitherto been any kind of an indulgence to either body or spirit. Bath time in Highgate was a complicated affair, involving the stoking up of the fire, the coaxing of the geyser, and then sitting on the slightly scratchy surface of the small bath as the water cooled rapidly in the unheated bathroom. And in Fitzroy Street, baths were regulated, one a week, with advance permission from Mrs Horton, grudgingly given, and with a strict time limit; ten minutes after the bolt was drawn on the bathroom door, Mrs Horton would be banging on the door, crying in lugubrious tones, 'Time's up'.

Polly lay in the huge bath, swirling her hands in the pale green water, and topping up with hot water, adjusting the tap with her toes. She was in limbo, out of time, out of place, perhaps she would come out to find everything had changed behind the bathroom door, the Roman house nothing but a dream, and the click-clack of Mrs Horton's heels to bring her back to earth with a bump.

She sat up and soaped herself. Reality nothing. Mrs Horton was a dreadful woman, but simply not in the same league as Katriona. Then she chided herself for ingratitude, for taking such a dislike to Oliver's sister. Oliver couldn't help having an unpleasant sister, he couldn't be held responsible for her unwelcoming, unmannerly ways. Out of kindness, he'd wanted her to have a treat, to get away from the melancholy madness that came over her on grey London days, and it was up to her to enjoy herself.

She was grateful, how could she not be? The light here at Rodoard was wonderful, a tonic in itself, the sea and the mountains were breathtaking. It was simply that she didn't fit in here, not for a day nor a week, let alone a month.

Yet, infuriatingly, her fingers itched to paint, with an intensity she hadn't felt for months. For more than a year, even longer. Only, if she were to stick it out, where could she work? Oliver, for all his knowledge and understanding of art, had no real idea of how an artist was seized by the urge to work, the intense pressure that built up and made the hours fly by.

She made her bed, and then stood looking at it in sudden doubt. Should she have left it for the maid, should she pull it all back, pretend she hadn't done anything to it but climb out and leave it for the servants to see to?

Too late, here was Marie, come for the tray, looking at the bed and saying something in rapid French that didn't sound at all pleased. She shook her head, and with tutting noises, swept the sheets and blankets completely off the bed, and bundled them in her arms before going to the window to shake them out and hang them over the windowsill.

Polly fled, but she hadn't reached the bottom of the stairs when she heard Katriona's knowing voice float down from the gallery, calling out to Oliver, 'Look what that ridiculous child has been up to, making her own bed, Marie told me, honestly, she's nothing but an embarrassment.'

Polly jumped down the last few steps, eager to get out of earshot. She skidded round a corner into the atrium and ran full tilt into Lord Fraddon.

'Is there a fire, an emergency of some kind?' he said.

Polly wanted to let fly at him, to tell him what a horrible place this house was, and how he should be ashamed of having a daughter with such a tongue on her, she might be a scrubby little suburban, but where she came from, no one would ever have treated or spoken about a guest the way Katriona did.

'You've been at the receiving end of some of Katriona's uncharitable remarks, I dare say,' he went on. 'Pay no attention, I never do. Do you like paintings? Of course you do, you're an artist. Come and look at my pictures, that will soothe your shattered nerves, great art has that effect, don't you find?'

And like a dog trailing along behind its master, Polly found herself walking behind Lord Fraddon. He opened a door and stood back to let her through, but she stood on the threshold, holding her breath, blinking at the beautiful room and, as her eyes caught first one and then another canvas, dazzled by the paintings.

'A Renoir,' she said, bounding up to a painting of a Parisian in a striped dress and a hat, all set for a day of delight. 'And this is a Cézanne, I don't believe it, and a Monet, one of his London paintings, one of the really good ones, and here's his garden. I love the Impressionists,' she said, turning impulsively to Lord Fraddon. 'I know people sneer at them, but when you stand in front of one, it's as though the world is twice as alive.'

She moved across to look at a painting of a bridge over a river, made up of hundreds of coloured dots, and then went back from the canvas, a step at a time, her head on one side.

'You're like a child in a sweet shop,' said Lord Fraddon.

'Pointillist,' said Polly, standing back and narrowing her eyes. 'Is it a Seurat?'

'It is. And if you care to go over there, you'll find some Post-impressionists, and several nice paintings by contemporary artists. Are you an admirer of Picasso?'

'I'm not sure I understand Cubism, which is a dreadful thing to say, but . . . Oh!'

She moved swiftly over to the far wall, where three paintings hung side by side, long panels of the same riverside scene, painted at different times of day. 'Corot.' She stood and looked in silence, then gave a deep sigh.

Lord Fraddon came to stand beside her, and side by side, they looked at the three paintings. 'These are my favourites,' he said. 'I stand and look at them every day, and they are never the same, and I never grasp all that's within them.'

How could one man own all these? 'What a collection!'

'It's one I've built up over many years. I brought some of them from England, others I bought here or from the artists themselves.'

How extraordinary to be that rich, to live like this, to have the money to buy paintings like these. No wonder Oliver knew so much about art and had such an eye.

'Why are you looking at me like that?' said Polly, suddenly wary. 'Have I got a smudge on my nose?'

'Not at all. It's just that, for a moment, you reminded me of someone I once knew. I can't think why, for now I look at you, you're not at all the same. I'm glad to see you looking less distressed. Do come in here whenever you like and look at my pictures. You're thinking, how can a man possess all this? I dare say you've never had much money, and you can't imagine what it would be like to be able to buy such paintings. Only you wouldn't want to, and you have something that I don't have, and which is to be envied.'

'Me?' Was he going to say your youth? Was he no more than an elderly lecher, charmed by a young woman?

'As a young man, I wanted to be a painter. Or an artist of some kind. However, although I have various gifts, an eye for a painting, an ear for music, the ability to turn a neat phrase on the page, I have no artistic ability. So you can console yourself that although I am rich and you are poor, you have something that money can't buy.'

All very well, but an artistic nature didn't put food on the table, and starving for one's art in a garret wasn't much fun after a while. Especially when one had honestly no idea if one were ever going to produce anything worthwhile, anything that someone would stand in front of and say, 'Now I understand, now I am aware in a way I wasn't before'.

'Don't let Katriona get you down, by the way,' Lord Fraddon was saying. 'She is the antithesis of you, being rich and discontented, and she lives shut off from the things that nourish the spirit.'

In the distance a telephone bell shrilled. 'That will be for me,' he said. 'If you will excuse me.'

'I was going to go out, for a walk. If that's all right. In the gardens.'

'Wherever you like.' And he walked away, leaving Polly with an image forming in her mind, of Lord Fraddon in a toga, and taking out her pen and notebook, she propped herself against a handy pillar and did a lightning portrayal of a senatorial baron, beaky nose held high.

THIRTY-SEVEN

Miss Saxe and Mrs Elgin had told Polly that they lived in Lord Fraddon's stables. Not, she supposed, literally in a stable, as in a loosebox on hay, but in a part of the stables that had been made habitable. Or in the groom's quarters, that would be typical, artists squeezed into the dark space reserved for the lowlife of the household in previous times.

She turned these revolutionary thoughts over in her mind as her feet took her in the direction that Oliver and Katriona had been heading when they returned from their ride. They must have been coming back; remembering the slight lather on the horses' necks, she concluded that they had been out for a gallop or at the least a brisk canter, and were returning to the stable at a slow pace, as was right.

Polly knew something about horses because as a girl, she had loved drawing them. She had worked on Saturday afternoons at a local livery stable, mucking out and cleaning harness, and when that work was done, and she was very glad of the money, little though it was, she would stay on and draw the horses and ponies, and the people who worked in the yard. Jimmy with his bowed legs who looked as though he had been born on the back of a horse, was one of her favourites. He had been a jockey before he broke one of his bent legs.

'I missed the racing, course I did,' he confided to Polly. 'But as long as I'm with horses, I'm a happy man. They're on the way out now, what with everyone having cars and tractors on the farm, but I'll end my days among horses, and if the good Lord is half what the parson says, I'll meet up with some of my old friends when I get to heaven. Stands to reason, it wouldn't be heaven without it had horses in it, now would it? You've not got Thunder's eyes right, you've made them look like he's thinking of nothing, which isn't the case, for he's a clever hoss, that one, always got something going through his head. No point in getting all those muscles and things right if you can't see through his eyes into what's going on in his head.'

Which was probably as profound and valuable an insight into the work of a painter, a portrait painter, at least, as Polly had ever been given, and she never forgot it, always telling herself when she painted people, or, indeed, animals, that the eyes were the windows of the soul, or at least the mind, and blank eyes meant a blank portrait.

Sure enough, there was a clock tower over an arch, which must lead into a stable yard. Which it did. It wasn't, Polly noticed with some thankfulness, a Roman stable yard, just a traditional quadrangle with a well in the centre, and stabling and offices set round it. All along one side, the stables were still used for their original purpose; an equine head looked over a half-door, regarding her in that inquisitive way of horses, wisps of hay dangling from his soft mouth.

A window opened above her, and a voice called down. 'Hooray, a visitor. It's Polly Smith,' she called back over her shoulder. 'Come in, the door's open, just give it a push.'

Polly did so, to find herself greeted with enthusiasm, and instructions to drop the Miss and Mrs. 'Then we can call you Polly.'

A clever conversion of looseboxes and the loft above had made a tiny cottage with a good-sized studio downstairs. 'The looseboxes are our studio, do you see?' Jo told her, as she and Maud showed Polly round. 'There's a bedroom in the old harness room, there are so few horses now, they don't need much room for the saddles and so on, so they use one of the stables on the other side. Upstairs, we have a little bathroom, you can sit in the bath and look out over the hills and if you take your bath back to front, then you can look out over the Med. And a spare room. Come and look.'

Polly climbed up the wooden ladder-like steps to the loft, and admired the tiny bathroom and the other room, bare, except for a table and chair, full of light, with wide polished floorboards. She peered out of the window that overlooked the stable yard. 'Were the stables built at the same time as the house? It seems so mellow, in comparison. And not at all Roman.'

'No,' said Jo. She pointed across to the roof on the other side. 'Look at those lovely old tiles. That was the original house, the one that was here when Lady Fraddon, that's Fraddon's mother, bought the land. She turned the old house into the stable and built her Roman extravaganza close to the sea. They made a good job of it, adding the other two sides in much the same style.'

Polly drew her head back in. 'It seems odd, to turn a house into stables, instead of the other way round.'

'Yes, but I expect it was the kind of house where the family lived on the first floor, with the animals below, so it wouldn't have been so much of a change. I believe it was virtually derelict back then, don't be imagining hard-working people turned out of their home for the aristocrats to build their follies. Maud, how about coffee for our visitor?'

Maud, who had stayed downstairs, called up to say that she had already done so, it was poured out, and to shut the window upstairs before all the heat flew out.

In the corner downstairs was a handsome stove, emitting a gentle glow of warmth. 'Not really necessary when the sun shines, even in December,' said Jo, 'but it gets chilly at night, so we keep it going.'

Maud handed Polly her coffee, observing that she looked a different person this morning, 'I felt so sorry for you last night, dark rings under your eyes, and obviously bewildered. I adore Oliver, but he can be completely thoughtless.'

'Yes, Maud and I were saying this morning that it was extremely tactless of him to drag you here at this time of year, when he must have known Katriona would be putting in an appearance,' said Jo. 'What a tiresome woman she is. I suppose she's been going around saying in a loud voice "Where's Rory going to sleep?"'

'Rory,' said Polly, her heart sinking. 'Who's Rory?'

'Her son. He's a nice boy, very like Fraddon, so he'll turn out all right despite his mother, with any luck. He's at school in England.'

'Does he usually sleep in the room I'm in?'

'Haven't a clue,' said Jo.

'There's plenty of room,' said Maud. 'There are all the staff rooms, apart from the ones in the main part of the house.' Maud explained to Polly, 'Most of the staff come in daily, from the village.'

'Fraddon wouldn't let them put Polly in a staff bedroom,' said Jo.

'I wouldn't mind,' said Polly. 'I'm sure Katriona thinks of me as being of far less consequence than a parlour maid or a valet.' She put her cup down with a decisive thunk. 'Actually none of it arises, because I've realized this is all a disaster. I should never have come. I'm going to go back to England, right away.'

Cries of dismay and disapproval from Jo and Maud made her laugh. 'Honestly. I'm not running away, and it's not self-pity or anything like that. Oliver's very kind, and I should love to stay, I've never seen anything like the light here in all my life, and I should like to paint from morning till night, and that's not possible, unless I sit outside, there's nowhere that I can see that I can. Oliver doesn't really understand.'

'No, of course he doesn't. It wouldn't ever occur to him, Most of the artists he mingles with have their own studios, and he isn't very good on practical matters, like a painter needing space and the right light and somewhere to leave your stuff laid out the way you want.'

'To be fair, my jackets are so small-scale, I can almost do them on my knee, in a bedroom.'

'Nonsense,' said Jo.

'You can't possibly,' said Maud. 'Not if they're to be any good. I know writers work in extraordinary conditions, but they only need a pen and paper, or a typewriter they can put down anywhere.'

'You'd better come and work here,' said Jo.

'Just what I was going to say,' Maud said.

They looked at Polly with pleased faces. 'There's the room upstairs. Half empty, that's deliberate, because so many of our friends who come to stay want to work while they're here. Can you cook?'

Polly longed to say yes, but honesty compelled her to confess that she was an egg and sardine person. 'I could try.'

'I thought as much,' said Maud. 'Jo cooks lunch here, and if you've any sense you'll watch and learn from her. Think how useful it will be when you're married.'

'When I'm married?'

'That is an engagement ring you're wearing, isn't it? Didn't Oliver mention a doctor?'

'You won't be doing much painting if you marry a doctor,' Maud said, in a voice almost too low for Polly to hear.

'So you'll need to cook, and cooking, as you can tell from the meal last night, is an art in its own right. How's your French?'

Polly made a face. 'School French, that's all. Pretty hopeless, I can't understand what people are saying, so I can't even try to talk.'

'If you've got a smattering, then you can come shopping with us. Buying bread and talking to the locals will bring your fluency on in leaps and bounds. You never know when it'll come in handy. That's settled then. We'll go across and tell Fraddon, and you can bring your painting things over. You won't need an easel for book jackets, will you, although there is a spare one if you want to paint.'

'I'm not sure – Oliver's been so kind, and—'

'You don't want to seem rude, decamping to the stables,' said Jo, who had a leggy walk, which made it an effort for Polly to keep up with her. Maud managed it by proceeding in a series of skips and bounds and little runs, a frolicking artist, thought Polly, and then, I should like to paint her, just like that, in mid motion.

'Far ruder to ask to be taken to the station, unless you were planning to send yourself a telegram saying "Come at once, all is discovered",' said Maud, slightly breathless.

'Can't do it, not here, not with the Post Office at Rodoard a clearing house for all the local gossip, it would fly round that you had sent yourself a telegram, they would know it was a fake even before it arrived.'

'Is the village far from here?'

'You go to the top of the drive, along the road a little way, and then there's a track through the trees. A steepish pull going, and a stroll coming back. It's where we do our shopping, except on Saturdays when we go to the market at Beauvoir. And it's where we go in the evenings, if we aren't summoned by Fraddon,' Maud added.

'Quite a few kindred spirits there, you'll find,' said Jo. 'Get one artist or writer or musician in a place and the others come rolling along like ants to a nest. Tulliver, the man you met last night, he's got a room there. Shares a place with a young painter, a reclusive sort, called Ivo. We'll take you there with us one evening, and introduce you. You'll soon feel at home.'

Polly had a sense of an irresistible tide flowing through her life and tossing her up on unknown shores. She wanted to resist, to think about it, to consider if this was what she really wanted.

'What's to think about?' said Jo. 'You aren't shaking the dust of Oliver's home off your feet, you're just moving your work down the road. Thus removing yourself for many hours a day from the oppressive presence of Katriona, who will be annoyed, let me tell you.'

'Oh, God, will she? Why?'

'Deep down she's delighted you're here, because it gives her a perfect target for her fretful temper. If you're not there, what will she have to complain about?'

'Don't worry,' said Maud. 'She'll find something, when has she ever not?'

THIRTY-EIGHT

Cynthia woke early. She hadn't slept well since America, and her hopes that the clear air and tranquillity of the house at Rodoard would work its magic had so far not been fulfilled. She usually woke in the early hours and then drifted back into a troubled sleep filled with strange and meaningless but disturbing dreams. This morning she hadn't gone back to sleep, but waited until the first pale light of dawn showed pink and yellow in the eastern sky, when she got up. She ran a bath for herself, Rose would be up and about downstairs, but she didn't want to talk to her or to anyone else. She dressed quickly, putting on a woollen coat because the morning air was chilly.

These last few days had been astonishingly warm, but André, who looked after the garden and saw to all the logs for the fires, had been stacking up extra loads, shaking his grizzled head and prophesying much colder weather. He pointed to the mountain tops, purple and splendid, but with thin wisps of cloud gathering over the peaks. 'Snow,' he said. 'Which is natural on the mountains, they should have snow at this time of year. But now it will fall at lower levels, it will come down below the heights of the mountains, to us.'

Cynthia believed that cooler weather might be on the way; snow was surely an exaggeration. She had never known it to snow in the South of France.

She let herself out of the front door, walking swiftly away from the house and through the gates before any well-meaning member of the household could call out to her. Harriet was fast asleep, she had looked into her room and seen her stretched out under the blankets in the total relaxation and deep sleep of youth. She envied her daughter her ability to sleep; she knew Harriet wouldn't wake of her own accord until after midday, when she would emerge, yawning and dishevelled, exclaiming how hungry she was.

She paused in the square, then walked to the edge, to breathe in air so fresh that it made one's head tingle, and to look out to sea, across the tumbling greenery and roofs below. The beauty of the view, the distant headlands, the wheeling birds, the changing light of sea and sky restored her equilibrium, and she crossed the square, planning to walk up the steepest of the winding streets to the higher square where the old church stood. It was a favourite place of hers, sheltered in summer and winter, and with a special calm to it. She wanted to think, no, not to think, to reflect. The questions still ran round inside her head, to tell Walter, or not to tell him. Or pretend to herself she was imagining it, that the last sixteen or seventeen years of her life hadn't been based on falsehood and misunderstanding.

She had her foot on the shallow step at the bottom of the street when a door directly on the street opened, and a man came out. He didn't notice her, he had a canvas bag slung over one shoulder, and he swung it around against his back before calling back through the door to someone, in English, 'Tell madame I'll be round at eleven.' He shut the door with a slam and set off up the street.

Cynthia shrank back into a doorway. Just one good look

at his face, his beardless face, and now she knew for certain that it was him.

What was he doing here in Rodoard? Was he following her, hounding her footsteps? No, she didn't think so. It was just a terrible coincidence that had brought him, of all the places in France where he might be, to Rodoard. Life was like that, it played wicked tricks on you.

Knowing that he was alive and not dead was one thing. Knowing that he had travelled on the *Aquitania* from America and was in England was another. But for him to be here in France, on her doorstep – that was insupportable. He would see her, recognize her, she hadn't changed so very much, not in those ways that survived the superficial differences that age and fashion brought to a woman's appearance. Her voice, her walk, the turn of her head – the very things that had made him so recognizable were the same. A man changed more from sixteen to his thirties than a woman did.

She would leave Rodoard. This very day. She would get Max to take her to the station as soon as Rose could pack a suitcase. What excuse? What could she say? And what about Harriet?

It was a wild idea and it didn't linger in her mind. She was prone to behave as foolishly as any other person, she was often impulsive and impetuous, but she wasn't a coward, she wasn't the kind of person who ran away.

On the other hand, she didn't want to see him now, not face to face. He might come back down the street at any moment. She almost ran back across the square, through the gates and hurtled through the front door, closing it behind her.

'Good God, Cynthia, what's up?' said Max, coming into the hall. 'You look as though you'd seen a ghost.'

'Oh, Max,' she said. 'That's exactly what I have done, I've just seen a ghost.'

Max took her into the sunny room they used for breakfast room, sat her down, rang for coffee and toast, and pulled out another chair. 'Now, tell,' he said.

Cynthia looked at him with troubled eyes. 'Max, I'm in a pickle.'

'I can see that. Is it Malreward? Because if so—'

'No, no. It isn't Walter. Well, I suppose it is a bit, indirectly. It's such a mess, I don't know where I stand, legally or morally, and what on earth I can do about it.'

'Start at the beginning. If it's a legal question, we can send a telegraph to Jarvis this morning. As to morals, well, let's have a go. Is it to do with the divorce?'

'No. Yes. I don't know.'

'Right, let's try another tack. Who or what did you see when you went out this morning that's given you the heebie-jeebies?'

Cynthia took a deep breath. She could trust Max. If there was anyone in the world she could trust, it was Max. 'I saw Ronnie, Ronnie Jones.'

'Ronnie Jones?' Max shook his head. 'Sorry, old thing, the name doesn't mean anything to me.'

'You don't remember him, although you did see him once. It was during the war, when I was sixteen, and helping Helen and Mother with their voluntary work.'

'Serving tea to soldiers, yes, I remember that.'

'One of the soldiers was Ronnie Jones. You saw me with him, we were walking in St James's Park, and you came past.'

'A handsome boy, and I remember hoping Mother wouldn't catch you walking and talking in a comradely fashion with a mere private. So that was Ronnie Jones. I suppose you had an affair with him, is that it? Is he blackmailing you? Because after all this time, it might be a minor embarrassment, but hardly more than that. Unless you became – ah, is that the problem? Harriet?'

'You are quick on the uptake, but no, I didn't exactly have an affair with him. Max, I married him.'

Now she had really startled him. 'You what?'

'I married him.'

'When? How?'

'In a little church, by special licence. He was on embarkation leave, he went off two days later. And I never saw him again. A month later, I got a telegram from the War Office saying that he was missing, believed killed. I was pregnant, and I didn't know what to do.'

'You could have told me.' His voice was sharp, but it was the sharpness of regret, not of condemnation. 'Why didn't you, you know I would have helped?'

'Because you weren't there. You'd done one of your mysterious disappearances, and no one at your office would say where you were or when you'd be back.'

There had been several occasions during the war when Max had been away from his office, away from London, and more than once, out of the country. Secret work. If he remembered rightly, he'd been away that time for more than two months, under cover in France, with not much else in his head but keeping alive and reassembling his network of agents who had been nearly destroyed by one man's treachery.

'They finally told me that you'd gone abroad, I thought to America probably, although they wouldn't say. So I knew there was no point in hanging on for you to come back, and there was no one else to turn to. Can you imagine how Mummy would have lammed into me? And Daddy, too, his little daughter the widow of a common soldier, with a baby on the way?'

'And by the time I came back, you were married, perfectly respectably, to Geoffrey.'

'Bigamously married, as it happens.'

Max fell silent. He didn't like to think that Cynthia had

tricked Geoffrey. The Harkness family were neighbours of the Lyttons, and Geoffrey and Max were much of an age. They had gone to the village school and then on to the same private school, had played together in the holidays, and while they didn't in the end have much in common, Max counted Geoffrey among his friends.

'Don't look like that, Max,' Cynthia said, her chin going up. 'I know what you're thinking, and it wasn't like that at all. Geoffrey found me crying one day. A pal of Ronnie's had come to see me, bringing some of his things. He said that the "missing believed killed" didn't mean there was any hope Ronnie was still alive, he'd seen him go over the top, it was a massacre that day, everyone was shot to pieces. He could never have survived, and the missing bit simply meant they'd not found his body.'

'So you felt sure he was dead?'

'Oh, yes, and that was why I was crying. I did love him so much, Max, can you understand that? People think that sixteen is all adolescent crushes and passing fancies, but that isn't necessarily so. And Geoffrey was awfully sweet and kind, he is a kind man, you know. In the end I told him all about it. And he said the best thing was for us to get married. Which we did.'

'Did you tell him you were pregnant?'

'Of course I did! Honestly, Max, you do have a low opinion of me. Geoffrey didn't mind, and before you express disbelief, he really didn't mind because he'd had mumps very badly at school, which had led to orchitis, and I expect you know what the consequences of that can be, the doctors told him he would be most unlikely ever to be able to father a child. So he said that by marrying me he could be a father and that . . . well, he'd been keen on me for a long time.'

So Cynthia had been carrying this secret all these years, as had Geoffrey.

'You weren't in love with Geoffrey.'

'No. How could I be, aching with unhappiness over Ronnie? I thought I'd never fall in love with anyone again. And I don't think I have,' she added, but so quietly that Max knew the remark wasn't intended for his ears.

'Let's be practical. When you got the telegram and the visit from Ronnie's fellow soldier, you assumed that Ronnie was dead, and therefore you were a widow and free to marry again.'

'Yes.'

'Did you hear from the War Office again?'

'Geoffrey went and saw someone there. The procedure was that if there was no more news of Ronnie, after a period of time I could make an application to have him declared dead, so that I would then legally be a widow and entitled to a widow's pension and all that.'

'You didn't want to do that?'

'You know I didn't. There wasn't time, not with Harriet on the way. Either I told the truth, announced I was Mrs Jones and that the baby was Ronnie's or I just pretended the marriage had never happened. You'd have helped me, if you could, but you couldn't support me and a child for years and years. I knew that Mummy and Daddy wouldn't. you know how ruthless Daddy is about class and all that. It would have been out into the snow with my bundle, almost. Or they would have made me give the baby up for adoption, and I couldn't have done that.'

'Who were the witnesses at the wedding?'

'Ronnie's best friend. He went back to the front and was killed himself, later that year, I saw his name in the casualty lists. The other witness was a complete stranger we pulled in off the street.'

'And the vicar who conducted the ceremony?'

'He died, too. He was young and he became a military

337

chaplain and was killed in a bombing raid in Egypt. I know because I went back to the church at the end of the war, I wanted to remind myself of Ronnie, it was a special place for us, where we were married. I spoke to the man who was vicar then, and he told me what had happened to his predecessor.'

'So no one knew of the marriage. Didn't Ronnie have any relatives?'

'None that he was in touch with. He ran away from home when he was fourteen. His father drank and his mother beat him up until he got too big for her to manage it. She hated his being good at art. She said it was effeminate, and she'd break all his fingers if he kept on with his drawing. That's when he ran away.' A sudden awareness came into her face. 'Of course! That's why he's here in Rodoard. It's nothing to do with me, it's simply that he probably is an artist, and this place is a favourite spot for artists.'

'So you were married to Geoffrey with both of you quite sure it was OK. You married in church. "Voice that breathed o'er Eden", everything right and tight.'

'So I thought.'

'And Harriet was born eight months later, which raised a few eyebrows and accounted, people would have said, for your marrying so young. However, even Mother and Father wouldn't make a fuss about that.'

'They washed their hands of me when I got married, as you very well know,' said Cynthia. 'They'd always considered me difficult, and since I hadn't made a brilliant match like Helen, I wasn't of any interest to them any more. If Harriet had been a grandson I suppose Daddy might have wanted to interfere, but he wouldn't bother about a girl. Lucky for Harriet,' she added, managing a smile.

'There are several unanswered questions,' pointed out Max.

'Yes, such as why, if Ronnie survived the war after all, he didn't come and find me.'

'Where's he been all these years? Why has he reappeared now? Does he know who you are?'

'And do I make a clean breast of it to Walter? Because it's going to have to be lawyers, isn't it? Does Ronnie being still alive mean that I'm still married to him? I can't marry Walter until I know how things stand, but I'm afraid he'll take it badly, or set about sorting it out himself, which I really don't want.'

'No,' said Max, with a fleeting sympathy for the unknown Ronnie if he fell foul of Walter Malreward; from what Lazarus had told him, it wasn't wise to get in Sir Walter's way.

'Let's be sure of one thing,' he went on. 'You are certain that this man you've seen – what, three, four times? – is Ronnie? Not his double or his twin brother?'

'Ronnie didn't have a brother. At least, he had an older brother, who died when he was six. Apart from that, he had three older sisters. No, it's Ronnie, I'm sure of it. I knew it was the moment I saw him, that first time when he was going aboard the *Aquitania* in New York. I saw him again disembarking at Southampton, and yes, however much I told myself I was wrong, I was deceiving myself. This morning, I saw him close to, and heard him speak. It's Ronnie. He has a slight American accent, he may have been living in America all this time, but I'd know his voice anywhere.'

No wonder Cynthia had been looking distrait since she came back from America. She'd been through a divorce to a man she had never been legally married to, and now didn't know whether she was free to marry again or not. Presumably not, if she had a husband living. What if he had married again? Why hadn't he come back to her after the war?

'Did Ronnie know you were pregnant?'

'I assume so. When I got his stuff back, the letter was there, opened.' She hid her face in her hands. 'That's where

339

Harriet gets her eyes from, her dazzling blue eyes. Ronnie's eyes,' she said in a muffled voice.

'And stunning they are, too. That's nothing to cry about.'

'I'll have to tell her.'

'Yes, you probably will, and you may be surprised by how well she takes it. She'll probably think it's all terribly romantic.'

'I was so angry with her over the nightclub, out of all proportion to the offence. She became quite distraught, and kept saying, "Mummy, it was only a nightclub, and with Archie and Uncle Max and you and Walter all watching me like hawks, what harm could I come to?" How could I explain that I don't want her to take the step I did at her age. I don't regret it, how could I regret Harriet, but all those years of being married to Geoffrey . . . It closed so many doors.'

'This wouldn't be half so difficult if you weren't about to marry Walter, would it?'

'Of course it wouldn't. Only I am, and I've had to put him off, and he hates to be thwarted. He had it all planned, you see. The Ritz, friends, flowers, food. Oh, God, Max, I'm so damn fed up with it all. That's why I came here, to my house, rather than go to the Villa Trophie. You've never been there, you'd hate it, it's the last word in luxury and opulence.'

'Sounds vulgar.'

'It is vulgar. Walter's vulgar, beneath the English gent he's a Turk, fascinated by opulence and subtle power. That's what makes him so attractive, most men seem half alive in comparison to him. You don't understand. You don't like him. No, don't deny it, don't lie, Max. I can tell you dislike and mistrust him. It's my life, not yours, no one is asking you to marry Walter. I want to marry him, and I'm going to. He's exciting, the life he leads is exciting, and I long for some excitement in my life.'

Max got up and went over to the window. Excitement!

Little did Cynthia know. And how could he warn her? She'd just scoff, say he'd made it up to stop her marrying Malreward.

By keeping his professional life secret all these years, even from Cynthia, he had lost any authority his work might have given him. He appeared to be no more than a well-bred, well-off idler, how the hell could he persuade her that he knew what he was talking about, and that his lack of enthusiasm for her marriage to Walter was founded on more than mere dislike?

THIRTY-NINE

'What makes the light so bright?' said Polly. 'I know it's much further south here than England, but it's extraordinary how clear it is.'

'I believe it's to do with the mountains and the sea,' said Maud. She was sitting at a table at one end of the stable studio, with a slanted drawing board in front of her, using a fine sable brush and painting with deft, delicate strokes. Polly was sitting at the window, drawing Maud at her work, while Jo, who had been doing something noisy with a hammer, had paused from her labours to brew coffee.

Polly was radiantly alive and happy. The light and colours filtered through her bones, and she responded to the warmth like a contented cat, for with a cloudless blue sky and not a hint of wind, the sun was astonishingly warm. From the window she could see a wall with fronds of greenery hanging down, pricked with white starry flowers.

'Jasmine,' Maud told her. 'And when the flowers are all out, the scent is intense. The patches of purple are bougainvillea, flowering far too early, that's because it's been amazingly mild.'

It was as warm as most summer days in England. No drizzle in these parts, Maud, a weather watcher, had told

Polly. Torrential rain, more rain on this part of the coast than in London, incredibly enough, but it came in downpours, and in the summer everything was parched and dry before it came back to green life with the autumn rain. 'Which leaves the sky even clearer, washed and pure and brilliant.'

Polly put down her charcoal and stretched. Her fingers were tingling with the pleasure of drawing, and the colours she would use when it came to painting were dancing in her head.

She slipped down from her perch on the windowsill. 'May I see?' she said to Maud, who pushed a strand of hair behind her ears and sat back so that Polly could have a look.

'Fairies,' she said, adding a touch of purple to a pointed hat. 'Fairies and more fairies. I sometimes think if I paint another fairy, I'll scream, but then I think of the next meal and somehow, the beat of their little fairy wings and their tinkling laughter doesn't seem so bad after all.'

'They are exquisite, though,' Polly said, genuine admiration in her voice at the delicate, intricate tracery of figures entwined with leaves and bells. 'Rather Arthur Rackham, but less macabre.'

'Fairy stories sell, and aunts and uncles and godparents love to give illustrated fairy stories to the kiddies,' said Maud. 'So macabre isn't such a good idea. It's a shame that the stories themselves are usually nauseating, but I did do some pictures for a really good collection last year, which had goblins and evil elves and mischievous sprites as well as winged fairies, which was fun. I get ghosts to do as well from time to time. I have fits when I long to go in for a touch of Jo's stuff, but it isn't my style. Before I came to France, I mostly did fashion sketches for the newspapers, and those were even less interesting than fairies.'

Jo had her working place at the other end of the studio. She was busy with what looked like a scrubbed table top, with the wood scraped away to expose the grain and roughness of the surface. Upon it, she was constructing an extraordinary three-dimensional landscape of brick and stone, pieces of broken shells, a rusty hook, and an implement Polly couldn't identify, folded sacking, slats of wood nailed in at odd angles.

Jo explained about the school of Neo-solidism. 'We're very advanced. The original Solidists were simply anti anything manufactured. Nothing after about 1890 was any good, and they hated Art Deco, so contrived, so made, so decadent, and I do agree with them. Only they worked on a human scale, and I see mankind overwhelmed by the structures that surround us. So these matchstick figures' – she pointed to some spindly creatures – 'show the scale of our existence.'

Maud was proud of Jo's work. 'It's important,' she told Polly. 'My illustrations sell all right, but it's decorative art, it doesn't make any kind of a statement, they're mere pretty pictures.'

Solidism was new to Polly, and at heart she was a figurative painter.

'Figurative art is finished, or at least in its death throes, thank goodness. That's not where the excitement and the new work is,' Jo said. 'Of course, one can't force oneself into a different style so easily, but one must strive to be original. Figurative stuff is purely derivative, art can only be art when it breaks out of the bonds of all those centuries of representation and dead tradition. Art must be existentialist, it needs to be about the profound pointlessness and negativism of human existence.'

Polly looked out of the window at the deep and varied colours of the yard and hills beyond. 'I like Dufy's work.'

'Oh, Dufy! He sells, of course, people like him, but there's no depth, no message, no meaning to his work. I used to paint landscapes, when I lived and worked in Cornwall. It was sterile, however, and when I came here and saw what the Solidists had been doing, I realized just where I had to go.'

'I've never been to Cornwall,' said Polly. She took the coffee that Jo was holding out for her, delicate cup with a light-as-a-feather biscuit in the saucer. She would have expected a mug and a chunk of carrot cake; it showed that one could never make assumptions about people.

'Maud insists on fine china,' Jo said. 'I made the biscuits, I love cooking.' And the two women exchanged smiles so full of affection that Polly felt for a moment excluded. Their relationship was far more than friendship. More of a marriage than most people had, however much people might condemn their partnership as unnatural.

Could she live with another artist? How would she feel if Roger were a painter or a sculptor, could she share a studio with him, how would it be to move in the same circle, not be the other half of a couple one of whom dwelt in the wholly different world of hospitals and medicine?

She knew a gifted cellist who had married a concert pianist. The price of that love had been for Jean to give up her career as a performer. She'd said ruefully that there could be no room in a marriage for two egos. And no, she didn't really mind, because she couldn't imagine being married to anyone other than a musician. 'How would he ever understand me, if he didn't live for music?'

Only Jean didn't live for music any more, she lived for Yves, and his career.

Polly saw in her mind's eye the third bedroom of the flat where she and Roger would live once they were married. It was to be her studio. She knew, with sudden clarity that he was humouring her when she spoke of light and shelves. He saw it as the nursery, and that was what it would become.

Bother Roger. He was far away. 'Out of sight, out of mind,' she said aloud.

Maud laughed. 'Could you be referring to your fiancé? What did you say his name was – Dr Harwood?'

'Harrington. Roger Harrington.'

'Is he like all men?' Jo asked. 'Full of kindly tolerance for women's efforts in whatever field they have chosen?'

'Not exactly,' said Polly, driven to defend Roger. 'His mother is a doctor, and his sister-in-law is a pharmacist. And his younger sister is going to study medicine.'

Maud gave Polly a straight look. 'Family professions can exert a different kind of tyranny. What does the sister actually want to do?'

Polly gave a rueful smile. 'She says she wants to be an actress.'

'I bet that goes down badly with the Harringtons,' Jo said.

'They aren't exactly keen on the idea.'

'Can she act?'

'I've seen her in a school play, that's all, she's only sixteen. She was good. Outstandingly so.'

'And Roger and his family don't approve of her ambitions?'

'You can understand why not. It's a feckless, reckless life, being an actress.'

'Or an artist, or a musician or a writer. You should tell Roger that it could be worse, she might have wanted to be a poet, or a ballet dancer.'

'I suppose he would say poetry is something you can do on the side.'

'And it wouldn't occur to him or his family that the mind and spirit that drive a person to poetry or the stage might indicate a temperament and outlook wholly unsuited to the medical profession, or any scientific pursuit?' Jo's voice was tart.

Polly was uncomfortable with the implied criticism of the

Harringtons. She might have her own doubts, but it was disloyal for her to listen to other people – who had never met them, after all – condemning them. 'They want the best for Alice, isn't that what parents are like? I was lucky, my mother encouraged me to do art.'

'Very lucky. Take Maud's parents. They haven't seen or communicated with her for the last five years. She left a miserable marriage and moved in with me, and then we came out here; she's happy and making a life for herself professionally – but that doesn't matter to them. They may say they want the best for her, but it's only words.'

Polly would have liked to know more about Maud's marriage. What kind of a man had her husband been? Another artist? A businessman? A doctor? But there was a tension in Maud's face and shoulders that warned her off.

Polly held out her sketch at arm's length, and changed the subject. 'Do you know Cortoni's work?'

'The French-Italian portraitist? Huge, rather mannerist canvases?' said Maud.

'A fashionable painter of fashionable women,' said Jo. 'I knew him, when I lived in Paris. One of my teachers had worked with him, and he gave me an introduction. Interesting use of paint, given his subjects, but of no great importance. He was a friend of Lord Fraddon's,' she added. 'How close, one couldn't say of course.'

Close friend, code for lover. Polly was surprised.

'Didn't you know about Fraddon?' Jo went on. 'I thought Oliver would have told you.'

'I'm sure Polly doesn't want to hear a lot of old gossip,' Maud said.

'Nonsense. Everybody wants to hear gossip, and besides, it's better if she hears it from us than gets a garbled version from someone else. It was quite a scandal, Polly. Scurrilous paragraphs in the papers, especially those rags Sir Walter

Malreward owns. That's why Fraddon hardly speaks to the man, although they're neighbours. Malreward has a house here, that sumptuous villa you can see from the Roman House. I sometimes wonder if he bought it in order to torment Fraddon, it's the kind of thing he would do.'

'I met Sir Walter in London,' Polly said. 'He looked at me as if I were an uninteresting worm.'

'You surprise me,' said Jo. 'With your looks and figure, I should have thought he'd definitely be interested, the man's a perfect tomcat.'

'Oh, that. Well, it was a lascivious look, but he was with Mrs Harkness so I don't suppose he was interested in anyone else.'

'Ah, yes, the fascinating Mrs Harkness.'

'I like Cynthia,' said Maud.

'So do I, but she's a fool to think of marrying that man. Perhaps she knows it, there seems to be some shilly-shallying going on there. Why is she staying in her own house and not at the Villa Trophie? Especially when all the servants thought she would be Lady Malreward before the year was out.'

'Jo knows all the servants at the big houses around here,' Maud said, almost apologetically.

'Of course I do. They're much better company than their employers, and talking to them improves my French wonderfully. Besides, I like to keep tabs on what's going on, and they know everything.'

'So why is Lord Fraddon an exile?' Polly asked, longing to know, despite her feeling that to gossip about her host wasn't quite right.

'On account of the scandal. It was all to do with a footman, who died in suspicious circumstances. Turned out he and Lord Fraddon had been very close, someone had squealed to the police, who were investigating the friendship – an unnatural friendship, they'd call it. So when the young man was found floating in the lake at Fraddon dead as a doornail, an empty boat drifting nearby, with a large bump on his head, the police moved in for the kill.'

'Lord Fraddon murdered a footman?' Polly was appalled.

'I doubt it. Fraddon's not the type. And at the inquest it was brought in as accidental death, the footman was full of booze, could have hit his head on the boat, or a stone near the shore. The evidence was all circumstantial, but there was the whole homosexual side. Lady Fraddon, a hysterical woman at the best of times, didn't help, and one day when the police came to ask further questions, they found Lord Fraddon had gone. Upped and offed to France. They've been over to question him, but they can't issue a warrant, they know the case isn't strong enough to hold up in court, and the coroner's verdict still stands, after all. Rumour says that the coroner's jury was biased, since everyone for miles around was a tenant of Fraddon's or depended on him in some way, or simply liked him. He's a good landlord.'

The brightness had gone out of Polly's day. 'I never heard anything so awful. All that hanging over him, and never able to go back. When he's such a grandee, it must be dreadful to be exiled from his house and lands.'

'He doesn't pity himself,' said Jo, 'so he doesn't need our or your pity. His life is a great deal better than most people's, he's rich, he has a lot of friends, his family come and visit him, as you see, although I expect he could dispense with Katriona's company, how she must remind him of his wife.'

'Is she dead? Oliver never speaks of her.'

'She divorced Fraddon, which was remarkable in itself, since the Fraddons are Catholic. Went off to America and married a wealthy New Yorker. Katriona is in touch with her, but I don't believe Oliver is.'

'They aren't what you'd call a happy family,' Maud said.

'Lord Fraddon is attached to Oliver, but they never seem to me to be quite at ease with one another. I suppose Fraddon thinks Oliver blames him for what he is and for what happened.'

Polly had heard enough, she wished she hadn't asked, or that Maud and Jo hadn't told her. She got up. 'You said there's a place in Rodoard where I can buy a canvas. How long does it take to walk there?'

'Quarter of an hour uphill, ten minutes back downhill,' said Jo. 'René's the man you want, he runs an artists' suppliers from a kind of dingy shop and warehouse in the Rue Gaillac. Number fifteen. If he isn't there, try the bar in the square, he doesn't keep regular hours in the winter, but he'll always open up to make a sale. He does most of his business in the summer when all the amateur painters stream to this part of the world to share the air that Picasso and Matisse breathe. And he speaks some English, especially to do with artists' stuff. Cash on the nail, though, he doesn't trust artists an inch, or I should say, a centimetre.'

Polly rummaged in her bag. 'I've got my purse.'

FORTY

The way to the village was no more than a path, winding upwards, with roughly-cut steps in the steepest parts. Each turn brought a new view of headlands, the sea, the hillside with its villas set among trees; what a lot of greenery there was for December. It was the pines that made the difference. The air was balmy, and Polly walked fast, springing up the steps, glad to be out and about in this enchanting landscape. At the top she paused to watch a hawk hovering overhead, watching some creature in the undergrowth.

Rodoard had a sleepy look, pollarded trees around a central square, intriguing-looking streets winding off in all directions. Polly considered exploring, but she could do that another time, for now she wanted to paint.

She had rather dreaded the bar, given her limited French, and if it were full of Frenchmen, how would she know which was René? Fortunately, she found him at his warehouse doing some form of stocktaking, by the look of the lists in his hands and the muttered counting that was going on. He had canvases of varying sizes and quality, stacked up against the wall. Polly, automatically drawn to the smallest sizes, found herself pointing instead to a much larger one. It would be awkward to carry back, but as she looked at the creamy surface, she knew that was the smallest her painting could possibly be.

Walking back towards the top of the path that would take her back to the stables, she almost collided with a man coming the other way.

He apologized, in French; but he wasn't French. She had heard that voice before, deep and distinctive.

'So we meet again,' Max said. 'I was right, you see, although I hardly expected to see you in France. May I help you with that canvas?'

'I liked him,' Maud said, as Max took his courteous leave of the three women. 'He's very like his sister, but there's a core of steel there.'

Jo's face had a shuttered look. She's jealous, Polly said to herself. She doesn't want Maud to like Max, or probably any man.

'He's cold,' Jo said abruptly. 'An iceberg, and one can't tell what the submerged seven-eighths of him are like. An ex-soldier, I suppose, with that limp.'

'It was kind of him to help me down with the canvas. I don't think I could have managed on my own. And the limp's from having polio as a child.'

'A severe childhood illness can set a person apart,' said Maud. 'I've often noticed it. Such people become self-contained, and I think that's what he is, more than cold.'

'Cold and reserved,' Jo said. 'Intelligent, implacable, and up to something. I wonder why he's here?'

'He's spending Christmas with his sister and his niece, he told us so.'

'He's never been here before. And he has those eyes that miss nothing. Thank goodness he wouldn't stay, he gives me the creeps.'

Polly opened her mouth to defend him, but then why

should she? She hardly knew him, and although she was sure Jo misjudged him, she felt it was better to talk about something else.

'I'll help you upstairs with that,' Jo said, dusting brick powder off her hands and wiping them on the long black apron she wore tied around her waist. Then she gave an exclamation and stooped to pick up something from the floor. 'Drat the man, he's dropped his passport. Shocking carelessness.'

Then she frowned. 'This doesn't make sense.'

'What's the matter?' said Maud. 'Isn't it his passport after all? Is he masquerading under a false name, isn't he Max Lytton?'

Aghast, Polly was fumbling in her bag. No, it couldn't be hers, she couldn't have been so stupid as to—

'How odd,' Jo was saying. She turned the blue book over in her hands. 'It's the passport for someone called Polyhymnia Tomkins. Who the dickens is Polyhymnia Tomkins?'

Before Polly could say a word, she had opened it. 'There's a ghastly photograph, the usual convict look. Good God, it looks like you, Polly.'

'May I come in?' Max Lytton was standing at the door. 'I left my sunglasses here, I believe.'

Polly saw her opportunity, and jumped forward to snatch the passport out of Jo's hand. 'Yes, it's my passport. Thank you.'

'So what's with the Polly Smith?' said Jo, eyes narrowing. 'We were talking of masquerading just now, but it seems we had the wrong person in mind.'

She shot Max a severe glance, and he gave a faint smile. 'I see that I'm *de trop*,' he said. 'If you would pass me my glasses, which I see on the table over there, I'll take my leave again.'

'Don't go on my account,' said Polly furiously. 'Here I am,

353

revealed as someone going under a false name. I'm sure you're as full of curiosity as these two, you have the nose of a curious man.'

'I am inquisitive, yes, but I have no desire to intrude or to upset you.'

'It isn't upsetting.' Polly was telling no more than the truth. She was angry, now, not ashamed. She would tell them the truth and to hell with what they might think of her. 'I grew up believing I was Pauline Smith, and then, when I went to get a passport I discovered I wasn't called Smith at all, and that Polly wasn't short for Pauline,' she rattled off defiantly. 'The woman I thought was my mother turned out to be my aunt, my mother's sister. My father, Ted Smith, wasn't my father. I'm illegitimate. My mother dumped me when I was a few weeks old, and neither I nor anyone else has a clue who my father was. Satisfied?'

Jo's expression had changed entirely. 'Good God! Tomkins. Polyhymnia Tomkins. It can't be a coincidence. I thought I'd seen you before, when I first met you.'

'You were wrong. We've never met.'

'No, but you're rather like someone I did know. It says in that passport you're clutching to your breast that your middle name is Theodora. Is the aunt who brought you up also called Theodora, by any chance? Or Dora?'

How could Jo possibly know that? For a wild moment Polly had thought Jo was going to declare that she knew who Polly's father was, but this was leading in a different direction.

'Because if so, I think Thomas Tomkins, the painter, must be your grandfather. Was he?'

Polly felt as though all the breath had been knocked out of her, and she could only speak with an effort. 'Since my mother – my aunt, that is – won't ever talk about her family, I don't know anything about my grandparents. A painter, did you say?'

354

'Yes, and quite a well-known one. Thomas Tomkins was my teacher at Walthamstow for a term. He lived and worked in Cornwall, in Newlyn, but came to the college to give a series of lectures on landscape. He invited me to go to Cornwall and work with him, which I did. I stayed with him and his family for over a year before I found a place of my own. He was married to a musician, Theodora Besant. A singer, a soprano. They had two daughters, Thomasina and Theodora.'

Polly sat down with a thump. She couldn't take it in. 'My mother's name was Thomasina.'

'There you are!' Jo was looking extremely pleased with herself. 'Do you honestly mean you had no idea that you were a Tomkins? That's where you get your artistic talent from. Tomkins, TT he used to be called, and that's how he signed his paintings, was well-known in his time. There's one of his paintings in the Tate, I think. Old-fashioned, keen on Arts and Crafts; but I suspect he'd have approved of the Solidists.'

'Is he . . . ?' Polly could hardly bring out the words to ask if he were still alive. Why had Dora kept all this from her? Why had she never told her that her grandfather was a painter?

'You're wondering if he's still alive,' said Jo, sympathy in her voice. 'No. He was already in his late sixties when I studied with him. His wife, your grandmother, was quite a bit younger, but they both died in the flu epidemic after the war. Thea always had a weak chest, so I suppose it wasn't surprising.'

A sudden flash of memory: of coming home from school one day to find her mother strangely distraught. 'Some people I knew have died. From the flu,' she'd told Polly. She was dry-eyed, but with a weary sadness in her voice.

'From around here?'

'No, people I knew long ago, I haven't seen or heard from

355

them for years. One grows apart, and the years pass, and then . . .' she shrugged. 'And then it's too late.' She had busied herself then with getting Polly her tea, but Polly had heard her in the night, a muffled sound that might be crying, which disturbed Polly; her mother never cried.

The next morning she had been her normal self, and Polly thought no more about it.

'So you never knew your grandparents,' said Maud. 'But was your aunt kind to you?'

'She brought me up as her daughter, and no one could have had a better mother.'

'Dora was like that,' said Jo. 'Kind and compassionate. Too much so, perhaps, for a talented musician. You have to be tough to succeed as a musician.'

'And Thomasina? My mother?'

Jo sighed. 'What can I tell you about Thomasina? She was wild and wilful and loved life with a passion I've never seen in anyone before or since, she was overflowing with vitality. You've got a touch of it, Polly, but with her it was sensational. As were her looks. She wasn't beautiful in a conventional sense, it was just that she stood out, you couldn't help noticing her. I have to tell you that neither of the girls got on well with their parents. Dora hated the whole Bohemian set up, she detested what she called artiness, and the way Tom and Thea fought, my God there was never a peaceful moment in that household. And Thomasina was jealous of Dora, who had her music, while she longed to paint, but simply had no gift for it. Thomasina ran away, one misty morning, leaving a note saying she was going to Paris. Which she did, and became a successful artists' model.'

'While Dora stayed at home?' asked Polly.

'Dora won a scholarship to the Academy, and she, too, in a quieter, less dramatic way, left home. She made her own life in London, and I think, secretly, her parents were relieved to have both girls off their hands. Some marriages are like that, they cared far more for each other than for their children.'

'Hardly happy families,' remarked Max.

He had been so quiet that Polly had forgotten he was there.

'I possess one of your grandfather's paintings, Miss—'

'You may as well call me Polly. At least that hasn't changed, and I'm not sure I'd answer to Tomkins. As for Polyhymnia, no one could use a name like that.'

'Thomasina called you that?' Jo said. 'How typical of her, she wanted everything about her to be different. Dora would have called you Jane, I expect. I met Dora in London, some time afterwards, and she told me she was going to marry a clerk on the railways. She said, "He's called Smith, Ted Smith, what could be more wonderfully ordinary? He'll never raise his voice or shout at me, and we're going to live in a suburb and lead a completely normal life."'

The question Polly longed to ask was frozen on her tongue. Max Lytton asked it for her.

'If this Thomasina Tomkins, what an enchanting name, by the way, left Polly on her sister's doorstep, what became of her?'

'I don't know, and nor does my mother – I mean my aunt,' said Polly.

'I never found out,' said Jo. 'When I was in Paris, before the war, I met Cortoni, as I told you. Thomasina had been his favourite model, but she vanished one day, just as she'd done in Cornwall, only this time she didn't leave a note. He heard she'd gone to America, with a Russian émigré.'

So her mother might still be alive. Polly's mouth was dry with sudden bitterness. Careless of the baby she'd abandoned. What kind of a mother could do that, leave her daughter like a parcel and take no further interest in her? Of course, she'd heard of it happening when the baby was the result of a rape, when the mother cared nothing for the father and only wanted to be rid of the child one way or another. Was that what she was, the product of a loveless, even a violent union? Or was her father the Russian émigré, a man indifferent as to the fate of his child?

She stumbled to her feet, wanting to get away, to be alone, but the sense of emptiness that swept over her was so strong that her knees buckled. Christ, she thought, I'm going to faint. And then she was back on the seat, with Max Lytton's arm around her shoulders, and his calm voice telling her to put her head down between her knees.

'It's shock, that's all,' he said. 'Mrs Elgin, do you have tea in the house? Good. A strong cup with plenty of sugar will do the trick.'

The faces and voices which had been receding came back into focus, as Polly lifted her head.

'I'm sorry,' she said. 'I'm quite all right, I can't think what came over me.'

'A person who has no family, or a small one, forms an idealized picture of family life,' said Max Lytton. 'In reality, most families are complex units, with a good deal of life-long hostility and volatile emotions, alongside whatever bonds of affection may or may not exist. I, for instance, am close to my sister, Cynthia, but not to the rest of my quite large family.'

Polly looked into his eyes, the grey-blue eyes that went with his fair hair. They gave nothing away, but she knew, with sudden understanding, that this insight into his emotions from a very private man was an offering of particular generosity.

For that moment there was a powerful link between them, seconds of an unusual intimacy, and then the spell was broken as Maud thrust a cup of tea into her hand, and urged her to eat a biscuit.

'Have lunch with us, Mr Lytton,' Jo said, no trace of her earlier animosity in her voice.

'I have already outstayed my welcome, and my sister will be expecting me.' He paused. 'I hope all three of you will dine with us one evening. Are you spending Christmas and the New Year here, Miss – Polly? I know my sister and Harriet would like to meet you again. Cynthia will be particularly pleased to know that you are Thomas Tomkins' granddaughter, since she admires his work.'

'If you don't mind, I think I'd better stay Polly Smith. I'm used to it, and I'll go on being Polly Smith until I become Mrs Harrington, by which time it will all be mere history.'

'Mrs Harrington, of course,' murmured Max. 'Just as you wish. I'm sure Mrs Elgin and Miss Saxe will keep your secret.'

'Jo and Maud will do,' said Jo. 'Don't worry, we can keep our mouths shut when we want to.'

'Do call me Max.' He tucked his sunglasses into the breast pocket of his jacket. 'And whatever names anyone may be using, I shall be in touch about dinner.'

There was silence as the door closed behind him. Then Jo let out her breath in a long whistle. 'Well, what a morning! Tell me, Polly Smith, does your doctor fiancé know who you really are?'

FORTY-ONE

Tulliver lifted the last of the canvases into the back of the aged Citroën van and slammed the doors shut. He dusted his hands together and nodded at Ivo. 'That's the lot, I'll be off.' He reached the crank handle and went round to the front of the van. He inserted it under the radiator, and, bracing himself, swung the handle, giving it an expert sharp jerk as it came up. Three strong pulls and the engine rumbled into life. Tulliver climbed into the driver's seat, released the handbrake, and with a grinding sound, the van set off at a snail's pace down the steep, winding road which led from Rodoard to the main road below.

He turned left at the bottom and bucketed along the Corniche, sending the van hurtling round each bend and twist in the road with an abandon that caused several perilous near misses, with much sounding of horns and waving of fists from the other drivers he encountered or passed on his way.

He came sweeping round a final bend, and there was the Villa Trophie beneath him, a magnificent cream mansion in the style of the Belle Epoque. At the turning for the Villa Trophie, he took a sharp right, sending spurts of white dust up from the wheels, and flew along the last, level part of the approach to the villa.

Sir Walter was out on the terrace, a cigar clamped between his teeth, watching Tulliver approach. He came down the steps to where Tulliver, who had jumped out with his usual swift energy, was already undoing the doors at the rear of the van.

'Good morning,' he said. 'Do you want these inside as usual?'

'Take them into the hall,' Sir Walter said. 'They'll be going out tonight, they can be wrapped there. What have you got?'

Tulliver carried the five paintings into the house, setting each one against the wall for Malreward to inspect.

'A nice Corot,' Sir Walter said. 'What's this? Monet, good, good. Another Monet, a Renoir and a Greuze, isn't it?'

'Worth a good few thousand dollars in anyone's money,' said Tulliver with satisfaction. 'Ivo does make sure the canvases go off looking as good as can be, he's a real craftsman.'

'Leave them there,' said Walter. 'I'll ring for some brown paper, and Lanyard can pack them properly later today. Come and have a drink.'

Tulliver, a whisky in one hand and a Turkish cigarette in the other, stood by the window, looking out at the formal garden where two men were solicitously trimming a box hedge to a state of rigid perfection.

'I have clients for the Monets and the Corot. Private collections. There's a museum might go for the Greuze, and the Renoir won't be a problem, those idiots just love Renoir. I'll get you good prices. You want me to have the proceeds deposited in the usual way and then sent on?'

'Yes,' said sir Walter. 'Your new man over there is trustworthy, I suppose.'

'Absolutely,' said Tulliver with a grin. 'He's my brother. Not as smart as I am, but he does what he's told, and he understands money.'

'Good, good.'

Tulliver had spotted another picture propped against the wall. This one was framed, but he could only see the back of the picture, as it was facing the other way.

'Is that another one to go?' he asked, frowning. 'Five is enough in one shipment. Six is too many.'

'No, I had this one sent over from the gallery. It's not for sale.' Sir Walter went across and swung the picture around. 'A Fragonard. Like it?'

Tulliver shrugged. 'If it's not for sale, it's not for me to like it or not.'

'It beats me how you can know so much about art and care so little about it,' said Sir Walter looking annoyed.

'I know the value of a painting, which is to say what it will fetch in a given market. I know that most artists never made much money from their art, whereas we can. And most art is bourgeois and uninteresting, and all private collections are an offence to the working man. What else is there to say? These paintings are a means to an end. If you choose to indulge yourself with a Fragonard, that's on your conscience.'

'You sound like your Puritan ancestors, Penn.'

'Shakers, not Puritans, and they had the right idea. America would be a finer country if it had adopted Shaker principles, instead of greed and capitalism and opening its doors to the dross of Europe, thus breeding degenerates and bums. Let alone politicians who have the belief that they need to come to Europe's rescue every time the old countries get themselves in a fix.'

'You're doing your bit,' said Sir Walter. 'With funding and influence, we'll build a new order, and have a government that rewards self-reliance and industry, instead of providing hand-outs to the degenerates and bums you talk about.'

*　　*　　*

On the other side of the closed door that led into the adjacent room, Lois and Myron Watson exchanged glances. They weren't sitting on the cane sofa, leafing through the selection of glossy magazines laid out on the table. Instead, they were standing close to the door, listening hard and taking in every word.

Footsteps, a swift movement, and the door opened to reveal Lois and Myron apparently just coming into the room from outside.

'Good morning, Walter,' said Lois, all smiles and widened eyes. 'I can't believe how warm it is. We were just taking the air.'

Myron's habitual look of stolid placidity had returned, leaving him with an impassive countenance, quite different from the animated one he'd displayed just a few minutes earlier, when he'd had his ear pressed to the door. 'One fine day after another,' he remarked. 'Only one of your fellows is trying to convince me the weather's going to break. At least, I think he is, but given how limited my knowledge of the language is, I could be wrong. He might have been referring to something quite different.'

The look of suspicion left Sir Walter's face. 'You've been outside? Good, good. And I think the gardener's right, there is a change in the air. Come on in and I'll ring for Lanyard to bring in the cocktails. Lobster on the menu for lunch today, I don't apologize for serving it again, I know how you Americans like lobster.'

'You Americans, indeed,' muttered Lois to Myron, as they followed Malreward into the other room. 'I hate a man who denies where he came from.'

FORTY-TWO

'It's colder today,' said Polly, who had set off from the Domus Romana in a skirt and jumper, and then gone back to put on a jacket.

Jo came in with an armful of logs, which she deposited in the basket beside the stove. Opening the curved door of the stove with a strange-looking tool, she thrust two large logs inside, shut the door with a bang and brushed the dust from the logs off her hands. 'There, that should pep it up a bit. It was very chilly this morning, and the locals are all shaking their heads and prophesying snow.'

'Snow!' said Polly in dismay.

'If it falls, it won't last, and it will be Christmassy,' said Maud. 'Useful for me, I need to do some wintry scenes. A brushing of snow would be just the thing, I can get out and paint some pink-cheeked fairies.'

'In bobble hats and gumboots, I dare say,' said Jo.

'Pay no attention to her,' Maud told Polly, as Jo stomped out, saying she'd get more logs. 'She's not in a good mood, she had a letter this morning from England. One of her nephews wants to read for the bar, and that's expensive.'

'Nephews?'

'Her brother's children. He was killed in the war, leaving his window penniless with three boys to feed and educate on a tiny pension. Jo has paid for their schooling and university, and now Timmy, the middle boy, wants to go in for law.'

'Can't she just tell him, nothing doing, go and get a job?'

'She could, but she won't. She says she hasn't got them this far to give up on them. Besides, he's a clever boy, hardworking, too, and Jo thinks he'll do well as a barrister. It's a good profession and well-paid once you're established, only rather expensive while you're training and so on.'

Polly thought about Jo's nephews while she worked on the portrait of Maud upstairs in the room that had become her studio. It was above the stove, and quite cosy; this was the first day she hadn't opened the window while she worked. School fees didn't come cheap, and university must cost an awful lot. How on earth did Jo provide for them? Surely her landscapes couldn't sell for that much. If they sold at all, from what Maud had said, buyers weren't queuing up for Neo-solidist works, 'Too avant-garde for the general taste.'

Maud's illustrations sold all right, and must bring in a regular income of sorts. Enough, perhaps, for two women to live on if they were frugal; not enough for an expensive education for three boys.

And Maud and Jo weren't frugal. They ate well, and even in the brief time since Polly arrived at Rodoard, Maud had bought a silver bowl from the little antique shop in the village – 'Always best to buy in winter, Clothilde puts her prices up shamelessly in the summer when there are so many visitors.' Jo and Maud's clothes weren't shabby or cheap, either, but well-cut and well-fitted, as though they had been made for them.

It was a mystery.

A mystery that was solved that very day. Maud and Jo

wanted to go up to the village, they would only be an hour or so, did Polly want to come?

Polly didn't. She was having enormous fun, experimenting with sweeping brushstrokes and vigorous lines of colour. She would stay at the stables, and carry on with her painting.

Half an hour after they'd gone, Polly heard a horn tooting. She paid no attention, until a knock on the door downstairs was followed by a cheerful English voice calling out, 'Anyone at home?'

She ran down the stairs, to find a strange man standing there. 'Hullo,' he said. 'Who are you? Where's Jo?'

'She's out, she's gone to the village. She'll be back quite soon. And if it comes to that, who are you?'

'Bernie,' he said. 'Bernard Defford, at your service. Are you one of the girls? You don't look it?'

One of the girls? Then Polly grasped his meaning and blushed. 'I'm working in the spare room,' she said with dignity.

'Another artist, eh? What's your line, Miss . . .'

'Smith.'

'I can't call you Miss Smith, far too sedate. What's your Christian name?'

His smile was engaging, and Polly found herself smiling back. 'Polly.'

'Polly. I like that. And it suits you. Well, Polly, I'm in a dreadful rush, did Jo leave the doings for me?'

'The doings? What doings?'

'Lithographs. Heavyish, she usually puts them in a wooden box.' He looked round enquiringly. 'That's them,' he said, diving under Jo's table and dragging out a small box. 'She'll have done pulls, I wonder where they are?'

Lithographs? Pulls? She hadn't seen Jo doing any lithographs, although there had been that smell of acid on that first day. Lithographs, then, odd that Jo and Maud hadn't mentioned them. And why had this man come to collect them?

'I can't let you walk off with Jo's stuff,' she said to Bernie, who was at the dresser, searching among the papers there.

'She was expecting me. I'll give you a receipt if you want.'

'Even so.'

'Would I breeze in if I weren't expected?' he said. 'Mind you, I have got here a couple of hours earlier than usual, I grant you that. I don't want to hang about, though. If I can find the prints . . . Ah!' He pulled out a thick sheet of cream paper. 'Here's one, and yes, here are the others. Cracking good stuff, the boss will be pleased. Tell her a cheque will be in the post, will you?'

'No,' cried Polly. 'I can't tell her that. Honestly, I don't know what to do.'

Bernie put down the box he'd just hoisted into his arms, the sheets of paper resting on top. 'We can't miss the deadline, this book's ready to go, we only wanted these last few lithographs from Jo.'

'Book?'

'These are illustrations for a book we're printing. The Venus Press, a specialist house, Jo does a lot of work for us.'

'Let me see the pulls,' said Polly, taking them before he could object, and laying them out on the table. 'Good God!'

'Our Jo could teach Aubrey Beardsley a trick or two, don't you think?' said Bernie in an admiring voice. 'His drawings were static compared to Jo's, and it's action that the customers pay for.'

Polly stared at the naked, entwined figures, couples engaged in the act of love in a variety of positions which looked almost impossible, especially given the extraordinary size of the men's genitalia.

'Jo did these?'

'She did, and fine work they are. Illustrations by Johanna

Kimski, that's the name she works under, add thousands of copies to our sales.'

'I'm sure they do,' said Polly, unable to keep her eyes off the pictures. Pornography. Elegant, stylish pornography. 'It's amazing, when you think that Jo—'

'Has no interest in naked men, let alone men in that state. Bizarre, isn't it? Don't ask me how she does it, we're just glad she does.'

'Does it . . . does she get paid a lot for these?'

'Lord, yes. She can almost name her price. Of course, it's all right in France, but it was tricky when she was living in London. She found the police on her doorstep one day, but she managed to wriggle out of that. It's why she and Maud live in France, this is a country that understands *l'amour* in all its forms and has no puritanical or prudish notions about art. Now, put those back like a good girl. Jo won't thank you if you make difficulties, this is how she earns her living, and, being an artist yourself, you'll know how keen she is on the cheque that will follow the safe delivery of these in Paris.'

Polly was on tenterhooks, waiting for Jo and Maud to return, unsure how she could broach the subject. Jo had never spoken of that side of her artistic career, which was hardly surprising. Was she ashamed of it?

'Nothing of the sort,' said Jo, when she got back, cheeks glowing from the cold and the walk.

'What an idiot Bernie is, to come so early,' said Maud.

'Yes, he always expects us to be here whenever he cares to turn up,' Jo said. 'Thanks, Polly, for handing the stuff over, I hope you weren't too shocked if you got a glimpse of the prints.'

'Oh, no, not shocked exactly. Surprised. And impressed,' Polly added quickly. 'They're awfully good.'

'If you like erotic art,' said Jo. 'Designed to titillate, amuse and arouse; to what extent it does any of those things depends on your sexual proclivities.'

Give Jo's sexual proclivities, how was she able to draw the virile men featured in her lascivious lithographs in such exquisite detail?

Jo laughed. 'I know exactly what you're thinking, Polly Tomkins, and let me tell you how much you resemble your grandfather, when he was thinking naughty thoughts. I employ models. I go to Paris, to various establishments where they are perfectly willing for me to sketch and photograph their activities. In return, I send them copies of the books, which pleases them no end.'

And, Polly reflected as she walked back to the Domus Romana, that was how Jo paid for her nephews' education.

She'd finished work early, finding that the vigorous, slashing strokes she'd revelled in were turning into erratic, undefined lines. She would give it a rest, sit outside and do some drawing, or just go for a walk.

Katriona's voice was audible as she went through the door. Tiptoeing, she headed for the stairs.

'Who's that? Oh, it's you. What are you doing, skulking in?'

Skulking? 'I came through the door in the normal way,' Polly said indignantly.

'Hullo, stranger.' Oliver leaned against a vibrantly-painted pillar, his arms folded, as he looked at his sister. 'You've succeeded in driving Polly out of the house for the best part of every day, Katriona. Why don't you leave her alone?'

'She's taken herself off, very rude when you're a guest.'

'She is the cat's grandmother,' Polly muttered to herself, but Oliver heard and laughed.

'You are back early, though, Polly. Good. Come and have tea by the pool. You can have a swim, if you like, there's bound to be a bathing suit that'll fit you.'

A swim! Swimming to Polly was the municipal baths, or the lido in summer. Swimming in this sea-green pool would be a different thing entirely. She ran upstairs to her room, should she fetch a towel from her bathroom? Or would that be another solecism? She'd bet on there being towels provided, like the bathing suit.

She'd get out her new sketchbook while she remembered; her other one only had three or four pages left. Where had Marie stowed her suitcase? She found it at the bottom of the shelves in the area outside the bathroom, and, crouching down, she lifted the lid of her suitcase, empty now except for some of her artist's materials. She reached in for the sketchbook, and paused. How odd. She had brought a half-used sketchbook with her, plus a new one, of the size and type she favoured. But there seemed to be two Winsor & Newton sketchpads in the suitcase. She took them out, had she brought one of her old ones with her? She flipped them open.

One was, as she expected, full of blank pages.

The other wasn't. It fell open at a drawing of a sailor sitting on a bollard. She remembered him, she remembered the drawing she had done on the ferry, as the boat was waiting to sail. Only this wasn't her drawing. This was by another hand, and God, what a brilliant one. She turned the pages of the book: faces, figures, details of hands, quick sketches of postures and movement jumped out at her, and here was an enchanting, expertly-drawn, rustic scene, a bridge, a horse and wagon, a man on the shafts, pure Constable.

She shut her eyes, thinking back to the boat. Of course, the man along the deck from her, sketchpad propped on the railing, working with a furious pencil, he must be the artist, this must be his sketchbook. How ever had it got into her suitcase?

The train. The sketchbook on the seat of the empty compartment. The artist was the man sitting in the corner, with the hat pulled down over his face. He had dropped this and left without noticing. Goodness, he'd be annoyed to have lost it. And since she had no idea of who he was, let alone where he lived or was staying, there was no way she could restore his property to him.

She picked up the pads, and left the room.

Oliver was waiting by the pool, two bathing suits dangling from his fingertips. 'These should fit you,' he said. 'White or black?'

'Black,' Polly said. White with tanned skin was one thing, white against pale English winter flesh quite another.

She went down the steps at the far end of the pool, and launched herself into the blissfully warm and clear water, exhilarated by the feel of it, and the delightful patterns of light flickering across the pool and the walls beyond. She floated on her back, just stirring the water with her toes, and then rolled over and dived down to the bottom.

Oliver sat relaxed, his legs stretched out, smoking a cigarette and watching her. He was joined by Lord Fraddon, who sat down and fell into conversation with his son.

Polly surfaced, saw her sketchbook lying on the table, and hoped Oliver wouldn't pick up and look through it. No, he didn't seem to have noticed it. There was the drawing she'd made of Lord Fraddon in Paris – was it him? Yes, she was sure it was – only, was the relationship with the woman, clearly a close and affectionate one, a private matter?

She recalled what Jo and Maud had said about Lord Fraddon and the footman. It was strange, that a man could love both men and women, as he must do. Married, with children, a fling with a footman and now a love affair in Paris. Oscar Wilde had been married and a father, of course. Polly's thoughts drifted away as she swam in a lazy circle. She knew and liked Oscar Wilde's son, Vyvyan Holland, and there was Bertram, Oliver's erstwhile lover, would he change his ways, become a model father, or would the tug of sex lure him into entanglements such as had ruined Oscar Wilde and driven Lord Fraddon into exile?

Easier to be Jo and Maud, people might make remarks or cold-shoulder them, but there was no danger of a tap on the shoulder, of a knock on the door, and a contemptuous policeman waiting to haul you before a court on a charge of homosexuality.

Polly sighed, inhaled a mouthful of salty water, spluttered, and swam to the steps. Oliver was waiting to wrap her in a vast towel, which enveloped her from shoulders to ankles, and, telling her she looked like a woman on a classical frieze, he rubbed her back and then pushed her into one of the cane seats before going off to ring for fresh tea.

'I looked through your sketchbook,' said Lord Fraddon.

Damn it, why had she left it there? A man like Lord Fraddon would think nothing of picking up a sketchbook; just like Oliver, who, she had discovered early on in their friendship, had no scruples about reading her letters or anything else she left about.

'You will forgive my curiosity,' Lord Fraddon said. 'I see you spent time in Paris before coming here. Tell me, did you know who I was?'

Polly went scarlet; she glanced at the sketchbook, open at the drawing of the man and woman in the café in Paris. So it *was* him.

She shook her head. 'I had no idea. I just . . . That is, well, I just wanted to draw you.'

'Would you let me have the drawing? I would consider it an honour, and my companion would be very pleased with it, I think.' He closed the sketchbook as Oliver reappeared.

'Of course,' said Polly. 'Of course, I'd love you to have it.' What else could she say?

FORTY-THREE

Max was as good as his word. He appeared at the door of Maud and Jo's cottage, bringing an invitation from Cynthia Harkness. Would they care to spend Christmas Eve at Le Béjaune? 'A light meal before Midnight Mass, and then the feast to celebrate *le réveillon* afterwards.'

Jo looked Max up and down, rather to his amusement. He liked Jo, but was under no illusions as to her opinion of him, or of most men.

'Who's cooking? Is that old rascal Henri still the chef at Le Béjaune? Because if so, and he's making *raïto*, I'm your man.'

'Henri does indeed rule in the kitchen. He's been telling me about *raïto*, which I confess I've never tasted, but which he says is a traditional Provençale dish for Christmas Eve.'

'It is, and it's delicious. A sauce of onions and garlic and tomatoes and pounded walnuts, with herbs and red wine and capers, all simmered in olive oil. Served with fish. Who else will be there?

'Jo!' said Maud. 'Don't give the poor man the third degree.'

'Why not? I'm not deceived, *Mr* Lytton may have a limp, but he's a toughie underneath that smooth and *noli me tangere* exterior. It takes one to know one, and he's not going to be upset by a few questions. Two elements are necessary for a really good *réveillon*: one is food, and the other is the company.'

'Quite right. There's my niece, Harriet.'

'Nice girl.'

'I'm fond of her myself.'

'Go on.'

'Archie McIntyre, who's staying with us for Christmas.'

'Winkled him out of Paris, have you? Not quite what he seems, Archie, but that's true of most of us.'

'And, after this, I'm instructed by my sister to call at the Domus Romana and invite Mr Fraddon, who is an old friend of Archie's, and Miss Smith, to join us.' He paused. 'Or perhaps Miss Smith is here?'

'No, she isn't, and you'll be disappointed if you hope to see her house. She's gone up to Rodoard, she was talking about getting mountings for her drawings.'

Max did feel a sense of disappointment, but he wasn't going to show it. 'In that case,' he said pleasantly, 'I may meet her on my way back to village.'

'What about Lord Fraddon?' said Maud. 'And Katriona? Mrs Rawlinson, Oliver's sister.'

'I don't have the pleasure of her acquaintance. My sister knows that Lord Fraddon and Sir Walter Malreward don't get on, and since she—'

'Yes, we know all about her and Malreward,' Jo said.

And how much was 'all'? Max asked himself.

'Fraddon's dining out, in any case, with Daphne Wolf,' Jo went on. 'And Katriona and her long-suffering husband and little boy, both of whom arrived last night, are going to Nice on Christmas Eve. Oliver told me, Maud, don't think I'm repeating servants' gossip. Oliver said he was planning to take Polly out on the razz in Rodoard, said she might as well make the most of being spared Katriona's acid tongue for at least one evening.'

'Do I take it that Miss Smith and Mrs Rawlinson don't get on?' Max said.

'You are inquisitive, aren't you? No one gets on with Katriona, she bears a grudge against her family, for what she thinks is a good reason, and against the rest of the world for no reason at all.'

Which was comprehensive enough. How did Polly Smith cope in that household? She couldn't be finding it easy, and that was presumably why she escaped to the less alarming company of Jo and Maud.

'Polly does all right,' Jo said, disconcertingly. 'She keeps out of Katriona's way, Fraddon regards her with an amused tolerance, I think she rather intrigues him, and she and Oliver are the best of friends.'

Best of friends. It was, in Max's experience, rare for women to make good friends of men. Especially where there was no sexual attraction, which he doubted there was in this case. 'Does Mr Fraddon make a habit of befriending young artists?'

'Oliver doesn't make a habit of anything, and he doesn't go in for befriending. He does spend a lot of time among artists, however, and he and Polly just clicked. And,' she added, with what Max could only call a malicious look, 'if you're interested in a spot of befriending yourself, just remember that Polly has a fiancé.'

'Who sounds a dead bore,' said Maud, swirling her paintbrush in a jar of water. She flicked the tip of the brush expertly on her sheet of paper, and a clump of pixie bells appeared beside a foolish-looking fairy.

'If you're going to hang about asking questions, you might as well take your coat off and sit down,' said Jo.

'Thank you, I will,' Max removed his coat and laid it over

375

the back of a chair. 'Cigarette?' he said, opening a slim silver cigarette case.

Jo took one and thrust it into a daringly long tortoiseshell holder. 'No good offering one to Maud, she doesn't smoke.' She inhaled and sent three rings ceilingwards. 'What's your interest in Polly? Don't pretend you haven't got one, I know better than that.'

'Do you? Tell me, is she a good painter?'

'Getting that way,' Jo said, after a thoughtful pause. 'Just breaking out for the first time, and still feeling her way. Not my style of thing at all, but it may take her somewhere. Too early to tell. She's done a portrait of Maud that isn't bad; she has the makings of a good portrait painter, which means she might make a living out of it. It isn't art, though, not in the modern sense. The portrait went the way of the dodo the minute the first daguerreotype was printed, and it's a pity to see a young artist hitch her wagon to an outmoded genre.'

'I've seen some of her drawings. Caricatures, almost.'

'She has a keen eye,' Maud said. 'And a sense of humour. She likes people, for the most part, and a liking for humanity is useful for a figure painter of whatever kind.'

'Can she support herself on her art?'

Jo gave a contemptuous snort. 'Which of us can?'

'Some do,' said Max. He nodded at Maud. 'Maud does, I'm told. So does Johanna Kimski.'

'Now, how the devil do you know about Johanna Kimski?' said Jo, taken aback. 'Don't tell me you're in the market for that kind of book, I shall think the less of you if you are.'

'Admirable although the artwork is, no, it's not my kind of book. I heard about Johanna Kimski from Regé Dussonet, who owns the Venus Press, as you well know. He's a friend of mine.'

'Regé Dussonet should learn to keep his mouth shut,' said

Jo crossly. 'I insist on discretion, and now it turns out he's a gabmouth. Really, it's too bad.'

'Don't blame him. I was talking about Rodoard, and the artistic community here, and one thing led to another.'

'I have a strong impression, Mr Lytton, that you are a past expert at getting information out of people and about people. Is your visit here purely to celebrate the festive season in the company of your sister and niece, or do you have an ulterior motive? No, don't give me that cold look, I'm too old to be frightened by you. But don't you go frightening Polly, nor leading her astray.'

Max was annoyed. Jo was getting too close to the bone. He rose. 'I assure you, I have Miss Smith's best interests at heart.'

'Heart,' said Jo, when he'd taken his leave and the door closed behind him. 'That man hasn't got a heart.'

'Oh, he has a heart, make no mistake,' said Maud. 'The sort that a sentimentalist would say had been broken in youth and ever since girded about with strong armour.'

Jo shot her a glance, half-defiant, half-worried.

'No, my dearest Jo, I'm not going to fall in love with Mr Lytton, although I imagine a lot of women might. I can see past his reserve; all right, call it coldness if you will, and I pity him for what I suspect is a lonely life. Now, if you don't get on with lunch, we'll be eating it at teatime.'

Despite his limp, Max's long legs covered the ground quickly, and he took the turns and steep patches of the path back to Rodoard in his stride. Halfway up, he stopped to go to the edge and look out over the rocky hillside that sloped steeply down to a sea suffused with purple light. And there below him, perched on a boulder, huddled in a jacket, with a red muffler round her neck and fingerless mittens on her hands, was Polly, sketchbook beside her, hands clasped round her knees, gazing out to sea.

377

He slid down to join her. 'Good morning, Miss Smith. I'm glad to have met you, I came down to the Domus Romana to find you and Oliver.'

Polly looked at him, frowning, her eyes remote. 'What? Oh, it's you.' She blinked. 'Sorry, I was miles away.' She shifted along the flat rock. 'Sit down if you want to. It's warm, the sun is astonishing, don't you think? Why did you want to find Oliver and me?'

He passed on his sister's invitation, and said that Oliver was happy to accept, and had provisionally accepted on her behalf.

'Oh, yes,' she said cheerfully. 'If Oliver's going, and I'm invited as well. That's kind of Mrs Harkness, please thank her for me.'

Max picked up the sketchbook. 'May I?'

'It's extraordinary how people always want to look at one's sketchbook,' Polly said without rancour. 'You wouldn't look into a friend's journal would you?'

'I might. It would depend on the circumstances.'

Polly laughed. 'At least you're honest about being a snoop. Most aren't.'

He didn't care for being called a snoop, but he had an irresistible urge to see more of what Polly had been drawing.

The sketch of Lord Fraddon and the woman jumped out at him. 'This is good,' he said. 'It's Lord Fraddon, isn't it?'

'I'm glad he's recognizable,' said Polly drily.

'Who's the woman? What an interesting face.'

Her own face lit up at that, and she turned to him. 'It is, isn't it? I should love to meet her. I don't know who she is, and Lord Fraddon didn't say.'

'He's seen the drawing?'

'Yes, he's as nosy as you are, and so was looking through my sketchbook. I'm going to work it up, and give it to him.'

'I, too, should like to meet this woman,' Max said, tracing the curve of the woman's shoulder with a long finger.

'I drew them in Paris, I expect she lives there.'

Now Max was looking out to sea, as Polly had done. 'Lord Fraddon has the reputation . . .' he began, and Polly interrupted him.

'Don't tell me you're another gossip. Yes, I know Lord Fraddon's reputation, and the scandal, and why he can never return to England, and yes, it's obvious, if I haven't drawn something that isn't there, that he and this woman are in love.' She shrugged and reached out for the book. 'It happens that way. And I didn't put in what wasn't there, by the way. Their affection was flowing out of them both. You couldn't mistake it.'

'Lucky man,' Max said.

'To feel like that about someone?'

'And to have his feelings reciprocated. Yes.'

He fell silent, and Polly looked at him appraisingly. 'What are you thinking about, Mr Lytton? About Lord Fraddon? About love? Do you think he's too old for that kind of thing?'

'Too old? Good God, no. Why should one ever be too old for that kind of thing, as you put it? And why have I sunk to being Mr Lytton again?'

'Max, then. You haven't answered my question.'

'No. Tell me more about yourself.'

'Is this out of one of those manuals to make your life better? "Take the trouble to listen to other people talk about themselves, and this will earn you their liking and trust." Is that it?'

'Just accept that I'm interested in my fellow creatures. Do you make a living from your art?'

'Of a kind,' said Polly, who had opened her sketchbook at a fresh page, and was sketching Max's profile. 'I survive on book jackets, mostly.'

'And your job at Rossetti's.'

'Not any more, they sacked me.' She couldn't keep the indignation out of her voice.

'Why?'

'Dunno. I was only a temp there, filling in for the usual receptionist. My real job at Rossetti's was doing up pictures, there's a workshop behind the gallery. I made tatty old canvases saleable.'

'Rossetti is well-known for its restoration work.'

'That's the pukka end, I didn't work in that part. No, we were more humble. You know, take a dismal late-nineteenth-century landscape or flower painting, and touch it up, give it a facelift.'

Max's face revealed nothing. He didn't care to think of Polly in bad odour at Rossetti's, which could all too easily mean in bad odour with Malreward, which could be dangerous. No, he was carrying this too far, why should Malreward be interested in a young artist with a temporary position in the gallery? 'Touch it up? Faking, do you mean?'

'Not really. A bit of repainting, improving. I told you, turning a dud into a painting that someone would be pleased to hang on their walls. That's all. Although,' she added, her temper showing through, 'they were a bit naughty in the gallery, they had a flower painting that I'd done, and it was labelled – well, never mind.'

'The art world is notorious for its paintings and sculptures and all the rest of it not always being what they seem.'

'I suppose so. I don't like the dishonesty, though. I had no idea that what we worked on in our workshop ended up like that. So perhaps it's as well I got the sack and was told never to darken the doors of the gallery or its premises ever again. My conscience might have got to me. Anyhow, my fiancé doesn't want me doing that kind of work once we're married.'

Max had taken a strong dislike to this unknown fiancé.

'Tell me about him.'

She bent over her drawing, smoothing a line with her finger. 'No, why should I? And why should you want to know, Max Lytton?'

'As I said, I'm interested in people.'

'Roger isn't your sort of person. He's a doctor.'

'What's his other name?'

'Harrington, if you must know.'

'The he's probably the son of Dr John Harrington, the nerve man.'

'Yes, do you know him? I can't see you needing to consult a nerve specialist.'

'No, we met under other circumstances.' Which had been during the war, when Dr Harrington provided expert assistance to his department in interrogation of suspects. 'He's a good psychologist.' And a dull man, heaven help Polly if her Roger took after his father. She would be wretched married to a man with no sense of humour.

Polly said nothing. Max watched her mouth, which was set in a determined line, and found himself wondering what it would be like to kiss her.

She looked up, her expression challenging, and her eyes far too perceptive. He got up. 'I'd like to see the drawing of Lord Fraddon when you've finished it.'

'It's a present for Lord Fraddon, so you'll have to ask him.'

'I will. Until Christmas Eve, then.' Polly watched him go. Drat the man, coming and disturbing her peace. Not that she'd been doing anything except letting her mind drift with the chill wind and the hovering gulls, but even so. He was a disturbing man in every sense of the word, and, echoing Jo's suspicions, she asked herself what he was up to.

FORTY-FOUR

Polly watched Max go, and then took out her sketchbook and little portable paintbox, anxious to catch the extraordinary colours of the sea. After a while, the thin cloud dissolved into the horizon and the sea returned to normal. She had enough on paper to remind her of how it looked, so she put her things away and got up from her rock to climb back on to the path into the village. At the top, where the path levelled out and became a narrow road, and the first outlying houses of Rodoard appeared, she saw a girl walking towards her. There was something familiar about her. Did she know her? The girl drew closer, stopped, and smiled at her.

'Hullo. Do you remember me? I'm Harriet Harkness, and I met you at the Blue Monkey.'

'Of course.' It wasn't that she didn't remember Harriet, but that she didn't recognize her. 'You look quite different, so at first . . .'

Harriet made a face. 'I know. I was dressed up then. It's not the same when you have your hair in a plait and have to wear tweed skirts and sensible shoes, is it?'

'How old are you?'

'Sixteen.'

Sixteen, and going out to nightclubs? Polly cast her mind back, seeing Cynthia's swiftly concealed concern and anger. 'You went out without your mother's permission, didn't you?'

'Yes, and in one of her evening frocks. I made Archie take me, we both got into a frightful row over it. Uncle Max told me you were here. Are you painting and things?'

'And things, right now. I'm going to buy some card to mount some drawings on.'

'At René's? Can I come too? I love art shops, they're always full of fascinating things, although I can't draw or paint for toffee. I saw René heading for the bar, so we'll have to winkle him out.'

Polly was glad of Harriet's robust assistance; the girl had no qualms about going into the smoky bar and inquiring for René, who was sitting at a metal table, a cigarette burning out in the ashtray as he argued vociferously with his companion, a ferrety-faced man in a beret. He finished his beer, wiped his bristly moustache with the back of his hand and led the way to his shop, where he disappeared into the back and returned with the card. Harriet pottered happily among the paints and paper and pencils and brushes and boxes of crayons and pastels that were stacked in some disorder in the dim recesses of the shop. Polly hoped the interior was brighter come the summer months, or how could he sell anything? A Rembrandtian atmosphere had its appeal, but she liked to see the colours she was buying.

'I suppose you've seen all round the village,' Harriet said when they came out. Polly heard the hopeful note in her voice.

'No, I haven't. My friends and Oliver promised to bring me up one evening, only it hasn't happened yet.'

'You'll be coming up on Christmas Eve, did Max meet you and tell you? You are coming, aren't you?'

'Yes.'

'It's great fun, Christmas Eve. Awfully jolly, and they have cribs and puppet shows and things. Look, they're setting up a crib over there, on that windowsill. Those figures are called *santons*,' Harriet told Polly. 'You can buy them in the market. Aren't they fun? I'd love to take some back to school, they'd be horrified and say they were idolatrous. Look at those three kings, with purple robes and gold crowns and little parcels in their hands. And I love the donkey.'

Polly was enchanted. She pointed at one of the figures, an angel waiting to be put in place, and, with eyes and hands and two words of French, tried to ask if she might have a closer look. The woman, with two round-eyed children clinging to her skirts, smiled and handed the angel to Polly.

'It's exquisite,' she said, tracing the line of the cream and gold angelic robe. 'Wonderful detail.'

'That's a bit of a grumpy angel,' said Harriet critically. 'I prefer the merry-looking one. You can tell he's longing to be done with his angelic duties so he can get back to the plum pudding.'

They walked on, pausing to look at other cribs on the way. It was a tradition in the village for people to have cribs on display in the windows that looked out on the street, or outside on a stone wall or in a niche beside the front door.

Harriet guided Polly up and down the twisting streets, which in some places were so narrow between the houses that they were almost tunnels. There was a strong smell of drains in places, and the cobbles underfoot were tough on the feet, none of which detracted from Polly's pleasure in exploring.

'This is the church square,' said Harriet.

Polly looked up at the church that filled one side of the square, awed by its looming, austere façade with its massive arch, inset with three rows of carved pillars. 'It's impressive.'

'Isn't it? There was a monastery here in the Middle Ages, an important one, and this is all that's left of it, no monkish cloisters or cells, I'm afraid. Inside, it's all dark and smells of incense. There'll be a crib in there, too, and lots of candles and dingy religious pictures. Do you like churches?'

Polly went up the steps. Like them? She had been into very few, and certainly none that smelled like this. She stopped to look at the carvings on the portal, exuberant beasts grinning out from twining greenery. Hardly very religious, or perhaps it was, simply not very Christian.

The interior took her breath away, with its ranks of pillars and the soaring nave. The altar was set at the top of a broad flight of steps, quite unlike in an English church. And the place was a hive of activity: men came past them with armfuls of hay, which a cluster of women were arranging in a crib set about with figures quite two feet high. A most lifelike ox was brought in by an eager little boy, its legs up in the air until he righted it and set it down behind the manger.

Harriet was right about the pictures although, to an artist's eye, one or two of them were far from dingy, and some of them, the frescoes, were extremely old. Polly liked those best, with their simple lines and plain colours. She could appreciate the quality of a large sixteenth-century painting which hung behind a simpering statue, but the dark agonies of St Sebastian weren't to her taste. She sneezed.

'It's the incense getting up your nose,' whispered Harriet. 'Wait until the service on Christmas Eve, they swish it about so, you can hardly see anything through the clouds of smoke. I like the smell; lots of people, especially English people, don't. My father hates it.'

Outside Polly blew her nose and breathed the clear cold air with some relief.

On one side of the square the ground fell away steeply, with a drop of more than fifty feet to the winding road below. Harriet knelt on the stone bench and looked down. 'I can see Uncle Max's car, doesn't it look tiny?'

Polly had a look, then quickly drew back. 'I don't have much of a head for heights. Where's he going?'

'Uncle Max? To the station, he's going to Paris.'

'To Paris! Isn't he going to be in Rodoard for Christmas?'

'He'll be back. He is inclined to rush off at a moment's notice, when he gets something into his head. Don't ask me why he's gone, Mummy asked him, and he just said he had some business to attend to. He's been on the phone a lot, to England and Paris. Mummy's cross with him going off like that. Do you like him?'

Polly was taken aback. 'I've only met him three times, I hardly know him.'

'Once is enough to tell, don't you think? Lots of people think he's cold, icy, actually, but he isn't really. I don't think the monocle helps, it makes him look grand and remote. I expect that's why he wears it. He's my favourite uncle, not that that's saying much, because the other ones are stuffy or gloomy or both. Mummy's family disapprove of him, because he's rich and can do what he likes, and because he couldn't fight in the war, they're all terribly keen on men going out and biffing the enemy. And they think he should get married, instead of having affairs.'

She stole a quick glance at Polly, wanting to see if she'd noticed the sophistication of her attitude. 'Affairs with married women, too, and they think it's dreadfully immoral.'

'So it is,' said Polly.

'If a woman's married to an awful man, I don't see why she shouldn't have affairs. Anyhow, people do, all the time.'

'It doesn't make it right.'

'I suppose not. Are you very down on that kind of thing?'

'You mean, am I a prig and a prude? No, I'm not. But your uncle might be happier married.'

Harriet drew Polly to one side as a man on a bicycle came up behind them, panting with the effort of climbing the hill.

He had two figures for a crib hanging from his handlebars, and the roof of the stable tied on behind.

'He wanted to get married once,' Harriet confided. 'He was in love with a woman called Isabella. Everyone was pleased, and she was a stunner, beauty of her generation, that type. They were a golden couple, apparently.'

'What happened?'

'The family version is that she didn't want to marry a man who wasn't out there fighting and doing his bit. The man she married instead was a war hero, you see.'

'That doesn't say much for her,' said Polly, unreasonably angry with this Isabella.

'The truth, according to Mummy, was that Isabella found Max cold-hearted. She said she couldn't bear to marry a man who was so reserved and emotionally frozen.'

'If he was in love with her, that's not being frozen.'

Harriet lifted her shoulders. 'I don't understand it either, but then I don't know much about love, not that sort. Anyhow, Isabella ran off with Bobbie Strachan; maybe the truth is she wanted to be a countess.'

'Countess?'

'Yes, she became Lady Strachan. Fearfully grand, only it all ended in tears. They didn't get on, which is what seems to happen to people who are married, and they got divorced. Mummy says Bobbie Strachan's frightfully bitter about it, because he's still in love with her despite everything.'

Lady Strachan. Wasn't that the name of the woman in the Cortoni portrait in the Rossetti Gallery? The painting she had enthused about, told Max he must go and see? What an awful faux pas!

'Is your Uncle Max still in love with her?'

'He wouldn't tell me if he were, and he's been running around with that spiky Thelma Warden, and others before her, so I don't suppose so. People say Isabella broke his heart.

Do broken hearts mend? Do people get over losing the love of their life? Or does time heal all, and there are lots more fish in the sea?'

'There are,' said Polly firmly. She didn't much care for hearing the details of Max's love life. He was probably one of those men who put their life into compartments, and women would only ever be a small part of his interest or concern. In which case, he and Mrs Warden were doubtless well-suited.

A moment later, all thoughts of Max Lytton's amorous pursuits were driven from her mind by the sight of a man coming up the street towards them. Suddenly, she knew who he was, it all came back to her. This man was the artist she had glimpsed sketching on the ferry and, therefore, given what was in the sketchbook, almost certainly the man on the train who had inadvertently left it on the seat in the train. She still had the sketchbook in her bag, and here was her chance to restore it to him; what a piece of luck to find him, how awful for him to be without a sketchbook so stuffed full of good work.

Telling Harriet she'd be back in a minute, she darted down the street. He had gone into one of the houses. Damn. She knocked on the door. No response. She waited for a moment, and then gave the door an experimental push. To her surprise, for it had the look of a firmly closed door, it opened. She hesitated, then pushed the door wide enough open for her to go in. In front of her was a flight of stairs, to the left a door. She could hear voices coming from behind the door. French voices, could he be in there? Or had he gone upstairs? She opened the door just a couple of inches, and a mouth-watering smell hit her. She looked round the door, and one glance was enough to tell that the door led into a bakery, and that the person she wanted wasn't one of the three people waiting to be served nor the man behind the counter, busily pulling a long loaf off a shelf.

She went slowly up the stairs to the first floor, feeling her way in the semi-darkness. Some light filtered through a closed shutter on the landing, and her eyes grew accustomed to the dimness. Off the landing was another closed door. She went up to it, and listened. Tap, tap; someone in there was using a typewriter. Her quarry? Unlikely, unless he'd settled at the typewriter the second he got in, and besides, he was an artist, not a writer.

The top floor, then. She went on up the stone steps, steeper here, and curving round. The door at the top was open, and smells as familiar to her as that of baking bread reached her nostrils: turps and linseed and oil paints. This was the right place.

A voice called out, 'Is that you, Tulliver?'

Polly paused, thought of announcing herself from the door, and then went in to a plainly furnished bedroom, an immaculately neat room, if spartan.

'It isn't Tulliver,' she said, advancing towards the other room where the voice came from. 'I've got something that I think is yours, a sketchbook . . .'

Her voice died away as she stood in the entrance to Ivo's studio. He was on his feet in an instant, coming towards her, crying out, 'Who the hell are you?' and trying to block her view of what was in the studio.

Too late. Her eyes had taken no notice of the usual paraphernalia of the artist, and had fixed on the canvas propped on the easel, a magnificent pastoral scene, glowing with colour and life and the rosy flesh of a woman with doe eyes and a pointed chin.

A Ruisdael, a characteristic Dutch landscape.

A Ruisdael, still glistening from the freshly applied paint. Her eyes looked through the studio to the window, open, even in this cold weather, and to another canvas, pegged to a line. And there, propped up beside the easel was a Corot, a Corot with a figure in the foreground that she had seen all too recently.

She flipped open the sketchbook that she had been holding

out, and found the page she was looking for. There it was, a preliminary sketch for the man in the Corot. The little bottles, the pestle and mortar, the eggshells, the iron in the corner; she knew exactly what was going on here.

At the same time, she knew that she had encountered this man before she caught a glimpse of him on the ferry. He was the man she'd seen coming out of Rossetti's, minus his beard, but she recognized his hands.

'You changed the signature on the Kolyov,' she blurted out. 'You moved it from the right-hand corner to the left.'

'Observant little devil, aren't you? You must be the girl Grandison and Folliott were so het up about. I take it you're an artist, or are you just a student of art history with an eye for trivia? No, I can see the paint on your fingers.'

He had given up his attempt to hide his work. His intensely blue eyes were no longer angry, but amused. 'You shouldn't go poking your nose into strange men's rooms, you know, you really shouldn't. You've landed me in a hell of a mess, walking in here.'

'Did you paint that? And that one?' Polly couldn't keep the admiration out of her voice. She went closer to the canvas to look at the brushwork. 'It's incredible, I don't believe it. And this one, it's completely different in style and technique, and yet it's perfect.'

'Old masters from any period up to the nineteenth century,' said Ivo flippantly. 'I leave the moderns to other, lesser mortals, although I have turned out a Picasso or two for fun.'

'Why?' said Polly. 'Why do this when you can paint like that?'

His smile was twisted, now. 'Why do you think? It pays, duckie, it pays. Every one of these I do brings me a fat profit. My own work?' He shrugged. 'I can't give it away.'

'What do you do with them when . . . Oh, my God, the Rossetti Gallery.'

'You're far too quick on the uptake. If I were you, I wouldn't make that suggestion to anyone.'

'I see you have a visitor.' The words came from the door, and Polly swung round, startled, to see Tulliver Penn leaning against the door, hands jammed into his trouser pockets. 'I heard words flowing down from above, and thought I'd come to see who'd ventured on to your hallowed turf, Ivo. You don't like people in your eyrie, do you?'

'A fellow artist, returning a sketchbook of mine, that's all,' said Ivo easily. And to Polly, 'Thanks a lot.'

'I'll show you out, Miss Smith,' Tulliver said, with a weasel smile that Polly didn't care for. 'We met at Fraddon's place,' he said over his shoulder to Ivo as he almost pushed her out of the room and down the stairs. 'Don't worry, I'll see to it.'

Polly was relieved to get to the bottom of the stairs, but as she tried to get past Tulliver to reach the door and make good her escape, she found her way barred.

'Now, you're a sensible girl, and I'm sure you appreciate the value of silence.'

'If you mean, am I going to go around shouting, "Listen everyone, a master forger lives in that house there," no, I'm not. Frankly, it's none of my business.'

'That's the right attitude, stick to it, is my advice.'

Polly had her back to the other door, and while he was speaking, she'd had her hand behind her back, feeling for the handle. She found it, and pressed it down, almost falling backwards into the bakery. Slamming the door behind her, she ran past astonished customers and out of the main shop door.

Harriet was waiting for her. 'You said you'd only be a minute. Why, whatever's the matter? You look quite barmy.'

'Do I?' said Polly, glancing around, fearful that Tulliver might come pounding after her. 'It's just running up and down a lot of steps in there, that's all.'

FORTY-FIVE

Tulliver went across the road to the bar, and straight to the telephone, which was tucked away inconveniently behind the door. He lifted the receiver, inserted a coin, and asked for a number. He waited, tapping his fingers against the wall.

'Lanyard? Get me Sir Walter. Yes, it's important and urgent.'

Sir Walter was in his study, a room decorated in Regency style, with fine panelling all around the walls. He sat at a vast, ornate desk, which had reputedly belonged to Napoleon, and which dominated the room. The telephone bell rang, and he picked up the receiver, not hearing the slight click as another receiver was lifted in one of the luxurious Louis-Quinze bedrooms upstairs.

'Who? What? Who is this Miss Smith? Wait a minute, Miss Smith, Miss Smith . . .' He clapped his hand over the mouthpiece, and pressed a buzzer on his desk, at the same time shouting for Lanyard, who came hurrying in.

'Remind me about that interfering woman at Rossetti's, the one who said a signature was wrong. Used to work under Padgett. What's her name?'

'Smith,' Lanyard said at once. 'A Miss Polly Smith.'

Malreward took his hand off. 'Is her name Polly Smith? It is? And you say she saw Ivo at the gallery? Bloody carelessness, the whole business. I can't stand inefficiency, Penn, and this reeks of inefficiency. And Ivo's not bothered? Amused? He'd better damn well wipe the amusement off his face and start being bothered. I'll leave it to you, Tulliver. Fix it, and fix it quickly. If money's not a possibility, then there'll have to be an accident. Don't go coy on me, you've done it before, you can do it again. The end justifies the means, you will recall.'

He slammed the phone down, opened the box of cigars which stood on the desk, and thrust one into his mouth. He sat back, chewing at the end of it, while Lanyard leaped forward with a lighter.

Upstairs, Myron softly replaced the receiver, and he and Lois looked at one another in silence.

FORTY-SIX

Oliver drove up to Le Béjaune in his Lagonda, and Polly sat in the front beside him, listening to the powerful engine throbbing as it took the bends with smooth force, while Jo and Maud, in the back, let out cries of warning about speed and dangerous turns. Oliver swung through the open gates of Le Béjaune, and came to a halt beside Max's Delage.

So Max was back. Polly felt absurdly pleased as she climbed out of the car, carefully holding Oliver's cloak out of the dust. She was wearing one of the frocks described by Katriona as a cocktail; it came to her ankles in a swirl of pleats, and made her feel astonishingly sophisticated.

Cynthia Harkness was at the door, with Harriet beside her, wearing red velvet of a style more suitable to her years than the one she'd borrowed to go to the nightclub. 'Mummy won't let me wear anything longer,' she confided to Polly as they went into the sitting room. 'Which is mean of her.'

Max was busy at the drinks table, while Cynthia explained the plans for the evening. 'It's not a regular dinner party, it can't be on Christmas Eve. So we're serving drinks and so on now and then everyone will want to go out into the village for the festivities, it's all very gay, and thank goodness, although it's cold, it hasn't snowed as our gardener insists it's going to.'

Harriet protested, 'Mummy, how can you not want a white Christmas?'

'It can snow in the early hours, if you like, but imagine having to slide about on those steep cobbled streets with a covering of snow.'

Max was beside Polly, handing her a cocktail.

'Did you have a good time in Paris?' she asked.

'Good time?' He considered her question. 'I wasn't out on the town, if that's what you mean. I achieved what I went to do, so it was a satisfactory visit.'

'Max is crazy,' said Archie, coming into the room and giving Polly a hearty kiss on both cheeks. 'My word, Polly, you do look striking this evening. No, I can't think what got into Max, dashing off and getting into Paris in the small hours, and then making the return journey only a couple of days later. At least he caught the sleeper back.'

What kind of business could take Max to Paris just so close to Christmas? And hadn't Mr Grandison said that he didn't have a profession, so why would he need to go? Perhaps Mrs Warden was there, or his stocks and shares were tumbling, and he had to consult; Polly had very woolly ideas as to the ways in which a rich man made and looked after his income.

'Don't eat too many olives and canapés,' Harriet said to Polly. 'Or you won't be able to fit everything else in. There's a chocolate log, that's a *bûche de Noël* in French, it's what you have on Christmas Eve. As well as *raïto* before midnight and turkey and chestnuts afterwards.'

'Yes, I'm afraid that Henri, our chef, has firm ideas about what's suitable for the occasion, so I trust we can do it justice,' said Cynthia.

The whole of Rodoard was out on the streets. Polly hoped

that there was no chance of encountering Tulliver in the throng, or Ivo if it came to that. She hadn't cared for the way Tulliver had spoken to her. She had thought of confiding in Oliver, telling him what she'd seen, but she wasn't sure how he'd react to her story. He might take a strong line and want to call the police, or go and tackle Tulliver; Polly had a strong idea that Tulliver was best left alone.

Or Oliver might laugh it off, shrug at the forgeries, say it was all part of life's rich pattern and make a joke of it.

Rodoard had been taken back to its early medieval glory this evening, to the time when it was the thriving town attached to a rich and powerful monastery. Flambeaux lit the streets, held in the old iron sconces embedded in the stones of the buildings. They burned with dancing flames and a smell of smoke hung on the air.

There were market stalls set out in the main square and overflowing into adjoining streets, selling trinkets and sweets, *santons* and nuts. A man in a beret was installed beside a brazier heaped with coals, on which he was roasting chestnuts. Polly stopped to savour the smell of the nuts as their shells burnt off with soft cracking sounds.

Many of Rodoard's artists had their wares on display, and Polly's eye was caught by some china figurines set out on a table; supple, Art Deco women striking extravagant poses as if caught in mid-dance.

'They're good,' said Polly, inspecting one, and discovering that the artist, a German woman, spoke some English, she plunged into technical talk with her. Polly had done a lot of pottery at college.

'I loved it,' she said regretfully, 'only I was never really good enough to take it further.'

The potter nodded her understanding. 'You paint, however, and I cannot paint at all, these figures move and dance, but on the page, everyone I draw is lifeless and awkward.'

Max was beside her, the others having moved on up the street. 'I think I shall buy one,' he said. 'I find them charming. You can advise me, which one do you like the best?'

'Oh, like,' said Polly. 'As to that . . . This one,' she said, pointing to a slender woman in a dress which flared out, her body arched back, her arms making swan-like gestures, 'this one captures the spirit of the time perfectly. It makes me smile.'

Max addressed the potter in fluent German. 'She wants to leave it on display, in case anyone wants to order a similar one,' he said to Polly. 'I'm to collect it from her studio.'

'And then you won't have to carry it around,' said Polly. 'You aren't really a parcel-carrying kind of man, so it's as well.'

He looked amused. 'Am I so effete?'

'No, but parcels are – oh, I don't know – domestic, somehow. You aren't domestic.'

'I'm not sure whether to take that as a compliment or an insult.'

She smiled at him. 'Take it any way you want.'

'Is Dr Harrington a parcel-carrying person?'

'Oh, yes. At least for now. Once he climbs up the medical ladder and becomes an important man in his field, then he won't be.'

For a moment her vital enjoyment in the evening and the novelty of the Christmas spirit abroad in Rodoard faded; she didn't want to think about Roger just now.

'Look at those candles,' she exclaimed, making for another stall, where Christmas candles in the shapes of angels and stars were burning merrily.

A group of children were standing around one of the cribs, which was illuminated by a forest of candles. The scene brought a lump to her throat, and as the children began to sing, in pure, high voices, tears pricked her eyes.

The tune was one she knew. 'What is it in French?' she whispered to Max.

'It's "*Les anges dans nos campagnes*". In a minute you can join in.'

'Not I,' said Polly, but as all around them, voices were raised to sing, '*Gloria in excelsis Deo*', she found herself singing, too, happily and without concern for whether she was in tune or not.

'I suppose you speak French fluently,' she said to Max.

'We had a French governess when I was little. Which is why I know the words of that carol.'

'How strange to have a governess. And then, I suppose, like Oliver, you went off to boarding school at eight, and then on to Eton and Oxford or Cambridge.'

'I was at Eton, yes, but before Fraddon's time.'

Polly laughed. 'I went to the local girls' school, and I was lucky to be able to. My father – the person I thought was my father – was killed in the war, but Ma used his savings to pay for me to go to that school.'

'Were you happy there?'

'As long as it was a day when I did art, yes. Were you happy at Eton?'

Max went very quiet, and Polly was close enough to him to see from his eyes, dark in the torchlight and even more expressionless than usual, that he was looking back to his schooldays, and with no particular pleasure. 'I wasn't ever cut out for community life,' he said finally. 'And I wasn't much good at sport, except for shooting, not with a gammy leg. To be good at sport at those kinds of schools is the great safety, it excuses everything. If you aren't a sportsman, then you're liable to be classed as a no-hoper.'

'No-hoper? You?'

'Let's just say you probably enjoyed your schooldays rather more than I did.'

At that moment, Polly heard a joyful cry and turned round to see what it was. She had no eyes for the arrival of the puppeteers at the far end of the square, which was the reason for the cheerful noise, for she had seen Tulliver, a few paces back. More ominously, the moment he realized she'd seen him, he ducked behind a tree and vanished into the throng of people pressing forward to get a good view of the puppets.

Max was watching her. 'What's up?' he said quietly. 'What did you see?'

'Oh, I thought I saw someone I knew, I was mistaken. The puppet show is beginning, it's the Christmas story. I love the donkey that Mary's riding on, what a resigned look he has!'

Harriet, holding Archie in a determined hand, came pushing through the good-natured crowd to join them. 'This is fun,' she said. 'I'm so glad we're here and not having to spend the evening at the Villa Trophie with Walter. He wanted us to be there, you know,' she said to Polly, 'only Mummy said, No, we'd go for Christmas dinner, not tonight. Come on, we can get closer.'

She tugged Archie off, elbowing her way through for a better view.

'How well do you know Sir Walter Malreward?' Max asked Polly.

'I don't know him at all. I met him for the first time at the Blue Monkey.'

'What do you know about him?'

Polly stared at him. 'Know about him? Why should I know anything? He's a rich man who owns magazines.'

'Did you know he owns the Rossetti Gallery?'

'Owns the . . . No, you must have got that wrong. Old Giuseppe Rossetti is the owner, he started the gallery and is still there.'

'A figurehead, no more. You didn't know it, but when you

worked there and in the workshop, you were employed by Sir Walter.'

'Was I? Was I really?' And then, as realization dawned, 'You don't mean that Sir Walter gave me the heave-ho?'

'More than likely.'

'I wish I'd known,' said Polly regretfully. 'I could have had a go at him if I'd known. Why does he keep it so quiet? I never heard Mr Padgett or Sam mention it, and if Sam had known, he would have said.'

'That would be Mr Sam Carter?'

'Yes,' said Polly, too busy hoping she could keep out of Tulliver's way to consider how Max knew Sam's name. 'Hadn't we better be getting back to Mrs Harkness's house, look at the time, almost half past ten, and she said to be back by then. I expect she'll be there waiting for us.'

FORTY-SEVEN

Cynthia wasn't waiting for them at Le Béjaune. Instead, she was out in the town, away from all the bustle and gaiety and music, walking up a quiet street behind the shadowy figure of the man she knew as Ronnie. He was heading for the church, she realized, and she followed him into the square, lit for tonight's celebrations by lanterns hanging from hooks high up on the church wall. It was deserted now; presently it would fill with people coming for the service. The church doors were open, and there were lights and voices inside, as the priest and his acolytes prepared for the mass.

Ronnie was leaning over the far wall, looking out over the countryside. There was a half-moon, which cast its pale, indifferent light over the landscape and the sea, silvery in the distance. Cynthia came up beside him.

She stood there in silence for a while before she spoke. 'Hullo, Ronnie.'

'I wondered if it was you,' he said, without turning his head. Then he tossed the cigarette he'd been smoking down into the bushes far below and swung round to look at her. 'Cynthia. It's been a long time.'

'More than sixteen years.' Cynthia sat down on the stone

bench which ran along the wall, and, after a moment's hesitation, he sat down a couple of feet away from her. 'What happened to you, Ronnie?'

'I'm Ivo for the present. What happened to me? Do you want the war story, to hear about the unspeakable, unimaginable horrors that were waiting for me in the trenches? Or the story of how I was taken up for dead by the Germans, who nursed me back to life and then put me behind barbed wire? Or how I escaped and stowed away on a ship that was going to America?'

'Why didn't you come back to me?'

'Circumstances intervened.'

'That won't do. I was your wife, I was pregnant.'

Ivo looked at his feet. 'That was the problem, you see. I loved you all right, but it was boy and girl stuff. Hearts and bodies and all that. A wife, a child? What did that have to do with me? I was only a child myself, for God's sake. I couldn't face it, that's all. Not going back to you, and most of all not going back to that hell on earth I'd been blown out of.'

'When the war was over—'

'When the war was over, it was too late. I was in America, with a new name, new life. Come on, Cynthia, it wasn't as though I left you destitute. You had family, money, all the things I never had. I knew you'd be OK. Whereas, if I came back to life, it would have meant nothing but trouble.'

'I grieved terribly for you.'

'Yes, I knew you would, and I was sorry for it. As much as I could be, there comes a point when you just stop being sensitive to suffering, your own or anyone else's. I told myself it was the best thing, for you to get it over with, start a new life yourself. I reckoned that by the time I'd got back, if I had, you'd have more or less forgotten me and would have been disconcerted and upset to discover I was still alive.'

'Never that.'

'Was it a girl or a boy?' he asked, looking directly at her now, his extraordinary blue eyes visible even in the muted light.

'A girl.'

'Better to be a girl. Less trouble, and no one will send you to the trenches when you grow up.' He paused, taking out a battered packet of Gauloises from his coat pocket. 'Want one?' he said, holding out the packet.

Cynthia shook her head. He took one, put it in his mouth and struck a match to light it. 'That girl who's with you now at Le Béjaune, what's she called?'

'Harriet.'

'Is she—?'

'Yes, Harriet's your daughter.'

'Does she know I'm her father?'

'No, she does not, nor does anyone else. When I learned that you were dead, I married a man called Geoffrey Harkness. She was born eight months later.'

'My God, you were quick off the mark. Covering your traces very niftily. You didn't fancy widowhood, I suppose.'

'As you say, circumstances intervened. Which made it advisable for me to have another husband.'

'She looks a nice kid. Can she draw?'

'No.'

'Pity.'

'You're an artist?'

'Of a kind.'

'Why Rodoard?'

Ivo shrugged. 'There are reasons, which it would be boring to go into.'

'And you make a living from your art?'

Ivo laughed, a laugh so familiar to Cynthia that her heart stopped, the laugh of the vital, confident Ronnie who had leapt out of her bed and gone off to war, promising to survive and come back to raise a family. 'Four children, you said you wanted.'

His laugh this time didn't have the same exuberance. 'It seems I've got what I wanted then. Three kids in America, and Harriet.'

'Three kids? And a wife, I suppose?'

'Yes. I married Conchita ten years ago.'

'Is she Spanish?'

'Mexican.'

'So we're both bigamists.'

That won her another genuine laugh. 'By God, I suppose we are. There'd be the devil to pay if Conchita ever found out, she's a good Catholic girl, she'd be horrified.'

'Do you suppose we should do anything about it? Legally, I mean?' Even as she spoke the words, Cynthia knew how meaningless they were.

'Are you mad? Unpick our lives for the lawyers to have a field day? Let sleeping dogs lie, Cynthia, there's nothing to be gained by doing anything else. How long have you known I was alive?'

'I saw you on the *Aquitania*, and recognized you.'

'Well done, after all this time. I'd hardly recognize myself, compared to how I was at sixteen, before I went to France.'

'Some things about a person don't change.'

'What difference could it make to you? You're divorced, everyone in Rodoard gossips about Madame Harkness's divorce.'

'Do they? Do they also gossip about the fact that Madame Harkness is going to marry Sir Walter Malreward, and this time, unlike when I married Geoffrey, I know I have a husband living, to whom in the eyes of the church and the law, I'm still married?'

Ivo's voice was sombre. 'Don't do it, Cynthia. Don't marry him.'

'Because I'm not free to do so?'

'Because he's a dangerous man, and I'd pity any woman who married him.'

'You sound like a character on the pictures. How do you know Walter?'

'I work for him. No, don't ask, for I'm not going to tell you, it's better that you don't know. Just don't do it. Don't for God's sake tell him about us, about the marriage, since that would mean the end of me – if he could ever find me, which I'll make damn sure he can't. Just back out. He won't harm you, however furious he is. If anything happened to you, there'd be too many questions asked.'

Cynthia was beginning to wonder whether Ronnie had been wounded in the head during the war, had been left not quite right in his wits.

'You think I'm nuts. I'm not. Look, Cynthia, face it, we'd have been washed up years ago if I'd come back to you. I thought I was grown-up at sixteen. Maybe you were, girls do grow up earlier. I didn't begin to grow up for another ten years, and by that time, I was a totally different person. So were you, I expect. So let's cut out the sentiment bit. I'm giving you the best piece of advice anyone will ever give you. Call it a parting gift. Accept it, reject it, the choice is yours.'

'Parting gift?'

'Oh, yes. I'm off. Nothing to do with you, honey, more to do with Sir Walter and his minions. I shall vanish into the night, and by the way, don't trouble to come looking for me. Ronnie disappeared years ago, and Ivo Johnson will vanish just as completely. It's a name I've used for various purposes, not the name by which I'm registered as a citizen of the great US of A.'

'How do you do it?' Cynthia exclaimed. 'How did you do it?'

'Escape, deceive, slide away from trouble? An instinct for self-preservation coupled with Celtic ancestry let's say.'

At that moment a breathless Harriet erupted into the square. 'Here you are, Mummy, I thought you might be, I know you like to come and mooch up here. Oh!' seeing Ivo. 'Sorry.'

Cynthia got up. 'It turns out that Mr Johnson is an old friend. Ivo, this is Harriet.'

Harriet held out her hand, and he took it, holding it instead of shaking it. Father and daughter looked into each other's blue eyes. He let her hand drop. 'I'm pleased to meet you, Harriet.'

Then his eyes met Cynthia's. 'It's goodbye, Cynthia. Take care of yourself.' He moved forward, and kissed her. And then, to Harriet's astonishment, he gave her a kiss on both cheeks. 'Be lucky, Harriet.'

And he was gone, leaving Harriet staring after him.

'What a peculiar man. It sounded as though he was blessing me, he must be potty. Do come on, Mummy, all our guests are there, tummies flapping against spines, and you nowhere to be seen.'

Harriet dragged her at breakneck speed over the cobbles, ignoring her protests. At the bottom of the street, Cynthia stopped. 'No, wait a minute, Harriet. You're not to say a word about meeting Ivo.'

'Mummy, what are you up to?'

'Nothing, but you must pay attention to this, Harriet. I mean it.'

'OK, it's a secret. Now, come on.'

FORTY-EIGHT

The church was full. Polly sat next to Oliver, having chosen to do so for the good reason that, being Catholic, he would know what to do, and she wouldn't find herself standing or sitting or kneeling at all the wrong moments.

She had never been to a service like it, and nothing had prepared her for the assault on her senses: the Latin, the chanting, the singing, the incense, the colours of the candlelit interior, the blaze of light and silver and gold on the altar, the rich vestments of the priest and his attendants.

The pre-church supper had been rather rushed, although tasty. Archie was keen to go to Midnight Mass. 'Quite a lot of us Scots are Catholic,' he told her, seeing her look of surprise. Harriet had insisted on going, she loved bells and smells, and she wanted to see Baby Jesus laid in the crib. 'I shall cry,' she announced, sniffing by way of practice.

Cynthia didn't want to go, she looked to Polly as though she had something on her mind and would be glad to be on her own. Maud and Jo said they'd go and slip out halfway; Maud, who was accustomed to keep early hours, was already yawning her head off.

Max had said he would go, and could keep an eye on Harriet.

'I don't need an eye kept on me, and besides, Oliver and Archie and Polly will be there.'

Max laughed. 'I'd like to go. Put on a thick coat, Harriet. If I know anything about churches, it'll be freezing.'

'No, it won't, all that religious fervour and candle power will warm it up.'

Max and Harriet were sitting with Archie on the other side of the aisle. Oliver got up from his knees and sat back, then reached for the order of service, printed on a faded sheet, which he gave to Polly. 'I know it by heart,' he said.

'Is it the same here as in England?'

'It's the same all over the world, they just pronounce the Latin differently.'

The service began, and Polly duly stood up and sat and knelt, the words flowing incomprehensibly over her. She gazed at the crib, at the angels and shepherds and the visiting kings in their vivid robes and crowns, the placid oxen and patient donkey, at bearded Joseph looking down at a serene Mary, who hung over the empty manger, waiting for the Christ child to be laid on the bed of straw.

Harriet had been right about the incense. A little boy, resplendent in a red gown with a lacy white surplice over it, swung the shining censer on its chain, each movement causing little puffs of intensely scented incense to rise into the air. Polly's nose began to tickle, and she pressed her finger against the bridge of her nose, to stop herself sneezing.

Her eyes were watering, and she knew that in a moment she was going to have to sneeze, she wouldn't be able to prevent it. And she'd go on sneezing, judging by the effect the incense was having on her nose.

People were moving up to the altar to receive communion.

Oliver stood up to go, gesturing to her to wait where she was. This was her chance. After the people on her other side had squeezed past, she crept to the end of the row, and, lost in the shadows behind the pillars, made her escape through the open doors and down the steps into the fresh, bitingly cold air of the square.

She bent her head and sneezed, again and again. Wiping her eyes, she was overcome with laughter at the absurdity of it; so much for religious experience, it was as though Ma's resolute shunning of St Jude's had caused a mirthful deity to curse her with sneezes for attending divine service. She pulled herself together, and, breathing deeply, went over to look at the moonlit view.

She knelt on the stone bench, the better to see across the moonlit hills to the silvery sea beyond, when she heard footsteps behind her. It must be a late worshipper, very late, to arrive more than halfway through the service. She turned round to see who it was, and saw, not a straggling member of the congregation, but Tulliver Penn.

'Hullo,' she began. 'What—' She was backed against the wall, unable to slide away, and here was this man advancing on her. A strong and relentless man, bent, Polly knew in an instant, on violence, not an amorous advance. In a moment, he had seized her by the arms and, thrusting her backwards against the wall, clearly had every intention of pushing her over the edge and down on to the rock-strewn ground so far below.

She yelped and kicked out, felt herself being remorselessly lifted, and then, miraculously, figures appeared out of the shadows. There, on either side of her, were Oliver and Max, tall, protective and a match for any Tulliver Penn. Tulliver loosened his grasp, and darted towards the street leading down into the centre, only to be confronted by more men coming out of dark corners and doorways. One of them grabbed him, wrestling him to the ground and twisting his arms behind his back.

Max called out to the man in French, and he, handing Tulliver over to his companions, dusted himself down and raised his hand in greeting, saying, '*Joyeux Noël*,' in the friendliest, most relaxed way, as though the whole scene were no more than a social encounter.

Joyeux Noël, indeed, Polly said to herself, thoroughly shaken. What on earth was Tulliver up to, was he drunk? Then she realized who the man who'd grabbed Penn was Ettore, the elegant, purple-sashed Ettore, now looking not at all like a rich woman's gigolo and every inch a man of action.

Was she dreaming?

'You can fall into my arms, if you like,' Max offered.

'No, thank you. What did Tulliver think he was doing? Is he drunk? Full of cocaine?'

'Not at all,' said Max. 'He was trying to kill you.'

Oliver cleared his throat. 'Why should anyone want to kill Polly?'

'I expect she knows something that Tulliver, by which one in fact means Tulliver's employer, prefers should be kept secret.'

'Rubbish,' said Polly, rubbing her arms, bruised from Tulliver's brutal hold. 'I don't know any secrets.'

'Walter Malreward thinks you do.'

'Malreward?' said Oliver. 'Are you serious?'

'Indeed he is,' said Ettore. He and Max exchanged glances. With the part of her mind that was still functioning normally, Polly noticed the look of understanding and complicity. They were two of a kind, now why should that be, when they were in every obvious way so very different?

'Now I and my men will proceed down the hill, to arrest Mr Ivo,' said Ettore.

'I think,' said Max, as Ettore vanished into the darkness, 'he will find the bird has already flown.'

In the distance, they heard the roar of a motorcycle. Oliver and Max went to look over the wall; Polly, who had no intention of ever going near there again, stayed where she was.

'Ivo, making good his escape,' said Max laconically. 'I doubt if they'll catch him, he's a wily character.'

'Ivo forges paintings,' said Polly. She was shivering from cold and shock, and her teeth were beginning to chatter. 'I saw them in his studio down the street. He's a brilliant artist.'

'Forger!' Oliver exclaimed. 'Here in Rodoard? What kind of a forger?'

'Old masters,' said Polly. 'So good even you, Oliver, wouldn't be able to tell them from the real thing,' and she began to laugh again.

'No hysterics,' said Max. 'Time to go home, Polly.'

'I'll run you back,' said Oliver.

'No, I'll take her. You wait here for the others and go back to Le Béjaune with them. Tell Cynthia I shan't be long.'

Oliver took Polly by the shoulders and looked closely at her. 'Are you sure you're all right?'

She nodded.

'The man's a maniac, I hope they put him behind bars for this,' he said.

'And for a few other misdeeds, I suspect,' said Max.

Oliver kissed Polly on her cheeks in a brotherly fashion; one, two. She felt a surge of warmth towards him, and laid a hand on his arm, thanking him with a smile.

She and Max walked back through the streets in silence, the sounds of the congregation leaving the church drifting down to them through the still, chilly air. And a few minutes later, Polly was sitting in the front seat of Max's car, and he was driving out of the gates and over the cobbles.

'I saw this car on the ferry,' she said inconsequentially.

411

'On the deck.' She yawned, and apologized, then yawned again. 'I'm sorry to miss the turkey and chestnuts and Harriet's chocolate log – what did she call it?'

'*Bûche de Noël*. I'll tell her to save you a piece.'

'Yes.' She yawned again. 'I'd fall asleep into my soup if I stayed. I'm exhausted.'

'Don't sound so surprised, it's not every day one survives a murderous onslaught. Are you sure he didn't hurt you? He's no weakling, and jumping you like that—'

'Thanks to the posse of rescuers, he didn't get the chance to do much.' Her eyelids drooped, and she came to with a start as the car stopped outside the Domus Romana, its entrance lit on that festive night with the same torches that flared up in Rodoard.

In the distance, a cock crowed. 'Silly bird,' said Polly sleepily. 'It's hours until dawn.'

Max had gone round and opened the passenger door. 'Come on, out you get.'

Reluctant to move, and with her arms feeling strangely stiff, Polly did as she was told.

Max looked up into the dark sky, with the moon riding through clouds, as the lone cockerel crowed again.

> '"Some say that ever 'gainst that season comes
> Wherein our Saviour's birth is celebrated,
> The bird of dawning singeth all night long,"'

he quoted softly.

'How wonderful,' Polly said, even more softly. 'Shakespeare?'

'*Hamlet*. From the opening of a tragic tale, whereas I hope tonight we've prevented the ending of another one.'

Polly yawned and stared at him, not sure what he was talking about. He looked at her for a moment, and then, without touching her, bent down and kissed her on the mouth.

A kiss that sank her into some velvety region, dark and promising, and . . .

The door opened. Lord Fraddon stood there, surveying them down his beaky nose. He was arrayed in a fabulous dressing gown of crimson silk, brocaded with a pattern of flamboyant dragons.

'Good evening, Polly, Lytton. Is something amiss? Where is Oliver?'

'Oliver is at my sister's house. I brought Polly back, she's had rather an exciting evening.'

'I see. Won't you come in?'

'I won't, sir. My sister is expecting me back. Goodnight, Polly, sleep tight. And Happy Christmas.'

'Happy Christmas,' echoed Polly, as the door shut behind him. She stood inside, blinking at the light from the torches that were set around the hall and through the atrium to the pool. Their gusting flames made the rich colours and gilt of the walls and pillars seem like an apparition from another world. The sense of detachment which had come over her after Tulliver's attack remained, and the sense of unreality was so strong that she wondered, for a moment, if she were caught in a dream.

Lord Fraddon looked her up and down. 'Are you all right?'

'Yes.' And then feeling she should expand on this, 'Someone tried to push me over the wall outside the church.'

'How remarkable. In Rodoard? But here you are, safe and sound. Did he hurt you?'

'Only my arms,' said Polly, removing her cloak and inspecting the damage. The bruises were already showing, dark marks where Tulliver's fingers had held her.

'You need a salve for that. Ah, Marie is awake,' he went on, as an alarmed-looking Marie appeared, wrapped in a flannel dressing gown, her hair pinned tightly to her head.

'Good. She'll bring you the salve and a tisane and aspirin and put you to bed.'

Polly opened her mouth to protest that she wasn't a child, but instead yawned, just managing to hide it behind her hand. 'I think I had better go to bed,' she said.

Lord Fraddon regarded her for a long moment, his hooded eyes invisible in the flickering light. Then he leant forward and kissed her on the forehead. 'Goodnight, and *Joyeux Noël*.'

Ten minutes later, Polly was in bed. As she lay in the tranquil darkness, she thought of the three kisses she had received that evening. One like that of a brother, one that of a lover, and one like that of a father. Only she had neither brother nor lover nor father. The recollection startled her into momentary wakefulness, before sleep overcame her and drew her down into forgetfulness.

FORTY-NINE

The note was delivered shortly after breakfast, which for Cynthia had consisted of no more than a cup of black coffee. She had dark rings under her eyes, testament to the fact that her few hours in bed had been passed in wakefulness.

Yet why? Because of her encounter with Ronnie, which had shaken her more than she could have imagined possible? Because of her uncertainty about Harriet – should she tell her who her father was, or leave her in ignorance? Because there had been that upset last night with police cars screaming through the town? Or because Max had returned from Lord Fraddon's house looking subdued and thoughtful, only coming out of himself when he told her that Ivo had done a flit, that he'd been busily engaged in forging old masters?

She couldn't possibly tell Harriet that her father wasn't the perfectly respectable Geoffrey Harkness, but the irresponsible if talented Ronnie – or Ivo, or whatever his name was. Artist, forger, bigamist, what an inheritance.

Max had disappeared, the tiresome man, saying he had some business to attend to. What business could he have on Christmas morning? And, moreover, she had a feeling he had fallen in love with that Smith girl. Not that Cynthia didn't like her, but she could hardly imagine two people less suited to one another. Perhaps he'd merely fallen in lust, in which case it would be no more than an affair, although Polly didn't strike her as the kind of girl who went in for casual affairs, whatever people said about artists' lax morals. Max usually found his amorous adventures among women of his own age and class, like that dreadful Thelma Warden, so why on earth he should be interested in a Polly Smith, she couldn't think.

She sighed, wishing the dull ache in her head would go away.

Rose gave a polite cough. 'The note, ma'am. It's from the Villa Trophie. Will there be an answer?'

'Oh, the note. Thank you, Rose.'

Cynthia looked at the envelope and saw it was from Sir Walter. She sighed again. A Christmas greeting? A card? A cheque?

The note was brief, and scrawled in a hand not at all like Walter's strong, deliberate writing.

I have to leave unexpectedly. My apologies, no dinner tonight. Goodbye, Walter.

Goodbye? What did he mean, Goodbye? What an extraordinary note. Was he drunk when he wrote it? She turned it over, as though there might be some explanation on the other side, but it was blank.

She was still staring at the sheet of paper when Max came in, calling for coffee, and asking if Harriet was still asleep.

'She won't be up for hours yet,' Cynthia said. 'She didn't go to bed until nearly three.'

'Nor did we.'

'We aren't sixteen. Max, I've had the oddest note from Walter.' She handed it to her brother and watched him with anxious eyes as he read it.

'He's done a bunk,' said Max.

'Done a— Don't be ridiculous. Why ever should he do a bunk?'

Max pulled out a chair and sat down. 'It's time you learned the truth about Sir Walter Malreward. And, not to put too fine a point on it, I don't suppose you'll be seeing him again, when he says goodbye, he means it. No wedding bells for you. I am sorry old thing, if it's what you really wanted. It's like this.'

Cynthia listened, aghast, not saying a word. She wanted to stop Max, to tell him it was all rubbish, that he was inventing this because he didn't care for Walter, didn't want her to marry him.

Instead, she kept perfectly quiet, and then, when Max had finished his succinct description of Malreward's career to date, she simply said, 'How do you know all this?'

'Can you keep a secret?'

'Isn't keeping secrets the story of my life? I know what you're going to say. You never did stop working for those people you were with during the war. Is that it? You're working for some government department, to do with intelligence?'

'That's it.'

'You've used your position to find out all this about Walter. Am I supposed to be grateful? Max, how could you do such a thing?'

'I didn't do it for that reason. Malreward's case was dumped in my lap by my chief. Don't you understand? Malreward is a crook, and his crookedness has made him a great deal of illicit money, which he's spending on bankrolling subversive elements in England and in America. Doesn't that mean anything to you?'

'Oh, that's just politics. Politics leave me cold.'

'Be that as it may, politics is why I've been looking into Malreward's affairs and history, and why he's now in deep trouble.'

417

Rose came in, holding another note in her hand. 'From Lord Fraddon, madam.'

'God, what now?' said Cynthia, still angry. As she read the note, written in a most elegant script, quite unlike Walter's effort, a look of surprise came over her face. 'He wants us to dine with him. He's heard that Sir Walter has unfortunately been called away, and since it's Christmas Day, he would like us to join him and a few friends this evening. It's kind of him, except that I don't intend to dine anywhere but here.'

'Which will be difficult, bearing in mind you've given the kitchen staff the afternoon and evening off.'

Cynthia had completely forgotten that. 'Oh, God, so I have. Well, we'll just have to fend for ourselves. Harriet can cook something, she learns domestic science at school.'

Max looked at her with amusement. 'One shudders at the prospect. And on Christmas Day, shame on you, Cynthia, for even thinking of such a thing. I should be delighted to dine with Fraddon, I suppose the rest of us are included in the invitation?'

'He writes, "and your daughter and brother and guest".'

'What's up?' said Archie, coming into the room with a bounce in his step. 'Have you heard that Sir Walter has rushed away from his villa? Driving at a hundred miles an hour, according to the good Jules. "A family crisis?" I asked, but Jules says, no, the *flics* are after him. All nonsense, of course.'

'The *flics* may be nonsense, but Walter has been called away,' said Cynthia. Damn it, why was she bothering to try and put a good face on it? If half of what Max said was true – 'Which means that we shan't be dining with him tonight.'

'Ah, trouble on the commissariat front,' said Archie. 'Is that coffee I see?'

'Lord Fraddon has kindly invited us to dine at the Domus Romana,' said Max.

'Excellent. He keeps a good table and his wines are superb. He's amusing company, too. Although it means we'll have to put up with ghastly Katriona.'

'Max is keen to go because Polly's there,' said Cynthia meanly, instantly regretting her remark as she saw Max stiffen. She hastened to mend matters. 'He's worried about her after the rumpus last night in the square.'

'Yes, Max, what was that all about?' said Archie. 'One hardly expects such drama in Rodoard.'

'Polly got in the way of a nasty piece of work called Penn,' said Max.

'Oliver will see she's all right,' said Archie. 'He's jolly fond of her. So am I, she's a honey.'

If she hadn't still been so angry, Cynthia would have laughed at the expression on Max's face at this fulsome praise. 'I suppose I'd better accept, otherwise it will be cold leftovers in the kitchen. I'll go and write a reply now.'

FIFTY

In honour of the festive occasion, Polly dressed with unusual care. She was wearing her red frock, and the moment she put it on, her spirits rose.

Marie exclaimed at the marks on her arms, and went away to come back with powder and a spangled shawl. One of Katriona's? Polly asked doubtfully, in her halting although much improved French.

Marie shook her head, and Polly gathered from what the maid went on to say that a guest had left it, but no one knew which guest, and so . . .

Reassured, Polly let Marrie apply the powder to her arms, and, more reluctantly, to her face. Then she draped the shawl to cover the bruises; she was ready for the fray.

As she went down the stairs, she grinned at the difference between this Polly, and the Polly of the first night at the Domus Romana. Then she had been a stranger, now she felt at home, and, moreover, she knew everyone who was dining there tonight. It was to be a large party, Oliver said. Daphne was coming, with Ettore; Gus Ibanez, the surrealist, would be a guest, and of course, Jo and Maud. And, since Sir Walter had left Rodoard unexpectedly, the party from Le Béjaune would be there as well.

Which meant Max. Polly didn't want to think about Max, so she quickened her pace, and went through to join Oliver and Lord Fraddon. He was wearing knee breeches and silk stockings, with court shoes, and looked extraordinarily grand and handsome. He congratulated her on her appearance, and summoned a footman, tonight, to Polly's secret amazement, dressed in full livery, to pour her a glass of champagne. Oliver, impeccable in white tie and tails, gave her a broad wink.

Katriona appeared, with her husband and little boy in tow. To Polly's surprise, Philip Rawlinson was a most amiable man, short and roly-poly, with a placid manner and a twinkle in his eye. He seemed able to ignore Katriona's sharp ways, and in fact, when he was there, she behaved rather better. Their son, Rory, was a shy, thin boy, all eyes, with an infectious giggle.

Katriona noticed Polly's frock at once, but only said, 'That's better.' Then she took issue with her father about the size of the party. 'Springing it on the servants like that, Fraddon, you should know better. And now I hear that apart from those people at that place in Rodoard, two Americans from the Villa Trophie are coming.'

'Sir Walter's guests, you wouldn't want them to dine alone on Christmas night, I feel sure.'

Polly let out an exclamation, and looked at Oliver. 'Is that the Watsons, the people at the Blue Monkey?'

'I imagine so.'

'The Blue Monkey?' said Katriona. 'I would hardly have thought—'

Her thoughts were not to be shared, as Fraddon's imposing butler, who had come to France with his master, announced the arrival of Mrs Wolf and Monsieur Aventurin. Close on their heels were the party from Le Béjaune. Archie was in Scottish evening dress of kilt and velvet jacket. He greeted Polly with a kiss.

'How glamorous you look,' she said. 'Is that really a dagger in your sock? Isn't it uncomfortable?'

'We call it a *sgian dhu*,' he said. 'And one gets used to it.'

More arrivals, Gus and Maud and Jo, and then the loud greetings and yelps of astonishment at the house from Lois Watson. 'Myron, did you ever see anything like it? Hollywood has nothing on this!'

More champagne, with Max at her shoulder, urbane, his sleek hair shining in the candlelight, his monocle catching the light as he asked her how her arms were.

'Fine,' she said. 'Tell me, I've been longing to ask you, do you have to wear that eye-glass?'

'Meaning, is it just affectation? No. Put it down to vanity. I have poor vision in one eye, and I don't care to wear spectacles.'

The sound of voices filled the room, and Polly, listening to an amusing tale of a fellow artist recounted by Gus, didn't catch the conversation that was going on at the other side of the room. Then she heard Lord Fraddon say, 'Polyhymnia Tomkins? Who the devil is Polyhymnia Tomkins? How extraordinary, but I do wonder—'

She went rigid, as he came towards her. 'Polly, is this for you? It's a wire, from England. Felix from the Post Office brought it down, in case it was urgent. It is addressed to Polyhymnia Tomkins, care of Fraddon, Rodoard.'

Polly took the telegram. A wire, for her? Who on earth – it had to be from Ma, but why would she send a wire? Was something wrong?'

'Open it,' said Max, 'and you'll find out.'

A silence fell over the gathering as Polly read the wire. The words danced in front of her eyes: *CABLE SENT ROGER. MARRIED VERONICA. LETTER FOLLOWS. NOT SORRY. MA.*

'What is it?' said Harriet. 'You looked stunned.'

'Not bad news, I trust,' said Myron.

'Perhaps it is a private matter,' said Lord Fraddon.

Polly stood stock still. 'I've been jilted,' she said, speaking more to herself than to the assembled company. She looked down at her ring, and then, slowly and deliberately drew it from her finger. 'Roger's married someone else.'

Voices rose in a hubbub.

'Good thing, too,' said Maud.

'Oh, Polly, how awful,' said Harriet.

'I didn't like the sound of Roger,' Oliver said to Max, who hadn't taken his eyes from Polly's face.

'Jilted?' Daphne's voice was amused. 'Never mind, plenty of men around for an attractive girl like you to pick and choose from.'

Lois nodded her agreement. 'And isn't that the truth?'

Cynthia watched Max watch Polly and said nothing, until Harriet nudged her, whispering, 'Don't you think it's awful?'

Cynthia whispered back, 'I don't think Polly minds so very much.'

'Doesn't she?' said Harriet, astonished. 'If she wasn't in love with him, why did she get engaged to him?'

'It happens,' said Archie. 'Give the girl another glass of fizz.'

'One moment,' said Lord Fraddon, in a voice that was quiet, but which commanded everyone's attention. 'Polyhymnia Tomkins. I thought your name was Smith.'

'I'm so sorry,' Polly began, crimson with embarrassment. 'I'm not an impostor, not really. It's that—' She floundered, and fell silent.

'Polly,' said Oliver, 'what have you been hiding from us? Don't look so distressed, nobody is going to throw you out into the snow, which has, if anyone is interested, been falling for the last half-hour.'

'Shall I explain?' said Max.

Polly nodded, thankful to let him do the talking.

'I wonder—' said Lord Fraddon.

'From what I learned in Paris,' said Max, 'I think your suspicions are well-founded.'

'Suspicions?' said Katriona, frowning at Polly. 'What suspicions?'

'Perhaps it would be best if I showed you a picture,' said Lord Fraddon. 'Come with me, Polly. And you, Oliver and Katriona. And Lytton, I think. Yes. If the rest of you will forgive us, we shan't be long.'

He led them into his study, where the portrait of the woman, with the only light in the room shining down on it, dominated the room.

Max made a sound of disbelief, and then said, 'A Cortoni.'

'A Cortoni,' said Lord Fraddon. 'A painting of his favourite model, Thomasina Tomkins.'

Polly let out a cry of amazement. 'Thomasina Tomkins? My mother was called Thomasina Tomkins. And she was an artist's model. Is that – is the woman in the painting her?'

'It's certainly Thomasina, and I can believe she was your mother. You are like her; not in feature, but there's a quality about you that reminds me of her.'

'I can't believe it.' Polly blinked, as tears filled her eyes. 'I don't have a single photograph, and now this. Did she really look like that, or is it all painter's glamour?'

'Cortoni almost invented glamour, but when he painted Thomasina he portrayed her as she was.'

Polly bit her lip, overflowing with an excited happiness that left her breathless. 'You knew her. You can tell me about her, about her life in Paris. And, oh, Lord Fraddon, is she still alive?'

'That is a question I often asked myself,' Lord Fraddon said. 'She went to America. I tried to trace her, without success.'

424

'Why did you want to trace her?' said Polly, although she knew the answer.

'I was in love with her; we were lovers. I had to return to England, and when I went back to Paris a few months later, she was gone. She told Cortoni she was off to America with a Russian. He had no address, no idea who the man was.'

'One moment,' said Max. 'I—'

He was hesitating, and Polly looked at him in surprise, hesitation was most unlike him. 'This may not be the time or place – however, it concerns both Polly and you, Lord Fraddon. It so happens that I have been undertaking an investigation for various reasons which I won't go into, in the course of which I have uncovered information about Thomasina Tomkins and Polly. That's why I was in Paris,' he said, turning to Polly.

Polly was taken aback, and opened her mouth to ask what he meant, but he was now speaking directly to Lord Fraddon. 'Thomasina was already four months pregnant when you went away, Fraddon. While you were in England, she gave birth to a daughter, Polly, and soon afterwards brought the baby to England to leave it in her sister's care. She confided in Cortoni's housekeeper, who is still alive, and told her that she couldn't marry the father because he was a married man, and a Catholic. She said that although the man was in love with her, he didn't know about the child. If he knew, he might want to leave his wife and children for her, and she didn't want him to do that. Instead, she intended to go to America to make a new life for herself.'

Lord Fraddon gave Max a long hard look. 'You seem to have been very busy about other people's affairs. Officious, one might say.'

'Not at all. I have my own reasons for wanting to find out the truth. Polly has a right to know, and you would already have known at least part of the story, Polly, if Dora Smith hadn't been so determined to cut herself off from her family.'

Oliver looked at his father, who was white about the mouth, and went over to stand beside him.

Polly's heart was thumping in a disagreeable way, and her mouth felt dry. She stared at Max. 'Are you saying that Lord Fraddon is my father?'

'Impossible,' cried Katriona. 'I never heard such a farrago of nonsense. And just who and what are you, Mr Lytton, a private detective? I think you're here under false pretences, what a nerve, coming here with these fantastic stories.'

'Polly is Fraddon's daughter, isn't she, Lytton?' Oliver said. 'She is.'

'What a Christmas present for us, Fraddon. You have a daughter, and I get a sister.'

Polly was speechless. Lord Fraddon her father? Oliver her brother – her half-brother? And she had a half-sister, and what a half-sister! 'I'm terribly sorry,' she said, the glowing image of family extinguished as the reality hit her. 'I think I'd better go.'

'Go where?' said Max, putting out an arm to stop her as she plunged towards the door.

'Anywhere. Lord Fraddon and Oliver won't want me – it's worse than being here under a false name.'

Lord Fraddon came across to Polly and looked down at her. Was there a glint of tears in those inscrutable eyes? She forced herself to look up at him, and they stood there for a long, still moment, father and daughter, regarding one another with a strangely similar intensity.

'Polly, my dear,' said Lord Fraddon finally. 'Could I possibly not want you here, for your own sake, and for the sake of your mother? You're all I have left of her, and although time passes, and I have loved other women, I could never forget her.'

He opened his arms, and after a moment's uncertainty. Polly accepted his embrace, muffling her own wet cheeks in the soft velvet of his coat, feeling the strength of him, while words echoed in her head: This man is my father. I have a father.

The embrace was interrupted by a cough from the doorway. 'Pardon me if I intrude,' said Myron. 'I couldn't help overhearing some of what you were speaking about, and I guess I have my mite to add to these interesting revelations.'

Oliver's face darkened. 'What the devil are you about, eavesdropping on a private conversation?'

'I apologize. Eavesdropping is an essential part of my professional duties, and as I say, I reckon Lois and I can clear up a few loose ends for you in this matter. I have to confess that Miss Smith isn't the only one here going under a name that isn't quite correct. Let me introduce the two of us afresh: we are Leo and Maisie Rasmussen, and we work for the Pinkerton Detective Agency.'

FIFTY-ONE

Pinkerton! There was a world of romance and danger conjured up by that name. 'Pinkertons get their man?' Polly said.

'We generally do get our man,' said Myron, 'and in this case, we've nailed down just what he's been up to, even if we don't physically have him behind bars.'

The other guests, hearing Myron's booming voice, had drifted towards the study. Max said to Lord Fraddon, 'I think, sir, I know what some of these revelations are, and if I'm right, they'll concern quite a few of those here tonight. Perhaps we might go back to the other room, so that everyone can hear what Mr and Mrs Watson – Mr and Mrs Rasmussen have to say?'

Myron held the floor; Lois sat in a senatorial chair beside him. Gone was the face of the eager American tourist, to be replaced by a keen, intelligent expression. Quite a pair, thought Max. They were, of course, the other parties Lazarus had mentioned coming across.

'Our quarry is the man you know as Sir Walter Malreward, and this was our purpose in coming to Europe.'

'"Know as"?' said Polly, who found herself filled with a

light-heartedness and light-headedness that made her want
to laugh. 'Not another person masquerading under a false
name?'

'I fear so, ma'am, but it's one he's used for some considerable time. He took on the name of Malreward when he
was a very young man, to better himself, and, through a
wicked murder, lay the foundations of his fortune.'

'Murder?' said Cynthia.

'Ma'am, I regret to say that although Walter Malreward
only killed once with his own hands—'

Here Lois interrupted. 'Hardly with his own hands. It was
arson, Mrs Harkness. He caused a fire to be started, which
killed two people. Ever since, he's paid or blackmailed or
forced other people to do his dirty work for him.'

Myron was nodding his head in agreement. 'You saw that
yesterday; Tulliver Penn made his murderous attack on
Miss—'

'Polly will do.'

'On Polly, here, on the instructions of Malreward.'

'How can you know that?' said Cynthia. 'It sounds to me
like pure supposition.'

'Ma'am, we are trained to make suppositions, however,
in this case, we heard Malreward speaking on the telephone,
giving Tulliver his orders.'

Cynthia subsided into her seat and began to pick at the
beads on her frock. Harriet looked anxiously at her, and
then, taking a cushion, went over to her and plonked herself
down at her mother's feet.

The story went on, the story that Max already knew, of
Malreward's time in Paris and then in England.

'Now why, you may ask,' Myron said, 'should Pinkertons
send two agents over to the United Kingdom at this time,
when Malreward has been out of America for so long? It is
because various official bodies, whom I cannot name,

approached the agency for assistance. Money has been flowing into the States, money suspected of coming from an illegal and untraceable source. And this money has gone into the coffers of various organizations that threaten the stability and good government of our country. We have groups far to the right that want to see America made racially pure, as they put it, and isolated, financially and militarily from any conflict that might arise in Europe. We have groups on the left that are plotting to overthrow democracy and place our country under state control of a Stalinist nature.'

'And this money comes from Malreward?' asked Archie, who was listening with keen attention. 'Why would he fund two opposing sides?'

'His own views incline to the fascist. He's an ardent supporter of Mussolini, as it turns out. And a good way to bring in a fascist government is to destabilize the systems that keep a democracy going.'

'And the money for this has come from forged pictures,' said Daphne Wolf.

She was sitting in another senatorial chair, dressed in her usual purple, and looking, Max thought, very much as one of the great Roman matrons might have done.

'Don't look at me through your monocle like that, Max Lytton,' she said. 'You may have been on the trail in England, and doubtless nosing around the Rossetti Gallery, which was the centre of Malreward's art business, but some of us over here have had our suspicions as well. Such as Ettore, who works for the French fraud investigators. And Gus, who forged Picassos and Matisses for Malreward as Ettore's inside man.'

'The extent of Malreward's misdeeds will doubtless be uncovered with the help of the authorities,' said Myron.

All Polly's gaiety had evaporated. 'Walter Malreward – and I worked for him.'

Lord Fraddon was beside her, his face full of a rare anger. 'I've disliked that man intensely for many years,' he said. 'I knew him for a blackmailer; I had no idea he was capable of the kind of wickedness you've revealed to us, Mr Rasmussen.'

'Have they caught him?' Jo said. 'Or has he got away to recreate himself again and do more mischief?'

'We have blocks on roads to Italy and checks on all other borders,' said Ettore. 'I do not think he will get away.'

'There is another death to be laid at his door,' said Max. 'One that again affects some people here. You, Lord Fraddon in particular. The death of the footman on your lake several years ago, which scandal said was murder, was. The footman wasn't a servant, he was an investigator in the employ of Malreward. He was sent to Fraddon Park to gather information which Malreward hoped to be able to use to harm Lord Fraddon. However, the young man became involved with a member of the household, and told Malreward he wasn't working for him any more, and certainly wasn't going to snoop on the Fraddons for him. So Malreward arranged for his death.'

As he finished speaking, the bell began to sound its hundred and one sonorous notes.

FIFTY-TWO

The butler stood in the doorway. 'My lord, dinner is served.'

Polly would never forget that Christmas dinner. The crystal, the silver, the gold and white china, the brilliant colours on the walls, eerie classical figures in their still dances just visible in the light from dozens of candles. The footmen in their splendid livery, the sound of a dozen voices, raised perhaps louder than usual after the tensions of the evening.

She was seated between Max and Oliver, and although part of her mind was elsewhere, whirling thoughts trying to make sense of what had happened, she felt a happiness of the kind that comes from comfort after struggle, the serenity of calm waters after a raging storm. Although there was still one point she wanted to clear up. 'Max,' she whispered, while Gus was telling a loud and lively anecdote, 'the footman wasn't involved with Lord Fraddon, was he? It was Oliver.'

Max nodded. 'Lord Fraddon took the blame by leaving the country, so that Oliver wouldn't be arrested.'

'That's a big sacrifice for a father to make.'

'He is fond of Oliver, and he valued the family name too highly to see it dragged through the courts.'

'Will he be able to clear his name now?'

'Not entirely, not without it being risky for Oliver. But I've made sure that the police know who was responsible for the footman's death. And word will get around, as it does.'

It was after midnight by the time the last of the seven courses had been served and eaten. Polly stood with Max, looking at the orange and lemon trees sprinkled with snow. 'Can they survive the snow?' she asked.

'It'll be gone by tomorrow, look, the sky is clear. Frost is what damages citrus trees, and there won't be a frost, it's already warmer.'

Polly looked up into the starry sky, her mind drifting with the trail of cloud floating in front of the moon.

When Max spoke, his voice was husky. 'Polly, will you marry me?'

Polly came out of her reverie with a start. 'What did you say?'

'I asked you to marry me.'

Polly stared down at her hands, looking at the faint mark still showing from her engagement ring. 'I don't want to marry anyone at the moment.'

FIFTY-THREE

Archie came down the next morning, yawning and stretching and demanding coffee. 'Good morning, Cynthia, you're looking uncommonly cheerful.'

'Ring for more coffee, Archie. This pot is cold. As it happens, I slept remarkably well last night, better than I have done for ages.'

'That's being shot of Malreward, I dare say,' Archie ventured, with a quick look at Max, who was standing by the window eating a piece of toast.

'Don't tease me, Archie. I shudder every time I think of that man, and how lucky I am to have escaped being Lady Malreward. I'd probably be on the run by now if I'd married him when he wanted.'

'You know what they say, marry in haste and repent in leisure. I don't suppose, if you're in the mood for a spot of matrimony, you'd consider me instead of Malreward? At least I don't go around killing people and dealing in fake pictures and causing riots.'

'No, you don't, Archie, dear,' said Cynthia, laughing.

'And Harriet would like me for a stepfather, she told me so.'

434

Cynthia stopped laughing. 'Harriet – why, the bad girl.'

'Just looking after herself and you, that's all. I know I'm not as rich as Malreward—'

Max turned round. 'Archie, don't you think it's time you came clean about just what you do live on? I know what your income is, and I can have a good guess at what your travel books make you, and the total amount wouldn't pay for one room in that flat of yours in Paris, let alone the car and other good things of life you enjoy.'

'Are you asking me what my prospects are, by any chance? Thought so.'

Harriet bounced into the room. 'Goodie, breakfast, I'm famished.'

'Good gracious, Harriet, what are you doing up so early?' said Cynthia. 'And how can you be famished after that meal you ate last night?'

'That was last night, this is this morning. I'm up bright and early because Polly's taking me sketching. She'll be here any moment, can I ring for some more food? Uncle Max and Archie have eaten it all. And what were you saying about Archie's money, Uncle Max?'

'Were you listening at the door?'

'I might have been. It's in the family, isn't it, secret investigations?' And she gave him a wicked look from under her eyelashes.

'I'll come clean,' said Archie. 'In case you're wondering, all of you, the source of my income is perfectly legal, although not of a nature that I choose to broadcast to the world. I write travel books, yes, but I am also the author of other books, which pay much better.'

'Pornographic literature?' said Harriet with a knowing air.

'Harriet!' cried Cynthia.

'Certainly not. I write popular thrillers, under a pseudonym, chronicling the exploits of Pete Maloney.'

Harriet was enchanted. 'Oh, but I adore Pete Maloney. Are you really John Madison? How clever. Mummy, you'll have to marry him, how grand to have a real writer in the family.'

At that moment, Rose announced Polly, who came into the room looking awkward. Max went over to her and took her hand, which he carried to his mouth to kiss.

'Goodness,' said Harriet, impressed. 'Are you in love with Polly? Mummy says you are.'

Now Cynthia was really annoyed. 'Harriet, that is enough. If you can't control your tongue, you must leave the room.'

'Sorry, Mummy. Sorry, Polly. Have I got time to eat breakfast before we go off?'

'Polly, sit down and have some coffee,' said Cynthia. 'Max has told me about the other astonishing revelation of last night. So Oliver is your half-brother.'

'Half-brother?' said Harriet.

'And you've found your father.'

'Oh, yes,' said Polly, her voice lifting with sudden happiness. 'I've got a new family.'

'Is Lord Fraddon your father?' said Harriet, accepting this without surprise. 'I suppose he must be if Oliver's your half-brother. And that means Katriona's your half-sister, well, sooner you than me. It isn't all good news, though,' she reminded Polly. 'Don't forget you lost a fiancé.'

Cynthia frowned at her. 'What are your plans now, Polly?'

'I'm going to stay in France and paint, at least for now. Mrs Wolf saw the portrait I did of Maud and she wants me to paint her. Oliver says she's very influential, and if she likes it, I'll get more commissions.'

'Will you live at the Domus Romana?'

'No. Lord Fraddon wants me to, but I'm used to a place of my own. So I called at the baker's on my way here, and

I'm going to rent Ivo's rooms, now he's gone and won't be coming back.'

'Good idea,' said Archie. 'That's one person settled. Amazing how good comes out of wickedness, isn't it? When are you planning to go back to England, Max, by the way? I've got some stuff I'd like you to take for me, if it isn't too much trouble.'

Max's eyes were on Polly, who looked gravely back at him. 'It won't be for a while, Archie. I'm planning quite a long stay here at Rodoard.'

Max walked outside with Polly while Harriet finished her breakfast, and they stood together overlooking the majestic view of greens and greys and browns that stretched down to the sea, calm and glistening.

'I heard this morning from a colleague,' Max said, rather abruptly. 'He's been helping me with this investigation.'

'Investigation? Into Malreward? Into my family? Max, just what are you?'

'I'm what Harriet hinted at. I work for the Intelligence Services.'

Polly turned to look directly at him for a long moment, before she switched her gaze back to the sea.

'Do you know what that means?' he asked.

'Yes. It means you'll be a busy man if what Malreward was up to proves to be a straw in the wind. No, don't tell me about it, I don't want to know. Sufficient unto the day, is my motto. What did your colleague say?'

'Not good news. He's been delving into police records, and particularly into an unsolved murder from twenty-three years ago, and has pieced together the answers to several questions. The murder of a young woman, who was shot and her body pushed into the Thames.'

'My mother,' said Polly. 'Is that what you're saying?'

He nodded.

437

Polly leaned on the wall, shutting her eyes, shocked by the sharp sense of loss and grief that swept over her.

Max said nothing, but waited.

Finally, Polly opened her eyes and took a deep breath before she spoke in a voice that astonished her by its evenness. 'Who murdered her? No, don't tell me, I can guess. Malreward.'

'It looks like it. Polly, I know you'd hoped—'

'Oh, hope. I can't grieve for her, not truly, because I never knew her. At least now I can think she might have come back for me, one day. That's something.'

'You have gained a family.'

'I have, yes. It's all rather overwhelming, but I'll get used to it, one does.'

'Isn't that what you wanted?'

Polly smiled. 'Orphan Annie comes home? I've had a yearning for a family, after just me and Ma, but now I know my family, and I think of the Harringtons . . .' She sighed. 'Perhaps family life isn't all it's cracked up to be.'

'Does it matter?'

Polly heard footsteps scrunching on the gravel and turned round to see Oliver approaching.

'Do I interrupt?' he asked. 'Good morning, Polly,' he went on, stooping to kiss her cheek. 'You look very thoughtful.'

'Thoughtful, yes, but do you know, I'm happy? Even if it doesn't show. All this started back in gloomy old Somerset House, you know, Oliver, when I discovered I wasn't who I thought I was.'

'And now you know exactly who you are.'

'Yes. I'm Polly.' She smiled at the two tall men. 'Polyhymnia, Polly Smith, Polly Tomkins, Polly Fraddon, even. It doesn't matter. I'm just myself.'

STOP PRESS

The yacht belonging to the missing tycoon, Sir Walter Malreward, the *Thomasina*, has been found floating at sea and brought back to land by local fishermen. No one was on board, and it is believed that Sir Walter has drowned. Police are searching for his body.

The True Darcy Spirit

Elizabeth Aston

A richly entertaining recreation of Regency London, as the next generation of Darcy girls have to make their way in a society that doesn't always appreciate their wit, determination and sense of fun.

This is the story of Cassandra, a young cousin to the children of Mr and Mrs Darcy of 'Pride and Prejudice'. She's a worthy heir to them in every way – she speaks her mind, is shrewd and talented – but, sad to say, she makes one very major mistake as a result of her impetuousness. Cast out of her respectable place in the world, she has to make her own way. But in a London that regards any attractive, independent young lady with deep suspicion, how can she avoid coming upon the town?

'Those who enjoy Austen will certainly enjoy Aston's work, as will historical readers who want an engaging plot and characters.'

Library Journal

ISBN: 978 0 00 724149 1

The Frozen Lake

Elizabeth Aston

The year of 1936 is drawing to a close. Winter grips Wetmoreland and causes a rare phenonmenon: the lakes freeze. For two local families, the Richardsons and the Grindleys, this will bring unexpected upheaval, as the frozen lake entices long-estranged siblings and children to return home for the holiday season.

Some are aware of what is happening in Europe; others don't want to know. Everyone's keen to put aside their troubles – money worries, love tangles, career problems, domestic rifts – and enjoy themselves skating while they can. But one visitor carries the seed of violence and not even the redoubtable matriarch of the Richardson clan can prevent the carefully buried secrets of the past from reappearing and transforming everything.

ISBN: 978 0 00 718486 6

The Villa in Italy

Elizabeth Edmondson

Four strangers are summoned to the Villa Dante, a beautiful but now abandoned house above the Ligurian coast. Each has been named in the will of the intriguing Beatrice Malaspina; not one of them knows who she is. Delia, an opera singer; George, an atom scientist from Cambridge; Marjorie, a detective novelist and Lucius, a Boston banker, come to Italy, only to find out that the mystery deepens.

Spring flowers into the joy of an Italian summer, and the Villa Dante, with its frescoes, and once-magnificent gardens, comes back to life. As water flows again through the cascades and fountains, the four visit the mediaeval tower close to the house, and find themselves face to face with their troubled pasts in a way they never could have foreseen.

The villa works its magic and slowly they are changed, as the sorrows of their wartime experiences grow into the possibility of hope. Now they can receive their unexpected inheritance and, as devastating secrets are finally revealed, the even greater gift of a new life.

Praise for Elizabeth Edmondson

'I loved it'   *Woman*

'A very interesting book, not only because it gives a flavour of life – it's a way of imbibing history'   *Oxford Times*

ISBN-13: 978-0-00-722377-0